JINX MAGIC

JINX MAGIC

Sam Stone

The Jinx Chronicles
Book 2

First published in 2016 by Telos Publishing Ltd
5A Church Road, Shortlands, Bromley, Kent, BR2 0HP

Telos Publishing values feedback if you have any comments about this book
please email feedback@telos.co.uk

Jinx Magic: The Jinx Chronicles Book 2 © 2016 Sam Stone

ISBN: 978-1-84583-111-0

Cover Art: 2016 © Jim Burns
Cover Design: David J Howe

The moral right of the author has been asserted.

British Library Cataloguing in Publication Data. A catalogue record for this
book is available from the British Library.

Part 1

Trafford City

1

Taylor Arch completed his morning run around the top level of the Trafford Centre Mall. His feet pounded the marble floor. Over the years, he had put aside his regulation army boots, favouring a pair of far more practical running shoes, and his camouflage uniform was replaced by jogging shorts and T-shirt. Taylor was in his mid-thirties – an attractive man – but his once clean-cut, all-American-boy good looks were slightly worn. The fine lines around his pale blue eyes had deepened in the last few years, and his light brown hair now had strands of grey streaking his temples.

As he ran, Taylor considered how easy it was to imagine that their lives were idyllic, to train his mind to ignore the daily grind, the constant battle for survival. The hardships had become the norm. That was life, there was no other choice; but Taylor couldn't fool himself that life was good, despite the enthusiasm of the other survivors. He was good at pretending, though, and it became a natural state for him to give positive speeches to rally the occupants of Trafford City. The burden of it all, secretly, wore him down.

He ran harder, circling the top floor of the mall once more. Sweat stained his armpits and ran into his eyes until he was forced to rub it away.

We are *fortunate*, he thought, forcing himself to believe it. The lights remained on in the mall – although they still didn't know how – and the electricity helped to make the survivors' lives a bit more bearable. Fresh water continued to run from the taps, again by means unknown. Of course, Taylor was deeply suspicious of these gifts and tried not to take their heat, light and water for granted, because, at any time, all of it could suddenly be taken away: just like the fuel – that had run out two years earlier, and so far they had failed to find any new resources within a 100 mile radius. They still had a few canisters of petrol for emergencies, but this could only be used in the direst of situations. So far they were managing successfully to avoid that, but Taylor wondered, as his feet drummed against the marble, if that day was closer than they thought.

As he rounded the corner, looping through the fake New Orleans streets of what was once the top tier restaurant area of the mall, Taylor heard the cooks setting up the mess for breakfast. It was 6.00 am, but the residents of Trafford City rarely slept in, they had too much work to do. Taylor ran around the top of the mess, taking in the false blue sky above his head, illuminated by powerful spotlights. One or two of the spots had worn out, and Taylor's right hand man, Lieutenant Donovan, had pointed out that they needed scaffolding to reach and replace them. It was possible to do, but so far the lack of illumination from a few lights hadn't become a problem, so it had not made it onto the repairs roster as yet. At that moment another light flickered out. Taylor shook his head. *Sod's law.*

Taylor reached the steep escalator and stepped on. Even though it was moving, he jogged in place, slowly cooling down his limbs before he reached the bottom. In front of him was a café bar. The shelves were empty, all produce moved to the store so that rations could be spread fairly among the survivors. The once shiny wood of the bar area looked dull and dusty. As he stepped off the escalator Taylor felt an urge to wipe away the grime but instead focused his energy elsewhere and stretched out, making sure the tension was released in each of his muscles.

This area of the mall had been the lower level of the food hall called The Orient, and it served the survivors as a main assembly area as well as the mess. Most of their social and democratic moments happened here. Taylor passed by Nando's and headed toward the McDonald's serving counter. Here the residents queued for breakfast.

Cramp gripped the lower calf of his right leg. He stopped at the old jacket potato stand, put his left hand on the wall and lifted his right leg up behind him. With his spare hand he pulled his foot back into his buttocks, stretching and pulling the calf gently until the pain eased.

Taylor closed his eyes, imagining the mall in all of its bustling glory. The image of shoppers stopping to have coffee, lunch and snacks filled his mind's eye. He remembered the smell of burgers frying on the grill, the spicy aroma of garlicky food wafting over the balcony from the Italian restaurant, the greasy odour of loaded pizza served by the slice. It was all so vivid, even though he had never been here before the world ended.

Taylor opened his eyes, and his gaze fell on a small female farmer. It was Kim, the wife of Sergeant Harvey. Once a strong, pretty girl, she looked frail and aged in her work clothing. The trousers, several sizes too big, were belted in, and she wore a grubby T-shirt that hung down past her small bottom. Kim nodded to him and turned away with her bowl of food. Her back reminded him of someone else he had once known, but the identity of whom evaded him at that moment. In the last three years his memories had dulled, as though someone had removed all thought of anything other than the present and the future.

The mess was full of people, as it always was during meal times, but despite this there was little noise, as the occupants were more interested in their food than in making small talk. Taylor passed a group of children aged around nine or ten, two boys and three girls. They sat silently eating. He knew this was abnormal, even though it had become the norm here. He missed the chatter and giggles of the children, and as he gazed into the eyes of one of the boys he noted the cold and bleak expression, the lack of humour that hung behind the child's gaze. He looked away and then around. A soldier sat in the corner, eating his ration and drinking from a cracked mug. A mother patiently fed porridge to a baby in a rickety high chair. An old man stumbled around looking for a place to sit, his shaking hands slopping the precious contents from his bowl. A pair of teenagers stared blankly into their empty bowls, behaving like doped-up patients in a psych unit. Taylor felt a wave of sadness roll through his empty stomach. This was Trafford City. There was no happiness, no joy. There was only hunger and depression. He had wanted to save them all from suffering. He felt like he had failed.

The weight of his responsibility came down hard on Taylor's tired shoulders. He bent his head, squeezed his eyes shut once more and imagined the sounds of the old world. Then he shook the thoughts away. Releasing his foot, he stood up and tested his calf again. The muscle cramp had gone and he was able to stand and walk once more.

As he approached the food dispensary, Lieutenant Steve Donovan looked up from his post supervising the rations: he met Taylor's eyes over the huge porridge pot. Donovan nodded, but his expression showed his concern as Taylor approached.

'Donovan?' Taylor said as he stopped beside the Lieutenant.

Donovan ladled a portion of thin porridge into a bowl and gave it to a woman Taylor had never seen before. She was in her fifties, wearing grime-smeared clothing, and her greasy hair was covered with a ragged piece of cloth.

'Over there,' Donovan told her, and Taylor followed her with his eyes as she moved away, noticing for the first time a new group of survivors clustered around the tables and chairs nearest the stage.

'They came in this morning,' Donovan explained. 'We can't keep taking them in like this, Captain. We've barely enough food for ourselves.'

Donovan rubbed his forehead with the back of his hand. His once dark hair was now almost white: he had aged dramatically in the last few years, and Taylor found it hard to remember that Donovan hadn't even celebrated his fortieth birthday yet.

'It would be impossible to turn them away ...' Taylor said, his eyes falling on a little girl who sat amongst the refugees. The child gulped down her food greedily, glancing around her as though she expected her ration to be snatched away at any moment. 'Our children should be playing and carefree. Not like this ...'

'Give the kid a few days. She'll learn that she's safe here and then we'll see some smiles.'

Taylor nodded. He couldn't bring himself to meet Donovan's expression again. Despite his upbeat tone, Taylor knew his eyes would belie his words, as he had seen the sadness there many times. It was how he felt too, and to acknowledge it would mean he could no longer keep his outward positivity going.

'We need to call a council meeting,' Taylor said over his shoulder as he turned away. 'We have to come up with a strategy to find more supplies.'

'Captain?' Donovan said.

'Yes?'

'Your ration.'

Taylor stared down at the bowl Donovan placed in his hands. He was starving, but he always felt such guilt every time he ate. He walked over to the table where the new arrivals sat silently. He could smell their fear mingled with the grime of the road and the stale stink of unwashed clothing.

Taylor held out his bowl to the little girl. Up close he realised she wasn't as young as he had first thought. She was around 12 or 13, but he had thought she was much younger because she looked so small and frail. *Starvation*, he thought. *Poor kid.* God only knew what else she had been through.

'Take it, please,' he said as the girl looked at him blankly. Real fear was in her eyes, and she backed away, burying herself in the arms of the woman beside her.

'She's been through a lot,' said the woman. Her voice was weak and cracked. It was as though she had spent years screaming in a wasteland with no-one to hear her cries. 'I'll take it for her.'

'You're safe here,' Taylor said. 'Welcome to Trafford City.'

'Captain?' a crackly voice said, and Taylor unclipped his two-way radio from his hip, pressing his finger down and opening the channel.

'Arch here. Over.'

'Captain, this is Andy. I'm outside on patrol.'

'What's wrong?'

'*Earthquake!*'

Taylor could feel the rumbling of the ground beneath his feet, and he was already running before Andrew Carpenter finished talking. He saw Donovan abandon his post by the pot, and the two of them raced through the mess toward the entrance near Nando's. Here there were two doors. One led from The Orient into what could be considered a long vestibule, the second went directly outside onto the car park. The two men ran through the first door and passed through the herb and tomato plants that lined the grand marble vestibule. As they reached the outside doorway they could see more soldiers pouring out into the grounds.

Outside, tarmac and flagstones were cracking and churning up, spewing grit and concrete dust into the atmosphere. An electric current burst like lightning from a particle in time and space and the sky shimmered. A pinprick of light began to grow and expand as Taylor and Donovan looked on.

A powerful wind picked up and erupted around the walls, thrumming against the glass doors. Taylor pushed at the doors, pressing back against the airstream. The doors held fast, but Trafford City shuddered.

A white Greek goddess statue broke free from the very top of the building, tipping over. It crashed down hard against the green sloped roof and rolled down to the edge. For a moment it caught on the guttered ridge, but then a new explosion shook the building and the statue toppled from the rooftop, plummeted down and smashed into the flagstones in front of the door.

Taylor threw himself aside, covering his face with his arm as glass exploded inwards into the mall and concrete shards battered the door. Behind him, he heard the refugees and civilian survivors screaming and shouting in panic. Within seconds, both he and Donovan were back on their feet and running through the now open doorway and out into the car park.

2

Andrew Carpenter ran full pelt toward the churning air as several soldiers poured from the mall behind him. It looked like a mini typhoon, but all of them knew it was the beginnings of an alien vortex. Andrew was 17 and a well seasoned fighter. He had been training with the soldiers since he was 14. In the early days there had been many attacks, but this was the first for a long time. Even so, Andrew hadn't forgotten the rule of stopping the inhuman Jinx: blow the vortex up before it had a chance to open fully. He stood poised with the other soldiers as the whirlwind focused and centred and the vortex opened. Down the turning mouth of the controlled tunnel they could see new and alien space developing out of thin air.

The air stank but it wasn't unpleasant; cleaner, fresher air than their own wafted toward them from the opening. Andrew breathed in, clearing his lungs of farming dust. In front of him the air continued to twist and writhe. There was the impression of sand particles swirling like crazed insects, and Andrew knew by instinct that the moment was almost there. He ran forward, grenade in hand, then threw with cricket-bowler-precision straight into the heart of the blossoming vortex.

'Don't shoot! Don't shoot!' yelled an unexpected human female voice from inside. 'It's me …' The pounding wind swallowed the sound, but the soldiers tensed, guns poised, as they waited for the vortex to explode. Nothing happened. It was as though the grenade had been swallowed by a black hole. The vortex continued to open. They heard yelling from inside, but the noise of the vortex masked the words. Then, unexpectedly, the grenade exploded and the wormhole imploded, rapidly disappearing as though it had never been there – but not before two figures hurled themselves out, tumbling and rolling on the cracked ground.

'What the fuck?' yelled Sergeant Harvey.

The wind dropped, the ground settled and the soldiers surrounded the newcomers only to find that they were a woman and a man.

Andrew raised his gun. 'Jinx!' he yelled.

'Wait!' said Taylor, knocking the gun aside.

The woman pulled herself up to a sitting position and raised her hands. Andrew and Taylor stared at her. She was so familiar, yet so alien with her long, clean dark brown hair and pale blue eyes. She was wearing some kind of robes. Andrew thought that these were the type of garments he had seen Bedouins wearing. He remembered a film about such a tribe being played to his class at school. Those days seemed so long ago, it was hard to remember the exact details, but however bizarrely she was dressed, it was still obvious that she was human and not one of the Jinx. The man however was a different issue. He sat up and, even on the ground, Andrew could tell how tall and imposing he was. He was most certainly alien: Andrew raised his gun once more, as did several of the soldiers around them.

They were a sorry pair, battered and bruised from the fall, and Andrew couldn't believe his eyes when Taylor stepped forward and helped the woman to stand.

'I can't believe it,' Taylor said. 'Jas? It's *really* you …?'

He helped Jas up from the floor, throwing his arms around her. Andrew stared on. It was as though someone had delivered him a massive blow. He stared at the woman. Once his saviour and companion, a surrogate parent and friend, Jas looked so far removed from the woman who had lived among them, pretending to be male, that he had trouble reconciling his memory of her with the person who stood before them. He couldn't quite get his head around the transformation, even though he had seen her change from man to woman many times in the past.

Now she was fully woman, no sign of the boy Jas at all.

'Captain! I urge you to be careful,' Donovan said. 'She didn't come alone.'

Taylor turned to look closely at the man that had exited the vortex with Jas.

'Don't hurt him. He helped me escape,' Jas said. 'This is Kale, and he can be very useful to us.'

Jas held out her hand to Kale and helped him to stand. He towered over her five-foot-eight frame by a good foot and a half. Andrew stepped back and allowed them to pass as the soldiers surrounded the two arrivals, escorting but ready to react if a threat should arise, and they all made their way back to the mall.

At the shattered doorway Kale hesitated. He was reluctant to cross the threshold.

'Is he a vampire or something?' asked Andrew. 'Does he need permission?'

'Oh my god! Andy! It's you!' Jas said.

Andrew blushed as Jas threw her arms around him; he didn't know how to react to her, looking like she did. She looked – beautiful.

'How can it be possible that you've grown up so much in one short year?'

'A year?' Andrew said frowning. 'You've been gone three years at least.'
'*What?*'

'It's true,' said Taylor. 'We thought we would never see you again.'

Jas looked at Kale and saw the shuddering that wracked his body at the thought of crossing the threshold into the building.

'What's going on?' she asked him.

Kale shook his head.

Jas took Kale's arm and tugged him over the threshold. 'Stop being a wimp and get in here.'

Andrew followed, his cheeks still burning. He wanted to know just what had happened to Jas but feared what she would tell them. She appeared stronger than ever, and there was a power resonating from her. Andrew had glimpsed this power before. It was something to do with her natural charisma: an inner strength that gave her the ability to control difficult situations. She was so different – so alien – to the residents of Trafford City, and always had been. Why hadn't he noticed that before?

Inside the mess, Jas and Kale were taken to a cleared area near the stage, and the survivors and soldiers surrounded them. Andrew heard the muted voices, the confusion of the mall's occupants, as Jas looked around, taking in the presence of children and women.

'Things *have* changed around here,' Jas said.

Jas pulled Kale down into a chair beside her. The Al Kuzemen was intimidated by the building and cast his eyes up at the ceiling, which was painted like a blue sky, with faded white clouds.

'I suspect he's never been inside a permanent structure before,' Jas said. 'He's not usually this quiet.'

A pretty female with warm brown eyes and faded blonde hair brought them both a glass of water.

'This is my wife, Caroline,' Donovan said. 'We found her and a few others just after you were taken.'

'Why, Donovan, you old rascal!' Jas laughed.

Taylor couldn't take his eyes off Jas. Andrew had never seen the Captain so taken by anyone. But Jas looked pretty and vibrant and so fresh and happy, unlike the rest of the men, women and children of Trafford City.

'As you can see,' said Taylor, 'we've grown in population. I'm a bit concerned you've brought a Jinx with you though. He now knows where we are.'

'I can't leave here without Jasmine,' Kale said. 'And neither of us can go back to Sharik or anywhere else on Emin.'

'He can speak English!' Taylor said. Somehow the idea that one of these violent and destructive alien beings could speak his own language made him very uncomfortable.

'I should introduce you. Captain Taylor Arch, this is Kale, Al Kuzemen to

Emperor Arven of Emin. In our terms, that means he's a magician or warlock I suppose.'

'I don't believe in magic,' said Andrew.

'Well you'd better start to, because Kale is the real deal, and he's taught me a few tricks too. The thing is, guys: Kale is not your enemy. He can't go back to Jinx Town even if he wanted to. It takes two mages to open a portal.'

'Jinx Town?' Andrew said.

'Yes. It's where they took me … that day. It's a slang name that the Earth women have for the place.'

'How did you get here …?' Donovan asked.

'It's a long story.'

'Well, time is something we all have,' Taylor said.

Kale abruptly leapt from his seat, and a female refugee who had been watching the proceedings squealed with fright. 'I have to get outside,' Kale said. 'It feels wrong here.'

'What is it?' Jas asked, kindly this time. She placed her hand on the Al Kuzemen's arm and stroked him with easy familiarity.

Andrew and Taylor watched this but said nothing. The Jinx mage began to chatter to Jas in his own language, and the soldiers were fascinated as they heard them speak together. It made them feel even more nervous of the alien and suspicious of Jas, who clearly understood every word perfectly. Andrew listened intently though; it was the first time they had ever come close to a Jinx, and the first time they had heard their strange language. Andrew felt an instant dislike for the alien. He didn't trust him one bit, and this affected his response to Jas's return. She was with the alien and could understand his jabbering language.

'*In anima dulerth …*' Kale said.

'*Il farin mien zoolik. Ien variam totea zcer,*' Jas said.

Jas patted Kale's arm again. Then looked around her as though she had briefly forgotten where she was.

'He says he can't see the sky,' Jas explained. 'I told him that this is no different from living inside their tents, which still block out the sky.'

'*Nah verin. In anima dulerth!*' Kale continued.

'Oh! You can't *see* the sky.' Jas turned to Taylor. 'I'll have to take him outside again and try to work out why this place is blinding him.'

'Blinding?'

'Yes. His third eye,' said Jas placing her head on her brow to illustrate her meaning. 'It's blocking his ability to see what's around it. It's as though he's wearing a blindfold.'

'Okay,' said Taylor. 'But you'll go outside under guard.'

Jas frowned, then nodded, and a handful of the men marched outside with Kale and Jas. Andrew stayed close. His curiosity was piqued so much that he had to find out more about both of these people. It was as though he had never known Jas. That the person he remembered was a dream, and this new being was the real thing. She, in her own way, was now just as extraterrestrial as the Jinx male was.

Kale leaned against the frame of the broken door, gasping in air.

'*Ich tenart*,' he gasped.

'Kale, I know you're upset, but please, speak English,' said Jas, looking around at the suspicious faces of the soldiers. 'He says "It's tainted",' she explained to Taylor.

'What is tainted?' asked Andrew.

'The atmosphere,' gasped Kale. 'The planet is dying.'

Andrew stared up at the fractured sky. These days it was more orange than blue, the air thick and heavy, and the temperature rising to extreme levels.

'I thought global warming had occurred because of the CFC emissions,' Andrew said. 'He's right, something is wrong. We've not been using our cars for years now. Why are things getting worse?'

'It *has* changed. It was pretty normal when I left. So what's happened?' Jas wondered.

Kale was silent, but his eyes seemed drawn to the haze above them. A thick heat-smog was settling several hundred feet above the ground. *It looks like the trail left by an aircraft*, Andrew thought. But he knew it couldn't be.

'Your world was always destined for this,' Kale said. 'It's why we chose you.'

'Jinx bastard!' yelled Sergeant Harvey diving at Kale. 'What did you do? What did you bastards do to our planet?'

'Not them!' said Jas throwing herself between Harvey and Kale. '*Us*. We did this to ourselves with *our* poison. Our technology. It's crippled the planet. We killed our world, long before the Jinx came. That's all he meant.'

As Andrew watched Jas defend Kale, he felt strongly that she had somehow switched sides. The air was thick with the anguish of suspicion, and Andrew couldn't help but feel it too. Even though his heart told him he was wrong. He didn't trust Kale, and because she was with him, this meant he couldn't really trust Jas either.

'What are you doing back here, Jas?' Andrew asked. 'If you like the Jinx so much, why bother coming back?'

Jas looked into his eyes. 'I wanted to come home.'

'Of course you did,' Taylor said. 'We're glad you're here, and your friend is welcome too. Please forgive us. Times have been hard and we have grown older and less forgiving. Come back inside, if ... Kale ... feels better now, that is.'

'Are we your prisoners?' Jas asked.

'Of course not,' Taylor said, and he looked around at his men, daring them to argue. 'But obviously it will take some time for people to learn to trust …'

'Kale,' Jas said, and Taylor nodded.

Andrew said nothing, but he watched the soldiers straighten up and lower the weapons they had been clutching so firmly since Jas and Kale had arrived. They would give Jas a chance, but they would be watching her and Kale for any sign of betrayal. Just as he would.

His heart hurt so much at the sight of her. Maybe it would have been better for all of them if she had never reappeared. He shook his head and blinked water from his eyes before any of the others noticed his turmoil. Her energy scared him. It was as though she and Kale were hundred-watt bulbs to their meagre ten.

3

'We're mostly farmers now,' Taylor explained to Jas. 'We soon realised that if we were to survive we'd have to start growing our own food again.'

Taylor sat on the edge of what used to be a large stage in the middle of the old restaurant area in the Trafford Centre.

'You're a town now …'

'Well, more of a commune, since we share everything,' Taylor explained. 'In the last six months, refugees have been arriving from all over the place. We now have over a thousand people living here.'

Jas noted how the mall still appeared bare in comparison with the footfall that used to pass through. She remembered hearing that over fifty thousand people would come into the centre to shop every Saturday.

'Where do they all live?' Jas asked.

'I'll show you …' Taylor said.

Jas looked over at Kale, who sat beside her with a bowl of porridge in his hands. He was eating it slowly and suspiciously. Jas had forced down some of the watery substance to show him it was edible, but the sickness that still clung to her insides felt like the cancer of fear. She hadn't felt well before they had left Sharik, and now she was worse. The atmosphere of Earth was not as welcoming to her as she had expected.

'How did you … become friends with this Jinx?' Andrew asked.

Jas's heart lurched as she heard the suspicion and disgust in Andrew's voice. She was surprised and hurt by it, but realised she shouldn't be. *How would I react in his shoes?*, she wondered. She sat upright on her seat and glared around her at the wary, ragtag army.

'Anyone hurts him and you'll answer to me.'

'I promise you, he has asylum here,' Taylor said.

'Thank you,' Kale nodded. 'I make promise to you that I am not here to hurt your people. I am here to protect Jas. She is special among my people. She is …'

'It's all right, Kale,' Jas interrupted. 'You don't have to explain anything. You helped me get back. That is all anyone needs to know.'

'I'm grateful to you,' said Taylor to Kale. 'I never thought I'd see her again.'

'You nearly didn't,' Jas said, thinking back to the race through the desert. Arven had almost caught up with them, but Kale had managed to open the vortex in the nick of time. 'The grenade almost saw us off … but thanks to Kale, the explosion was isolated until the vortex was large enough for us to jump clear.'

Taylor weighed up Kale carefully. 'You need to debrief us. What happened? Where have you been all this time?' he asked.

Jas nodded. 'A year away feels like a lifetime now.'

'Three years to us …' Andrew reminded.

Jas was spaced out. Home was foreign, but she knew she would get used to it if she could rid herself of this terrible, dark fear in the pit of her stomach. Only now did she realise how safe she had been in Sharik, the capital city of the Arrak Nah Tiaman planet, Emin. She had had power there, had been revered as the Empress and wife to their Emperor Arven. The memory of Arven came rushing back in a flood of anxiety. She *missed* him. It hurt so much that the sickness came back in a wave. Could the magic of the bonding she had taken part in still have some power over her, even on Earth? Or were her feelings what she most feared: *real*?

A small, petite and curvy mousy-blonde woman weaved her way through the crowd. She was holding a small child in her arms; a little girl with sandy hair and round grey eyes.

'Aren't you going to introduce us?' she said to Taylor.

'This is Dawn,' Taylor explained. 'And our daughter, Lucy. Dawn, this is Jas.'

Dawn held out her hand, and for a moment Jas stared at it as though she had forgotten what to do. She stood and shook Dawn's hand, using the opportunity to examine the other women's face. Dawn was attractive, but strangely faded, like everyone else in Trafford City, even Taylor. It was as though something was sucking the living energy from the people here. Or as though they were old, washed-out paintings of an era long forgotten. The place lacked colour and life; the dust and grime all around only added to this effect, and Jas wondered if Earth had always been this way but she had never noticed it before.

'I like your clothing,' said Dawn. 'It's very colourful.'

Jas glanced down at the kaftan. It was made of silk and had an intricate gold and green pattern woven through the fabric. It reminded her of the willow pattern used on china, even though it was colourful and not just blue and white. Underneath she wore a long pair of lightweight trousers. The kaftan had slits up the sides and was practical and comfortable. When Jas had made her escape from Jinx Town with Kale, she had thought carefully about her clothing choice, but there was nothing in her wardrobe that was plain, even though most of it was easy to wear.

'Thank you,' she answered, the old polite terms coming back.

Around her the people looked ancient. Jas could see sadness and hardship reflected in their eyes even when they smiled. Since her year spent in Jinx Town the world had changed significantly. The people had been worn down and had become more hostile. Even the children looked tired. For the first time, Jas began to wonder if they had arrived on the right planet. Earth was a grey world, and so unlike the vibrancy of Jinx Town that she couldn't help but make comparisons.

As Dawn turned away to talk to Taylor, Jas moved back to her chair at Kale's side. Kale was observing Dawn and the other women carefully. His eyes were grave, and for the first time she noticed that the swirling lights weren't dancing within them. The magician, and all of the Jinx, had strange pupils: they twisted and pulsed with hypnotic movement, changing colour. At first, when she had arrived in Jinx Town, she had found it hard to look into their eyes, particularly Arven's. On Earth, however, Kale's eyes appeared human. They were a deep and dark brown.

Jas took a breath, about to ask why that was, but thought better of it with so many people in earshot. The question could be asked later when they were alone.

'What happened with the time zones?' she asked instead. 'There's a huge discrepancy between our time and theirs.'

Kale shrugged. 'I don't know. Perhaps your lack of training? You didn't focus on the time, but on the place.'

Despite his height, Kale appeared more human than he usually did. The shrug was not something she had ever seen him do. Jas noted that he was examining the humans carefully. Perhaps he was adapting to make himself appear more benign?

'If my focus was off, then why did we arrive in this time? Luck?' Jas asked, while around them the residents of Trafford City were chattering with rare excitement. Jas didn't know that she had really given them something new to be interested in and to focus on.

'I don't know. But I feel it is not an accident that we arrived now,' Kale murmured.

A debate was going on around them.

'We can't just let a Jinx roam freely around our city,' a grey-haired woman in her early sixties was saying.

'Sylvia, that's a debate we can take up in the meeting. We need to gather the council members.'

'I'll do it,' she said, and walked away.

Jas was dazed, and the smell of the burnt and watery porridge wafted under her nostrils. She buried her head in her hands. The sickness bit so deep that the smell of the food made her want to vomit. She thought about

Arven, and then looked over at Taylor as he took his daughter from the arms of Dawn. He was so different from the last time she had seen him.

There is something very wrong here.

She could see Dawn's lips move but couldn't hear the words as a pounding sound began to build up in her ears.

Andrew pulled up a chair beside her. 'Hey, are you okay?' he asked, showing concern for her for the first time since she had arrived back.

Jas shook her head. The emotions that were raging through her made tears spring to her eyes. The same panic that had gripped Kale earlier had now taken hold of Jas. She forced her breath to steady as she thought about her irrational emotions. She had achieved all that she wanted to now, hadn't she? She had proven that Andrew was still alive. Her sacrifice on the day the Jinx had taken her had not been in vain. Taylor had found the women he wanted to make life better for his men. He even had one for himself. They were rebuilding their lives, having children, growing food and rearing livestock. They didn't need her, did they?

Of course, she realised, and her face registered the realisation as Andrew reached out and took her hand in his. *She* had needed *them*. She had believed she was crucial to their lives, especially Andrew's, and now she had been proved wrong. *This wasn't about them at all. It was about me*, she thought. *I had to learn that they were safe.*

All the time she couldn't settle to her life in Jinx Town, she had been concerned and worried about those left behind. Maybe it was guilt, but she had used it as an excuse not to let herself be truly happy. She had fought against her enforced marriage to Arven, but had found the happiness in it. Now that was all gone, and Jas realised how foolish her machinations had been. It had all been for nothing. *Why couldn't I see it before?*

Her mother had once told her 'You should never look back', and Jas had always tried to remember that. Maybe she should not have returned to Earth. But she could never go back to Jinx Town now. Surely Arven would not understand that this was all she had needed to do? She had wanted to see her friends one more time, because her past had crouched and festered in the back of her mind like unfinished business.

She suspected that her feelings for him were real. More real than the dream of the old world had ever been. This faded old world that felt nothing like home. But how could she forgive him everything, despite her unchecked emotions? Arven, and the Jinx, were murderers. They had killed innocent people, even children, and tried to justify it because of the need for their own survival.

I'm a fool, she thought. *I had everything. Why didn't I realise it?*

'What have I done?' she murmured.

Kale looked up from his food, examining the distraught woman before him.

'What have we *both* done?' he said, understanding better than she that there really was no going back.

'Would you like a tour?' Andrew said. 'I could show you where you and this …'

'Kale. He's called Kale,' Jas corrected.

'Yes. Of course. Kale. I can show you where you can both sleep. Are you … *together*?'

Jas looked into Andrew's eyes. 'No, of course not. But we can share the same area. Kale wouldn't …'

'She belongs to the Emperor,' Kale said. 'And no-one else may have her.'

Blood rushed into Jas's face as the Al Kuzemen sat upright. He spoke the words clearly and loudly as a warning. The residents of Trafford City felt the impact of his words, and the chatter died down around them. Their eyes fell upon Jas. She felt the heaviness, the suspicion and the sick curiosity. She belonged to an alien emperor. What did that make her in their eyes? Jas could only imagine what they were thinking.

Taylor said nothing, but he stared down at Jas's bent head. She could feel his eyes more intensely than all of the others, but she refused to look up at him.

'God, you've really got to tell me the story of how that happened,' Andrew laughed, and Jas looked up to see the boy she once knew smiling back at her.

'They are bonded,' Kale said, weighing the boy up carefully.

'A marriage?' asked Taylor.

Jas nodded. What was the point of denying it now?

'An Empress, no less. I always knew you'd go on to better things,' Andrew smiled.

'It was, sort of, an accident,' Jas said, smiling back. 'I'd love that tour, Andrew. I want to see all the changes here.'

The crowd parted as they stood. Especially when Kale rose to his full height. He towered over them and walked with such confidence that the residents remained intimidated despite his benign behaviour.

'The council will meet at ten hundred hours,' Taylor said, and then he turned to follow as Andrew led Jas, Kale and two armed soldiers away from the mess.

They passed the old lifts and toilets, which were disguised by the decor of an Egyptian tomb. Pharaonic statues stood proudly to either side of the lifts. Jas remembered them well, and little had changed except that the brightly painted faces were as worn and dull as those of the humans around them.

'I still live in our old shop,' Andrew said. 'With a couple of other guys my age. We tend to share space by age groups, unless you're a couple or part of a family of course.'

They turned left, passing a shop that was once called Zara. The mannequins in the window were now bare and the clothing rails empty. Instead the huge shop space contained several erected tents.

'There are several communes within the whole of Trafford City ...' Andrew continued.

'Trafford City?' Jas said.

'Yes. That's what we call it now. I guess we became a city when the population rose to a thousand. It was Donovan that started it, and it kind of stuck.'

Jas nodded. 'Sounds like Donovan ... Please go on. You were telling me about communes ...'

'They gathered by faith at first. Religious or common interests. Now they live in their little ghettos. This group are Chinese.'

At that moment a little old Chinese woman came out of the tent carrying a small boy. 'They managed to hold out in Chinatown for a while, then when the food situation got worse they were forced to leave Manchester. We found them wandering around and brought them back here,' Taylor said.

The old woman saw them. She looked at Jas curiously and then started in fright when she saw Kale beside her. She backed up into her tent and peered out at the group with wide, frightened eyes.

'A scouting trip? I remember them well. I'd enjoy going on one with you again,' Jas said.

'We don't go out like that anymore,' Taylor said. 'We can't afford to use our emergency fuel.'

They walked in silence after that. Jas was amazed to see more of the communes gathered within the bigger stores. Debenhams held over a hundred tents and camps. It seemed that people still enjoyed their privacy and the tents gave them something of that among their still small communities. Jas couldn't help making comparisons between the townships on Emin and here. Were they so very different?

There were many children among the survivors now. Jas saw a fragile young girl of no more than 15 clutching a baby to her breast as she sat on the steps of the marble staircase outside Selfridges. The girl's eyes were flat and dull and she said nothing as the small party passed her, but her arm tightened around the baby as her eyes fell on Kale. She shrank back into the staircase, blending in with it in a bizarre chameleonic shift before anyone but Jas noticed. The strangeness of her disappearance, in this somewhat normal setting, made Jas realise it must be the same magic the girl had used to hide herself from the Jinx in the first place. It was how she had survived so long.

Like herself, when she had disguised herself as a boy.

As the group moved away, Jas remained, her eyes focused on the staircase. She couldn't see the girl and her baby at all now. It was as though they had completely vanished, and yet she *knew* that the girl was still there.

'Magic,' she murmured.

She turned away and followed the others into Selfridges, noticing how one of the soldiers had waited for her in the doorway.

So, it's like that, is it? We are *prisoners.*

In Selfridges there were more camps, more tents, and cordoned off areas that created rooms. In the electrical goods area, comfy sofas had been positioned around a huge flat-screen that was rigged up to a DVD player. A group of teenagers sat together watching an old horror movie. Jas had never been into horror and didn't recognise the film at all.

'*Fright Night,*' said Andrew as though he knew she wouldn't recognise it. 'With David Tennant. He was the tenth Doctor Who, you know.'

Kale stared at the screen, horrified.

'I guess you haven't seen one of these, then?' Jas said.

Kale shook his head. 'What is it?'

'It's a television set. These are actors playing the parts of characters in the story.'

'They've taken their souls into that box …'

Jas smiled. She could see how it might look to someone like Kale. 'It's just technology. It can't take a man's soul.'

'That is exactly what your science does,' Kale explained. 'Can't you see that? Here?'

Kale placed his hand on Jas's forehead, and the smile fell from her lips. She *could* see it. And although the television was a novelty after all these years, she felt no urge to sit down and lose herself in it. *It would be dangerous to rely on anything brought from the old world*, she thought.

'Let's move on,' she said to Andrew, suddenly suspicious of the television herself.

Andrew and Taylor showed them the training area, which hadn't changed much since the time she had left. The weapons were firmly locked up in cages, the target area was empty. The floor was covered with blue exercise mats. Around the edges of the room were various hand weights, a running machine and a cross-trainer.

'Those are new,' Jas said, pointing at the machines. 'This place has really turned into a gym now.'

'We've started to make our own bullets, out of necessity, but we don't have practice sessions often. We can't afford to waste any of our firepower,' Taylor explained. 'Physical strength is more important to our survival now. Particularly with the heavy manual farming equipment.'

Jas nodded. 'Understandable.'

'For obvious reasons, this area is off-limits to you and Kale,' Taylor continued. 'I hope you don't take it wrong, but we have to be sure we can trust your friend here.'

Jas smiled. 'Believe me, Kale wouldn't know what to do with a gun.

Besides, he doesn't need one. If he wanted, he could bring this entire building down around your ears. So, Taylor, you're going to *have* to learn to trust him.'

Taylor frowned, and Jas turned away, walking confidently out of the training area with the giant magician following her like a lapdog.

There were several empty shops along the way, which surprised Jas considering the new size of the community.

'There is still so much space here,' she said.

'It's a big place. A perfect place for a new city to be founded,' Andrew said. 'And because we're under cover we are somewhat spared the elements.'

They came to a halt near Waterstones bookstore. The shelves of books were still intact. Jas remembered how the store stretched back so far that you could almost lose yourself inside. The shelves were dusty, and she was disappointed to realise that the shop was barely used.

'This could be the centre of your new city,' Jas said to Taylor. 'The books are your library. Your education system for the children.'

'No offence, Jas, but you haven't been around for the last few years. Education hasn't been that high on our agenda. We've been trying to survive here.'

'I know,' she said. 'But maybe I can help with that, now that I'm back.'

'We could set up a school,' Andrew said. 'It's something the council has been discussing recently.'

'This is where we'll live from now on, Kale,' Jas said, crossing into the shop.

Kale entered the shop; his long fingers ran over the books with delight.

'Yes,' he said. 'I can rest in here. Nature is with us.'

'Andy, can you arrange a couple of mattresses for them?' Taylor said.

'Sure.'

'Good. I'll leave you then in Andy's capable hands,' Taylor continued. 'I still live in the old leather shop. If you need me, you know where I am.'

Jas nodded and watched him go. She wasn't sure where she stood at all with Taylor now, but there was no urge to rekindle their relationship in any way other than friendship. He, Andrew and the others weren't how she remembered them. Not at all. She watched the two soldiers set themselves up to guard them from outside the shop. Well, at least they would have some privacy inside.

She took Kale's hand and led him down to the back to talk.

4

In the back room of the leather shop, Taylor removed his sweat covered T-shirt and joggers. He filled the small sink with cold water. Then, using a torn-off piece of old towel as a wash cloth, he began to clean away the grime that clung to him. He reflected on Jas's sudden reappearance. Somehow he had always known she was alive. She was a survivor. She was tougher than anyone else he had ever met.

He wondered when he had stopped thinking about her. He couldn't remember the exact moment, and it seemed so long ago when he and Dawn had started their relationship. Lucy had come along rapidly after that, and they had gone from being a couple to becoming a family: something that Taylor had never thought he would have.

He loved Dawn, and adored his daughter. They were the only real things left in his life.

Now Jas had returned. She looked so different, so vibrant. Her strength and power were like Technicolor to their washed-out greyscale world. What had happened to her during those missing years?

He had always known she was different, enjoyed the fact that she had some inner magic that could transform her in an instant from female to male, even though he had never understood it.

Before the Jinx had destroyed the planet, Taylor had been a realist. The supernatural in his life had always been technology. He didn't believe in anything that wasn't born from science. How could he? But Jas was the real deal. Some primal instinct had issued warning shocks to his system the day he had met her and Andrew. Back then, he and all of his men had believed she was a boy, and they hadn't seen through the disguise at all.

They had been training together when he had learned the truth. It had been a freak moment of realisation, as though her mask had slipped. His eyes had seen the boy, but as they had fought together, his body had felt the woman beneath that disguise.

At the time, Taylor had thought that it was something to do with her ability to act like a male. He had seen the physical changes that had occurred but his mind had not really accepted them. He had watched her carefully, and when she had been around the others, Jas had definitely been a boy. He could not explain how that had happened or why, when he had been with her alone, she had been completely female.

I need to sit down with her without that goddamn Jinx in tow! We need to talk about all of this. I want some answers.

Taylor dried his hands, face and body with a small threadbare towel and pulled on a pair of clean joggers. He walked out of the bathroom and into the living room.

Dawn had turned the shop floor space into a real home. Scatter cushions decorated a comfortable sofa, a small coffee table sat on top of a Persian rug. There was a vase of fake flowers placed on a small table that also held an elaborate lamp. The old serving counter was moved aside and now held a selection of bottles containing expensive liquors: brandy and whisky among the meagre offerings. But they only ever drank when there was something special to celebrate. Nothing was to be wasted in Trafford City, as no fresh supplies would be forthcoming.

Their bed had been cordoned off with two Chinese screens and filled the left-hand corner of the shop. It created the effect of another room and gave them some privacy. Lucy's room was on the other side. Taylor had built the partition that gave the little girl her own cubicle, and the plain plywood wall was decorated with pictures and postcards of butterflies, rabbits and puppies. Taylor had thought the images twee at first, but when Dawn had explained her reasoning, and told stories to Lucy about the animals, he had realised that his wife was right. They rarely saw domestic animals now, and those they did see were rabid or feral. He wanted Lucy to know about pets, and he wanted her to know as much about the old world as possible. Inside the cubicle was a small futon-style bed with a metal buffer on the side so that the little girl couldn't fall out during the night. Beside the bed was a low cupboard that held a nightlight, and a battered teddy sat in the middle of the duvet. This completed his daughter's room, and it made their home feel 'real' somehow.

Taylor went over to a chest of drawers and pulled out a clean T-shirt. He slipped it over his head and turned, tripping over one of Lucy's toys.

'Shit!'

Dawn was out. He wasn't sure where, but knew his wife had duties to attend to, which meant that Lucy would probably be in the day-care centre with the other toddlers.

I have things to do too. This is all too much of a distraction.

He bent down, picked up the toy – a baby doll that cried when it had batteries in – and placed it down on the sofa, leaning against a red velvet cushion.

Taylor left his home and walked back toward the mess. The emergency council meeting would be taking place shortly and he had to be there. As he passed the bookstore, he saw Andrew and another young soldier dragging mattresses and bedding into the back. He paused, glancing down, but the rows of bookshelves restricted his view and he couldn't see Jas or Kalo.

He was confused by Jas's return. His feelings for her ran deep, but he had committed to Dawn and would never hurt her. Even so, he wanted to see more of Jas, talk to her, and learn about her once more; because the Jas that had returned bore little resemblance to the Jas he had known. The mystery of the new Jas was aching to be solved.

Taylor arrived in the mess and he found the council members gathered on the chairs and tables positioned around the stage. Taylor took his seat beside Donovan as Harvey joined them. He saw several of his men, including Corporal Kline, sitting among the civilian council members. They had each been voted into place, and all meetings were open to any of the civilians to sit in on. The small society they were building was based on transparency. Each resident of Trafford City was entitled to have his or her say, and that was why the meetings never took place in an enclosed area.

'Are we all present?' asked Harvey, as he quickly ticked off names on a list. Once done, he stuck his pencil behind his ear and looked around at the group of 15 people. They each took turns to chair the meetings, and today it was Harvey's turn.

'Mack can't make it,' said Sylvia. 'He sends his apologies, but he is in the middle of fixing the irrigation system. I guess he thought that was more important.'

'That's okay, Sylvia,' Harvey said.

Sylvia Bennett nodded. Her greying hair was hanging out of her bun, and she pushed some strands away from her face. She was in her sixties, one of the first of the refugees to stumble on the survivors in Trafford City three years ago, and she had become an integral member of the council. The men and women respected her, and listened to her advice. Mack Bennett, Sylvia's husband, was an engineer, and the two of them had become an asset to the town.

'Welcome to this emergency meeting,' Harvey continued. 'As you know, we've had a surprise today. Our former comrade, Jas Regis, has escaped from capture by the Jinx and returned to us. For those who don't know Jas like we do, which I guess is most of you, she and Andrew were the first civilians to sign up with us, and she became a part of the troop. We fought the Jinx side by side.'

'This is the woman who pretended to be a man?' asked Sylvia.

Taylor felt his cheeks flush as Sylvia's enquiring gaze fell on him.

'Yes,' he answered. 'Her disguise was … flawless.'

'Interesting. She is … an unusual creature,' Sylvia said.

'Now she's returned,' Harvey continued, 'I'm sure she will debrief us on the Jinx situation.'

'Let's talk about the Jinx magician she brought with her,' said Gerald Avery.

'Doc Avery,' Harvey acknowledged, and he bent his head and wrote Gerald's name on the list. 'I didn't see you there.'

'Obviously we haven't had an opportunity to talk properly to Jas or to this … magician she calls Kale,' Taylor said. 'All we know is that he helped her escape. Why he did that, I don't know, but naturally we do have a guard on both of them at this time.'

'Then you don't trust her?' Gerald asked.

'I didn't say that,' Taylor said. 'Of course I trust Jas …'

'Why do you trust her?' asked Sylvia.

'Because I know her …'

Gerald snorted, laughter bursting from his lips in a harsh gasp. 'Of course you *know* her, Captain. We all realised that when she was revealed to be a female. Her disguise, like you said, was flawless. Yet somehow you had been in on the secret. I'd still like to know how she achieved it, though. Even with you helping her, it is hard to believe that none of us noticed she was a girl.'

Taylor had never told anyone what he had learned about Jas. He had never revealed his suspicion about her ability to disguise herself, any more than he had told them about the conversation they had had about glamour. Taylor had spent time in the bookstore over the years, though, and he had read up on magic. It was myths, mostly, but in some of that research he had found information that made him believe in her. Before the council, and particularly Gerald, he didn't know what to say. To tell them now would be betraying Jas, and he had promised her, even though that did seem to be in another lifetime, that he would never reveal her secret. Taylor sighed. Besides, none of these people would believe in magic, would they?

'It was magic,' a voice said, and the council turned to see Jas and Kale standing behind them. 'You wanted to know how I did it? That's your answer.'

The councillors, seven men and eight women, stared at her.

'Taylor, you made a promise to me, and I release you from that promise now. You may tell the council what you know about me. I think that knowing will help you and the people of Trafford City. You can see by looking at Kale that we aren't that different from the Jinx. In fact, we were all born from the same primordial soup.'

The two soldiers who had been monitoring Kale and Jas suddenly came running into the mess. They were panting and disorientated.

'We … they … just suddenly disappeared!' said the youngest. His name was Joshua and he was only 19, but he had a deep frown line furrowing his brow. Joshua, like so many young people in Trafford City, appeared to be much older than his years.

Jas gave a half smile, 'We didn't "disappear" so much as give you the slip …'

Taylor stood. 'Please join us,' he said. 'The council are naturally very curious about where you have been.'

Taylor couldn't take his eyes off her. The weirdest thoughts had been going through his head since he had learnt of her marriage to the alien Emperor. She walked and talked like an Empress, and her – the word *aura* came to his mind, but he couldn't remember where he had first heard it – glowed with a vibrancy he hadn't seen before.

'Please sit down,' Sylvia said. 'You're welcome here if you plan to enlighten us.'

'Of course,' Jas nodded. 'I think you need to be able to trust us, and the only way I can see of gaining that trust is to tell you everything.'

As Jas's story began, Taylor sank back into his chair and listened. His heart beat hard in his chest as she told the story of her capture.

'On the night I left here, Kale came through a vortex and took me back to Jinx Town. I learnt there that I was on another planet, that the place the women called Jinx Town was actually Sharik and it was the capital city of Emin. Within days, I was married to the Emperor, Arven …'

Taylor noted how Jas's voice softened when she spoke the alien's name. His stomach churned as he waited for the horrible details of their wedding night, but Jas didn't speak of it. She told instead of the bonding ceremony, the marriage auctions and the way the Jinx lived.

'Enforced marriages. How awful,' said Sylvia.

'Yes, I agree,' Jas answered. 'The women were well treated though. It was seen as an honour for a Jinx male to bond with a human. We were the aliens on their planet, and yet they chose to accept us, for all our faults.'

'What happened to you?' asked Taylor.

Jas paused, and not for the first time Taylor wondered about the detail she was avoiding describing.

'I was unharmed,' she said finally. 'Arven treated me well, and I gained the respect of his people.'

'Then … why did you come back?' asked Sylvia.

'I guess I was … homesick,' Jas said. 'I felt all the time that I had to get home. I never really settled.'

'That is understandable. Surely no one could be happy in that situation? You were kidnapped and forced to …' Sylvia said.

'No-one wanted to go to the marriage auctions, but afterwards they adapted,' Jas explained. 'I put it down to the magic of the bonding ceremony.'

'You've used that word a lot,' said Harvey. 'But we don't really believe in magic, Jas. We've come from a world of science.'

'I know. And I wouldn't have believed it myself, but I have seen things … Besides, didn't it ever occur to you that the Jinx technology wasn't scientific at all? They don't use machines to open the portals – they use the power of their minds.'

A debate struck up among the councillors: the idea of magic was preposterous to some, but not to others.

'We're getting off the point,' Taylor said. 'And I think there is something crucial here that we are missing.'

'There is. Kale tells me that things aren't right here,' Jas explained.

'What are you saying?' asked Harvey.

'The planet is dying. The air is poisoned. Kale can sense it.'

'How?' asked Gerald.

Jas turned her head and recognised the doctor. '*You!*'

Kale moved to Jas's side, his eyes on Gerald Avery: his pupils began to swirl and move for the first time since he had arrived on Earth.

'This man …' Kale said, 'has tried to hurt the Empress …'

Jas put her hand on his arm and shook her head. 'It's in the past, and we must forget that if we are to move on, if we are to regain the trust of these people.'

Taylor found himself staring at Gerald, and the memory of what he had done, or tried to do, to Jas came flooding back. How could he have forgotten that the doctor had tried to blackmail her into a sexual relationship? It had been because of Gerald that Jas had left the safety of the mall and ultimately been captured by the Jinx.

'What is wrong with the planet?' Sylvia asked, bringing the discussion back to the issue at hand.

'I don't know, but something is killing the atmosphere,' Jas said. 'Kale, do you know what it is?'

'Your science has done this, and you don't have much time,' he said vaguely.

'How?' asked Taylor.

Growing panic flitted around the room as the councillors fidgeted.

Kale closed his eyes and concentrated hard. 'This place is like a thick black veil over my eye. I can see, but not see.' He shook his head and pointed to the doorway. 'There is something out there causing this. It makes the air poison, while the culprits hide below. It is all I can see right now.'

'We need to talk,' said Sylvia. 'Will you and Kale excuse us now, Jas? For obvious reasons, the council must speak freely without you in earshot.'

'We'll go outside,' Jas said. 'Maybe Kale can learn more. There's something in the building that is blocking him.'

'Lead,' said Dawn, appearing from behind the stage. 'We discovered that the Jinx don't get along with it.'

'More poison,' said Kale again, and he shuddered.

Jas and Kale walked away from the councillors and headed toward the door.

'How long were you there?' Taylor asked Dawn.

'Long enough.'

Taylor felt a flush of guilt colour his cheeks as he wondered at Dawn's meaning. Who had she been observing as she hid behind the stage wings?

I haven't done anything wrong, he thought. But his eyes had followed Jas, and his curiosity and interest were obvious.

'This is all very interesting,' Sylvia said. She exhaled slowly. 'I must admit I am fighting the terror I feel at being in such close proximity to the enemy.'

Murmurs from the other council members confirmed their own mutual response to Kale.

'Kale cares deeply for Jas, and if the alien is capable of feeling emotion, then surely we can come to some understanding with him?' Sylvia continued.

'What do you mean?' asked Harvey.

'She had power over him. Seeing our enemy like this makes me realise that they too must have their reasons.'

'What reason can possibly justify the murder of millions of people? Men and boys mostly,' said Gerald.

Taylor frowned at the doctor. He would never quite get over his dislike of the man. If it weren't for the fact that they needed him, Taylor would have sent him away soon after the betrayal. But the man had his uses. And he couldn't disagree with him about the Jinx. It was what they all felt. The deaths and devastation they had suffered were down to these monsters. No matter how human they appeared to be.

'His loyalty to Jas does not mean we should automatically trust him,' Taylor said. 'But he may have his uses as an ally for now.'

5

The broken mall door had been sealed with rough pieces of wood, and two teenage boys were now cleaning up the glass. Some tomato and herb plants that had been in the lobby area had been moved away to another door where the light streamed through.

'They were using this area as a greenhouse. Our arrival ruined it,' Jas said to Kale as they approached.

The area inside was oppressive, but Kale became jittery again as they approached the exit. He didn't like crossing the threshold. Jas took his hand and smiled up at the giant mage. Then she pushed against the door and pulled him outside as quickly as possible.

It was midday and the sun had risen fully over the car-park. The heat was intense and suffocating. The air was thin, and a still and dull haze hung over their heads like a thick miasma.

Kale was silent as they walked around the car-park, but Jas noticed the beads of perspiration that spotted his brow. Sharik had been warm, but the heat there had been dry and comfortable. She had never seen Kale sweat, and the only perspiration that had ever appeared on Arven's pale skin had been generated by the exertion of their love-making. Jas rapidly pushed the thought back into a blocked compartment in her brain. She didn't want to think anymore about Arven. Those days were gone, and thinking only brought back the hurt that her own actions had caused. She wondered instead about the temperature on Earth, but this only drew another comparison as she remembered how everything was balanced on Emin: there were no extremes of pain or suffering, but pleasure was heightened. Earth was the antithesis: Trafford City was the exact opposite of Sharik. There were so few people here – and yet they were quite clearly starving. In Sharik – *and why do I keep thinking of it now by its Jinx name when 'Jinx Town' was sufficient when I lived there?* Jas thought – there was a huge population, but an abundance of food. There were no street beggars, no-one homeless. Her mind stumbled over the painful thoughts. But the analysis wouldn't end. She compared Sharik with Trafford City and she came to a very outlandish conclusion: Earth was the yin to Emin's yang, and Sharik and Trafford were poles on opposite sides.

This is insane.

Food was scarce in Trafford City, that much was obvious, and the people here worked hard for their livelihood. On Emin, there was an abundance of fruit, fresh produce, meat, cheeses, bread, and she had never questioned where it came from. *Where* did *it all come from? There was no suffering at all. How was that possible?*

'We look after nature, and it looks after us,' Kale said, as though he were reading her mind. 'These people have not respected their world, and now it punishes them.'

'Can you get a fix on where the contamination is coming from?' Jas asked.

'A "fix"? I'm not sure I …'

Jas sighed. Sometimes she forgot that the Jinx didn't speak English well, and using a colloquial term was apt to confuse them.

'I mean, can you find out where the pollution is coming from?' she asked again.

'There is little point in trying. It's too late for the planet, Jasmine. We need to leave here. I have to protect you.'

'And go where?' Jas said.

Kale shook his head. With another skilled Al Kuzemen he might have had a chance to find somewhere more habitable for them to live, but Jas was new to magic and it would take years to train her. Years that Earth didn't have left.

'We may have to return to Emin,' Kale said.

'You know we can't go back.' But the thought of return, of seeing Arven again, made her feel an intense hope. Even though she knew she could never explain her betrayal in any satisfactory way to him.

Kale said nothing, he stared up at the sky and tried to trace the poison. Its contamination stretched far and wide, but the focus was somewhere below ground. He made a gesture, a sweep of his hands across his face and chest. It reminded Jas of the sign that Catholics made as they entered a church. Jas had not been religious herself, but the school she had worked in had been run by a diocese, and she had been forced at times to genuflect during assembly to be seen to be following the school's ethos.

'What is that you're doing?' she asked.

'There is great evil here, Jasmine.'

'I've never known you to be superstitious.'

Jas knew, of course, that there had been little for Kale to fear on Emin. His home planet had nothing truly dark or evil in it. Before they had brought the Earth women there, the Jinx had been a simple race, and they mostly abided by their own rules. Even so, before she and Kale had left Jinx Town, there had been cracks appearing in their society. The Arrak Nah Tiamen had begun to commit murder among their own kind, and their perfect world had begun to unravel. Why? Because of jealousy. Some of the Jinx wanted what they couldn't have – wives. They were not used to being denied anything, if the truth be known. And this one commodity was not available for everyone. There simply were not enough women to go around. When she thought about it, Jas couldn't really understand why that was. She had assumed that the Jinx had merely been corrupted by their contact with humanity, but now she saw that the focus of their jealousy was something that should have been easy to solve. In some ways, they were like spoilt children who were being told 'no' for the very first time in their lives.

'Where were all the women, then?' Jas said suddenly, and Kale looked over at her, surprised at the place her mind had wandered into. 'Kale, how many Arrak Nah Tiamen are there? What was your population size before you raided Earth?'

Kale closed his eyes and thought about the question. He didn't know why she wanted to know the answer, but reasoned it must be important in some way.

'Emin is a big planet – bigger than Earth – and there are just over a thousand towns like Sharik,' Kale explained. 'Each town had a population of around five hundred thousand to one million men. It was why Earth seemed so perfect for us. You had so many more women than we could need.'

'I reckon the population of the United Kingdom alone was around 65 million at the time you attacked. There has always been a pretty even balance of men and women, but generally at that time there were slightly more women than men. So we're looking at around 32 to 35 million females in this country. Worldwide there must have been maybe three and a half billion women. Where did they all go, Kale? Even if there are as many as a billion males in the Jinx population, they could each have had a companion taken for them, and that would still have left two and a half billion women remaining here.'

'Not all women were suitable,' Kale said. 'Like the one inside called Sylvia. She would not have been taken by our men.'

'Yes, I remember …' said Jas, recalling how a Jinx soldier had put an old woman to death before her eyes. 'Of course you were looking for women to bear your children, so others would have been … disposable.'

Jas felt strangely distant from the past events. She couldn't criticise the choices Arven and Kale had made; she herself had been responsible for the deaths of many in her attempts to ensure her and Andrew's survival. Looking back, she could almost excuse the Jinx their choices, but it didn't mean that all of this was right.

'How many old women were killed?' she asked.

'I don't know. The soldiers had no orders to kill them, only to bring back the suitable ones and despatch any of the men who tried to retaliate. If they hadn't resisted, they wouldn't have been killed.'

Jas knew this wasn't how it had happened though. The Jinx soldiers, despite their orders, had killed the innocent along with anyone who resisted. Jas recalled finding a row of dead boys, all under the age of ten, lying rotting in the streets, their bodies eviscerated by the Jinx. The dead had born witness to the lie that Kale told, but as Jas reached out and touched his arm, a ripple of magic connected them, and she realised that Kale believed what he had said. The soldiers would not kill randomly. They would do so only if attacked.

Her mind went back to the theatre, the random slaughter of men old and young; but then she saw the moment with more clarity than she had ever recalled it before. The men *had* resisted, and the children had fled, screaming and running. What would have happened if they had all simply stood still and let the Jinx walk among them, taking the women they wanted?

She shuddered at the memory. She remembered hearing the screams of her pupils as the Jinx poured onto their coach, while she and Andrew ran and hid inside the theatre.

Kale's normally pale cheeks went paler. He had seen into her thoughts as surely as she had seen into his.

'We did not kill for the sake of it,' he said again. 'And those images I see in your head, they are not the work of my people.'

'I saw your soldiers descend on the bus,' Jas said.

'Yes – but you did not see them kill the children. They would have taken the female ones, killed any adults who resisted, but they would not have killed the boy children.'

Jas's head hurt suddenly as she recalled the screams. They had haunted her dreams for years and fed fuel to the fire of her hatred of the Jinx. Even when she had lived among them, and grown to love Arven, she had found it hard to see beyond the slaughter he had caused in the name of saving his race. Jas's mind's eye ran over the dead bodies she had seen. A decapitated fireman, the ragged wound ripped into the stomach of a small boy, the throat of an old man cut so deep his head tipped back to show the scored bone of his spine.

'If not the Jinx, then who?' asked Jas.

Kale didn't answer, but he looked upwards again and frowned.

The sky held the unhealthy taint of orange as Jas squinted upwards once more. The firmament, she knew, was not really blue; that was just an illusion created by the natural process of sunlight passing through dust and moisture, which filtered out the reds and oranges from the spectrum and left just the blues. This was why Jas couldn't explain why, on what appeared to be a cloudless day, the sky looked orange. It was an impossible occurrence and meant that something was definitely not working in the usual way in

Earth's atmosphere.

If she was to help, then she had to find out what was wrong here and try to fix it.

'What you wish for is impossible,' Kale said.

'How can you read me so easily?' Jas asked. This was not a skill that Kale had shown on Emin.

'I don't know,' he said. 'Now we are here, I just can.'

6

Five Years Earlier.

Major Douglas Handley relaxed in the picturesque gardens, watching his wife, Clarice, snipping flowers to place inside the house. Clarice loved the garden. But then she was the epitome of an Anglophile. Everything English charmed her, even their godawful coffee and that strong brown tea they drank. It all tasted bitter and metallic to Handley, but Clarice claimed it was the best tea there was.

Handley was happy in England. He had an expensive house in the charming English countryside – which his wife was in love with – a fat salary, an easy command and the benefit of diplomatic immunity. What more could any American Major hope for when technically he had been put out to pasture?

Since they had lived in Cheshire, Clarice had taken to 'doing lunch' with the local ladies and had become interested in the meaningless politics that occurred in their small community. He had never seen her quite so contented, and Handley was grateful for anything that pleased Clarice. He had spent years trying to please her and her family. Sometimes with little success.

Clarice Beaumont, of the New Orleans Beaumonts, had come to Handley with a stack of social credentials and the financial impetus that could have swept him successfully into politics – if he had been of that mind-set. In those days Handley had been slimmer, fitter, and dashing. He had known right away that Clarice would make the perfect complement to his career. He had, quite literally, swept her off her feet.

Clarice brought a rose over to the garden table and placed it in a small narrow vase.

'The day is gorgeous,' she said. 'Don't you think so, Doug?'

Handley nodded, but continued to read his paper silently.

'Have you seen this beautiful rose, Doug? England has such stunning flowers. Especially this time of year.'

Handley picked up his glass of lemonade and sipped it, then placed it back down on the table.

'It's idyllic here,' Clarice continued. 'I'm so happy.'

'I'm pleased for you,' Handley said, his tone indifferent.

Clarice poured lemonade from the jug into her own glass and topped up Handley's as she looked around the garden again. The weather was warmer that day than it had been of late, and Handley was happy to spend time in the garden with her, but his indifference struck home once again.

Soon after they had married, Handley had given up his excursions to the gym. He enjoyed his food and wine and indulged himself on his wife's money. But he had kept his army career; it gave him respite from Clarice, when the intensity of her expectations became too much. There were always missions to plan, especially since Clarice's father had bought him his promotion to Major. Handley didn't know quite how that had happened, but one day he had received the notice, the next he had been a Major. Jonathan Beaumont couldn't have a son-in-law with lower social standing than that.

The Beaumonts were very powerful people: they had their fingers in many pies. One might even say that they were something of a mafia in their own way. Not that Handley had ever heard of any really illegal dealings, but people deferred to Clarice's father, and whatever Beaumont wanted, for him or his family, he usually got it without too much fuss. Of course, Handley had known exactly what he was getting into and had welcomed it. Money, power and notoriety had always been things he had craved.

'Cook is making us a Caesar salad with roast chicken for lunch ...' Clarice said.

'Tell her not to forget my fries,' Handley said.

'Oh, Doug! You don't need fries with every meal. I thought we'd have a healthy lunch.'

Handley placed down the paper and looked at the lemonade glass.

'And I'd like a gin and tonic, too,' he said.

At that moment Sturgeon, the butler, came out into the garden.

'Julia Forrester is here to see you, Major,' said Sturgeon.

'I wasn't expecting her,' Handley said. 'Send her into the office and I'll be there shortly.'

'Oh, Doug!' Clarice complained. 'Today's your day off – why is your assistant here?'

'I don't know,' Handley said. 'It must be important.'

Julia passed Handley a set of confidential orders, the contents of which at first seemed to him to be routine. He accepted his new assignment with the usual indifference he showed to all of the army's machinations. The enemy was attacking, and he was called upon to act as the American liaison for the British/American alliance. As he packed his case, Handley paused to read the instructions again, more carefully.

There was always an enemy. Always a crisis. He had seen this type of urgency so many times before that he didn't really take it seriously – until he learnt that all flights out of the country had been cancelled.

Handley ignored Clarice as she watched Sturgeon place his case in the boot of Julia's car. They had an urgent meeting, which meant Clarice would have to eat lunch alone again, but Handley felt no guilt, only his usual indifference. He climbed into the car next to Julia. She was a slender, sophisticated girl, but far too staid for Handley's taste. Even so, he took advantage of his position and ran his hand over her thigh as she started the car.

Julia said nothing; she neither responded to, nor rejected, his advance.

Interesting.

'What I'm about to tell you is highly classified,' said Colonel James at the consulate. 'It cannot leave this room.'

'I understand,' Handley said.

Handley was expecting to be told about a fighting strategy that the Colonel's paranoia wouldn't let him share with his most trusted officers. He didn't expect to hear that there were aliens among them, who had begun a series of strange attacks all over the world.

'We've known about them for a while. We have evidence they've been here before.'

'What evidence?' Handley sat upright, and his heavy midriff groaned as he leaned forward to give Colonel James his undivided attention.

James held out a file. It was a thick brown folder, and it had the word *CLASSIFIED* stamped boldly across the front. Handley took the file, placed it on the table between them and began to flick through it.

At first he didn't know what he was looking at. The folder contained photographs of some obscure art.

'Cave drawings,' James explained. 'Found in the Amazon. Those date back over one hundred thousand years.'

'I don't know anything about cavemen,' said Handley, frowning.

He studied the pictures carefully. The images showed crude drawings of beings towering over what Handley assumed were self-portraits of the cave dwellers themselves. He turned another page, saw more photographs, more caves, more strange beings.

'Egyptian,' James pointed out as Handley studied a picture of a faded carving that contained hieroglyphs as well as images. These pictures were less crude, but Handley was struck by their amazing similarity to the others.

The tall beings were drawn wearing some kind of armour, reminiscent of that used in China at the time of the Ming Dynasty. Armour that couldn't possibly have been made in the eras when the pictures were drawn.

'Leonardo Da Vinci predicted helicopters,' Handley pointed out. He liked to be cynical and found conspiracy theorists a bore.

He turned over to the next page. He found images of artwork he had never seen before. His wife liked art, and often ensured a gallery visit was included on his leave trips. He didn't mind traipsing around looking at old paintings, and some of the information about them had stuck. He recognised the style of Turner, for example. A picture of an autumn forest and a wild deer captured caring for her young. However, in the background, Handley could see a tall, armour-clad figure hiding behind one of the trees. At a distance it could have been mistaken for part of the foliage, but close up, Handley could see the jewel-covered helmet and the Ming Dynasty-style armour that covered a long arm. Tapering and elongated fingers clutched a mighty sword. The sword had a glow around it, as though it had absorbed the light from the moon above.

'Jesus …' Handley gasped.

'We have more images like this,' James said.

'How has this gone unnoticed?'

'This painting was confiscated from the artist at the time. Like I said, the government have known about the sightings for years – centuries in fact.'

'That's some history and knowledge. We're talking the 18th Century, and a governmental body existed to watch over these things?'

James nodded. 'And it wasn't a new organisation even then.'

Handley turned the page and found a photocopy of a letter. He read the contents aloud:

'An earthquake shook the ground beneath our feet and a great void opened up before us. Briefly I looked down into a light-filled tunnel. I thought then I must be dead, or dying. I saw mighty warriors pour from the mouth of the opening, and they swooped on our men, and the enemy alike, swatting them down like flies. They swarmed the bunkers, taking food, clothing, tents. Everything that you would expect, except they avoided the weapons, leaving the bayonets scattered and trampled as though they had no value at all. Mother, the doctors don't believe me: they say it's shellshock and that I'll soon get over it …'

'That letter is dated 12 September 1915,' James pointed out. 'Luckily it never reached the boy's mother and the censor placed it in departmental hands. The boy died soon afterwards. He had gangrene in his wound. It was just as well. We didn't have the technology in those days to brainwash information away.'

'You mean you do know?' asked Handley.

Colonel James gave a thin smile. 'The time for that is gone.'

Handley read on. The file contained more sightings, more letters, more photocopies and photographs of artwork, but nothing truly new after that. In a way, the dossier was less complete than Handley had hoped.

He wanted answers now, wanted to understand who the enemy were; but for all of the centuries of accumulated knowledge, all they had were sightings. It was proof enough that the aliens existed, but that was all.

Later, James showed him some amateur camcorder footage of one of the alien giants' raids. Handley's eyes widened as he saw the slaughter, heard the screams of the desperate women who were taken by the aliens, and watched the vortex close, leaving behind sheer devastation: hundreds of people dead.

'I don't understand how this helps,' Handley said.

'Major, for years these aliens have attacked our world. Small, inconsequential raids. Sometimes there have been reports of people being taken by the aliens and experimented on.'

'Cranks,' Handley said.

'I agree,' James nodded. 'There have been reported pregnancies too. Women who said they were abducted and forced into liaisons with the aliens. All unproven, as most of these incidents happened too long ago. Our investigators at the time believed that in *most* of these cases the women in question had simply had straightforward sexual encounters, later found themselves pregnant, and felt they had to lie about it for one reason or another.'

'You say *most*?'

'We can't explain why in some cases people are born to parents of less than average height, yet they are exceptionally tall. Modern science calls this "throwback" – and yes, it's true that a white couple can suddenly have a black child, because of a throwback gene in one or more of the parents' ancestry.'

'You think the aliens have been fucking our women?'

James held out another file. This one was much thicker than the first. 'We think these may be genuine cases.'

Handley took the file, but hesitated to open it. He wasn't sure what he would find inside. 'Maybe summarise this one for me,' he said.

'Okay. Inside you'll find the complete story of Anna Solace. She was a young girl who lived in Maine in the early part of the 19th Century. When Anna was 20, she went missing from her parents' locked house. Anna was a good girl: she went to church on Sundays, did charitable works, and was being courted by the vicar's son, Jeremy Johnson. At first the parents thought that Anna and Jeremy had eloped. The father stormed around to the vicarage and found, to his horror, Jeremy fast asleep in his own room. He knew nothing of Anna's disappearance. The area was searched. Anna wasn't found.

'Six years later, in the middle of the night, Anna's parents heard cries coming from their daughter's old bedroom. They ran in to find Anna, not a day older than she had left, still wearing her nightshirt, crying in the corner of the room. When asked what had happened, the girl couldn't explain where she had been. All she could remember was a man in armour taking her away.

'Nine months later, Anna gave birth to a child. It was stillborn, and the family hushed it up as best they could.'

James paused, then went on: 'The file is full of similar stories, although generally the children survived. Further investigation, wherever the records could be found, revealed that the children in these cases, male and female, grew to be taller on average than their parents and grandparents. They were said to have unusual characteristics, too.'

'What characteristics?' asked Handley.

'Superior strength, and they didn't seem to age as quickly as those around them. Looking young for many years.'

'How far back do these records go?'

'The earliest report, again a similar story to the Anna Solace case, tells of a girl born in Cornwall in the 17th Century. She was only 16, and her mother claimed she was a virgin. When she fell pregnant, her parents were so ashamed that they took her from the village and hid her in an abandoned woodcutter's cottage. When the labour began, the village midwife was brought to the girl. As the girl lay dying, she told the midwife about a demon who had taken her from her bed one night. She said that a tall and monstrous devil had forced himself on her. When the child, a baby girl, was born, of course she looked human. The midwife never told anyone what the poor teenager had said as she lay bleeding to death – the birth having damaged her too badly for her to survive. She pitied the girl and believed that she had been raped.

'The baby girl was adopted and raised by a couple in the next village, who couldn't have children, and the whole thing was soon forgotten. But as the baby grew into a woman, a woman of exceptional height, rumours began to abound. It was said that she was seen in the woods running naked on a full moon, and soon the cry of witchery was raised. The midwife, on hearing these rumours, finally confessed to the local priest what the girl's mother had told her. The priest set up a trial and they took the girl, now a teenager, from her adoptive parents.'

'They burnt her?' Handley asked.

'Yes. Eventually. It was the only solution feebleminded peasants could come up with. But first they subjected her to the usual tests – drowning, torture – all of which she survived, because she was also uncommonly strong.'

Handley fell quiet. He flicked through the file, seeing other stories similar to the two that James had described. He began to feel strangely alive and interested for the first time in years. This was not the mundane or the norm. This was different. Despite his excitement, though, he remained cynical.

'So what you're saying is, these aliens have been fucking our virgins and impregnating them? It sounds … preposterous. It sounds B-movie …'

James rubbed his forehead. 'To be honest, I don't know what I'm saying, Handley. But these monsters are now blatantly taking our women. At least, those women that seem capable of bearing children … And this time, they aren't returning them; which would suggest to me that they don't have any of their own. How that happened we can only guess. They've taken some before – we know that – but never on this scale.'

'What do you think we can do about it?' Handley asked.

James took back the two files and turned in his chair, reaching out to the filing cabinet behind him. He opened the first drawer and dropped the folders inside, then locked it, removing the keys that dangled from the top.

'There's nothing we can do. They are going to keep raiding until they have what they want. You know already that our weapons are no use against them. If we stand up to them, we'll die, and they'll still take the women.'

'We could try to negotiate. There are plenty of women to go around,' Handley suggested. 'Last time I checked, the Earth's population was over seven billion, and more than half of those were women.'

'We could try to negotiate … In fact we'd like you to be *seen* to be trying to come to an arrangement with the aliens.' James dropped the cabinet keys into his pocket, then met Handley's eyes. 'But the thing is … we've been prepared for this for a long time.'

Handley listened to James's plan. His eyes barely widened when he heard about the bunkers strategically placed all over the world; about how the chosen few were going to go underground and leave the rest of the world to be picked clean of females and resources. The important detail was, if Handley followed his orders to the letter, he had a place of safety reserved for him.

Soon after Handley's meeting with James, the shit hit the proverbial fan. Handley remained in London until halfway through the battle that ultimately destroyed the city, then left with his selected team and returned to the main base to place it in lockdown. Then he headed toward the location he had been given by James. The location of the base later known as MD59.

7

MD59 – Present Day.

MD59 was a city underground. Handley hadn't been expecting that. He had presumed he would find a glorified bunker with a few computers, lots of provisions – probably no bigger than a military base. But Colonel James had been true to his word, and now Handley controlled the large facility, and the rations given to the people under his command. He also controlled the breeders and the P-class females based there.

Major Handley, Colonel James and some key government officials had gone to ground with over 5,000 military staff and 4,000 preselected fertile females, and the underground city of MD59 had been activated as Taylor Arch's men had lain dying at the hands of the Jinx. Since then, Handley had had few regrets.

It was the best way to live. He was, as he had always wished to be, ultimately powerful.

Now Handley walked through the P-class domain and headed toward the room where Gina would be waiting, prepared for him. He fed his voucher into the scanner and the door opened.

Gina looked at him solemnly. She was sat on the sofa by the bed, dressed in the clothing he preferred. The woman was in her twenties, but her small frame leant itself to the appearance of youth. She was wearing a short kilt, a tight-fitting blouse stretched over her small chest. The tiny buds of her small breasts pressed against the material, and Handley felt himself harden immediately. Here his penchant for the 'schoolgirl' image was not frowned upon. No-one cared what turned people on; the constraints of their old society meant nothing.

Gina was P-class. A pleasure drone. A girl who was incapable of breeding due to some unfortunate genetics and so served, with others of her sort, to relieve the tensions of the military force. Of course, those married soldiers who had chosen to bring their wives and families with them into the bunker were not allowed to use this service. It was merely for those who, like Handley, had no partner with them underground. So Handley got to use Gina whenever he wanted.

Gina stood as music flowed through the speakers, and she began a dance routine for Handley's amusement. He sat down on the bed as she gyrated, stroking herself between the legs with one hand while cupping one of her breasts with the other. The music intensified and Gina began to remove her clothes.

Handley barely noticed that her expression never changed. Gina made no sounds, did not smile, did not cry, but her face remained passive. He knew why she was compliant, of course. The girl was drugged. Not enough to make her limp, but enough to control and persuade. This was the effect of the conditioning drugs that Handley's boss, James, had once hinted at. They could make anyone behave any way they wanted, with a combination of medication and conditioning.

To start with, all of the P-class women had been difficult. They had screamed and fought, accused their clients of rape. But as the months and then years had passed, each of them had slowly become the thing that they were being conditioned to be.

Gina, always the sexy schoolgirl, removed her blouse, but retained the kilt as she squatted down between Handley's thighs, parting her knees so that he could see the white panties she was wearing underneath. She didn't touch him, though, and Handley began to remove his own shirt and trousers. Once he was down to his boxers, Gina pulled his cock free and began to suck on it enthusiastically. It was as though she really believed she was sucking on a tasty lollipop.

Handley's large bulk flopped back on the bed. 'You like the taste of me, don't you?' he gasped, as pre-cum leaked into her small mouth.

'Yes, Major. You're so sexy, Major,' Gina said in a flat, monotone, emotionless voice.

But Handley enjoyed that deadpan sound. He edged back onto the bed, and Gina climbed over him. She pulled aside the panties and positioned herself over his cock. Then she slid down over him.

She was dry, and it hurt slightly, but this was how Handley liked it the most. It felt like she was unwilling, and so he always requested no lubricant. It was also the only time that Gina made any genuine sounds. She always winced a little, which pleased Handley. It made him feel that his less-than-average-sized cock was bigger than it was. Gina rocked over him. Her small legs were muscular from the exercise, and she never seemed to tire as she rode up and down. Handley found himself looking at her almost-flat chest, and he reached up to cup her small breasts in his hands. He pinched her nipples until she winced again, and then he shot his load deep inside her.

Once he came, Gina remained still until he told her to move. She responded to commands in much the same way a robot might. And indeed the pleasure drones were like emotionless sex dolls. But it made it easier for all of the men to use them while they were like this. Some of the soldiers had even convinced themselves that the girls were merely toys, not real people at all. It added to the pleasure, removed all guilt, and meant they could do whatever they wanted to them without any sense of responsibility. The P-class women were a necessary part of the running of MD59. An important way of maintaining control and keeping testosterone surges among the soldiers down to a minimum. Handley understood this, and used it all to his own advantage.

He slipped away from the bed, taking his clothing with him. He didn't turn and look at Gina, but he heard the other door behind him open and knew she was being taken away to be washed and changed for her next client.

Handley opened the door to the small shower cubicle attached to the opposite side of the room. Once inside, he dropped his clothing over a chair and stepped into the shower. He washed carefully, then took his time to dry and dress. By the time he had finished, he could hear music coming from Gina's room again. Another customer was being entertained. Handley briefly wondered who it was, then shrugged. He left the cubicle via a different door that led back to the corridor, not giving the girl, or her client, another thought.

8

'I made a terrible mistake,' Kale said as he and Jas settled down for the night on their new mattresses. 'This is no fit place for you, Empress.'

'Go to sleep,' Jas said. 'We're both tired and overwrought. Things will look better in the morning.'

Jas turned over on her mattress and pulled the duvet up over her shoulders. Her mind was a whirlwind of unrest and she couldn't settle. She was deeply distressed by all she had seen so far on Earth and, like Kale, she fretted constantly that they had made a mistake coming here.

Despite the efforts her former friends were making, she knew that they had no future. Her mind flashed to the aged look of Donovan, of Taylor even. Three years couldn't account for how sallow and drained everyone appeared. It wasn't enough time for relatively young and fit people to have aged so significantly. If they had told her 15 years had passed then she might have found it less difficult to believe. But no, it was three years – Kale had confirmed it, and Jas knew in her heart that it was true.

She wondered again at her motives for insisting on returning. Andrew, for all the poison in the air, seemed to be okay. She had needed to know he was still alive, but now she was even more concerned about the boy's future. As for Taylor, she didn't know how she felt about him anymore, and now that he had Dawn and Lucy, it was obvious that she hadn't been missed. Not that she had truly worried about the Captain during her absence. Sexually, her relationship with Arven had been the most satisfying experience she had ever had. She was his Empress, his lover, his wife. *What is the matter with me?* Jas thought. *When I was with him I pined for home, now I'm here I pine for Arven and … Sharik …*

Yes. Sharik was *home.*

She tried to push the thoughts and angst from her mind. *I've ruined that now. There's no going back.*

'Empress,' said Kale. 'We could go back, throw ourselves on the Emperor's mercy. He loves you. He will not turn you away.'

'Stay out of my head, Kale,' Jas said.

'I cannot help it. You are projecting so loudly I'm surprised that others cannot hear you.'

Jas sighed. 'Sorry. I just don't know what's the matter with me. This place … it feels … wrong. It's as though we came back not only to the wrong time but to the wrong place …'

Kale was silent for a moment.

'I have explored this possibility,' he said. 'But never in all our travels, our history, have we discovered, let alone travelled to, alternate or parallel universes. This is the world you once inhabited. But the problem is, you no longer belong to it. Emin has embraced you. You are Arrak Nah Tiamen now, even if you don't want to believe it.'

'What's an Arrak Nah Tiamen?' asked a voice from the front of the bookstore.

Jas sat up and looked down toward the front. The shop was dark, but she could make out a shape standing just inside the door near the old payment counter.

'You spying on us, Taylor?' she asked.

'No. I was passing and wanted to see if either of you needed anything.'

Jas pulled the duvet up around herself. She had stripped away the robe and now only wore a thin shift.

'You didn't answer my question …' Taylor said.

'Come in properly,' Jas answered. 'Pull up a chair.'

Taylor came forward, and Jas reached for the small bedside lamp that she had brought in and positioned inside the shop beside their makeshift beds. She switched the lamp on.

'Arrak Nah Tiamen, exact translation is, Warriors of Space. It is what the Jinx call themselves.'

'A pretentious name …' Taylor sneered.

'Not really. The Jinx are very literal about who and what they are. They wouldn't have thought of this in any other way. They are warriors who travel through time and space. It is that simple.'

Taylor pulled a chair away from a reading corner and sat down opposite Kale's and Jas's beds.

'So … you're one of *them* now?' he said.

'She is the Empress,' Kale said. 'She belongs to us.'

'Whether she wants to or not?' Taylor said

'We do not choose our destiny,' Kale answered. 'It chooses us.'

'I am present and can speak for myself …' Jas said.

She folded her arms over the duvet. She noticed how Taylor's eyes followed her movement and rested briefly on her breasts.

Destiny was indeed a peculiar thing, Jas thought. She had wanted to see Taylor again and now, faced with him, she felt none of the old feelings. She wasn't even slightly attracted to him. In fact now all she could think about was that she wanted to return to Emin, to Jinx Town, and more importantly to Arven. Even so, Jas refused to accept it was possible. She couldn't imagine herself grovelling at his feet and begging for forgiveness. Nor could she imagine admitting that she had been wrong.

A terrible pain twisted in her gut at the thought of never seeing Arven again. It made her wince.

'What's wrong?' asked Taylor, concerned.

'Nothing …' she said.

Kale looked at her in silence.

'Returning would be for the best …' he said eventually.

They would kill you! she thought back at him. *You know this.*

They can talk to each other telepathically, Taylor thought. *She's changed so much, yet she is so much more attractive than she was. Mysterious. Dangerous.*

Jas turned her eyes back to Taylor as though she had heard his thoughts, but she said nothing. They looked at each other for a moment. Then, unable to remain silent any longer, Taylor began to talk.

'The council asked me to speak to you,' he said. 'They are intrigued by this use of magic. And, despite what Harvey said, we have seen many displays of it in the last two years.'

Jas thought about the girl who had blended into her environment, effectively making herself invisible.

'There are women among us who have the power to make plant life grow in the worst possible soil,' Taylor continued. 'Some of them have a talent for finding things: water, animals, fuel sources; although, granted, we haven't been fortunate in that way recently. It's like a sixth sense among them. Others have the power of persuasion. Sometimes, when I'm talking to the council, I'm aware of how influential Sylvia is. It's as though she has a talent for convincing you to do something. A charisma maybe. Perhaps that's why she was in politics before this happened.'

Jas listened as Taylor revealed the skills he had observed in others of the women. Some, like Jas had been, were natural soldiers. Some had healing ability. Others had musical ability. They was all things that one might naturally have accepted as raw talents, and yet the way Taylor described them implied that they were executed with an unusual flair.

'It is as though the less technology we have, the more these abilities exhibit themselves.'

'Your science magic is failing. Therefore your inherent power is returning,' Kale said. 'However, it is not usually women who carry magic. It is a trait in the Earth women that I have observed, though.'

Taylor grew thoughtful, and Jas remained silent as she considered everything that both men had said.

'Science is evil magic. It is the poison that taints this planet,' Kale said.

'But how? We have nothing here. We are going back to the basics, growing plants the hard way, using horses, manual ploughs. We have no machinery to aid us.'

'And yet you have this …' Kale observed, waving his hand at the lamp. 'You have the box with captured souls inside. You have machines to take you places, to fly through the air; and there are those machines below the ground that are causing the real corruption.'

'Below the ground?' Jas asked sharply. 'Where, Kale? Can you see them now?'

Kale shook his head, 'I can feel them, but as yet cannot *see*.'

Taylor walked back to his home, but he didn't hurry. He had to think before he faced Dawn: before he felt the loving arms of his wife and daughter around him. He was shaken by Jas's return, by the newfound knowledge she and the mage shared. If he was to believe everything they said, then their world was limping to a final end. Their efforts were worthless. It made him feel as though he should merely give up trying to survive.

Jas being back perplexed him. He wasn't sure how he should feel about her, though she interested him more now than she ever had. And what about this marriage she had endured to the alien Emperor? His mind stumbled over the thought of her giving herself to a Jinx.

Kale made him feel odd. He had spent so much time trying to kill the Jinx, and now he was letting one have free access to their city. It was all so confusing. If this Emperor was similar to Kale, and Jas had to have sex with him, what would that have been like for her? The thought brought a pang of combined jealousy and disgust. It was perhaps the same feeling he would have if anyone forced themselves on Dawn. His imagination went into overdrive and, without realising it, his mind repeated all the questions that the human women had, held the fears that they had shared, all because he didn't know the implications of the Jinx/human bonding any more than they had known before it had happened.

Jas had explained to the council that it was something you couldn't understand until you experienced it. She had made it sound as though 'bonding' was a deeply spiritual experience. They had not asked her for details of her sex life with the alien, and Taylor knew he had no right to. She was not his anymore. But still there was this responsibility that he had to all of the survivors. Somehow he had let her down, and now she was, by virtue of her experiences, no longer a part of them. This realisation made his heart hurt in a way he had never expected or experienced.

Jas was as alien as Kale was. This was the reality. And yet the council had chosen to allow them asylum. In fact they believed that they could learn from both of them. It was all about protecting their new and fragile society. But what if this all meant nothing, as Kale and Jas had said? What if the

Earth really was going to end? How long did they have?

Taylor halted a few feet from his home. He couldn't go back inside and pretend that nothing had changed in their lives when everything had; all in the space of a day. He began to wish that Jas had never returned, and then he quashed the thought, horrified with himself that he could even think it. Yes, she was as complex as ever. True they had come with bad news, but she was alive and he was grateful finally to know what had happened to her, even if he didn't like it.

Of course the reality she told of the Jinx confirmed the human suspicions of what had happened to their women, but at least it didn't sound quite as bad as they had imagined. Taylor's thoughts stumbled again. No, it was worse. Far worse. What was he thinking? The Jinx made wives of human females, but wasn't it just the same as rape when it came down to it?

'It's not rape,' Jas said behind him.

Taylor turned, shocked that she had been reading his thoughts.

'I don't know how I can do it,' she said with a smile. 'But, like Kale, since we arrived here, I've been picking up *some* stray thoughts. Not all, and I'm not reading your mind. I just caught that last thought.'

'Where's your minder?' he said, looking round for Kale.

'I ordered him to stay behind.'

'And he always does as you say?'

'Not at all, usually. But strangely, *here* he has become more … I guess I am the nearest regal influence, now that he is away from Arven.'

Taylor heard that softness in her voice once more as Jas spoke the name of the Jinx ruler.

'Not rape,' he said, hoping she would elaborate.

'No. Believe me, after the bonding occurred, I was *willing*. More than willing.'

She turned around, then and headed back toward the bookshop.

'Jas,' Taylor called. 'I thought you wanted to tell me something.'

Jas stopped walking, but she didn't turn around. 'I just did.'

He stared after her even as she rounded the corner. She walked with a straight back, for all the world like a real Empress.

Dawn was standing in the open shop doorway as he turned back toward his home.

'What was all that about?' she asked.

Taylor shrugged. 'Where's Lucy?'

'In bed. It's pretty late.'

'Sorry. The council reconvened for a brief recap, but the meeting went on way longer than expected.'

'Not surprising, really. Her arrival is a bit of a shock to us all,' Dawn said. 'Do we still have guards outside the bookshop?'

'Jas isn't a threat to us, Dawn,' he said.

Dawn sighed, walking away from the door as he entered.

'I don't trust her,' she said.

'Let's not get into this. I'm tired.'

'We're *all* tired, Taylor,' Dawn said.

Dawn fell quiet, saying little more for the rest of the evening. Taylor was relieved: he hadn't wanted a full-on row over Jas; he was still trying to work her out himself.

Later, when they retired to bed, Dawn slid her hand down his body and found him hard. Despite his turmoil, Taylor was led along. Dawn had a way of seducing him, even when he didn't feel like it. He wondered if this was her magic. Her power. He pushed the thought away as he entered her and buried himself in as deeply as he could. She was soft and smooth and she groaned under him. He moved in her until Dawn's orgasm spasmed on his cock. She gasped against him, wrapping her legs tighter as he rose to the occasion and pumped her hard just as she liked it. Then, as Taylor came, he buried his head into her hair and he smelt, for the first time, a faint, unpleasant odour.

As he rolled away from her, the smell followed. Taylor raised his arm and smelt his own flesh. What was it? *Death and decay*, he thought. *Age and rot.* And it wasn't just on Dawn, but on his own skin too.

He thought back to the shining vibrancy that came from Jas and Kale and realised that they held some inner light that the survivors appeared to have lost. He shrugged. Maybe it was just poor hygiene, something they all lived with generally, but he was surprised he could even smell it at all if that was the case.

As he began to slip away into a relaxed sleep, Taylor had a vision of Jas in the arms of Arven. He didn't know what the Jinx ruler looked like, but in his mind's eye he saw an attractive man, tall by human standards, passionately embracing Jas, while she gasped and cried out in pleasure. Jealousy surged forward again, then Dawn's hand touched his thigh and the feeling receded. He wondered if the inner turmoil he was feeling was obvious to Dawn and it was causing her just as much uncertainty and pain as it was him.

9

MD59 had always been connected to the Trafford Centre. Had always controlled the lighting, the heating, the water supply. And it had amused Handley to leave things as they were. He liked to see the men and women above ground strive endlessly against the fate that nature had in store for them. Besides, as the women lived and bred there, they became another resource for MD59 to use.

They had observed the arrival of the Jinx magician and the woman a few days earlier, and the welcome they had received from the Trafford survivors. The woman was oddly dressed, wearing a kaftan of sorts made from rich silk. It was vibrant but regal, and Handley noted that she moved as though she were important.

'Strange,' said Handley. 'Why would they let a Jinx among them? Who is the woman? Is she some emissary from the aliens?'

'Our informant tells me that she was formerly a soldier with Taylor's army. Before they found the women,' Corporal Caine said.

'But there were no women among the soldiers …' Handley pointed out.

Caine showed Handley video footage of Jas training with Taylor. He had all of it to hand. A click of the mouse and the images came up on his screen.

'She hid it well,' Caine said, placing a file before Handley. 'A former teacher.'

Handley opened the file and saw a picture of Jasmine Regis in the uniform worn by the teachers at the school she had worked in, and then a shot of her in front of the classroom. They had a whole file on the woman. Her education, her hobbies, former lovers. Every detail of her life prior to the arrival of the Jinx was laid out before him.

'Why do we have this information on her?' Handley asked.

'She had been earmarked as a breeder with A-class potential.'

Handley was intrigued. He couldn't understand what was so special about the girl that James and his apocalypse team would have considered her that important.

'Why her?' he asked as he glanced down over the file.

'She was an unusual case,' Caine began. 'Obviously highly intelligent and resourceful. She had been steered into a teaching career even though it wasn't her first choice. We needed her to be in the right place at the right time. She didn't disappoint, either. Somehow she saved one of the pupils … a boy unfortunately … and managed to hide out from the Jinx, and from us. Remained undetected for several years.'

'I still don't get it.'

'She's chameleonic. Has excessive strength for her build. Charismatic. A natural leader.'

'Not breeder material at all then …' Handley said. 'Sounds like trouble to me.'

'Her blood group is rare. Rhesus negative,' Caine explained.

'Ah. She is potentially a throwback,' Handley said.

Over the years since his recruitment, Handley had been fed information from James via Caine. It was always on a need-to-know basis, but it didn't worry Handley that he never saw the full picture. What he had learnt, and what was relevant to Jas, was that the Jinx half-breeds were all rhesus negative. Somewhere in Jas's ancestry was Jinx blood: there was no 'potentially' about it. She was definitely of the bloodline. And there were more half-breeds on the planet that anyone had realised. At least, anyone who wasn't in the know like James.

Since Jas and the male Jinx had arrived at Trafford City, Handley and MD59 had been monitoring the changes that had began to occur in the centre. And there had been many. The female, Jas, now dressed as any of the other women did, was holding some form of counselling session with small groups of the women. These took place in the large area that was also used for the soldiers to train in.

'Of course the microphones haven't worked in that area for quite some time. We can only speculate what is being discussed in there,' Caine said.

'Is there no way we can get someone in there to fix it?' Handley asked.

'Not without exposure.'

'What about our insider?'

'Unfortunately they don't have that kind of technical expertise, and again the risks are too high …'

Handley dismissed Caine and was left to his own thoughts. Although they had little contact with James at MD1, he wondered what he was supposed to do. Their above-ground supply store, formerly known as the Trafford Centre, had long been compromised by Taylor's soldiers. Handley could have sent a team up to remove the survivors, take back the food that had been left there for MD59 to fall back on, but he had chosen to observe them instead. At that time, Taylor and his men had also attacked one of the nuclear plants that fed energy to the underground bunker and kept places like Trafford City with electricity and fuel.

Handley hadn't expected the soldiers to last long, but they had managed to hold their position for almost three years now. Attempts had been made to build a life, and despite all expectations, they were somehow managing to grow food in the contaminated soil. Taylor's continued survival was a source of both agitation and amazement to Handley.

Now, this new anomaly had thrown a spanner in the works, and Handley knew that Caine would report back to James all that he knew. What James would do about that, he wasn't sure, though he suspected that he would probably send in men to kill the soldiers, capture the Jinx: the remaining women would come in useful going forward also. It was James's *modus operandi*, after all.

Five Years Earlier.

An ambulance was blocking the route to Hersham Power Plant as the convoy of trucks and limousines turned into the main thoroughfare. As Handley would have expected, the streets were otherwise deserted, but as the lead truck, a huge machine carrying twenty soldiers in the back, pulled into the kerb, a man wearing a paramedic uniform opened the back doors of the ambulance.

'Thank god! You've got to help us. I've got some kids in here, and my wife and daughter are missing.'

Within a few minutes, more survivors – men, women and children – had come out of their homes.

Handley had been in a limo behind the third truck, with Colonel James. James opened the window, called to one of the soldiers, who hurried back to listen to his superior officer.

'Clear the way,' James ordered.

'Yes, sir,' said the young soldier. 'But we've found some survivors. What shall we do with them?'

'Are there any females?' James asked.

'Yes, sir.'

'Good. Load them into the back of the truck.'

'What about the men and boys, Colonel?' asked the soldier.

'Kill them,' James said. 'In the style of the Jinx.'

The soldier stared at James for a moment.

'I gave you an order, soldier,' James said.

The soldier backed away, then turned and hurried toward the front truck. By then there were over 100 people milling about the streets, waiting to see how the soldiers would help them.

The doors of the first truck opened and the squad poured out, weapons loaded and ready.

Though he was in the back of the limo, Handley could see through the front windscreen of the car. The car was soundproofed, and what unfolded was like a scene from a silent movie. The soldiers began to the load the women and female children into the back of the truck. One woman was proving to be difficult; she didn't want to leave behind her male child. The soldier clubbed her with the butt of his rifle, and she was unceremoniously pushed, slumped, into the back of the truck.

An soundless uproar ensued as the civilian men reacted to how the woman had been treated. As the back doors of the truck were slammed shut, soldiers turned, aimed and fired at the rioting men. As several fell to the ground, the others capitulated and stopped their fighting, but this meant nothing to the soldiers, who had orders to kill them anyway.

On their knees, hands on their heads, each man was executed.

'The paramedic could be useful,' Handley mentioned casually.

'True,' James said. He opened his window once more and gave the order.

The man was brought to them. James once again lowered the window.

'We're going to give you a unique opportunity,' James said to the man. 'You can live today and come and work for us.'

Around them, the screams of the dying male children, and the cries of the men as they were murdered, shattered the serenity that had been in the limo earlier.

'You bastard,' said the paramedic. 'You're killing them. It's you. It's all you. There are no aliens … You've lied to us all.'

'No, of course we haven't lied. This has just given us a unique opportunity,' James said, 'to have the kind of coup that no-one will ever see coming.' His voice was so cold that even Handley felt a shiver of fear run down spine, and he knew that he would never cross the man no matter what atrocities he was responsible for. 'Kill him,' said James, then he closed the window as a soldier pulled out his hunting knife and slit the man's throat.

The paramedic fell forward, mouth open as he made an attempt to object, but his soundless cries ebbed away into the tarmac along with his life's blood.

When all of the women were loaded in the back of the trucks, and the men were dead, James finally left the car.

'Lay them out on their lawns,' James said. 'It will warn away anyone curious enough to come this way. They will think it was the Jinx.'

Now, Handley considered again what James would do when he heard the news. He felt a momentary panic that he might be blamed for letting Taylor Arch's soldiers remain and use the resources for so long. It had been a game for them all initially. See how long they lasted, with a view to ending it any time. But perhaps James would think the time had long since passed, and that Handley's judgement had been impaired.

I can always justify it because of the surveillance, Handley thought. *And because of my informant.* It had been an experiment. One that would show the determination of humanity's will to survive after all. And it had been productive in many ways. They were in need of breeding stock, for example, and many of the women at Trafford Centre had proven themselves capable of that. Arch himself had a daughter, after all: James would certainly enjoy the irony of taking the Captain's child and making her a breeder or a whore.

Handley's mind turned to Julia. His former assistant was now in the breeders' unit. He shut down the computer, left his office and climbed into a small, electric-powered golf cart.

He wanted to check in on Julia. He didn't know why, but he liked to keep an eye on the girl. She was on her third pregnancy since being classified five years ago. She was doing as well as could be expected, but her turn out was a little disappointing. Like battery hens that produce too few eggs, some breeders would be put out to pasture. Julia was likely to be demoted to P-class if her next pregnancy took as long to take as this one had. For the moment, though, she was carrying a baby, and that made her useful.

He drove the cart through the underground tunnels, turning left at the first junction, which took him from the residential area to the medical wings. He parked the cart outside the breeders' unit and walked to the main entrance.

Despite being underground, with people they believed were trustworthy, they still had security on the medical buildings and on the armoury. Handley had a team of military police that patrolled the streets day and night to ensure that the soldiers were always aware that there was a higher authority than them. Drunken soldiers could be far more dangerous than drunken civilians, and they needed law and order just as much.

Now, Handley passed through security into the breeding house. He had triple-A clearance as the most senior officer on the base and was never questioned.

The breeders' unit was sterile. This was a hospital environment: all the women were impregnated via medical procedure, and sexual contact was not permitted. Handley passed several operating rooms where implantation took place. Julia, though, was over on the ward, and he made his way there. As he reached the corridor, he paused by the two-way mirror to look inside at the women. There were twenty of them in this particular ward, but Handley wasn't interested in the others

Julia was confined to bed for most of the process, permitted up only to walk to the toilet and back. Now she was sitting up, reading a book. Handley wondered where she had got the paperback from, but then recalled how Dr Tremaine had insisted that library books be brought down to the women for entertainment.

Handley had wondered if it would be better to have the women asleep through the pregnancy in a chemically-induced coma. That way, the medical staff could implant and remove at the same time without the fuss of having to care about entertaining the women. When he had suggested this to Dr Tremaine, the man had looked at him as though he were a complete monster. Handley had laughed it off, pretending it was a joke. But it had infuriated him that Tremaine would dare treat his opinions as a joke.

'Major,' Tremaine said as he walked along the corridor toward him. 'I didn't know you were planning to visit. I've just being doing a procedure.'

'A successful implant?' Handley asked.

Tremaine shrugged. 'Time will tell, but I suspect so.'

Handley looked back into the ward. A male nurse was now taking Julia's blood pressure. 'How is it going with this one?'

'Good,' said Tremaine. 'We are taking her down to surgery this afternoon, though. She's been suffering quite a lot with high blood pressure. We don't want any stress to reach the baby.'

'A girl, I believe?' said Handley.

Tremaine nodded. 'We are breeding only females this year. Next year will be a mix again.'

'And I become a father for the first time,' Handley said.

Tremaine scrutinised Handley carefully before answering. 'I was surprised you put yourself forward for this, Major. Most of the hierarchy aren't bothering. I guess it's because you have no family down here.'

Handley had no reason to worry about his lack of fatherhood, and he would not be involved at all in the life of this child. The girl would grow up with the same privileges, or lack of, that all the women on the base shared. She would be classified according to her own ability to breed. If she was lucky she would be chosen to be the wife of one of the single soldiers. It would all be based completely on her fertility.

Handley knew this, but he wasn't overly concerned. Females had their place, and he would probably persuade some ambitious soldier to marry the kid before classification was enforced – that was, if she wasn't a complete dud.

Handley glanced once more inside at Julia. It was a pity they wouldn't let him implant her directly. The breeding process was all so sterile. All so controlled. Unfortunately, though, the breeders were given better consideration than the P-class women. Handley wondered if this directive could be changed and why he hadn't chosen to enforce his seniority on the breeding houses before now. He toyed with the idea of impregnating some of the other women, then shrugged. It was a fun idea, but in reality he didn't have the energy or interest to deal with the battle Tremaine would give him. Tremaine and his bleeding heart conscience. Handley wondered how he had even qualified to be down here, when there had been so many fertility doctors to choose from.

'Let me know when the child is born. I'd like to see it,' Handley said.

'Of course, Major,' Tremaine nodded. 'We're doing a caesarean. Not sure if Julia will be able to have another one. There has been no end of problems with this pregnancy.'

'She will have to be reclassified, then.'

Tremaine nodded. 'I won't perform a hysterectomy at this time, though. I think we might give her one last chance … See how she heals.'

'Yes. We have so few good breeders, it might be worth trying again,' Handley agreed.

Handley left the area feeling odd about the whole antiseptic experience of his fatherhood, but his thoughts remained with Julia and her possible reclassification.

All the women in P-class, having proven unsuitable or unable to breed, were given hysterectomies. This meant there was never any inconvenience caused by their monthly cycle and they could work all the time. He wondered what it would be like to have Julia in the pleasure area, then felt the urge to revisit Gina again. He imagined bending her over the bed while he took her from behind. The idea excited him briefly. Then he replaced Gina's face with Julia's. She would hate being a whore far more than being a brood mare. Handley wanted to be the first to use her; he even fantasised about having four men hold her down instead of giving her the drugs and conditioning first. But then, that too was against James's rules.

10

The tent was as Jas remembered it, although it seemed less kempt than when she had left it a few days ago. She looked around. The wardrobe curtains were open, her clothes still hung from the rail inside. The bed sheets were thrown back just as she had left them, and she could still smell the odour of their sex in the air.

It was night on Emin; Jas could tell by the red glow that filtered in through the slit in the tent behind the bed. A slit she had made when she had escaped from the town and run with Kale across the desert in a desperate bid to flee back to Earth.

How am I back here? she wondered.

Then she saw him. The pain in her chest eased a little, but then intensified with fear as she wondered what reception she was going to get. Arven was slumped across the strategy table, maps spread out underneath his head. Instinct made her realise that he was sleeping from sheer exhaustion. Somehow she knew that he hadn't slept in hours, possibly days. Not since she had disappeared before his eyes into the vortex created by his own treacherous mage.

Her heart went out to him. The enormity of what she had done weighed heavily on her chest. The pain of parting hurt like a dagger cutting deeply into her stomach. A dagger that twisted and turned with every moment she was apart from him.

She walked toward him. The urge to touch his skin, to feel the electric and sexual pulse that leapt between them whenever they were in close proximity, wouldn't be denied, no matter how afraid she was of the consequences. She had to admit her presence now. There was no other choice.

Her fingers felt cold against his hot skin. She stroked his head, easing the sickness and pain for them both. He stirred under her hand. Waking from his tortured sleep to look at her.

'How?' he asked.

She shook her head, tears in her eyes at the reunion. She saw love in his eyes, not anger, not recrimination. And then the look turned to passion, and the lust that was created the day they bonded swept over them.

He lifted her up into his arms. She was like a fragile flower, a heroine in some obscure love story, and then Arven laid her down on the bed, rapidly pulling away both his clothing and hers.

'I'm never letting you go, Jasmine,' he said. 'You're mine.'

Jas opened her arms to him. His kisses rained down on her face, her lips, her bare breasts, and she arched against him, craving the touch of his mouth and hands.

'Arven …' she sighed.

He entered her gently. It was so far removed from the last jealous possession they had shared, that Jas gave herself completely to it. She felt loved, even though he never said the words. Jas knew it, and the words didn't matter anyway. Even so, she wanted to tell him now how she felt, how foolish she had been, beg for forgiveness as he took her.

She came, writhing and twisting and pushing back onto his cock. No longer afraid of him, or it, knowing it wouldn't hurt her beyond that pleasure-pain that was truly erotic and sensual.

'Jasmine …' he gasped, pouring into her.

This time, however, as his orgasm filled her she felt something different. There was no alien pod bursting into her womb, imparting rapture as it fought to join with her. The orgasm felt … normal.

'Oh, Jasmine,' Arven gasped against her breast. His movement inside her brought her to climax again.

What did it mean? Was Arven becoming human?

'It's happened,' he gasped. Laughter and breathlessness rippled from his expansive chest. 'It must have been the last time.'

He lay gasping on her breast. She felt happy, loved. And then the strangest thing occurred. She could no longer feel his skin. His body seemed to sink through her as though her form were dissolving into the ether.

'Jasmine …' he cried, but the sound was muffled in her ears.

Jas was shivering as she woke. The lamp beside her mattress was switched off but light filtered through the shop from the Trafford Centre concourse, and she could see Kale sitting on his mattress opposite her. His eyes were wide and afraid.

'You! Did you …?'

'No, Empress. Never. I would never touch you. I couldn't … This is so … *What are you?*'

Jasmine pulled the covers over herself. She smelt sex and perspiration on her body. She tasted Arven on her lips. She felt the concentrated sensitivity in her breasts and vagina that followed the intense sexual contact she shared with Arven.

'I dreamed he was with me.'

'I know,' said Kale.

'You saw it all in my mind?' Jasmine blushed.

'No … You weren't there. Then you returned …' Kale stuttered. He was shaking his head as his brain denied what his eyes had seen. 'I can smell him on you,' he said.

'It was a dream. It had to be.'

Kale closed his eyes and turned his head, as though the sight of her was too much for his eyes to bear. 'I have to take you back,' he said. 'There has never been a bonding like this. You have to go back to him.'

Jas drifted back to sleep, a sated smile on her lips. For the first time since she had left Jinx Town, she no longer felt sickness or pain.

Kale did not dare take his eyes away from Jas as she slept. He believed at any moment she would fade away again and leave him there with the Earthlings: a prospect that he did not relish. For, unlike her, he did not have the power to return alone.

'I need to start training again,' Jas said as she joined the new recruits in the training area the next day.

As always, Taylor was there to lead the morning session, and he noted that even with her boyish combats, trainers and T-shirt she looked so different from his former lover that he couldn't bring himself to touch her. Maybe it was the long hair, or maybe it was because she no longer had the need to hide what she really was. She had curves now, too. Taylor recalled that she used to bind her breasts to make them unnoticeable, but it was more than that. She had filled out a little, and he realised that this was because she had been well fed on the Jinx planet. *She'll go too lean again now she's back on rations*, he thought. *It will be a shame.* He liked her curves so much better.

'Do you remember anything of the combat instruction I gave you before?' he asked.

'Of course. All of it. I just haven't been practising.'

Kale was with her, as he always was. The Al Kuzemen had taken a seat on one of the exercise benches at the side of gym. He looked as though he hadn't slept well, but he barely took his eyes off Jas as she interacted with Taylor.

Taylor agreed to the training session, but he was reluctant. It felt odd to be around Jas. He hadn't touched her since the first day. She was like an illusion: some strange part of his mind believed she would disappear by some sleight of hand if he didn't keep an eye on her.

He set the recruits to work in teams, and then the martial arts session with Jas began.

They fought tentatively as first, as though each of them believed the other would break, but soon the adrenaline of fighting a worthy opponent kicked in, and Jas and Taylor kicked, punched and moved around each other like enemies, not former lovers. The recruits stopped working and turned to watch them. Jas moved with agility, an ability that appeared to be more reflexive than trained. There was a rawness about the way she fought and moved, and Taylor responded to it, rising to the challenge. The recruits had never seen him fight better. But when the session ended, none of them could say who had had the upper hand. It was equal: both strong and vital. Taylor appearing more so, the more he responded to Jas's moves.

When they had finished, both still standing but panting with the exertion, the recruits applauded them.

Jas laughed. 'That was fun. I think I've missed the exercise.'

Taylor nodded; his breath was strained, and he wasn't up to speech.

He glanced over to Kale. The magician was watching them both closely, but his eyes were mostly studying Jas. She was like a specimen to him; a confusing character to study and understand. Taylor realised she was as much a mystery to Kale as she was to him.

He thought back to her words a few nights earlier. He had told Dawn he hadn't understood what Jas was saying. He had refused to accept the obvious about her. But her words had come back to him again and again: she had enjoyed her coupling with the Jinx Emperor. Yet here she was, seeking him out and wanting to fight him. In the old days, a girl had been known to punch a boy in the arm to show her affection for him. Was Jas here to show Taylor that she was still interested in him? He was confused by it. What signals, if any, was she giving? She was unfathomable. Bizarre to say, because her behaviour was open and friendly to all. She also appeared less alien that day. It might have been because of the change of clothing. Taylor wasn't sure. Or maybe she was doing her usual trick of blending in, becoming a part of her surroundings as camouflage, just as she had done when she had pretended to be a boy.

Sweat-covered, Jas left the exercise area and went over to Kale.

'Impressive, Empress,' he said.

Taylor blanched at the formal way the mage addressed her around him and the others. He wondered if it was a reminder to them that she was important to the Jinx. That she was, in fact, off limits to all.

'Thanks for the workout!' Jas called back. She and Kale then headed toward the door of the training room, but as they reached it, Dawn appeared.

'What workout?' she said.

'Training,' Jas said.

'*You've* been training? What on Earth for?'

'I like training.'

Dawn glanced inside at Taylor. 'You've been working out with her?'

Taylor was aware of the jealous undertone and the implication of Dawn's words.

'Of course,' Jas said. 'It was all completely above board, Dawn. We even had an audience.' She nodded toward the chattering recruits.

'I need to speak to you,' Dawn said to Taylor.

'What is *her* problem?' Jas fumed as she walked away with Kale.

'They are bonded,' Kale said. 'But she sees you as a threat. On Emin, this would be a wasted emotion. He cannot betray her, any more than you can betray the Emperor.'

'It's not like that on Earth,' Jas said.

She glanced back to Taylor to see Dawn talking intently with him. She had her hand on his arm, and a strange expression was on his face. Jas frowned. Confusion furrowed her brow.

'You see,' said Kale simply.

'Things are *changing* here,' Jas said.

'The people are. But not quickly enough to save themselves. They believe too much in their old ways.'

'You talk in riddles as always, Kale,' Jas said.

'Open your eyes, Empress. See what is really happening and then you will be able to do the thing that has drawn you back here.'

'What thing?' Jas asked.

'Only time will tell …'

11

'We don't believe in magic,' said the youngest girl in the group.

'That's understandable,' said Jas. 'I didn't either. Not until the magic was proven, which is why I have asked Kale to show you some things.'

Kale stood up and walked forward. They were once more in the exercise area, where Jas, with the permission of the council, was trying to identify which of the women had latent magical ability and assess if they could be taught to control it.

Kale held his staff out in front of him. Jas nodded toward Andrew, who was waiting by the door. The boy turned the lights off and the room was plunged into darkness.

There was a collective gasp as Kale's staff tapped twice on the hard floor. Then a burst of light came from the end and floated above them like a bubble holding a vibrant firefly.

'It's a trick,' someone said.

Jas nodded toward Kale again. The mage moved his arm, turning the staff around so that colourful circles formed in the air. Each circle became another ball of light, and soon the room was illuminated as much as it had been with the electric light.

'Where does his magic come from?' asked Sylvia, who had been observing the whole scene from the back. She sat on a bench with three other council members.

'Kale?' asked Jas.

'Everything in the planet, in the universe, has energy. It is what we are all made of. I merely channel it.'

'Is that like … Reiki?' asked a woman sitting on the front row.

Jas turned to look at the woman. She realised it was Caroline, Donovan's wife. She had over the last few days been the kindest of the women, and Jas had often sought her company.

'I don't know. I've never heard of that …' Jas said.

'I'm a Reiki master,' Caroline explained. 'It's a healing thing. The belief is that you channel universal life-force energy to help to raise the vibrations in a person's aura. It is supposed to heal them. By that I mean physically, mentally or spiritually. Whatever is needed. Though we were never permitted to call ourselves healers as it opened us up to being criticised. Or blamed if it didn't work.'

'And you believe in this?' Jas asked.

'Yes. At least I did, before –' As she spoke, Caroline's skin began to glow gently. 'I have always tried to maintain my belief. I give our two children treatments, and Donavan of course. It seems to helps us all. The thing with Reiki is that when you give it, you also receive it. I always feel less tired once I've shared it with my family.'

'My god! She's *glowing* …' gasped one of the women sitting closest to Caroline.

'It is indeed the same energy,' Kale said. 'You have a strong sense of it. It's flowing through you, and because you have already accessed this energy, you have more control than you should have at this stage of your magical development.'

'What do you mean?' asked Caroline, looking down at her hands and seeing the faint white glow that came off her skin.

'You've been tapping into it to do something good. Magic should be used only for good things.' Kale explained. 'It is why you can manipulate it so well.'

'Shame you didn't think that before you raided our world and killed our sons and husbands, you murdering bastard!' yelled a woman from the benches.

'Please Margery!' Sylvia said. 'We are here to learn. This … magic … may help us.'

'I can't sit here and listen to this monster tell us how to live,' the other woman retorted. 'I watched my son being pierced through the heart by one of 'em.'

'We all lost someone,' the young girl who had spoken first said. 'But, things weren't that great before, were they?'

All heads turned to the girl. The room fell silent, and Jas realised this was because on some level they all agreed that the world had been broken long before the Jinx arrived.

'What's your name?' Jas asked her. The girl was about 15 years old. She had mousey blonde hair that fell over her long face. Jas observed that she was tall. Taller than average. Taller than herself.

'Natasha,' she said. 'Natasha Healy. I was in a foster home before. It wasn't good there. They weren't nice people … They …'

'You don't *have* to tell us,' Caroline said.

'I do,' Natasha said. 'I knew I was different, you see. I knew I wasn't the same as them.'

'What do you mean?' asked Jas.

'It wasn't just my freaky height. My mother put me in care when I was five. They never told me why, but I'd always felt she didn't want me. Couldn't cope with me.'

Natasha began to tell them a story of her unhappy childhood as she grew up in care. Her mother, she had been told, had carried an unwanted pregnancy to term because of her religious beliefs. But the child was a constant reminder of her father, who had abandoned her mother as soon as he learned she was pregnant.

'I believed this was true at first. That this was why my mother had left me. But it all turned out to be a lie.'

'What do you mean?'

'Before the Jinx arrived, I learnt where she lived. I went there.'

The group waited while Natasha collected her thoughts.

'She looked like me,' the girl said eventually. 'And I know she recognised me … but she pretended she didn't.

'I said, "Mother, why did you send me away?", and she answered, "I don't know you. I'm no mother. I can't have kids. Now go away."

'I knew it was a lie though. There was something in me that recognised her. I hadn't been given any pictures, and my memory of her was too fragmented, but I *knew* her immediately. It was like recognising part of myself. When she rejected me like that, I started to cry. Then she took pity on me. She looked around, as though checking to see if anyone was watching, and then she said, "Look you aren't safe here. You can't be around me. Just believe me when I say you must never try to see me again." Then she walked away.

'I didn't know what to make of it. I thought she was just giving me the brush off, but later, when I thought about it more, I preferred to believe she'd given me up for my own safety.'

'Why would she do that?' asked Caroline. 'Who was she hiding you from?'

'I don't know. But it was obvious that she was afraid of something.'

'Sometimes someone is forced to give up a child. If they can't look after it. Maybe she had … issues. The paranoia would suggest …' Sylvia said.

Natasha shook her head. 'You've asked us to come here and listen to Jas and Kale with an open mind. I think you can listen to me with one too. My mother was not mentally ill, or abusive. I *know* she gave me up for my own safety. You see, after I left her, I went back to the care home. As I walked up the driveway, I saw this black car parked by the door. Some instinct, I guess it was a sixth sense, made me duck down behind the fence by the gate as a man got out. He was in plain clothes but he walked like …' Natasha nodded toward Andrew, 'a soldier … you know?'

Jas nodded. 'I do. Go on.'

'There were a few of them in the car and they were flashing badges to one of the carers, like they were important. Then they went inside. I stayed where I was for a while. I don't know why, but I knew it would be a bad idea to go inside just then. After about half an hour, these men came out, and they were carrying a black bin bag. Another man had remained in the car while the others went in. He was a big man … fat, really. He got out and opened the bag. That was when I knew they had all of my things. You see, they pulled out a teddy bear I'd had for as long as I could remember. It was the only thing I'd had when they took me into care.'

Natasha grew quiet.

'What happened then?' Sylvia said gently, while Caroline placed her arm around the girl's shoulders.

'The fat man became really angry that I hadn't been found. He started shouting about closing the home down, how they had failed to take care of an "important asset". "The shit's hitting the fan and you assholes have lost one of 'em. I ought to have you court-martialled …" Then he got in the car. One of the other men threw the black bin bag into the boot and they all climbed in and drove away. I stayed hidden until they were gone, then I ran in the opposite direction, even though I didn't have anywhere to go. I just knew I couldn't go back.'

'What did you do?' asked Jas.

'Well, like the fat guy said, all hell was about to break lose, and the Jinx came. I just hid myself away like everyone else did. Later, I went back to my mother's house to find it had been raided. The door was wide open, so I went inside. The place was wrecked, and there had been some kind of struggle in there for sure. My mother was nowhere to be found. I walked outside and looked around. The street was quiet, like everyone in the whole world had magically disappeared. Then I saw one of those vortexes arrive for the first time, and I knew that the Jinx hadn't taken my mother. I thought it was the fat man that had her. I don't know why I thought that, but I did. After that, I ran away before the thing opened, back to the home, because I didn't know where else to go, but when I got there it was empty. All the other girls and the carers were gone. It was like something out of some kind of horror movie. Where you wake up and find that everyone has vanished and you're the only person left …'

'I'm sorry,' said Jas. 'It's an awful thing to be so young and be alone.'

'We've all been through similar,' Natasha said. 'I guess my story isn't anything different than anyone else's, except …'

'Yes?'

'I know about the magic. I mean … I believe I have something. It's saved me, hidden me, many times until now. I always know when something is going to happen. I thought it was a sixth sense. Like a survival instinct or something. But I know now that this is more.'

'What are the symptoms of this magic?' asked Kale.

Jas looked at him, surprised by his turn of phrase. He was becoming more human in his speech patterns every day that he remained among them.

'Symptoms? Well … I get this nervous sickly feeling in my stomach first. I usually wake up with it. Thought it was normal for most of my life … Then the hair stands up on my arms, usually right before something happens. It's then I always know to run. To hide. The minute I feel like that, I just can't help it …'

'Precognition,' Kale said. 'It is the same response an Al Kuzemen would get if his skill was in predicting the future. There have never been any women with this skill in our society that I know of …'

'That seems irrelevant now. Besides, Natasha is human …' Sylvia said.

'No. Not completely,' Kale said.

'What do you mean?' asked Caroline. 'Of course she is …'

'He's right. I've known it all along. My father was a Jinx,' Natasha said. 'It's why I've always been different. And those men knew it. It's why they wanted me.'

'What would they want with you?' Jas asked.

'I don't know. But, I'm not afraid of the Jinx – I was terrified of those men though. There was real *evil* in the fat man.'

The group was quiet and thoughtful for a moment. Then Kale began to show the women how to test their abilities.

By the end of the session he had diagnosed that all of them had some latent ability.

'What does this mean?' asked Taylor.

They sat on the benches while the last group of women dispersed. Jas was drained from the whole day of explanations and assessments. She had demonstrated her own skills over and over by showing the other women how she could turn into a boy, or read some of their thoughts. Her body ached as much as if she had been in battle all day. Some of the groups had been stronger than others, some more negative, some more open minded. But all had shown an amazing capacity for magic.

'It could make them extremely powerful. I don't know how far this power stretches. But our hope is that if they all learn to work together, use this strength, then the healing of the planet can begin,' Jas explained.

'How?'

'I don't know. But with Kale's help we may be able to find out.'

'Perhaps you need to test the men as well …' Taylor said. 'Starting with me.'

'I already have,' said Kale. 'There is no magic in the men at all. I suspect it is because you are too attached to your technology. If you all learn to let go as much as the women among you have … You have to rid yourself of all of this … *made* power …'

'Made power?' Taylor asked.

'Electricity,' explained Jas. 'Kale says it blocks the natural energy from flowing through the building. It's why most of the women are only latent. The energy isn't flowing through them properly yet either.'

Taylor ran his hand over his forehead. 'This is all baffling.'

'You have to change,' said Kale. 'All of you. Or this planet is doomed and you will all die with it.'

At that moment, Donovan entered the training room.

'Captain! We need you to come to the medical room right away.'

By the time Taylor, Jas and Kale reached the medical centre, Donovan had explained what they had found.

'She stumbled onto one of our hunting grounds. She's in a bad way,' he said.

'Doctor, we need to interview her,' Taylor said as they entered.

'No more until she's recovered. She's lost a lot of blood,' said Gerald.

'How? Is she injured?' Jas asked.

'She has recently given birth. Perhaps within the last few hours.'

'Oh my god. Where's the baby?' asked Jas.

'I don't know. She was haemorrhaging badly by the time the men brought her to me.'

'Maybe the child died,' said Donovan.

'No,' Gerald shook his head. 'This is a professional job. She was given a caesarean. My guess is that the baby is still alive. She'd torn some of the stitches but I've patched her up the best I can.'

'Did she tell you anything?' Jas asked Donovan.

'She said she'd escaped from an underground facility.'

'Escaped? Surely she would have wanted to be there, safe from the Jinx?' Taylor said.

'No. She said she had been held there for the last few years. Against her will. That she had been … a breeder.'

12

MD59 – A Few Days Earlier.

Pain woke Julia. She was bleeding heavily: a thick pad had been roughly shoved between her legs to mop up the post-birth blood. Her stomach hurt from the operation. She reached down, repositioning the pad more comfortably inside the disposable underwear, then sat up and looked around the darkened ward. All was quiet; even the male nurse at the table at the bottom of the ward had fallen asleep in his chair, head down on his desk. Julia was glad. That particular nurse was cruel to the women, handling them roughly as though they were nothing more than breeding cattle. And – she supposed – that was all they were to him and the other men on the base. They had no consideration for their health, beyond their ability to carry yet another child that would be taken, moments after its birth, and given up to some other unspeakable horror, brought up to be used and abused like every other woman on the base. But Julia pushed the thought from her mind. She couldn't think about the sweet little baby that had been ripped from her as she slept. She would never see it again. Never have time to love and nurture, and certainly never be told if she had carried a boy or a girl. She reasoned, although it still cut her as deeply as the surgical knife that had opened up her belly, that this was the best thing for them all. If she learned to love the child, it would hurt more to know where and how it was used. And the horror of possibly having given birth to a girl was something she couldn't bear to face.

'Julia …'

She woke again. Startled because she hadn't been aware of drifting off. The slow release of morphine to keep her quiet and pain-free must have kicked in again and sent her to sleep. Dr Tremaine stood above her. She noticed that the drip had been removed from her arm.

'You'll begin to wake up now,' he said. 'Then you need to get dressed. I couldn't get you any proper clothing, but I brought you all some surgeons' uniforms.'

Julia stared at the green, pyjama-like trousers and top.

'I can't do this anymore,' Tremaine was saying. 'Anything, the Jinx, it's got to be better than you all living like this.'

Julia sat up and turned her feet over the edge of the bed. Tremaine helped her dress in the robes. She noted that Adam, the nurse, didn't move.

'You drugged him?' she asked.

'Yes.'

'Are you coming with me?' Julia asked.

'If I can. I've been planning this for a while. The moment is right. It has to be tonight. Handley's men are tanked up in the mess. They won't be expecting any rebellion, certainly not from me. And I've aided their early sleep with something in the ale ...'

Once dressed, Julia and Tremaine went from bed to bed to wake the others. All the women were groggy, but Tremaine injected them with something that soon had them alert again.

'It negates the effects of the drugs they've been pumping into you,' he said.

There were around twenty in this ward, all of them nervous and afraid. Some, like Julia, were recovering from a recent birth; others were in various stages of pregnancy.

'This way,' Tremaine said. 'Please don't talk or make a sound.'

Used to obeying orders without question, they followed him quietly. Passing, for the first time in years, through doors that had been locked to them since they arrived.

'There's a hatch that leads outside. It's an emergency exit that only a few key personnel know about. If you think of secret tunnels that fortresses had, this is something of the equivalent. It is also their weak spot, though they don't realise it,' Tremaine explained to Julia.

They passed down a corridor that led them close to the officers' mess. As they turned the corner, a young soldier, drunk on cheap homemade booze, stumbled out of the mess and began to walk toward them. Tremaine pushed the women back into the previous corridor, then walked up to the soldier. Julia peered around the corner in time to see Tremaine inject the man with something. The soldier slumped. Tremaine dragged his body over to a service closet, then stuffed the man inside. Then he slid over to the mess door, looked inside for a moment, before indicating to Julia to lead the women forward.

They followed her meekly. And the doctor hurried to show the way as soon as they had all passed. Another corridor, and Julia realised what a maze the place was. She had no idea where they were, or where the doctor was leading them. Was this all some cruel trick? She hoped not, as the doctor had always tried to be kind to them.

Tremaine extracted a key from his pocket and used it to open up another door that led into a cavernous area with several large boilers and some generators. He glanced at his watch. 'The mechanic is on a break. We have only a few moments before he'll return. I put something in his drink earlier. He'll have needed the bathroom a lot.'

He smiled at the thought, but Julia had no sense of humour. It had all been bled from her over the past few years.

'This way ...'

They followed again. No questions. No sound. All too afraid. All conditioned to obey.

As the last of them slipped through the next passageway, Julia thought she heard the outer door, leading into the area, open. The mechanic must have returned. She found herself hurrying; heart pounding now. Was it really possible they could get out of there? Could they really escape that awful place forever?

The next corridor was full of long pipes that groaned and creaked. Steam came off some of them, and Julia realised this must be the base's main heating system.

'This is the hard bit,' Tremaine said. 'The fittest of you must go first. We have to allow time for you to escape, and I don't know how much time we have before your absence is noted.'

'I'll go first,' Julia said.

Tremaine opened a broad hatch. It led into what appeared to be a vertical metal shaft, attached to the side of which Julia saw a ladder that led so far upwards that she couldn't make out the top.

'Start climbing. Don't stop until you get to the top. Once there, there's an escape hatch, and you need to key in the passcode. That's 1066. The year of the Battle of Hastings. Can you remember that, Julia?'

Julia nodded. Then she began to climb.

It was dark, but she climbed. One rung after another. Her stomach hurt, blood leaked into the thick pad, but she didn't stop; she had to lead the others out. She ignored the claustrophobic feeling of darkness and the closeness of the sides of the shaft. It was as though she had been climbing forever, and maybe an hour or more passed before her head bumped against the escape hatch that Tremaine had mentioned. She ran her fingers up and around it, and was aware of someone climbing up under her, and almost reaching her.

'I'm at the hatch,' she whispered down. 'There's no keypad.'

Her fingers probed around the edge, ran over the centre, and then she felt buttons under her fingers. The keypad lit up. She pressed 'Cancel', for fear that she had accidentally hit the wrong key. Then she keyed in the correct code and pressed enter. The hatch hissed above her. Then slowly began to open. As soon as it was wide enough, Julia scrambled out, then looked down at the others. At that moment, an alarm began to sound below.

'Hurry!' she called, holding out her hand to help the next woman out. But at that moment the hatch began to close. The woman found herself half in and half out.

'Get back in!' Tremaine called from below to the woman struggling to climb out. 'The alarm has triggered a lockdown!'

Julia pulled back her arm as the woman slipped down inside the hatch and it closed above her. She found herself alone outside.

The air smelt bad compared to the fresh, air-conditioned atmosphere of the base. Faintly, she could still hear the sound of the alarm.

She waited, wondering if the others would manage to open the hatch once more. Then it occurred to her that if it did open, soldiers might be on the other side. She slipped away and began to walk.

It was night. The moon gave off an unfamiliar light. The earth beneath her feet felt alien, covered in rocks or shale of some sort. She was high above ground, and the moon lit up a valley below. This place was once her home, now it appeared to be a desolate and unrecognisable wasteland. Had the world changed so much in just a few years?

Instinct and fear propelled her forward across the challenging landscape. She was sure she was in mountainous land, but couldn't remember or place the scenery in the night. Some part of her drug-dulled brain began to search for the knowledge of the area of the base. She knew where it was, but just couldn't remember.

She found herself on an overgrown path. What had once been smooth tarmac was now moss-covered. Plants burst through the cracks in the path as though the earth was determined to reclaim the land once more. It was like an alien terrain: Julia had never felt less at home.

By dawn she was exhausted. She stumbled and staggered on down the path until she came to an old car-park. There was a structure that looked like an old tourist centre, but the place was obviously deserted, cars left abandoned. Again plant life was bursting through the once controlled ground.

She was sure that her escape would by now have been noticed, even if the doctor had managed to get the others back to the ward without anyone finding out. Paranoia overwhelmed her. She needed to drink. She glanced inside the tourist shop. It had long since been looted, but maybe there was something inside. At least it would afford some shelter. She climbed over the broken door, swayed in the doorway, close to fainting, but some inner strength forced her forward.

Around her, tourist leaflets were strewn on the floor, a small two-seater sofa was tipped over, and a food and drinks machine was smashed open, its contents taken. She staggered up to the point of the broken glass, glanced at the carnage with dull eyes. Then, as she began to turn, she saw something glinting in the bottom of the dispenser. It was a can of lemonade, obviously left by the looters, but fortunate for her.

She broke it open, trying to remember how much time had passed since the fall of Earth. Did it matter anyway? She sipped the drink, found it tasted okay, and so drank it slowly, trying to make it last. Then she looked around the centre and realised that this was not the safe place she had hoped to find. She stumbled once more over the fallen door and made her way back to the car-park.

Outside, she fell into one of the cars and, closing the door, slept fitfully for a few hours on the back seat.

When she woke she was parched again, and hunger gripped at her insides. Fear clenched them further. What would she do out here? Surely outside was worse than being in the base? There was nothing. There was no-one left. She believed it a terrible certainty that she would die alone in this alien land.

Something moved outside. Julia saw soldiers streaming through the car-park, felt a sudden and irrational fear of being found. They would kill her. Or worse. She was to become a whore. Surely death outside was preferable to that? She cowered down, even though her stomach hurt her to bend.

Thankfully the soldiers didn't look in the cars. Maybe they weren't searching for her after all?

After a while she ventured out of the car. She didn't notice the keys that hung from the ignition as she headed away from the direction that the soldiers had gone.

Days and nights blurred into one. Julia staggered on. She now had a place to head for. She knew it. The map of its location was burned into her photographic memory. It was the only thing she could focus on, and she knew without doubt that there she would find sanctuary.

The pathways became roads with churned-up tarmac and concrete. Signs that the Jinx has been there, or maybe scars from military grenades that had been used on the enemy. She didn't know. She didn't care. Here and there she found a clean stream and risked sipping the water to keep her going. Once she even tried to wash away the dried blood that seeped down her legs.

Eventually she found herself on a semi-deserted former motorway. Old and rusted signs seared into her mind and led the way to her subliminally-remembered destination. She could see the files on her old desk; the words and pictures were scorched into her memory for all time.

She fell down behind an abandoned lorry as she saw soldiers in the distance hurrying along the motorway. They, like her, appeared to know exactly where they were headed, and Julia realised she was near now. She didn't know why; but some part of her fevered, fear-filled brain realised that these soldiers weren't dressed quite so formally as Handley's men at MD59.

She stumbled forward. Her slipper-covered feet were blistered and bleeding but she barely felt any pain as she saw the dome in the distance.

'There …' she gasped. 'I remember … Trafford Centre …'

13

Jas went back to her makeshift home in the bookshop. She was frightened, and so tired from exercising her magical energy to show the disbelievers among the women that she didn't think she had anything left to give.

Kale had stayed in the medical room and used some of his healing powers to help the woman recover.

'What's her name?' he had asked.

'I don't know,' Gerald had replied. 'She never told me.'

Kale had been wary of Gerald, and Jas knew why. She hadn't told him of the doctor's previous behaviour toward her, but she suspected Kale knew what kind of man Gerald was. And it was the same kind that had done this awful thing to the woman lying in the infirmary bed. It was why, she knew, Kale had decided to remain there with the woman.

Now Jas was alone in the bookshop, but she didn't feel unsafe, far from it. The Trafford Centre had always felt like a safe haven to her. Though she couldn't understand why. Even so, alone with her thoughts, she began to make comparisons between the Jinx's treatment of women and that of this military organisation that was somehow hidden below ground. It was hard to imagine humans doing these things. Or was it?

'I'm growing soft,' she murmured.

It wasn't that long ago in her own time line when she had had to fight off the amorous attentions of some of the remaining men on this planet. It was after a near rape experience that she had first chosen to disguise herself as a man. A skill, she later learnt, that was a form of magic she hadn't realised she possessed. But even in that disguise she hadn't really changed inside: she had still had female emotions - and those feelings toward Taylor had caused her disguise to slip, giving Gerald the ammunition he had needed to try to blackmail her into being his whore. But that was all water under the bridge now. Or was it?

Jas sat down in the armchair by her mattress and gazed blankly at the collection of books on the shelf opposite. These were horror novels, some of which depicted the end of the world, but none of them had imagined it happening quite like this. There were zombie apocalypses, alien attacks, viruses, deadly Cthulhian monsters coming up from the sewers, atomic explosions that turned humanity into misshapen creatures. The horror and reality of the real end of the world as they had known it were far worse.

She began to tremble with the onslaught of memories of her past there. How monstrous it had all been. Being in the Jinx world had deadened the memories somewhat. The nightmares had stopped, but now they would return, and she knew it was all her own fault.

Jas pondered once more her treatment at the hands of the Jinx. Yes, the captured women had been herded like cattle into a harem of sorts, then gradually paired off with Jinx males, but Jas could hardly say she had been that unwilling. Even now, she could feel the tug of her bond with Arven. It was stronger than any attraction she had felt with Taylor. That mini affair seemed nothing more than a trivial dalliance now. A way to relieve boredom, a way to satisfy the woman that was inside her, hiding behind those male clothes. With Arven though … it was love. She knew it now, and her eyes watered as she thought about her own stupidity.

If I did nothing else, I proved to myself that the feelings were real, she thought. *I want to go back!*

But wasn't that just like her? She always wanted the very opposite of everything she had. *When did I become this annoying? I was tough once.*

She wasn't going to cry though. What was the point? She felt a tremor in the pit of her stomach. A fear she couldn't define. Perhaps it was that she was afraid she could never return to Emin. Or maybe it was something else.

A prickle on the back of her neck - a feeling like she was being observed - made her turn. She stared at the bookcase opposite her. The sensation wouldn't diminish, but instead intensified.

The light from the lamp beside her caught on something on the bookshelf. It glinted like a hidden jewel. Keeping her eyes on the spot, Jas stood and walked toward the shelf. She stared at the books on the row. All of different heights and thicknesses, they seemed to have been placed illogically. Perhaps some of the occupants of Trafford City had been reading them and had replaced them, but not exactly in their original order? Jas frowned at the row. One book, obviously smaller than the others, occupied the space nearest the right-hand side of the shelf - closest to the wall.

Jas bent down and looked closely at the book. Then she pulled it free of its space and flicked through it. It was an ordinary-looking paperback. Nothing special at all. She went to replace it, and then her eyes fell on something in the wall behind.

A small button that looked as though it was made of glass seemed to be attached to the back of the shelf. Jas peered closely. Though it was tiny, she realised that what she was looking at was the lens of a camera.

She reached forward, fingers probing the area. If it hadn't been for the light from the reading lamp she might never have noticed this.

She was confused, worried. Were the occupants of Trafford City so paranoid that they needed to watch her and Kale at all times? What should she do? It angered her suddenly that her friends couldn't trust her, and she pulled hard on the bookshelf. She pushed aside the remaining books from the shelf, throwing them off onto the floor with uncharacteristic disrespect. Once the shelf was cleared, she pulled it away from the wall. Then she looked behind. The wire attached to the camera fed all the way into the wall. This clearly wasn't a new addition to the shop, but had been placed there some time ago. Maybe even when the shop was first fitted out. *How many years ago had that been?*, she wondered. Ten? Maybe even 15? Perhaps longer. She couldn't remember when the centre had been built or how long the bookshop had occupied that particular location.

On impulse, she hurried from the shop. Dawn and Taylor were standing at the next corner talking very quietly together.

'Taylor!' Jas said, ignoring the look of irritation on Dawn's face. 'I think you'd better see this …'

Taylor followed her back to the bookshop, while Dawn lingered behind, aware she wasn't wanted but afraid to leave her husband alone with a woman she saw as a rival.

'My god,' Taylor said. 'This is military issue.'

'How did it get here?' Jas asked.

'I don't know.'

'There's more of them,' Jas said with a growing certainty. 'I feel it somehow.'

'Jinx magic again?' Taylor said.

Jas nodded.

'We need to sweep the whole centre. How did you find it?' Taylor said.

Jas shrugged. 'It was luck, really. I spotted it while I was looking at the books on the shelf.'

Taylor went away to order the sweep, and then Jas looked around the shop, wondering how often she had been observed, and by whom. The thought made the hairs on the back of her neck stand up again.

It was many hours later that the council of Trafford City gathered in The Orient to hear the news that someone had been watching them from the beginning. Cameras had been found in every shop and every space in the centre. There had even been some found in the training room, but those it seemed had suffered natural wear and tear and appeared to be no longer working.

'Maybe we shouldn't be too paranoid,' Sylvia said. 'It could be that these were security cameras from the days when the centre was open.'

'There is no evidence to support that, unfortunately,' Donovan replied. 'We know where the original security system did operate. We know every inch of this place, and these cameras aren't linked to anywhere in the operators' rooms. The information has been fed to somewhere else. Outside.'

'But where?' asked Sylvia. 'And why?'

'It's possible that wherever it was no longer exists and no-one is monitoring them,' Donovan said. 'But, with the arrival of that woman in the infirmary, I don't think it's unreasonable for us to be paranoid. There clearly is a base somewhere nearby, full of survivors who may have food, equipment, weapons and any other means to survive for as long as they need to be below ground.'

'That would mean a hell of a lot of provisions,' someone said from the crowd. 'And if they are there, why haven't they let us know?'

'I feel like a lab rat,' Dawn said. 'It's like they've been watching everything we do for some weird form of experiment.'

'Let's not get hysterical,' Jas said. 'It's possible that the cameras might not even be working.'

Taylor had remained quiet during the exchange, but now he spoke up. 'Archie? Are they still live?'

A young soldier Jas didn't recognise stepped forward. He was taller than some of the other men, African-American, with close-cropped hair.

'Yes, Captain. There is definitely a live feed going through some of them. Others none at all. Which obviously suggests that whoever is running them can't get here to carry out maintenance. Once a feed goes down, it stays down.'

'Is there any way of figuring out where that feed is going?' Taylor said.

Archie shook his head. 'Not without the right equipment.'

'So … what do we do?' asked Sylvia.

'Disable all of them,' Taylor said. 'That way, if we are being observed, we cut off the source of information, and hopefully they will be forced to reveal themselves. Or leave us alone.'

It was agreed, and those soldiers with the relevant experience went away to take care of the cameras they had found.

The council dispersed, but as Jas turned and began to leave The Orient, Taylor caught up with her.

'Jas, will you come back to the infirmary with me?' Taylor asked. 'Our refugee is awake and ready to talk. I think it would be nice for her to have a woman present. It might reassure her.'

Jas was surprised. 'What about Dawn?'

'I think, with your extra skills, you might be able to assess if all she says is true,' Taylor said.

'You think she's a plant?'

'No. But … it doesn't hurt to be certain of all sources of information.

Things are getting weirder and weirder around here. I can't believe we've had those cameras here all this time and I never noticed them. It's as though I'm blind to the obvious. I feel like I've lost my edge.'

'You haven't,' Jas said. 'But my skills, as you said, might have made it easier for me to see what was happening.'

14

Inside the infirmary, Kale sat beside the woman. She appeared calm, unafraid of the large Al Kuzemen.

'I've given her a draught,' Kale said as Jas met his eyes.

'I'm really not happy that this quack is administering his hocus-pocus drugs to my patient,' Gerald said. His face was blood red, and he appeared to be at the limits of his endurance.

'The patient looks well on it,' Taylor said. 'And we really do need to learn as much as we can from Kale. I'd prefer it if this patient were left solely in his care for the time being.'

Gerald went very still for a moment. 'You put this Jinx's magic before my medicine?' he said through gritted teeth.

'Gerald. Be warned. You are here because I allow it,' Taylor said. 'I do not trust you, and I never will after how you have behaved in the past.'

Angry, Gerald stormed out of the infirmary, leaving Kale and a female nurse alone with the woman in the bed.

'Thank you,' Kale said.

'The time for us being enemies is not now,' Taylor said. 'We all need each other, and I won't allow anyone to treat you with prejudice.'

Taylor and Jas pulled up chairs beside the bed. They introduced themselves to the woman.

'And you are?' asked Jas gently.

'My name is Julia. And I remember Captain Arch.'

Taylor stared at the woman in surprise.

'You don't recognise me,' she said. 'I'm not surprised really. We met only once, just before the ...' she cast an embarrassed glance at Kale, 'Jinx attack. I was Major Handley's secretary.'

Taylor's mind flew back to the brief meeting, moments before he was hurried into the incident room to hear the bad news that they were under attack.

'Yes. I do remember.'

'I've changed a lot,' Julia said. 'I've had three babies in the space of five years.'

Jas was sickened. She knew already that the information Julia brought would turn her stomach more.

'Ever since the main attacks on London, I've been below ground. I thought that I was going there to continue my work as Handley's assistant. But it seems I was taken for another purpose. Almost immediately, I was placed in the breeders' ward and subjected to IVF treatments, and was impregnated within the first month. Since then I have been pregnant five times. Only three of the pregnancies were successful. No sooner was I recovering from one birth than I was made pregnant again.'

'That's horrible,' said the nurse, who remained in earshot. 'Inhuman.'

'I would expect nothing else from those savages,' Kale murmured.

'A few days ago,' Julia continued, 'I had a caesarean for my latest pregnancy. Only to learn this would be my last. I was to be … permanently sterilised. Then I was going to be integrated into the pleasure unit.'

Jas frowned. 'Pleasure unit?'

Julia looked down at her trembling hands. 'I was no longer fit for carrying any more children. The process had irreversibly damaged my uterus, my cervix was too weak to carry any more. Therefore I would …' her eyes filled up, '…be fit for only one thing. As a whore for the soldiers.'

Jas reached out and took one of Julia's cold hands in hers.

'I'm so sorry. As Kale says, those men are animals.'

With some prompting, Julia began to describe the situation in the underground base.

'I didn't have the freedom to move about as A-class females did, but over the last five years I learnt what was happening in the base. Some women, ex-wives of some of the commanders, were brought into the breeders' unit after a couple of years of having freedom on the base. Their husbands had grown bored with them, and they had been reduced in status – a situation they had never considered possible … They had thought that as they were married to those in charge, they would be safe. They told me that there were apparently many classes of women, none of which was desirable. If you were A-class it was the closest you could come to being untouchable, but only if you had a male protector and for the time that he wanted you. This meant that all women lived under the rule of their husbands. It was like being back in the dark ages. We had no rights of our own and could be demoted at any time, just because of an argument or a cross word, or even on a whim. B-class – breeders like me – were considered important because of our ability to produce new children, and the girls were to be incorporated into the system that was being built. W-class are workers. Older women who did all the menial jobs around the base. Cleaning toilets, cooking, housework. And then there were the P-class women, in the worst position of all; whore to anyone who wanted them, unable to refuse, drugged and brainwashed into submission.'

'That's rape. Pure and simple. It sounds like a 1980s B-movie scenario,' Jas said.

'Where does Handley come into this?' Taylor asked.

'He runs this base. The others are manned by some of his superiors.'

'There are *other* bases?' Taylor said.

'Yes. Many. I was privy to that information before I went below. All kinds of sensitive material came through Handley's office. I remember it all, but I'm unclear on the locations of some of the bases.'

'How did you escape?' asked Jas.

'Dr Tremaine, the fertility doctor, got me out. He eventually took pity on us breeders, I guess, although in the end I was the only one who managed to reach the surface before the alarm sounded. He had been following orders, like everyone else down there. No-one dares to go against the order of things, for fear of what will happen to them. You see, even the men aren't safe. Insubordinates are killed. Without trial. It's a dictatorship. A horrible, Nazi-ish camp. It's the most atrocious place in the world. And we had been told that we were to be cared for – that we were being saved from the Jinx!'

Julia broke down and cried. Jas held her hand until she was fit to speak once more. After a while, she continued her story.

'Handley wanted us all hooked up and fed drugs, virtually brain dead, just human incubators for their future race. But Dr Tremaine wouldn't allow it. He said it would be bad for the babies, although I suspect that was an untruth. He didn't approve of what they were doing. In his eyes it was unethical. So, when he heard what they had planned for me, he helped me escape.'

'Strange,' Taylor said. 'That was a major risk for him.'

'It was,' Julia said. Then she began to explain exactly how the doctor had helped her, and tried to help the other women too.

15

'*What* did you remember?' asked Taylor as Julia finished her story. He knew the rest: she had stumbled into the mall, confused, bleeding, and they had taken her immediately to the infirmary.

'The Trafford Centre. That's what this place is, isn't it?' Julia said.

'It was. We call it Trafford City now.'

'I saw this place once. Or rather, a file on it.' Julia explained.

'A file?' Jas said. 'What do you mean?'

'I have a photographic memory. I never told Handley or any of my superiors. It would have made me unsuitable for the confidential work. This place, the Trafford Centre, was designated as a reserve food area. For the base. For MD59. They left some C-class drones to take care of it. Keep it free of looters.'

Jas and Taylor exchanged glances. 'The red coats?'

Julia nodded.

'What does C-class mean?' Taylor asked.

'Controlled. They were warped, altered by drugs and conditioning. There are things going on there … Experimentation. Brainwashing. They have a team of scientists working on confidential stuff that most of the soldiers don't even know about.'

Jas remembered all too well her first time at the Centre, when two men, dressed in red blazers, had been found by Taylor's troops. The food around them had been untouched – the grotesque men had been cannibals instead. They had kept the place free of looters. Julia's explanation finally made some sense of the drones' behaviour. If the scientists at MD59 were responsible for turning ordinary men into cannibals, what else were they working on? The thought terrified her.

Jas shuddered as the memory of the half-eaten, but still alive, female victim of those freaks flashed into her mind. She could never forget it. A horrible time.

'I've just realised something,' Taylor said. 'This means you probably know the exact location of the base.'

Julia nodded, but the colour drained from her face, as though she had just realised she was no longer safe among the residents of Trafford City.

'It's not far if you have transport. Maybe a couple of hours' journey away. Walking, it took a lot longer,' she murmured. Then tears burst from her eyes and began to stream down her face, until Kale laid a soothing hand on her arm.

Jas felt the power flood over Julia and into her own hand. She pulled away, not wishing her senses to be dulled, for the effects resembled those of morphine as the power ran through Julia's aura.

Julia slumped back on the bed and her eyes closed.

'We need to find this place,' Taylor said.

'Why? What are you going to do?' Jas asked.

'You heard what she said. We can't leave those women down there. Suffering like that.'

'I don't see what choice you have. It's a military base. They'll be fully equipped to fend off any attacker.'

'Yes. But they won't be expecting us to attack,' Taylor said. 'Nor to get in through their escape hatch.'

Jas said nothing for a moment. 'It will need careful planning. A recce first, I'd suggest.'

Taylor nodded. 'Send for me when she's able to talk again. We need to know the location exactly, and anything else she can tell us about the hatch.'

He excused himself and left the infirmary to go and seek out his men and to arrange another council meeting.

Jas turned to Kale. She saw his tired expression and knew that he needed rest. The atmosphere of Earth wasn't kind to the Al Kuzemen. Although the power should have been unlimited, using it often drained him – unlike on Emin, when he was energised by his own power.

'Go and get some sleep,' she suggested. 'I'll stay with Julia.'

Kale looked at her for a moment, and Jas could see he was considering arguing, but eventually the mage stood.

'You won't leave her?' he said.

'Not until you return.'

'I don't trust the doctor …'

'I know. Neither do I.'

16

After Julia had given detailed directions to the underground base, it was decided that a reconnaissance mission would be arranged. Taylor chose his most trusted men to accompany them, among them Andrew and Donovan. He left Harvey behind to take care of the security of the survivors.

'I'd like to come with you,' Jas said.

'No. It might not be safe, and we need you here to continue training the women. This may be their only way of protecting themselves,' Taylor said. 'We should be gone only a few days at most. We won't be attacking until we know what's there, and then we will need all of our soldiers.'

Jas watched as Taylor said his goodbyes to Dawn and Lucy, but she wasn't satisfied. It would be strange, and perhaps more hostile, without his continued presence in the town. He always had a way of calming situations, and as she watched him leave, Jas wondered if Kale would still be safe.

She returned to her bookshop, where she found Julia lounging on the new mattress they had added to their area. Kale felt oddly responsible for her and had invited her to live in their space as soon as she was well enough to leave the infirmary. Jas found his interest in the woman intriguing, but didn't comment on it. She welcomed the company, though, and was glad to offer the other woman some stability and security.

'How are you feeling?' she asked as she sat down on the easy chair beside the sleeping area.

'Much better. Kale has done wonders for my healing. The scar has already gone silver. I thought I'd have numbness there for many months, but already my abdomen is feeling normal. That is, if I can even remember what normal is, after all the pregnancies.'

Jas observed Julia closely. She did appear to be healing well. The colour had returned to her cheeks, her figure was slimming down to what must be her normal size, and she was already starting to look as though she had never been pregnant in the first place.

'One of the other women told me that you ... lived with the Jinx for a while,' Julia said.

'I'm sure gossip has been bouncing around,' Jas laughed.

Julia smiled. 'I guess. I'm just … intrigued. I mean, they wanted us for pretty much what I was used for … right?'

Jas was quiet for a moment. On the surface, the Jinx's motives were obscene. 'It appears that way,' she said eventually. 'And I can't say I ever approved of their motives or methods. But, as time goes on, I can't help making comparisons between them and Earth men. The Jinx, although they did kill our men and take our women, are nowhere near as vicious as the soldiers seem to have been to you. It seems worse to me that our own people are capable of this. I find it hard even to see those men as human. It's barbaric.'

'And the Jinx *aren't*?'

Jas wasn't sure what to say. How would the world of the Jinx appear to Julia's eyes? She had been badly abused. Her body used to breed, as though she were an animal and not a woman. How was that any different from what the Jinx wanted from the Earth women they had captured? Yet somehow it was. It was very different. The women taken to Emin hadn't been hurt, not really, and no bonding was unwelcome in the end, was it? Jas thought back to her sexual encounters with Arven and felt that familiar surge of lust rush between her legs. She still wanted him. Just as she had said to Taylor: it was never rape. She had been willing. But was the Jinx's use of magic any different from the drug-induced coercion of the base that Julia had described? Jas wasn't really sure. All she knew was that she still craved Arven's touch, and as time passed, that desire did not diminish; it grew stronger, if anything, not weaker. She reasoned, and hoped, that this meant she couldn't be addicted in any sense to the magic that had been in Emin's atmosphere, or generated by her bonding ceremony with Arven – because if it had been a form of addiction, then surely she would have gone 'cold turkey' by now?

'He's different though, isn't he?' Julia said, cutting into Jas's thoughts.

Jas looked over at Kale. He was standing by the bookshop door, looking out nervously.

'He's a mage,' Jas said, as though that explained everything. 'He's not a warrior and never has been.'

'He's a healer,' said Julia. 'It isn't in him to cause pain.'

Every night since the first night she had arrived back at Trafford City, Jas had found herself back in Arven's arms. Just as though she were really there on Emin. And yet, even though those moments could surely be only dreams or visions, she couldn't shake the thought that she really was with him.

Jas curled up in her bed and turned over, facing the wall, with Julia behind her. She wanted to see Arven all the time, but in the daytime she was able to push this urge aside. At night, in bed, the feeling became irrepressible. Jas closed her eyes and thought about Arven. In her mind's eye she could see him sitting at his desk as though waiting for her. His hypnotic eyes appeared to pierce through space and time. He paced the room, wringing his hands sometimes, anxious and lonely.

Jas rolled over onto her back and opened her eyes. The vision faded. She wondered what was happening on Emin. It was weeks since she had left. Was the time the same for Arven, or was it merely days?

She heard Julia's soft breathing as the woman slipped into sleep.

Kale returned. Jas didn't ask where he had been. She knew that sometimes the mage had to go outside, because the interior of the Trafford Centre drained him more, for some reason, and the moon, as pallid and distant as it was, somehow helped him restore his energy levels.

She closed her eyes again. Arven was waiting, not patiently now, but anxiously. Jas felt that rush once more in her sex. Heat flushed her body, and as Kale watched from the darkness, she slowly faded away, leaving Earth behind to answer the call of her lover's needs.

'We have to sort things out,' she said, holding Arven at arm's length.

He pulled her into his arms, and the lust carried her away as she let him strip away the rough human clothing.

'This is ugly,' he pointed out, tossing her jogging pants to the floor. 'This is beautiful.'

His hands stretched around her small bare waist, the tips of his large fingers almost touching near her spine.

'Jasmine,' he breathed against her lips, pulling her into the kiss he longed for most of all. It was at these times that he felt closest to her. Kissing, this human oddity, was so intimate, and he never tired of the feeling it gave him.

His tongue slipped inside her mouth, raking over hers until she shuddered against him. Arven loved the arousal that rippled through her, and the way her skin glowed with passion. He lifted her, carrying her easily to the bed, and lay her down, naked and willing before him.

She tried to talk again. Every time she came here he promised himself he would listen, but the need for her was too much and he couldn't control himself.

She gasped under him as he spread her, positioning the head of his penis between her legs. As he entered, her tightness pulled small sounds from them both. He worked her until she screamed beneath him, letting go of all of her angst in one rushing orgasm.

The pods didn't come now. His orgasm was still good, but not the same as before she had returned to Earth. She still writhed beneath him, coming again as though his pleasure excited her as much as her own. The excitement for her appeared to be the same without the pods burrowing into her. He knew he ought to explain to her why they no longer did, but there was never time. Their frantic lovemaking always took precedence, and then afterwards she would disappear again, as though she were some mirage that came to his fevered and love-starved mind.

Now all he wanted was for her to remain, for a few moments at least, to let him hold her until the tremors ceased and they could both think enough to talk.

'Stay,' he murmured as the fading began, and for a moment she seemed to have control of it. Her body solidified once more, and she placed a kiss on his lips.

'You need to know that ...'

But she was gone. Just like that. Away and back to that dying planet.

Arven stared at the indent in the soft pillow, then pushed aside the covers. The room smelt of their sex; he breathed it in, willing her to return, but he knew it was useless. Her will was what brought her here, not his.

'Damn it!' he said. His heart hurt, but he was unable to do anything at all to stop the pain. 'Come back to me. There will be no punishment,' he said. But these words meant nothing when she couldn't hear them.

Why was his tongue so tied when she appeared? Why was it that his thoughts cleared only once they had made love? Once she was fading again and there was nothing he could do to bring her back or make her remain?

But there was of course something he could do ...

Arven walked to the doorway of his tent and looked out at the two red moons of Emin. The magic was flowing here. The new Al Kuzemen had arrived from one of the other towns, and Arven knew he could find Jasmine any time he wanted. His men were ready for one word, spoiling almost for the fight, but he had no stomach for the slaughter now: Jasmine had changed him.

There were also the words that Garuk, his new mage, had said when he had arrived and looked into the divinity pool: *She is full of her own magic and wonder*. It had frightened the new mage to tell Arven the truth about Jasmine, but he had been forced to speak. Garuk had expected the Emperor's anger, but his prophesy had been greeted with stoic silence. Now Arven thought about it all again ...

'She is full of her own magic and wonder. There is a mission she must fulfil, lord. This is the thing that drives her. Yet ... I feel this great love she has for you. These Earth women are complex. They don't understand or *feel* our ways as we do.' Looking deeper into the pool, Garuk gasped.

'Yes?' Arven said, his tone demanding more.

'She carries *your* child, lord.'

Arven knew this already of course. He had known as soon as the pods had stopped trying to find their determined way inside her womb. But – she was carrying *his* child. That was the confirmation he wanted most.

'What of Kale?' Arven asked.

'The mage was misled. Foolishly. But he was never untrue to you. Sometimes things happen because destiny makes them happen. And the Empress is strong, determined. She had to return for her own destiny to be fulfilled.'

'I must bring her back. And Kale,' Arven said.

Garuk shook his head. 'Not yet, Lord. I implore you! If you go after them now, they will run and hide, and she may never return to you.'

'Then I must have patience?'

Garuk nodded. 'The time to act will present itself. This I am certain of.'

Now Arven breathed in the night air of Emin. Frustration curled like bile in the pit of his stomach. It gave way to the anger that was always there, barely suppressed, beneath the surface of his normal controlled wisdom.

Damn her! Why did she have to be so difficult? So stubborn? Why couldn't she accept that she belonged to him?

He sighed. Of course, that was exactly why he loved her, wasn't it? She was different, strong, human. Yet underneath it all, he knew she had heart.

He let the flap on the tent drop. The cool air from outside was immediately cut off. He wanted to bathe, but the thought of washing away the traces of her scent from his skin horrified him.

He paced the tent. Then, realising that his actions were futile, he returned to the nest of their bed. He needed sleep. Had to remain strong until the time came when he must travel once more to that dying planet to bring home his wife.

Jasmine's scent was all over the sheets and pillows. He inhaled her, trying to push thought from his mind as he nestled his head down on her pillow. One thing was certain: she would be with him again the following evening. It had been this way ever since she had passed through the portal with Kale and they had disappeared back to Earth. He closed his eyes, determined to make the next time better. Determined to tell her the truth about the changes that would soon occur in her body. Determined to beg her to return before the poison on Earth hurt her and his child.

By morning his resolve had crumpled. He had to go and find her. He had to force her to return. No prophesy would keep her away from where she belonged. He had to save her and his unborn child. He didn't care about Earth or its occupants; they could fight their own wars.

17

After leaving the trucks several miles away, Taylor and his small reconnaissance team set up camp in Llanberis Pass, near a tourist information centre that Julia had described. It was decided that they would retrace Julia's steps from this point on, in the hope of finding the hatchway that led to the underground bunker.

'It would be good to give that bastard Handley a shock,' said Kline as they set up a discreet camp on the hill above the centre.

'We mustn't let our hatred foul our common sense,' Taylor said. 'That son of a bitch will get what's coming to him, but we have to do this right. This is a recce. We need to rally and pool what we know before we go in guns blazing.'

Donovan chewed on the end of a cigar and said nothing, but he always agreed with Taylor's logic – even though he, like Kline, wanted to stick a blade in Handley's fat throat.

'This whole thing was planned,' Taylor continued. 'From the start. They knew for years about the Jinx. At least, that's some of the intel that Julia picked up while being in the base. We also have to get over our horror at what those men have done in the name of survival. If Handley hadn't cut us loose, it could just as easily have been us taking orders to behave like that down there.'

Donovan looked hard at Taylor. 'I wouldn't have. There's no way I could have done those things.'

Taylor thought back to other missions. Other things he and Donovan had done together. He didn't remind him about the camp in Vietnam, as he pushed the memory of the whoosh of napalm burning through that sleepy, and probably innocent, village. It had burnt everyone – man, woman and child – to death as they slept. All because Handley had said it was a terrorist camp. Sometimes Taylor heard the screams of the dying in his dreams.

'I'd like to think we wouldn't have,' Taylor said. 'But we were all loyal until Handley screwed us over. We were conditioned to take orders and not to question. So are the men he chose to take down there with him. It could just as easily have been us behaving like that.'

'That don't mean we can let this all go now,' said Kline, accepting what Taylor said. 'We've changed, and we all have families, women we care about, and kids.'

'Yes,' said Taylor.

'We'd never let that bastard get his hands on them and do this shit ...' Kline finished. 'Everything we have is worth fighting to save. The Jinx made us strong, not weak,'

Taylor nodded. It was a speech he frequently gave, and it shocked him how his own words were being quoted back to him now by Kline. Maybe he was responsible for his own form of brainwashing. But at least he believed what he said and considered that what they did was for the greater good. Unlike Handley, whose methods were just sick and frighteningly dictatorial.

'It's like a throwback from the Second World War,' Donovan said, as though reading his thoughts.

'Yes. Lesser humans don't matter in the military scheme of things. Nothing really changes, does it?' Taylor said.

Leaving some of the men behind at the first camp, they marched on until nightfall. They set up a second camp in an area that Taylor suspected wasn't far from the hatch.

'Let's do a recce of the area. Just be aware that Handley may well have surveillance in place,' Taylor said.

Andrew remained behind at the second camp with their meagre provisions and heavy equipment while Taylor and Donovan pushed onwards. They found the hatch around half a mile from their camp.

'Looks like this was originally camouflaged,' Donovan said.

Taylor looked down at the fake grass that must have been shoved aside as Julia had opened the hatch.

'We could open it ...' Kline said.

'It's alarmed,' Taylor said. 'Besides, if I was Handley, I'd have made sure the code was changed.'

Taylor shone his torch over the area. Dried blood stains confirmed Julia's earlier presence. Everything was as she had said.

'Odd though ...' he murmured.

'What?' asked Kline.

'No other footprints. But I can see hers ...'

'Meaning?' asked Donovan.

'That the soldiers didn't pursue her this way.'

They walked on a few metres and found themselves at the top of what appeared to be a slate quarry.

There was a huge metal door that clearly led down into the underground bunker. Taylor, Kline and Donovan crouched low, then lay down on their bellies as they observed the area.

Taylor raised a pair of infrared binoculars up to his face. The lenses zoomed in on the opening, and he could see the keypad and camera security that protected the door. There was no obvious military presence outside, however.

'They are afraid,' he noted.

'What of?' Kline asked.

'Being seen. Everything here is low-key. This place could just as easily be the slate quarry that it appears to be. Yet inside there, immediately beneath us probably, is a military base housing thousands of people. Not just that, but according to Julia there are many such bases around the world.'

'What does it matter if anyone finds it?' Donovan said. 'After all, they are safe and sound in there and have the firepower to deal with any attempts at intrusion …'

'Firepower doesn't work on the Jinx, and they are the only thing to fear … At least, that's what Handley believes,' Taylor said.

They watched for a further hour, saw no movement, and so made their way back to the camp.

18

'I don't know what your problem is with her,' Caroline said. 'This morning I used the power I've always known as Reiki to move a glass of water from one end of the table to the other.'

'Oh, she's got her uses,' Dawn said. 'I just don't trust her. I mean, how can I?'

'Donovan told me it was down to Jas that they even found us. She was the one who heard our original message.'

'I know.'

Dawn picked up her cracked teacup and swigged neat rum, carelessly sloshing it over her lips and onto her already stained top.

'I guess we'd better call it a night,' Caroline said.

'No ... I still have another bottle of this shit hidden away ...' Dawn giggled. 'Come on, we haven't had a girly night for ages.'

Caroline laughed and let Dawn refill her mug. She glanced over at the sleeping children. Lucy and Caroline and Donovan's two children, Jamie and Selene, were huddled up on a mattress in the corner of the shop that she shared with Donovan.

'Here's to the future,' Dawn said, pulling the other bottle of rum from the bottom of a canvas bag.

Caroline sipped the rum: it was going to her head too quickly. She wasn't used to it anymore, not like in the old days when alcohol was a way of easing her loneliness ...

Long before the Jinx, Caroline had often drunk too much, then woken up the next day in bed with someone she could barely remember. Those mornings had meant grief and self-loathing and overwhelming isolation. But she would drag herself back into the rat race, day after day, always falling into the same trap the very next night.

She discovered Reiki when she fell for Philippe. He was into all the new age stuff, and was a self-proclaimed Reiki guru. Caroline followed him, took in the beliefs that he taught and rapidly fell in with the hedonist lifestyle that he believed in. Tantric sex, a fad for some, was a lifestyle for Philippe – along with the abusive relationship that he indoctrinated her into before she realised how unhealthy it was.

He wasn't really a Reiki master, that was just something he used as a pick-up line, but Caroline, newly attuned, attending the same group healing meetings as him, had no reason to doubt he was telling the truth.

She wasn't the first to fall in with him, and, still desperate for something to make her feel important, fuelled by her lack of belief in her own self-worth, she was ripe for the picking.

There were orgies. That wasn't much of a leap from her old lifestyle of one-night stands, and somehow seemed validated as acceptable because others appeared to have no hang-ups, no guilt, about participating. Alcohol featured prominently, alongside prescription drugs that Philippe said opened their minds to other spiritual possibilities. He wasn't even a child of the '60s; he was way too young for that. But he believed in it all, or convinced Caroline and the others that he did.

It took five years of degradation before Caroline discovered that Philippe was a fraud. By then, she was an advocate. All the things he taught so convincingly, but did not really believe, Caroline now knew were actual truths. Particularly Reiki. He was like the proverbial devil: he gave the facts, but they were clouded by temptations that led her away from enlightenment.

Her closest friend, Kaitlin, was a strong-willed, fiery woman, a little older than herself, who already had a man, and a child. All the things that Caroline craved but couldn't find. Kaitlin questioned her constantly about her beliefs, and then, somehow, always managed to point out that Philippe didn't live the life he preached. Caroline shrugged it off. That was his French heritage. The French loved wine, women and song; everyone knew that. But all that Kaitlin said sank into some subliminal part of her brain that also began to question Philippe.

Even though she never said a word to him, it was all bottled up inside her, waiting to explode, like a bottle of fizzy pop that had been shaken.

Then, things between them changed. It was, she thought, all for the better. The group sex and swinger sessions had ceased when a new fad presented itself.

Philippe was now focusing on her.

He had been studying the *Karma Sutra*, along with some ancient teachings in the Koran that advocated pleasing your lover. Caroline saw his sexual experimentations with her as love. He became kinder to her too. It was all so nice and romantic, and the sex was the best they had ever shared. She didn't realised that Philippe was deriving a different kind of satisfaction from playing her sexually. He saw this as a vindication of his prowess.

Like a pimp, he had always made her use protection when farming her out, but when it came to his own pleasures, he hated wearing condoms. Caroline was taking precautions though. He stood over her every day while she swallowed that little pill that promised 99.9% protection, never knowing she would become one of the 0.1%.

The pregnancy came as a shock to them both, but it was also a wake-up call for Caroline. The drugs had to stop, as well as the alcohol. She was excited, delighted, and convinced that Philippe would be too.

'I'm pregnant,' she told him, after making dinner and plying him with champagne that she didn't share.

He stood up from the table and held his arms out to her. She went to him. Happy. This was perfect, this was what would make them truly a couple.

'Don't worry, love,' he said. 'We'll get you booked into a clinic as soon as possible. I'll take care of everything.'

Sickness bubbled up into her throat. She ran to the toilet. Just made it.

That night, he screwed her so hard that she thought he was trying to murder the child inside her. She was afraid of him for the first time.

In the morning, she was lethargic and sick. She rang work and told them she was ill. As she put the phone down from the call, Philippe came in, mobile phone in his hand.

'I've booked you in for this afternoon. The sooner the better, hey?'

Caroline was almost speechless. 'I don't want an abortion,' she said after a moment. 'How can you even expect that from me?'

'Listen love, it's up to you. Your body and all that, but if you're having a kid then you'll have to move out. That's not for me,' Philippe said. His voice was not cold, merely indifferent. It was then that Caroline realised he had never told her he loved her.

'But ... this is *your* child ...'

'I don't want kids.'

He wouldn't move on it. Wouldn't budge one little inch.

Caroline let him take her to the clinic, even though she cried as they sedated her for the procedure.

Six weeks later, Philippe arranged another of his parties. This one featured three women, including Caroline, and six men. Caroline knew what he had in mind, but she wasn't interested in playing. She couldn't get over what he had forced her to do. It went against all her beliefs. All the things he had told her that mattered in the world.

'Why aren't you dressed?' Philippe said, coming into the bedroom. 'Everyone will be here soon.'

The dress he wanted her to wear, a sheer black fabric with PVC strips down the sides, was lying across the bed. Caroline was wearing a tracksuit.

'I'm not in the mood,' she said.

'What do you mean? You're always in the mood ...' He kissed her on the back of the neck.

Normally his touch would have aroused her, but Caroline was sickened by it. She'd had nightmares over and over about her unborn and innocent child. Waking in the night, she had studied Philippe, sleeping as though he didn't have a care in the world, and she hadn't liked what she saw. And it was true: he didn't have any worries. Philippe didn't care, and that was something she could no longer ignore.

'I said, no. I'm not interested,' Caroline said.

Philippe froze. 'What's up with you? You've been a right miserable cow recently …'

'Really? And you have no concept of why?'

'I'm not getting into this now. Get that dress on. We're gonna have a good night. All you need is a drink, a good bit of dick …'

'Oh god! Is that all you think about? Get away from me. You make me sick.'

Anger flushed his face.

'You. Are. Going. To. Put. That. Dress. On.'

'I'm not. I'm not whoring with your friends anymore,' Caroline said.

He grabbed her shoulder, spun her around and threw her on the bed. His hand swooped back and he slapped her. Not hard, but it stung, and she knew she would have a bruise on her cheek where his fingers had smacked against the bone.

Caroline was shocked. Frightened. Angry. He had never hit her before. No-one had.

'Get dressed.'

Philippe left the room. Caroline stood up. Looked at the dress. Then took some nail scissors from her drawer and began to slash through the fabric. It gave her amazing satisfaction. A sense of peace. A way of venting the fury and pain his callous behaviour had inflicted. She opened Philippe's wardrobe and, even though it was challenging with such small scissors, destroyed all of his designer clothes.

She left the shreds of fabric all over the room. Then she packed a bag, taking all of her essentials, plus a wad of money that Philippe always kept in a hole in the floorboards. She was shocked to find around £5,000 there, and took it all. It was the very least she deserved!

Downstairs she heard the arrival of the first guests. She recognised their voices and knew that Philippe would have taken them straight into the lounge to give them a drink, maybe light up a joint.

Picking up her bag, she stuffed the money inside, then pulled on a light jacket. She crept downstairs and out of the back door.

Hurrying down the alley to where her car was parked, Caroline heard a yell from the window upstairs. So he had found the damage. He would be mad now. Really mad. Maybe enough to kill her. She paused. Perhaps that was what she wanted after all. It would ease the pain of what she had done to her unborn child. Punish her for her sin.

'You fucking *bitch!*'

Hearing his voice spurred her into motion. He wasn't out of the house, didn't know which direction she had taken yet, but would know where her car was parked. She turned and ran away from the vehicle, down the alley in the opposite direction. He would never expect that. And, despite herself, that survival instinct kicked in.

Ducking down behind the dustbins, she saw him come out of the back and run down the alley toward her car. Then, the strangest thing happened. The earth began to shake, and Caroline thought, *This is it. I'm finally being punished for what I've done. For murdering my baby.*

She saw the vortex open. Saw Philippe, caught in the swirling wind, and then the giant creature wearing jewel-covered metal armour stepping out.

Rick and Sophie, a couple Caroline knew well, came out into the alley to see what was going on. The monster from hell withdrew a sword, pierced Philippe through the stomach. The whole thing seemed to happen in some sort of slow motion. Philippe's intestines fell to the ground before he did. Rick yelled, Sophie screamed. The monster reached her, took her up in his arms and then fell back into his portal.

The wind stopped howling. The tornado vortex vanished. Caroline cowered behind the bins, afraid to move in case it returned. She didn't realise that payback had been well and truly delivered to Philippe not by the devil but by the Jinx. At the time, they seemed one and the same thing.

'You've gone quiet,' said Dawn.

'I was remembering before ... What life was like,' Caroline said.

'Really? I don't remember it at all. I feel like we've always lived here.'

Caroline laughed. She shook away the maudlin memories and focused on the good that the Jinx had brought into her life. Donovan had been her salvation, as had Jamie and Selene. When she had given birth to Jamie, that awful hole in her heart had been finally healed.

She glanced at her children. She would never let anyone or anything hurt them. A fierce and violent protectiveness surged up inside her. She would kill to protect them from harm. Wouldn't any mother?

19

'There's been no movement at all,' said Kline. 'I'm not convinced that the external surveillance still works.'

'We can't rely on that, though,' said Donovan. 'It could be a trap. We may well have been watched all along.'

'I don't think so. I suspect that they aren't as diligent as they once were,' Taylor said. 'Look down in the quarry. I'm sure that I can make out mines.'

Donovan picked up his binoculars and examined the area carefully. 'You might be right. At the very least, the opening is booby trapped. What better way to prevent the Jinx, or us, from attacking?'

'We need to get back to Trafford City, regroup. Maybe get a team out here to try to go in through the hatch. Wish we had brought Archie along to have a look.'

'Yeah,' Kline agreed. 'What Archie doesn't know about tech stuff isn't worth knowing. I got pictures of the lock. Hopefully that will be enough for him to suss what to do with it.'

They made their way back to the lower camp. Once they had collected Andrew and their equipment, they all walked down the long pathway back to the truck.

In the abandoned car-park near the information centre, where just a few days ago Julia had found the can of lemonade that had possibly saved her life, Kline and Andrew siphoned fuel from the tanks of the abandoned cars. There was enough to refill the truck's tank and to fill several canisters.

'It was worth the trip just for this,' Taylor said as they stowed the canisters in the back of the truck.

At that moment shots rang out somewhere in the distance.

They climbed into the truck, but let it freewheel down the hill, both to save fuel and to avoid being heard.

'What do you think that was?' asked Kline, when Taylor finally turned on the engine.

'Not sure, but we aren't in a position to go and investigate,' said Taylor. Then he turned the truck back toward Manchester.

Taylor had a sense of failure. He felt impotent. He knew they didn't have enough resources to tackle the base. To stand any chance at all of rescuing the women inside, they would need more weapons and soldiers. It was hopeless.

He thought back to the time some years ago when they had attacked the energy plant. Jas had helped with the planning; they'd had more men then too. He felt a momentary sadness at the deaths of so many good soldiers through one cause or another since then. He wasn't sure he could justify losing more. Especially when those remaining now had families and lives worth living for. Or did they?

'Look at the sky,' Donovan said, almost reading his mind.

Taylor glanced in his rear-view mirror. The sky was bright orange: a colour they were growing used to, but abnormal whatever way you looked at it. And a purple thread of vapour was bleeding up into it from the direction of the base.

The Jinx mage, Kale, had been adamant that something was wrong, and that seemed to be borne out by this sign that some form of pollution was being expelled into the atmosphere from the base.

Taylor pushed the thought away. It was something he could do nothing about, and what was that old proverb his mother used to say? Something to do with worrying about the things you can change, and accepting the things you can't. He tried to focus on the exact words. His mother had had a plaque hung up in her kitchen. Now, like so many things from the past, he couldn't remember it clearly.

'That purple is coming from the base,' Kline said. 'My guess is its nuclear.'

Taylor frowned. Of course, that was exactly what Kale had said.

'It's some kind of wastepipe, you mean?' Andrew asked.

'Probably. They can't pollute their own air below, after all,' Kline confirmed.

Taylor braked, pulling the truck slowly to a halt. He stared at the purple streak through his side mirror.

'I've got an idea, but it will require a bit longer recce,' he said.

'Whatever it is, we are with you all the way,' said Donavan.

Taylor turned the truck around on the empty motorway and began to drive back the way he had come. It didn't matter that he was driving in the wrong direction on the motorway; after all, who was left to stop him?

'Try thinking outwards,' Kale said. 'A bit like the skill I taught you to find your focus to bring us here.'

'For that, I summoned up a picture of this place,' Jas said. 'This is different though, isn't it?'

Kale placed his hand on hers. Her sent a mental picture. The image had no real shape or substance; it was more of a feeling. It was like a light sweeping over the surface of her brain. Sometimes it went deeper, became intrusive.

'Stop that,' she said, pulling her hand away.

'Did you feel the light?' he asked.

'Yes, but I didn't like the probing feeling.'

Kale was quiet for a moment, then he touched her hand again.

'The light is the search. The probe is the focus. Look into me. See how I sharpen the focus.'

Jas did as he suggested. Her mind reached out for his, and she experienced the sensation from his viewpoint as he stretched his beam outwards. The sensation of warmth, of light, like sun filtering through a parasol, and then the beam narrowed, tightened. She could feel how Kale flexed his concentration, and she knew exactly how to do it too.

She withdrew from him, sent her own focus outwards. She was like a creeping vine, sweeping over the land, and then it hit blackness. A blank.

'What is that?' she asked.

'That is what we have to fear. Something evil. Out there.'

Jas probed gently, then moved around the spot. It was as though someone had placed a massive dome around them that she couldn't penetrate. She pulled back, sent the beam in another direction. Many miles on, maybe 400 or more, she hit another wall. It was bigger than the nearest one. A dark fury buried beneath the ground. But its influence was affecting the air.

'You're right. Something is there.'

She could feel Kale's fear beside her, and his exhaustion.

'You haven't been sleeping well, have you?' she said.

'I have to protect you.'

His fear sharpened.

'What is it?'

The mage shook his head, but his eyes were swirling and he was holding magic in abeyance, ready to use.

'Something is coming ...'

Taylor was aware that following the purple fog was like trying to search for gold at the end of a rainbow. They skirted around the area, which seemed to stretch for at least five miles. Far from the hatch, and the opening they had seen in the slate quarry, they noticed a row of four tall, wide chimneys. The purple smog poured from the tops of them. They were definitely venting something from below.

They halted a couple of miles from the site. Taylor took out his binoculars and checked the area.

'It's an energy plant of some sort. These sorts of places usually burn coal for electricity, but I'm pretty certain that the waste coming from those chimneys isn't coal smoke.'

'What is it then?' Andrew asked.

'I don't know,' Taylor said.

'Now we know this is here, let's get back and think through what to do,' Donovan suggested.

Taylor glanced at him, then nodded.

'Let's get some photos,' Andrew said, taking a camera from his pocket.

As they turned around and headed back, Donovan studied the images on the camera monitor. 'This was definitely already there before the Jinx. These towers are old. Industrial. Though I don't remember seeing them before.'

'We saw some further north,' Taylor said. 'While we were still on the move.'

'Yes. All inactive, as I recall,' said Donovan.

Taylor grew thoughtful. The pollution had started only a short time ago. It had been only in the past year that they noticed the changes in the sky, and the constantly hovering fog. Did this mean that the base had recently begun to burn some new kind of fuel? Did it mean that their nuclear plants were no longer of use?

'Where was that nuclear plant we visited?' he asked, aware that his brain just wasn't functioning at all.

'Haversham?' Andrew said.

'I wonder if it's still operative.'

'Maybe we should check it out?' Donovan said.

20

It was night, and Jas was restless. She was afraid to sleep, knowing that she would be back with Arven as soon as she closed her eyes. This was a skill that she was frightened to asked Kale about. An ability that she was certain he wouldn't be able to explain. She could feel the urge pressing on her, the tiredness growing, but she wanted to think. To analyse it.

She wandered through the book aisles, searching for mystical and occult books. Maybe it could be explained somewhere without her having to face Kale's scrutiny, and perhaps even recrimination? Because surely if he knew of the liaisons with Arven, he would insist on their return to Emin.

Of course, her refusal to do that made no sense even to herself. She knew now that no harm would come to either of them. Kale would be forgiven, because he had been led astray by the Empress. How could he refuse anything she asked of him anyway? And by their own laws, the Jinx would be unable to prosecute her. Did they even have a law that punished treason? Jas doubted it. She even doubted that the Jinx had any concept of treason in the first place. Their laws and beliefs were so different from all that she had grown to accept as true.

On Earth, all explanations, all excuses, made more sense than her running away ever had. Especially now. Arven loved her. He wanted her back. She was creating pain – terrible suffering – for them both, but … she couldn't return. Yet. Something else held her here, and it wasn't any emotion toward Taylor or Andrew, but an urge to learn the truth. *Perhaps.*

This possible reality struck home, and Jas paused in the back of the shop. *I could be needed here. I could help set up schools for the children, make this makeshift city a real community.* But the thought was absurd. If this society managed to survive, it could do it nicely without her. If anything, her presence complicated things.

Jas sighed. Her heart hurt in her chest. Somewhere, out in the universe, in a completely different galaxy, Arven sat at his desk waiting for her. He, foolish though it was, was even willing to have these fleeting moments. And why? Why? What held her here? What was it that she couldn't leave? What was the truth that she needed to learn?

That day, Caroline had shown a surprising amount of telepathic ability. Natasha was expanding her precognitive focus too, and many of the other women were learning to control and build the operancy of their own magic. It was miraculous, wonderful, but how on earth was it going to make any difference to their lives?

'While you lot are dabbling in here, the crops are being neglected,' Dawn had pointed out. So far she had refused to participate in any of the classes.

'Oh, come on, Dawn. You just won't accept what we all know. And you have this ability too. I've seen how plants respond to you,' Caroline had said. 'The chores will wait. Maybe what we are learning will help us all survive.'

Dawn had stormed off. She was not convinced, and Jas could feel the hatred pouring from her. Dawn didn't like her, or her influence on the others. Jas couldn't work out if this was a good or a bad thing. At least Dawn kept out of her way for the most part, and she couldn't help but dislike the woman back. There was just something so … annoying about her.

'She's just jealous,' Caroline said to Jas. 'She knows that you and Taylor … Hell, we all know …'

'I'm not here for him,' Jas said.

'Then why did you come back?' asked Sylvia.

Jas knew that the older woman was exerting her own influence as she spoke. Sylvia had a calming effect on the group, and Jas was far from immune to it. But she was at least aware of it, even though she wasn't certain if Sylvia was.

'When I know the answer to that question, then I'll tell you, Sylvia. But, for now, I don't.'

And that was the crux of the matter, wasn't it? Jas really didn't know, and she couldn't force a reason no matter how hard she tried.

Her hand ran over the texts in the aisle again. Mystical books, witchcraft … *Tales of the Occult: Magic and its Origins.*

She picked this book up, flipped it over and read the back.

'Discover the mysteries of centuries-old superstitions …'

She placed the text back onto the shelf. It wasn't here.

'These books cannot give you answers,' Kale said.

Jas started. She hadn't heard him, and it annoyed her that anyone could sneak up on her like that. She had really lost her edge.

'Then where can I find them?'

Kale smiled. 'The answers will come to you when the time is right. Jasmine, you have fought your entire life to be here, at this moment, and now we are on a pathway that leads to your destiny.'

Jas sighed again. Kale's constant talk of destiny didn't help.

'Go to him. It hurts you more the longer you leave it,' Kale said.

'You *know?*'

'From the beginning …'

'How? How is it possible that I can go back *there?*'

'Empress … Jasmine. You have the power to go wherever you like. You just need to will it. The problem is, your heart will take you where you truly wish to be, even when your mind does not want to go there.'

'I need to control it. Stop it from controlling me …' Jas said.

She sank down into a seat at the end of the aisle. She was exhausted. Sleep was pulling at her, almost as much as the urge to return was.

'Something bigger than our will is in force here. You need to accept it. Only then can we both return.'

Jas was quiet. Kale's words both pleased and concerned her. He had stopped asking her to return with him. Yet, he often said they needed to leave. The contradiction of his words confused her more than his complaints that Earth was poisoned.

She pushed her mind outwards in the way he had shown her, but the ripple of light fell only a few feet beyond her.

'You're tired. You need rest.'

'I will get no rest if I travel back to Emin again,' she said.

'Then *will* it not to happen tonight,' Kale said.

Jas mulled over his words. Willing it *not* to happen was a possibility she had not considered. But she was tired and drained. The thought of facing Arven, of the intense guilt, and love, that consumed her in those moments, was not one she relished.

She pushed the thought-beam inside herself. Instead of projection she searched for protection. She chose to stay. Then was overwhelmed with guilt at leaving him alone, even for one night. It would be excruciating: he would be afraid. How could she let him know that all was well, without returning?

A dream. As she rested, she could try to send him peace, in a dream.

Jas lay down on her mattress. She felt sick – something that was becoming all too common lately – and she knew that her mind and body needed this break.

'It's astral projection …' she commented, as Kale took up his place on the mattress near hers.

'Oh no. It is much more than that,' Kale said. 'Rest, Empress. No-one can deny that you deserve it.'

21

Blood poured from Dr Tremaine's nose and trickled down his chin. One eye was badly swollen, his top lip was split and a few teeth were loose in his mouth. He was tied to a chair in an interrogation room, down in the bowels of MD59, head bowed.

'You've been very foolish, doctor. How on earth did you hope to escape with twenty breeders?' said Major Handley. 'Obviously, you will return to your duties. You will, of course, no longer have the triple-A status you have so far enjoyed.'

Tremaine didn't answer.

'Julia is probably dead. Exposure, or eaten by wolves. Such a waste of a potentially good whore,' Handley continued. 'I would have enjoyed helping to indoctrinate her into her new duties.'

'You're a sick bastard, Handley,' Tremaine said. Blood and saliva dribbled over his already blood-stained shirt. 'I'll speak to Colonel James about this …'

'And do you think James will have any sympathy at all for a traitor? You broke rank, Tremaine. Count yourself lucky that I didn't have your fingers broken … It *was* tempting. But then, you'd be no use to us anymore, and we have so few doctors …'

Handley left Tremaine in the hands of Caine. The man wished to interrogate him further, but Handley was bored already with the game. Tremaine had given in to guilt. Anything else didn't matter to Handley. Except Tremaine would be watched from now on. Already one of his subordinates had replaced him in the breeders' unit. Tremaine would be moved to more mundane general practice. Taking care of the wives of some of the soldiers would make the man feel less guilt. And the new doctor, Tony Gardner, was more receptive to Handley's methods than Tremaine had been. Any thought of resistance from Gardner, of course, would be curbed when he learned about Tremaine's demotion and beating.

Outside the interrogation unit, a young soldier waited for him in a golf cart. Handley climbed in beside the man.

'Where to, Major?' asked the soldier.

'Conditioning,' Handley said.

The soldier turned the cart around and headed down a long straight corridor. The underground routes stretched for miles and miles, linking together all manner of government offices and complexes. Eventually, he turned into another corridor and headed toward a guard post in the restricted area.

Handley left the man outside as he swiped his card and entered through a sterile white door.

Once inside, Handley was met by a female officer who was monitoring the reception area. Like all female workers that were not suitable for either breeding or sex, Gloria was in her early fifties.

'Hello Major,' she said formally. 'How can we help you today?'

'I want to see the experiment,' Handley said.

Gloria nodded. Then she pressed a button under her table, and a panel in the wall slid open to allow Handley to enter.

The panel silently closed behind him, and Handley stood patiently. Another panel in the wall opened, revealing a white coverall hanging inside, with a spacesuit-like helmet next to it: it was a hazmat suit.

'You need to wear that,' Gloria's voice crackled through a speaker somewhere above his head.

Handley squeezed his bulk into the suit and placed the big helmet on his head. It barely fitted over his thick head and wide neck. Once his suit was secure, another panel slid aside and Handley entered the lab.

Inside were a few men and one woman, suited identically as they examined a body that was lying naked and cut open on a mortuary slab.

'Ah, Major,' said one of the men. His voice echoed inside Handley's helmet.

He was a scientist by the name of Derek Brinton. A man who was leading in his field before the Jinx had come into their world. His expertise lay in chemical warfare, and he particularly specialised in creating mind control drugs. It was Brinton's work that made their conditioning of the P-class females so effective.

Beside Brinton was a woman. She was one of the rare A-class females in the base. She had triple-A clearance, and this was because she was not only Brinton's wife but a scientist of particular value to MD59. Hilary Brinton was an expert in genetics. With her knowledge and Brinton's skill, the couple were experimenting with a drug that could control many natural urges.

Handley looked down at the body on the slab and realised that the man, cut right down his middle, with stomach and guts laid open for all to see, was still alive and awake. He did not move, nor did he show any sign of distress.

'As you can see, subject 239 is completely relaxed and in no pain,' Hilary said.

'Which compound has the man been given?' Handley asked.

'It's Zobec 6. A derivative of 5, but with a little something added,' Hilary explained.

'Zobec 5, as you recall, was used on the drones living outside that were protecting food resources,' Brinton elaborated. 'Most of these drones were killed by looters, or in the case of the Trafford Centre, by ex-soldiers. We felt the reason why they were so ineffective was that the drones still held too much emotion, and could feel pain. This soldier doesn't feel anything. Emotional or physical. He does, however, respond to orders, and will fight to the death.'

Handley looked at the open wound with only a small feeling of disgust. 'Show me,' he said.

'Carlson, stand up,' said Hilary.

Carlson sat up on the slab. Blood seeped from his open wound, but he gave no sign of feeling pain. Then he stood. His organs moved, more blood oozed outwards, dripping down his naked sex organs and over his thighs.

'Jog in place,' Brinton ordered.

Carlson did as he was commanded. Soon, weakened by blood loss, his body began to grow limp, but the soldier continued to move until he was told to stop.

'Let's get him back on the table and close him up,' Hilary suggested.

'Yes – we've spent quite a few months on the conditioning of this unit, we don't want him to die unnecessarily,' Brinton said.

Carlson lay back down, and one of the doctors on hand began to sew up his abdomen while a nurse placed a cannula in his arm and began to administer a transfusion.

'The thing is, he has no natural defence to make him stop. He would just bleed to death, but he would take his opponent down with him, because he also has no fear or pain that might otherwise stop him.'

'I'm disappointed,' Handley said. 'I thought you were trying to create super-soldiers. This is just one that's too stupid to know he's dying.'

'Major, what we have here is the beginning of that process. All we need to discover is how to stop blood-flow when the soldier is wounded. If we could do that, nothing short of decapitation would stop our men. We could go topside again, and we'd have no fear of a Jinx attack,' Brinton explained.

'It sounds like a pipe dream to me,' Handley said. 'If doctors could stop blood-flow you'd have done it years ago.'

'We did,' said Hilary. 'The problem is combining the two drugs and keeping them stable.'

'What do you mean, you did it years ago?' Handley said. Once again he was being fed information on Colonel James's 'need to know' basis, and it was starting to irritate him.

'Desmopressin is a drug commonly used for haemophilia. Which is when a person starts to bleed but the natural clotting doesn't occur. The haemophiliac will continue to bleed, depending on how severe their condition is and what type of haemophilia they suffer from,' Brinton explained. 'The problem comes when we treat a normal person with the drug, or in this case a souped-up version of the drug.'

'Enlighten me. What happens?' Handley said.

'Excessive clotting. Not just at the source of the wound but internally, which can lead to thrombosis. The candidate could die from that alone. All it takes is a blood clot to find its way to the heart. Of course it depends on whether or not that matters. If the candidate is badly injured, he probably won't survive from the wounds anyway.'

Handley thought for a moment. 'It sounds like the right way to go. Why aren't you doing it?'

Hilary sighed in her suit. 'There's a clash between the two composites. Sometimes the desmopressin compound starts to clot the blood inside the subject, even though we have altered it to react only when the blood hits the air. I guess it's about finding the exact amalgamation. It takes time, unfortunately, Major.'

Handley frowned. 'Time is running out,' he said.

'But I thought –' said Brinton.

'What? That we could stay down here forever? We are safe for another twenty or so years, but after that we need to think of building resources above ground again. By then, hopefully, the Jinx will have forgotten us, and the survivors will have suffocated in the smog we're generating. The planet will be ours to do with what we want.'

Handley nodded to underline his words. This was all part of the plan.

'Right,' he said. 'Now. Show me the new conditioning for the women ...'

The observation room itself was sparse, containing two chairs and a table fitted beneath a two-way mirror. There was a control panel, a computer and speakers.

Through the mirror, Handley saw a young woman sitting naked on the floor in a padded cell. She was unnaturally still as she stared into the mirror. Handley could see she was pretty, though her body bore the marks of the many pregnancies she had previously endured.

'This is what she is hearing,' Brinton said as he pressed one of the controls. A high-pitched sound burst from the speakers, followed by the mandatory conditioning tape.

'You are nothing ... You are worth nothing ... You will do as your client tells you ... Your only aim is to serve ... You like sex with your client ... You want sex with your client ... You will feel no hatred ... You will feel no disgust ... You must never say no ... You are nothing ... You are worth nothing ...'

'Who is this one?' Handley asked.

'Former breeder. Her name was Susan, but she'll be Dominique when she goes over the P-class area. She was fixed six months ago and we've been working on her ever since. She's responded well, but today is the moment of truth,' said Brinton.

Handley didn't question the name change of the girl, as he knew that it was all part of their conditioning. The brainwashing removed everything that they had been and gave them a completely new personality.

In the cell, the tape stopped playing.

'Ah. Her *first* client?' Handley said.

Brinton nodded. 'Your timing was impeccable, Major.'

'Who volunteered?'

'Colonel James has come over specially. He enjoys breaking them in,' Brinton said.

Handley hadn't seen James in the flesh for years. He hadn't even known this detail that the man came to MD59 regularly, even though he still received communications and orders from MD1. He felt a pang of jealousy that this man had been granted the privilege of starting the former breeder on her new classification, but he quashed the emotion quickly, because he wouldn't put it past James to have some secret device that could read thoughts. He would never do anything to jeopardise the cushy position he had in the new order.

'I assume that's why no-one is in here monitoring.'

Brinton smirked. 'Yes, but it's being recorded. James has requested a copy already.'

'Unzip me,' James's voice sounded husky through the speakers. Handley noted how much the man had aged.

The girl inside turned her head to look at James. She was spaced out, drugged to the eyeballs, but still a flicker of fear crossed her face.

'That little blip will be gone after today,' Brinton said.

Handley knew that meant the following interaction would consolidate her coercion, and he could tell the man was getting off on seeing the girl becoming a whore for the first time. He felt a surge of excitement brewing in his own loins. James was a bastard to the women. If she survived this and fell into the robotic mode of conditioning, this girl would be up on the rota for use within hours. Handley would probably try her out sooner rather than later too. There was something less blank about the newly conditioned, as though they hadn't quite lost themselves in the role that was given to them, as though there was still something inside that might rebel.

The girl made no move to do as James told her.

'Interesting,' said Brinton.

'She's resisting?' Handley said.

'Some try. The struggle won't last long. It never does,' Brinton said.

'I said unzip me,' James said. He stood over the girl now, blocking her from Handley's and Brinton's view through the mirror. But Brinton rectified that by changing the image on the viewing monitor to the side-facing camera.

The girl stared at James's crotch as though she were a trained monkey trying to assimilate a new instruction. Then she reached out a hand and gently pulled down his zip.

After that, her hand flopped by her side.

'Take my cock out, you stupid bitch,' James said.

The girl looked up at him again. That tremor of fear passed over her features once more.

'What do you want?' she asked. Her voice was small, tremulous. She sounded young and afraid.

'I want you to suck my dick,' James said.

Instead of ordering her to do what he believed he had the right to insist on, James now changed his tone. He spoke to her as though she was a slightly unintelligent child.

'Suck it. Just like a lollipop.'

'He's good ...' said Brinton. 'Very persuasive.'

'He's had years of practice,' Handley said.

The girl's hand went inside his trousers and retrieved James's already swollen penis. She stared at the tip for a moment and then opened her mouth, taking him inside.

James groaned.

'She's gonna be a great P-class,' Brinton said. 'She's sucking him like her life depends on it.'

Handley knew that Brinton's joke was far too close to the truth to be really amusing: if she didn't work out as P-class, there would be only one place she would end up. She would be fodder for the drones.

Now she was on her back while James pumped into her enthusiastically.

'You like it, don't you? You've always wanted to shag lots of men, haven't you? You were made to be a whore ...'

'No,' the girl said, and Handley heard tears in her voice. It aroused him.

'She might need a little more work,' he suggested.

'Nah,' said Brinton. 'It's the last bit of fight. Makes fucking her even more fun.'

'So. This is one you'll be trying out?' Handley said.

'Me? I'm a married man. 'Gainst the rules ...' Brinton winked.

Handley laughed then. He knew that Brinton was a regular in the P-class rooms. As James poured himself into the girl, who was now sobbing uncontrollably, despite her inability to resist, Handley left the room, and Brinton to his own devices.

Everything was going to plan, and Handley loved his world. How could things be any more perfect?

22

It was a difficult night for Arven. He waited for Jasmine to appear, but unlike on the previous few nights, she never did. He began to regret listening to Garuk. The mage had talked him down again, telling him to have patience.

'There is a divine plan, Lord. You just need to wait.'

Arven was afraid to wait, though. Jasmine was on Earth, and the planet's pollution would in time, according to Garuk, affect her. Now he paced the tent, waiting for her to appear, and with every passing moment fear gripped his heart. Where was she?

He stopped pacing and went to the divining pool. It was sure to locate her if he thought hard enough. All he needed was reassurance that Jasmine was safe. It wasn't much to ask for.

He stared into the water. At first nothing moved, but then his swirling pupils detected a faint trace of movement before the water cleared. He saw Jas sleeping. Blue circles were evident under her eyes. He wondered at the tiredness. The paleness of her skin appeared sickly compared with the usual robust colour she had in Sharik.

The image faded. Reassured that she was at least unhurt, Arven began to undress, then he slipped naked into the bed.

He lay, waiting, hope that she would still come, but overwhelming tiredness seeped into his limbs and began to numb his thoughts. He fell into a dream.

The ghost of Jasmine sat beside the pool. Arven dreamt that he opened his eyes. She smiled at him.

'I'm fine. Just tired. Don't know why. It's probably this damned planet ...' she said, but her lips never moved.

The image of her shimmered, faded. She was too weak to materialise fully.

'Come back to me,' he said.

She stood, walked toward him and then faded, completely disappearing.

Arven's eyes opened and he stared at the pool. It was a dream, nothing more, and the disappointment he felt made his eyes sting. But still he stared at the spot, refusing to give up hope that soon Jas would appear, as solid and real as ever.

Garuk stared into his own divining pool.

'What do you see?' asked Marlin.

'The Empress has a strong connection with the Emperor. The bond between them can never be broken. Not even with this distance.'

'It would be better if she were to die on Earth,' Marlin said. 'The people call for change. Arven has been weak. He let the love he feels for this *human* colour his judgement.'

Garuk looked at Marlin. He had chosen to hear the councillor out, but was scandalised by the tone in his voice and the words he dared to utter. The thought that the Empress should die horrified him. He did not tell Marlin that Jasmine was with child; the Emperor had sworn him to secrecy. But the talk of Arven being anything but perfect went against the training and beliefs of the mage, and he did not wish to hear it.

'The Emperor is never wrong. All decisions he makes will lead to better things for the Arrak Nah Tiamen,' Garuk said. 'We have to trust that Almia[1] will guide the Emperor.'

'Times are changing,' Marlin said. 'Maybe her flight was fortuitous after all.'

'What do you mean?'

'I spoke to Prestin,' Marlin said.

'Shandalin's mage?'

'Yes. He tells me that he can trace the Empress. That the trail leads to a place with many women. There are men here who would happily kill more Earth men to find a wife.'

'The Emperor has forbidden it. There are to be no more unnecessary deaths,' Garuk said.

'Do you deem all that we have achieved as unnecessary?' Marlin said. 'Even the Emperor bonded with one of them. Though she has proved to be troublesome. Some are angered that he even entered the ceremony before the needs of his men were met.'

Garuk picked up a goblet from a table that stood in the middle of the room. He sipped the water in the cup. It was cold and refreshing, and he needed a moment to think before replying to Marlin.

'We all know that destiny plays her music in the ceremony,' Garuk said. 'No Arrak can resist the call when the song for his mating is played. Arven found his mate. I believe she is perfect, if something of an anomaly. Did the

---

[1] The Arrak Nah Tiamen Goddess of wisdom.

mage of Shandalin not tell you of the Empress's calling?'

Marlin looked sharply at Garuk. 'He told me that he saw two fate lines. One that led to an uncertain future. The other that showed us bringing her home. It all depends on choices the woman makes. Which is why I feel we should attack now, before she makes the wrong one. Surely the Emperor will not be angry if we bring the Empress back? And if a new influx of women should accompany that return, then the unrest among the warriors would settle for a time.'

'But only for a time, as surely there still would not be enough for all,' Garuk said.

Still, Garuk couldn't argue against Marlin's logic. He had seen the two possible destinies but had also looked beyond the choice that Marlin would make. He had seen Jasmine returned, but not completely safe, and something was blocking his vision as to why.

Maybe it was because the future was still in flux. Maybe Marlin was right. He knew that Arven would be happy to have Jasmine back, to see his child safe. But he would be going against his own advice to leave her for now. To see where her real destiny lay. And, he would be going against his Emperor's wishes to avoid further bloodshed.

'It is what she hates about us,' Arven had explained. 'To these women we are savages, no matter how hard we try to make amends, make them happy. I cannot destroy her trust. I promised I would kill no more of her people.'

Garuk shook his head. 'The Emperor said no. He may yet go to collect her himself, but he will go in love, not in war.'

'And how will his peaceful visit be greeted by the humans?' Marlin said.

Garuk closed his eyes. He knew how it would go, which was why he had urged Arven to remain. The humans would fight, more would die. Arven's promise would still be broken, and Jasmine's anger might place a permanent wedge between them.

'I need to think,' Garuk said. 'And consult my runes. The future might not be set, and our actions could take us down a path we do not care to tread.'

'I understand,' Marlin said, but a faint smile curved his lips. He quashed it when Garuk once again opened his eyes.

When Marlin had left him, Garuk sank into a chair beside the pool. He gazed at the visions it showed him.

'Show me what might happen if we leave the Empress on Earth,' he murmured.

Scenario after scenario played out, none of them to a positive conclusion. He saw Jasmine dying at the hands of treacherous soldiers, her unborn child shrivelling within her womb; Jasmine sipping a drink containing poison while a jealous woman hid behind a bookcase; Jasmine suffocating to death as the contaminated air of Earth burned her lungs: around her the carcasses of other women rotted.

Wherever he looked, the future was showing him terrible options. He could, of course, go to Arven with his fears; but that would mean that the Emperor would leave for Earth immediately, and the fight he feared would take place. There was a possibility that Arven would die … and with no heir, there would be bloodshed on Emin too, as warriors fought for the right of succession.

Garuk was horrified by it all. He did not know what to do.

'Show me what will happen if I allow Marlin to fetch the Empress,' he instructed.

The water swirled, clouded up, then cleared. He saw devastation on Earth – nothing new there, the planet was doomed no matter what – but … the Empress was returned. Her baby born and safe, and more women were rescued from certain death on a dying planet. They would be enough to appease, and they would learn to accept Arrak Nah Tiamen ways, just as the others had. It seemed like the only positive future.

Garuk made up his mind. He would help Marlin cross through a vortex to Earth. It was the only sane option if he wanted to save Arven, and life on his own planet, as well as the Empress.

23

'You were gone longer than I expected,' said Dawn as Taylor collapsed onto the mattress beside her.

'One thing led to another,' Taylor said. 'We discovered a working power plant; not nuclear, but something else.'

'Wind farm?' she said.

'No. That at least would make sense, and would not kick out pollution into the air.'

'Pollution?' said Dawn. 'Is that what's up with the sky?'

'I guess so, but I really don't know. Whatever it is that's coming out of those chimneys it's not healthy, that's for sure.'

Dawn was quiet. It was dark and she couldn't make out his expression, but she felt his worry as he cuddled up to her.

'What shift are you on?' he asked.

'Afternoon.'

'Good. Can I hold you? Just while I sleep?'

Dawn kissed his forehead and nestled comfortably under his arm, resting her head on his chest. It wasn't long before he fell asleep and, as his breathing levelled out into a low snore, she slipped away from him and out of the bed.

In the seating area she sank down onto the sofa and pulled her knees up to her chest. She stared at the wall, her thoughts skipping around like a panicked cat locked in a cage. His words had frightened her more than he could know.

The pollution of the air could affect them all. It was also completely against everything *they* had told her. Everything *they* had promised.

Dawn shook her head. *Who were 'they'?*

She heard Lucy stirring in her room. Taylor had done a great job of building them privacy, but the wall was still thin, and every sound seemed to carry. Lucy wasn't one for staying in bed late. It was a situation that would probably change as the girl reached puberty, but for now she was little more than a baby, and she woke as hunger and bathroom needs called.

Dawn considered how her child had been unplanned. She hadn't wanted to bring an innocent into this horrible world, but it had happened. She recalled her horror at discovering she had given birth to a girl. An unnameable phobia had clawed at her insides. And there was such regret in those first few moments after the birth, as she recalled refusing Dr Avery's offer to abort when she had first discovered she was with child.

Of course that had been out of the question once Taylor knew she was pregnant. She had never seen such happiness on his face before. He had seen this as the road to a future. A stepping stone on the pathway to building a new world. Dawn loved him. She couldn't deny him that perceived future. That hope.

She considered her life here. It had been hard, but mostly happy. So much so that she had barely thought of the past. Now, that past was pushing at the sides of her memory like a boil ready to burst.

She hadn't lied when she had told Caroline that she couldn't remember the past. All she recalled was the day she had found Caroline and the other women, hiding out in Prestwich. It was as though before that day she had never existed.

'I'm a friend,' she had said as the barrel of the shotgun was directed at her. She had frozen, hands in the air, fearing that the woman facing her would get nervous and pull the trigger anyway. But Caroline had lowered her gun and hugged her. Dawn had taken an immediate liking to her. In this world, being a woman meant you were trusted. No-one asked you awkward questions about your history. Unlike men, who were always viewed with suspicion.

'How many of you are there?' Dawn had asked on that first meeting.

'Twenty-three. We've been lying low for a few months now. But we've seen a group of soldiers around. Yesterday they answered our call and we had to watch as they fought off a Jinx attack. We were too afraid to reveal our whereabouts after that.'

Dawn had nodded. 'I've been travelling. It's hell out there. The sooner we mix in with a bigger group, the more chance we have to survive.'

Caroline had agreed, and so they used the two-way radio they'd found to call again.

As the soldiers had arrived on the site, Caroline had suddenly become afraid. 'What if they are … weird?'

Dawn had laughed. She had convinced them all it was safe to trust Taylor's men. She couldn't recall how, but she had known they were safe to be around, and getting in with the group had been somehow important.

They had all been willing in the end to join up with the soldiers at the Trafford Centre, and relationships had rapidly formed.

'All this time we've been trying to find and help survivors, and you show up and they suddenly come out of the woodwork,' Donovan had commented to Caroline.

Dawn knew how to find others. She had an instinct for it: a bit like the Jinx, if the truth be known, because until they had all moved into the lead-covered dome of the Trafford Centre, any woman had been a magnet to the enemy. Dawn knew that lead could hide them from the Jinx, but it didn't hide them from her.

She had done so much good in the early days. Bringing in the waifs and strays, helping the Centre become their city. Growing crops with the magical green thumb that seemed so effortless for her. And she believed in it all, believed that they could make a difference and have a future.

She hadn't looked back, only forward, and had never questioned it.

Now, as Taylor slept and Lucy stirred, Dawn found herself questioning everything. Why had she been unable to remember anything other than her name? Why had she never thought to be concerned about it? Partly it was Taylor's fault. He had avoided asking her questions about the past, and she knew this was deliberate. They all had stories, some worse than others, but it wasn't worth dwelling on them. What was important was now and the future, not what had happened before.

But something was jogging in her memory of a past forgotten. It hurt to think of it, but she forced her mind to focus. A headache formed around her eyes, threatening to become a migraine. She shook her head. She had to remember something. It was crucial, but she didn't know why.

White hot pain exploded behind her eyes. She was like a blind person trying to see. A veil formed before her eyes. It looked like quarantine plastic sheeting, hung up around military cots. She was remembering a hospital environment. Or maybe it was some kind of hazmat situation. But the memory wouldn't shape into anything coherent. She pressed and squeezed, picking at it like an itchy, painful sore.

Then, the boil burst.

Dawn had always been a good soldier. One that followed orders to the letter, as Taylor and his men had once done. She had been one of the first to be taken down into the underground base before the final days. There had been many soldiers, male and female, working down there. Dawn had been underground for almost two years before the Jinx forced the others to join them.

'Lieutenant Cawley,' James said when she arrived in his office on that final day. 'It's time you learnt about the future of Earth. And the final days that you and your team have been preparing for.'

The news was not good. James told her that the world above had gone to shit. Dawn and her team were to prepare for some new work. She was, he said, crucial to the future of humanity.

A course of specific drugs and vitamins were prescribed for her. James told her she needed to be strong, but it was the indoctrination that was the hardest to accept.

She listened to it all with an open mind. The news of how female status had changed was a difficult pill to swallow. But Dawn took it in her stride. It didn't mean *her*. She was a soldier, and therefore exempt from the rules that governed the civvies among them.

The drugs they gave her made her feel calm all the time. All things would be good. The new world would be better than the old. She had a status that protected her from the breeders' wards and the P-class pleasure area. It never occurred to her to question why there were no P-class males to service the women, like herself, who were on the periphery of it all.

'Gone are the politicians who dictated how we lived. The rules have all changed,' James preached. And Dawn saw him like some religious leader teaching a long-forgotten doctrine.

'I'm very pleased with how you're turning out, Dawn,' James said.

By then Dawn was so brainwashed she would do anything for him. She frequently went to his rooms and spent time in his bed, pleasuring him, not like the P-class whores, but because she wanted to. At least, that was what she believed.

The questions came into her mind only when she saw the changing status of one of the other female soldiers.

'I don't want to be a breeder,' Beverly Stains said.

'The doc says you're fertile,' said the soldier who took her away. 'Plus, you aren't quite working out in this programme.'

'Why isn't she working out?' asked Dawn, coming into the mess area during the commotion.

'Dawn, you've got to help me,' begged Bev. 'Talk to Colonel James ...'

'I'm sure this is a mistake,' Dawn said, and a feeling of anxiety leaked through the drug-induced calm. 'Bev is a good soldier.'

'She's a girl. With a womb that works. She'll be better off somewhere else ...' the soldier said.

Dawn watched at Bev was led away. The male soldier's eyes had been dead when he spoke to her. That was when Dawn realised that the men she worked with, had fought alongside, had all changed their view of her, and of the other female soldiers.

A few of the others had shared her concern as they watched the exchange between Bev and the soldier. No longer could they kid themselves that they were safe. They were female. They had no rights. They were no longer soldiers.

Soon after that, a few more of the females were taken. Dawn became even more concerned. But she also knew she was favoured by James, and felt that maybe he was even her protector.

She went to his rooms a few days later.

'I'm shipping out of here,' he told her. 'I have another base to run. Handley will be in charge of MD59 from now on.'

'Handley? Is that why things have changed?' Dawn asked. She felt secure lying naked in his bed, with the taste of his cum still in her mouth.

'What d'you mean?'

'A few of the female soldiers were taken from my unit this week. Their status was changed. Some went on to the breeders' wards. Others to the P-class area.'

'Just think of it as them being deployed where they will be of better use ...' James said. Then he climbed on top of her and fucked her. Dawn couldn't think of it in any other terms than that. It wasn't love making, it was screwing. Nothing more.

While she was lying under him, Dawn recalled that their sessions were never that pleasurable for her. It was all about James and what he needed. The awful thought occurred to her that she too had been deployed and had not realised it. She was James's P-class: his own private whore. Now he was moving on, where did that leave her? She was afraid to ask.

James had plans for Dawn, of course, and it was a relief when she heard that she wasn't remaining behind at MD59. She hated Handley. The Major sickened her, and she had caught him looking at her a few times when she had been training in the gym. As the number of females among the soldiers rapidly diminished, Dawn noticed that more and more of her male colleagues started acting strangely around her. Gone was the camaraderie that she had enjoyed with them. Gone was the feeling of equality.

'You'll have a new task soon,' James said as she joined him in the carriage of the underground train.

'I'm looking forward to it,' Dawn said, but his words terrified her. She didn't know at all what awaited her at MD1.

They travelled underground in the network of tunnels that the military had built prior to the invasion.

'I didn't know there was such a big network,' Dawn said.

'Well, it's all need-to-know. You'll have to forget you've seen this, of course. It's not knowledge a woman should have,' James said.

'Where is MD1?' Dawn asked.

James looked at her. His gaze was cold and measured. Dawn realised that he had no feelings for her at all. She saw the same expression that the other soldiers had now when they looked at her. It was as though she were a toy that could be put aside whenever the Colonel tired of playing with her. Dawn knew her place. She got onto her knees and began to excite him. If she was to be a whore, better it was for just one man.

They reached MD1 some hours later. James was relaxed, and Dawn followed him into the base, and to what she thought would be their joint accommodation.

'Well, I'll be sorry to lose you,' James said. 'You've been very responsive to the treatment.'

'What do you mean?' Dawn said. Her heart began to pound in her chest.

'You're entering a new programme today, Dawn.'

'No. Not me. You can't turn me into a …'

'No. Of course not. You're way too talented to become a breeder. We have something entirely different in mind for you.'

Dawn's face flushed. The thing she most feared was about to happen. She would become a P-class.

'No. You can't do this to me. Please don't do this to me. I'll do anything … anything you want.'

'Dawn. My dear girl. Calm down. I know you'll do anything I want. I've trained you well. Now it's time to forget all about us until the time is right,' James said.

'What do you mean?'

'You're going undercover. Oh, not yet. In a little while, once our scientists are happy that you've been conditioned to behave exactly how we want you to. Don't worry. When your mission is done, your triple-A status will be your reward. '

'Triple-A?'

'Yes.'

'What do I have to do?'

'Mummy? I want some juice …'

Dawn snapped back to the present. Her stomach lurched, and she ran past Lucy and into the back room. She heaved up bile, then sat shuddering as she leaned over the toilet bowl. Her head hurt so much that she couldn't think straight. Even so, images of her former life burst into her head, like newly acquired recollections. It hurt. A lot.

Everything she had done over the last few years had been a lie.

24

Taylor, Donovan, Andrew and Kline were huddled around one of the tables in the mess when Jas and Kale came in. It was late afternoon and the four men still looked, and felt, tired.

'Jas. Over here,' Taylor said.

'I'm glad to see you back safe and sound,' Jas said. She took a seat at the table, and Kale, after a little coaxing, did the same. 'Did you find anything out?'

The four men exchanged glances. Jas realised that they were considering whether or not to tell her anything. She held in a sigh and waited while Taylor made up his mind what to say.

'There's definitely an underground base. Everything that Julia said was accurate,' he explained.

'Did you doubt it?'

'No. Of course not,' Donovan said. 'But we always err on the cautious side at first.'

'So what are you going to do? It sounds like some women in there need rescuing,' Jas said.

Taylor frowned.

'The truth is, I don't think we can do anything,' he said.

'What? You can't *leave* them there.'

'The thing is,' Kline said, 'we don't have the manpower, or the weapons, to do much other than cause a ruckus. If we do that, then we risk bringing them, and any military power they have, down on us. On our families.'

'Of course. That is a major risk,' Jas said. She was thoughtful.

'Even so,' Taylor said, 'I plan to head back out there with a team. Archie used to work for a security firm. What he doesn't know about electronics, surveillance and safe-cracking isn't worth knowing. If anyone can open that hatch, and gain us some access to the base, without them knowing, then he can. Fortunately, Julia really does have an excellent memory. She has been working with an artist today to sketch the layout of the base.'

'That's something, at least. But I agree that you shouldn't take unnecessary chances,' Jas said. 'When will you be setting off with Archie?'

'Tonight. We will probably be gone for a few days,' Taylor said.

'Better go and tell my wife,' Donovan said. Then he stood and left.

The other soldiers rapidly dispersed, leaving Taylor, Jas and Kale alone.

'I believe you've been doing some good work with the women,' Taylor said, addressing Kale.

'They are a rare talent,' Kale said. 'It is all unexpected, but does explain why, when we searched for a planet, Earth seemed the most promising and compatible to us.'

'How many other planets are there with inhabitants?' Taylor said.

'Many, but Earth and Emin have the only humanoid life-forms we know of. We came from the same source,' Kale explained.

'What do you mean?' Taylor asked.

'Human and Arrak Nah Tiamen are two tribes. We were both born under the same sun. One tribe chose magic, the other science. That was when the divide began.'

'You're saying we're all from the same gene pool?' Taylor said. 'Did you know this, Jas?'

'It is part of the history that the Jinx teach. Physically we aren't dissimilar at all. If you take away the exceptional height of the Arrak Nah Tiamen. And the lack of nipples in the males of the species.'

Taylor laughed. 'They have no nipples?'

A smile flickered briefly over Jas's lips. 'They have no need for them. I suspect men of our own species will evolve the same way eventually.'

'Why did they evolve before us?' Taylor pondered.

'Your science holds you back,' Kale said.

Taylor frowned. 'It's all we know.'

'Then learn something new,' Kale said.

Taylor stood, bringing the strange conversation to an end. 'I have to go. Lots to do before we leave.'

Jas watched Taylor leave, and then turned to Kale. 'Perhaps you need to go a bit lighter on them. They are trying to adapt. It's a lot to take in. Here, we are the aliens.'

'Not you. Just me,' Kale said.

'No. I'm every bit of an oddity as you are. I've never felt less at home than I do here,' Jas said.

'I need to make sure Julia is well,' Kale said. 'They may tire her with their demands.'

'Okay. I'm going to do some more work with Caroline and the other adepts this afternoon.'

She watched Kale go. His interest in Julia was something rare indeed, and Jas was grateful for it. It meant that he was less by her side, less of a reminder that she didn't belong here.

25

Dawn stared out onto the former car-park of the Trafford Centre. She had a lot of thinking to do. The change had occurred so quickly that she wasn't sure how to respond and behave in a normal way amongst the other occupants. She didn't belong there. How could she have forgotten that? And now she was experiencing a peculiar sensation. Her fingertips tingled, and every fibre of her body was numb and cold, as if the drug she had once been taking daily at the base was now back in her system.

She mulled over the problem. She was a soldier, sworn to do her duty, even when she hadn't agreed with it. Now she understood all those feelings of anxiety she had experienced when Lucy was born. She was unable to protect her child, and it wasn't the Jinx that she feared. Even so, duty was all she had known. She was conditioned to it. Now it pushed aside the other emotions that struggled inside her. The feeling of helplessness was subdued with them.

James had told her this day would come. She remembered now.

'You'll be fully submerged into their society. You'll have relationships, lovers, maybe even children. But you'll be activated when you're needed, and you will respond.'

There had been no threats made at that time. James was sure of her indoctrination. He was certain that she would come back into the fold and bring all of the occupants of the Centre with her.

'There you are!'

Dawn turned to see Taylor by the door of the Centre.

'I needed some air,' she said, but her excuse sounded unnecessary even to herself.

Taylor came to her, took her stiff body into his arms. 'I have to leave again.'

Despite everything, Dawn relaxed against him.

'I know you probably won't understand,' he said, 'but we have to try to get in. Maybe help the women in there.'

Dawn pressed her face into his chest. 'I do understand. You're a soldier and you want to do your duty.'

'Yes.' Taylor hugged her fiercely and then pushed her back so that he could look into her eyes. 'I love you. You know that, right? Take care of Lucy and I'll be back as soon as I can, with or without the women on the base. In the end, the safety of everyone here matters more.'

'I know.' Dawn hid her face in his chest again. She was afraid that he would be able to see inside her, see the guilt and the betrayal that lay hidden there. She didn't know what she was going to do, but she had been 'activated', and that meant things were going to change. Her life was never going to be the same again.

She watched him leave after a tentative and tender goodbye. She marvelled at how easy it was to slip into that mode of loving wife, even though she now knew it was a lie.

She went back inside as the trucks containing Taylor and thirty or so men drove away, following the path of the old car-park out onto the deserted motorway. A couple of hours' drive was all it would take to get to the base, especially now, when there would never be traffic to hold up the truck.

Dawn knew the base well. She knew it like the back of her hand. She would be able to lead them, easily, through the hatch and down into the breeders' wards. But how could she share that information without revealing who and what she was? Why should she, anyway?

It was a question of survival, one that hadn't changed at all with her newly recalled knowledge. She intended to survive. She was determined to gain her triple-A status. And maybe her child would be given the same privilege too? After all, the base needed children, women, and loyal soldiers.

Inside, Dawn walked through the mess. She saw Sylvia, Caroline and several other women following Jas and Kale to the training area. They would be looking once more at expanding their powers. Dawn almost laughed aloud at the absurdity of it. *Magic indeed.* They were fools to believe this nonsense. It was probably all trickery. Tricks of that Jinx bastard and that slut he claimed was their Empress.

A dark shadow fell over her heart. It was some ruse; now she could see it, though she had been blind to it all like everyone else at first. Her fear before had been that Jas had come back just to pick up where she had left off with Taylor, but now that silliness no longer mattered to Dawn. Taylor was a casualty of the war.

'They are already dead …' James had said. 'Each of them with their pathetic struggle to live. It all means nothing. The only law is down here with us. The only chance of survival is in the bases.'

Dawn believed it was true.

She went over to the day-care centre.

'Is Lucy okay?' she asked Clara, the receptionist.

'Sure. Wanna see her?'

Dawn hesitated. 'Okay.'

Her daughter was playing in the ball pool with Selene and Jamie. The three children were close, but Dawn saw it for what it was. As Lucy grew, she would become a commodity, like all women, and so would Selene. The thought sickened her more than anything else in the world since the Jinx had invaded.

'I have to get back to work,' Dawn said.

'You okay?' asked Clara. 'You look a little pale.'

'A bit under the weather, but I'll shake it off,' Dawn said.

She left the day-care centre and walked back toward her own home. A shiver ran over her as though someone had walked over her grave. She looked up, then saw Gerald watching her.

'What are you doing here?' she asked.

'Bringing your supply of pills,' Gerald said. 'Thought you would have collected them as usual. You're two days late.'

'Pills?' Dawn said. She glanced down at the package that the doctor held out to her. 'With all that's been going on, I ...'

She took the package and watched as Gerald walked away. Then she entered her home, sat down on the sofa and opened the package.

Inside was a tub containing two different kinds of capsules. Dawn stared at them, rifling around in her memory to recall what they were for, and why Gerald was prescribing them for her.

Vitamin supplements perhaps? Something in the back of her mind jogged. She saw Gerald frequently supplying her. Her eyes fell on the old shop counter in the corner of the room. Nowadays they used it as a bar. Random bottles of alcohol stood on and behind it. Not that she, or Taylor, indulged much, despite her blowout with Caroline when the men were away.

Dawn stood, made her way to the back of the counter and examined it. Behind was a row of shelves, on which was a box containing various knick-knacks, cotton and needle, spare buttons, and various patches of fabric that she used to extend the life of their clothing.

There was a solid beam that passed through the counter. A support beam, Dawn thought. The Trafford Centre was a huge structure, and the roof and upper floors needed to be supported by huge columns that were placed at intervals around the building.

Dawn tapped the beam. Something she hadn't done before, or didn't recall doing. And then a strange thing happened. The tap echoed. Which showed that the beam was hollow, and therefore fake. She bent down behind the bar, looking over the bottom carefully. A half-remembered dream floated back to her. She recalled touching this column before, in such a way that –

A panel opened in the side. Dawn glanced up at the packet of pills she had placed on top of the bar. She reached up, pulled them down and stowed them inside the panel, where no-one could find them.

Her thoughts were hazy. Merging the two halves of her was the cause, and she now understood the real reason why her old memories had come back. She hadn't been activated at all; she had accidentally stopped taking the meds Gerald had been supplying her with to *suppress* the memories.

Dawn looked around her home. She had been happy here. But was it *all* a lie? Could she begin to take the drugs again? Hide the truth once more from herself and continue playing house with Taylor? The thought appealed to her. A happy bliss, an ignorant fool, living in a fantasy, a dream-like state that hid all the truth from her. But why?

And why, more importantly, had she failed to continue taking the pills?

It was obvious, really, now that she was awake. It was *time* for her to *act*. Clearly the doctor was somehow involved. Dawn did not think she had met him before coming to the Trafford Centre, but recollection of seeing him frequently since then, and of his supplying her with the medication, came flooding back. She had never liked Gerald: she cared for him even less now.

She poured herself a drink from a decanter containing Jack Daniels. She sat on the sofa again. It was barely three in the afternoon. She had a lot she needed to do, but it was more important to *think*. She was in turmoil. Part of her wanted to contact James and warn him of Taylor's possible breach of their defences. Part of her wanted to go to Sylvia and the other council members and tell them the truth.

The problem was, the two halves of her were at war.

'I could go back to oblivion …' she considered aloud, gazing at the column. 'Just take the pills and damn the consequences.'

The image of Lucy playing in the day-care centre, innocently enjoying the friendship of Selene and Jamie, came back into her mind.

The base was bad. *Evil.* Her logical mind could see that the horrors they inflicted on women were horrendous. No amount of brainwashing had taken those images and that understanding away. Fear was the only reason she had participated in all of their experiments. All of the awful things they had done to make sure she would remember her duty.

The Trafford Centre was home. She could never betray the people here. Never put her child at risk, and never hand Taylor over to those brutal men. What would they do with him if she did?

Her head hurt suddenly. The pain felt like someone had pierced her with red hot needles that singed her memories and stole away her emotions. She dropped the glass she was holding, spilling the contents over the sofa, as her conditioning kicked in, reminding her that there was no way to fight, and no escape.

'We own you,' James's voice echoed inside her head. 'I know your every thought, every deed. I know what little heart you have left.'

'No …' Dawn said. 'No …'

She pushed back at the pain, felt it recede until she could think.

It was all the fault of the Jinx. They did this. They destroyed everything. And now they had let one into the Trafford Centre. She would never be free while they were allowed to live. Lucy, and Taylor, would never be safe.

Dawn stood. It was time to act. Time to get the revenge she had always wanted and James had promised.

'Lieutenant Crawley reporting for duty, sir,' she saluted thin air. Then she turned and left the room.

PART 2

Betrayal

1

Al Kuzemen Garuk raised his staff to the darkening sky. The Ah Min Zins, the two red moons that circled Sharik, brightened, and the resulting glow gave the impression of infrared light. They were in the desert, a stealth mission of fifty Arrak Nah Tiamen, all found by Councillor Marlin, who now stood beside the mage as he summoned up the portal. Garuk knew that each of these men was loyal to Marlin. What promises the councillor had made to secure this loyalty he could only guess, but he noted that all of them were single warriors, who had either not been successful in the marriage tents, or had never been fortunate enough to be called.

Garuk reached out to Prestin, the mage from Shandalin, a town some several thousand miles south of Sharik, and together they projected across time and space toward the spot that Garuk could see so clearly. It was a place taken directly from the mind of the Empress on one of her many nightly visits back to Arven. Garuk had stood, unseen, in the tent while the couple's ardent lovemaking had distracted them both from *feeling* his presence.

'You're sure this is the place?' Marlin said. 'Prestin tells me that something is blocking his view.'

'A metal substance,' Garuk said. 'I learnt this from her mind. She was projecting the whole time she was here.'

Marlin studied Garuk carefully. 'How was she able to materialise? Does Kale help her?'

Garuk shook his head. 'I have been unable to determine how. But there was no Al Kuzemen magic present. This is something she has learnt to do on her own.'

A faint breeze wafted over the desert, raising the top layer of the sand up into the atmosphere, as an electric-like energy began to crackle in the air. The hair stood up on the back of Garuk's neck as he felt the touch of the other mage, and they mind-merged to raise the vortex.

The air began to turn slowly, then the eddy collapsed in on itself and Garuk and Marlin took a step back. The vortex sprung into life as though it were a tornado that had been turned inside out.

'It's ready,' Garuk said. 'I just need to focus the direction …'

Marlin and Garuk stepped onto the pathway. The sides of the tunnel spun. The fifty warriors began to follow, and soon they were all inside the vortex as it wended its way across the universe to Earth.

Garuk's mind-meld suddenly came to a halt.

'What's wrong?' asked Marlin.

'The block … it has been raised,' Garuk gasped. 'I can see beyond the veil, and now know … *You!*'

'Ah!' said Marlin. 'Prestin couldn't keep you completely from seeing inside his mind then. We wondered if that would happen. But surely you realise that this is all for the best?'

Now completely connected with Prestin, Garuk could see that Marlin had lied. That Prestin himself had formed the false futures deliberately to deceive Garuk. Every possible outcome that Garuk had explored had been counterfeit. Jas's future, and that of the Emperor, had not yet been determined in any way.

'Treachery!' Garuk said.

'No,' said Marlin. 'I'm taking care of the Emperor's business because he is unable to.'

'You lie! Arven doesn't want this. He promised the Empress and would never break that vow.'

'Precisely. This way he is not responsible. He will thank me for this … in time.'

The vortex shuddered around them. The fabric of time and space began to unwind.

'You'll kill us all!' Marlin said.

Garuk pulled back his focus. There was no way back now, only forward. A fact that he knew Marlin and the treacherous mage, Prestin, would have been banking on. To stop now would be certain death for them all.

'I intend to bring the Empress back unharmed,' Marlin reassured. 'I want Arven's throne safe. He is a good Emperor and has seen us through many bad times.'

Garuk sighed. He heard truth in those words and could not deny the reasoning, despite the manipulative way Marlin had behaved. He forced his mind to re-merge with Prestin's, but the other man's guard was now firmly in place. There was still something they weren't revealing; they were still untrustworthy. But for now he was forced to concentrate on the task at hand.

The vortex reached its destination with a vague thump, but Garuk knew that on Earth the pressure of its arrival and opening would be devastating. He tapped his staff twice on the pathway. The spinning slowed on either side of them. Garuk checked the date and time of their appearance. It was just a few weeks after Jas and Kale had arrived, but at the very same spot in the car-park of the Trafford Centre.

He waved his staff before the vortex, and the gateway began to open like an airlock to a wormhole.

Marlin stepped forward. Then he turned and indicated to the warriors behind. The men flooded around the mage and councillor, like a human shield.

Marlin smiled. Garuk wondered if the man was looking forward to the fight: it wouldn't surprise him. Already he had glimpsed a savagery that he hadn't wanted to see inside another mage. He raised his own mental barriers, blocking out Prestin, even as the thought of reporting this betrayal floated into his mind. He loved the Emperor and would never intentionally betray him. *In my urge to protect him, I have done just that,* thought Garuk.

The vortex veil began to clear. Garuk looked out and saw ...

The earthquake shook the Centre so hard that it was as though the very fabric of the structure was being ripped apart. A crack appeared in the painted sky ceiling in the mess. Dust and brick fell down onto the inhabitants as they scattered for cover.

In the day-care area Clara and two other carers, Felicity and Anna, called the children out of the ball pool and off the climbing frame and slide. There were currently three little girls and four boys in their care. Clara and the other women huddled down in a corner and sheltered them with their own, larger bodies.

'What the hell's going on?' asked Felicity. She had only just started to look after the children and was much younger than Clara and Anna. She had been at Trafford City for only a few months.

'I don't want to scare you but it feels like ...' Clara said.

'Jinx?' Felicity said. 'Ohmegod. Ohmegod. I thought we were safe here.'

'Get down here,' Anna said, grabbing the girl's arm. She pulled her into the huddle. 'We have to protect the children. No matter what.'

'Lucy!' Dawn said, running into the reception.

'It's okay! She's here with us behind the counter. What's happening?' Clara asked.

'Jinx attack, I think. Oh god! Taylor and the men are gone – we're short-handed. How can we ...?' Dawn began.

Then Dawn's demeanour changed. It went from panicked and frightened mother to something else entirely. Clara watched the change with a vague fascination. It reminded her of stories she had heard, when the world was civilised, about how parents had found superhuman strength in order to save their children.

Now Dawn possessed an extraordinary quality. She was a mother that would do anything to make sure her child survived – or so Clara thought.

'Stay here,' said Dawn.

'Where are you going?' said Clara.

'I'm going to kill the Jinx. What else can I do?' Dawn said.

Clara stared after her. Her brown eyes glowed with a new understanding that she didn't like. She could see something was wrong with Dawn. She just wasn't sure what it was.

'She's crazy. She's going to get herself killed,' murmured Anna.

Lucy began to cry beside her.

'There, there. It was only a silly joke. Your mummy's going to be fine,' Clara said. She gave Anna a look that said, *What were you thinking?*

Dawn hurried out into the main area and looked around at the carnage. A woman was crying as she hunched in a corner holding her wounded arm. A man staggered drunkenly against a table as blood poured down his face from what appeared to be a serious head injury. All around her, carnage reigned, but for once Dawn knew what to do. She ran through the chaos, jumping over fallen bits of ceiling and the static bodies of wounded, perhaps dead, people. Heading toward the armoury, she detoured briefly back to her place. She knew where Taylor kept his set of keys, though she had always been careful never to reveal this fact to him or to anyone else.

Dawn pulled the key ring from underneath their mattress and began to rifle through the keys. Her hands were trembling, not with fear, but with a familiar surge of adrenaline that she hoped would give her the edge. She was soon on her way, like a trained runner, through the Centre and to the training area.

The training area was empty when she arrived.

'Good,' she muttered.

At the back of the room was a partitioned section. Here was a cage. A huge metal structure secured to the floor with massive bolts.

Dawn inserted a key into the padlock and opened the gates. Inside was a stack of rifles, handguns, boxes of bullets and grenades.

She stuffed two of the grenades into her jacket pocket, then took up one of the rifles. With rehearsed expertise she loaded the weapon and put a handful of spare bullets into her trouser pocket.

Within seconds she was running full pelt back toward the mess, and to the car-park.

Several of the remaining soldiers had surrounded the vortex by the time Dawn arrived. No-one looked at her; they were so focused on the anomaly, and the attackers within.

'Get ready,' said one of the soldiers. Dawn recognised him as Lieutenant Barry, and was horrified to realise that he was the only officer left at the base with any knowledge of how to protect them – other than Harvey, who seemed to be nowhere in sight. She knew that Barry, a little long in the tooth and way out of practice, was less than adequate.

She pulled one of the grenades from her pocket, popped the safety pin but held down the clip. As the vortex opened, the soldiers began to fire. Ducking below the line of fire, Dawn ran forward, throwing the grenade. Unfortunately, she didn't have the practice of the other soldiers. The grenade hit the side and was repelled by a sharp gust of wind. It bounced away from the vortex.

Lieutenant Barry dived on it as it bounced back toward the waiting soldiers. He grabbed, gripped and pulled back his arm to throw. The grenade left his hand, but not fast enough. Barry screamed as half of his arm exploded, sending blood and gore out into the group of soldiers. He fell to the ground, his body peppered with shrapnel, rapidly going into shock, while his life's blood drained out onto the flagstones.

Dawn wiped blood from her eyes and raised her gun as the vortex continued to open. She felt cold, inside and out. Her emotions and fear completely in check. It never even occurred to her that she had caused the death of one of their men by her sheer lack of practice and skill in throwing the grenade. Instead she pulled out the second grenade.

Bullet rounds pounded the void without any effect. Then, a loud tapping took up behind Dawn. She turned her head and saw Kale, his staff held tight in his grip as he pounded the ground with the bottom of it.

The vortex began to close. Sweat poured down Kale's face, and Jas, standing by his side, placed a hand on his arm. Dawn observed that it was as though Jas poured strength into Kale. The mage grew in height, and then he raised his staff once more, slamming it down one final time.

The pavement beneath his feet cracked with the force, as a huge rush of air careered toward the vortex.

Light surrounded the opening. Through gunfire smoke, Dawn could see another magician inside, his clothing, moustache and height all similar to Kale's. Then the space around the vortex contracted. The void closed and disappeared into the air.

Kale tumbled to the ground. It was only then that Dawn noticed Julia at his side. The girl rushed to help the mage up, and a surge, like a red mist, came over Dawn.

'Don't touch him. He's a murdering Jinx bastard. He brought them here!'

'No, Dawn! Kale just *stopped* the attack,' Jas said. 'Surely you all saw that?'

The soldiers had turned silently to look at Kale, as Jas and Julia helped the mage back to his feet.

'We'd all be dead if Kale hadn't used most of his strength to thwart them,' Jas said calmly, once Kale was back on his feet.

'He was helping them,' Dawn said. 'And so was she. This whole time, she's been here to lead them to us.'

'No. I came …'

'Why did you come?' Dawn asked.

'I came to make sure that Andrew was all right. I was homesick … I …'

'I don't believe you. Why leave that idyllic world that you've been preaching to everyone about? That world of magic where you are an *Empress*. Why would anyone leave *that* to come *here*?'

'She has a point,' said Gerald, appearing with his leather doctor's bag, followed by two men with a stretcher. 'Get a tourniquet on Barry's arm …'

'Too late,' said Dawn. 'He was dead before he hit the ground.'

'Okay, let's get the body away from here and get any wounded inside,' said Gerald.

'Not you,' said Dawn. Her rifle was pointed in the direction of Kale.

'You won't stop us coming back inside,' Jas said. 'Taylor will …'

'What will Taylor do? He isn't here to side with you this time, but my daughter is inside there, and I won't put her at further risk.'

'Nor my kids!' said one of the soldiers.

'What are you doing?' Julia said. 'These people are helping us. They aren't the bad guys. Look at what we've learned from them so far …'

'If you like them so much, then you can go with them,' Dawn said. 'We have enough mouths to feed around here anyway.'

'You can't tell us what to do …' said Jas.

'Yes I can,' said Dawn. 'I'm holding the gun.'

'Now wait …' Jas said. She stepped forward as Dawn turned to walk back to the building.

Dawn spun, raising the weapon once more. The gun went off as Kale stepped in front of Jas, but the bullet bounced off his staff and fell, crushed, to the ground, as though it had hit an impenetrable wall.

'*She* is not one to trust,' Kale said, pointing at Dawn.

'Oh and *you* are?' said Gerald. 'A Jinx? A *murderer*?'

Kale studied Gerald carefully, and then he backed away, taking Julia and Jas with them.

'Surely you don't want to go with them?' Gerald asked Julia. 'You are welcome here.'

Julia shook her head, 'I trust this man with my life.'

'Then you're a fool,' said Dawn.

'Get behind me,' said Kale.

Julia slipped behind them, Jas took her hand and they all slowly backed away from the soldiers and the murderous intent in both Dawn's and Gerald's eyes.

'They are *drones,*' Julia murmured.

'Dogs,' agreed Jas.

'I need you to concentrate,' Kale said over his shoulder to Jas. 'Take us out of here. Somewhere you feel safe ...'

Jas focused her mind as Kale began to raise a vortex.

'See!' cried Dawn over the howling wind. 'He's taking her back! They *were* planning to trick us!'

'No!' said Jas, stepping around Kale.

At that moment a large pocket of air surrounded the three of them.

'Forget them. I need your help now,' said Kale. 'Concentrate.'

Jas placed her hand on his arm. 'I can think of only one place. Though god knows what kind of safety remains there.'

The vortex surrounded them, smaller than those used to travel through the universe, but no less strong.

Bullets fired openly on them now. Julia screamed into the vortex wind, but the bullets disintegrated into thin air as they came into contact with the void. The futility of their actions reflected on the faces of the frightened soldiers, and the three of them knew that the men couldn't help themselves. It was conditioning, after all. Everything they had done for years had been about warding off the Jinx; now they were showing themselves to be every bit as dangerous and powerful as the enemy that the occupants of Trafford City feared. It was all down to fear in the end.

Take us to the Lowry Theatre, Jas thought. Her hand held Kale's, and he saw the image in her mind. Julia clung onto Jas's other hand but said nothing as the vortex closed and they vanished from the car-park of Trafford City.

2

The vortex reopened in the desert. Marlin and Garuk stumbled out with the warriors close on their heels.

'Kale is a traitor and will be dealt with,' Marlin said.

'*You* are the traitor. You and Prestin *lied* to me,' Garuk said.

Garuk turned and began to walk away, back toward the camp where the warriors had left their mounts. It was full dark now, but the Ah Min Zins lit his way with natural infrared.

As he reached the camp, Marlin caught up with him.

'Wait!' Marlin ordered. 'We need to be clear on our story if anyone saw us leave Sharik ...'

'I don't need a story. If the Emperor asks me, I will tell him the truth of what I have learnt.'

Marlin laughed. 'What have your learnt? That we wanted to make the Emperor happy, when you advised him against this action?'

Garuk continued walking. He reached his tethered el lien meck, and began to untie the reins of the camel-like, double-humped animal.

'Garuk?' called Marlin.

Garuk ignored him.

'Garuk ... this is your last chance. Turn around and talk to me.'

Garuk pulled the reins over the el lien meck and tugged the animal so that it knelt down, allowing the mage to begin to mount.

Then the air was knocked from his lungs as the most excruciating pain shot through his spine. In that split second, Garuk knew that a warrior's sword had swept through the air, cutting a path through his spine. His legs gave. Blood poured from his back, and his kidney, severed by the sharp sword, flooded the sand with urine and blood as the warrior pulled his sword free.

Garuk's mount reared with fright, tugging at the reins even as the mage's eyes turned lifeless and his body slumped over the creature. The animal stood, taking the Al Kuzemen's body with him.

A warrior stood over him. Long dark hair flowed freely over his shoulders. His eyes were multi-coloured, and twisted and swirled with an excited energy.

'Well done, Elidon,' said Marlin. 'Send his body off into the desert. I'm sure something will pick the bones clean before dawn.'

Elidon wiped his sword on the mage's robe, then sheathed it. He took Garuk's el lien meck, pulling it roughly away from the others. Then he slapped the animal hard on the rump. The creature, already spooked, galloped away in the opposite direction to Sharik, carrying the body away from the oasis.

'The rest of you disperse back to your towns. We will need another Al Kuzemen to help finish our work, but when the Emperor finds Garuk missing, I'm sure he will send for one from another of the smaller towns. I may even suggest one to him …'

The men quickly mounted their el lien mecks, then waited for Marlin to give his final instructions.

'You'll all have your reward for this,' Marlin said. 'And wives to choose from. Now go. Be ready for my call.'

Elidon galloped away first. The others soon followed.

Marlin kicked sand over the bloody spillage, the only evidence that Garuk had ever been there. Then he climbed up on his own mount. He didn't look back at the oasis, nor did he give the murder of the mage another thought, as he headed back to Sharik as quickly, and quietly, as he could.

'What's wrong?' asked Julia.

'Garuk … is dead,' Kale said. He held his back, gasping for breath.

'Who is Garuk?' asked Julia.

'Another Al Kuzemen. The one controlling the vortex …' Kale said.

'How do you know he is dead?' asked Jas.

'At the final moments he connected with me. I didn't have an opportunity to tell you, but he helped me close the portal …'

'Why would he do that?' Jas said.

'I don't know. He began to tell me, but his explanation was cut off.'

'Someone killed him?' Jas said.

Kale nodded. 'I was still connected when …'

Julia and Jas helped him stand upright.

'Did you see who it was?' Jas asked.

'The connection was so fragile … but I have my suspicions.'

They stood at the back of the Lowry Theatre. Jas's mind was reeling with the attempt that Dawn had clearly made on her life, and it was odd being back at the Lowry after all this time. If it hadn't been for Kale, she was sure that a rifle bullet would have been buried deep in her heart. She tried to recall when she had seen such hatred before.

'Why did they behave like that?' she murmured.

'They weren't in their right mind,' Julia said.

Kale's strength was slowly returning as he recovered from the shock of Garuk's death.

'This place is destroyed,' Julia said. 'We can't even get inside.'

The front was as Jas remembered it. A year ago in her timeline, but three years ago in Earth time, Kale had opened a vortex on this very spot. The front of the theatre had been destroyed, leaving Andrew trapped inside. Seeing it now brought back painful memories to Jas. But also good ones. She and Andy had been safe here for a time.

'Round the back,' Jas said. 'There's a stage door. Andrew and I mostly went in and out that way. Less conspicuous.'

The door in question was hanging off its hinges. Jas ran her hand over the frame, noting it had been broken outwards. Maybe it had happened when Andrew had freed himself from the wreckage?

They entered the building with caution. Kale took up the front and Jas the rear, keeping Julia safely between them. It was dark inside, but their eyes soon adjusted to the gloom, and they walked through a corridor toward the rear of the stage and the former actors' dressing rooms.

'We had a secret stash of food,' Jas said. 'If it's still here, then we won't go hungry for a time …'

They reached the star dressing room, and Jas came forward and opened the door. There was a scurry of rats inside.

'Urgh,' Julia said.

Kale tapped his staff on the floor, the tip of it illuminated and light spilled into the room. Jas could see an old discarded sleeping bag on top of a mattress in the corner. The mattress was chewed and rotten. Animal faeces and cobwebs covered the room.

'You *lived* here?' Kale said.

'It wasn't quite like this when we did. But yes. Times were hard following …' Jas stopped. She didn't want to remind Kale of what he already knew. The Jinx had destroyed her world. But the unfinished sentence hung in the air like an accusation.

'I'm sorry,' said Kale.

'No need. It's all old news now,' Jas said.

'We can't stay here,' Kale said. 'This isn't good for you in …'

'We could clean it up,' Julia said.

'No,' Jas decided. 'Kale's right. In your state of recovery, this isn't hygienic. I'm just at a loss as to what else to do.'

Jas took them up to the main theatre stage. Here, she and Andrew had stored cans of food, and even though they had later merged most of their provisions with the stocks held by Taylor and his soldiers, Jas had erred on the side of caution and hidden a chest full of cans under the stage, in an old trunk.

'How do we get down there?' Julia asked. She looked around, as though nervous of the appearance of more rats.

'This way. There's a trap door under the stage. The trunk is on it. I rigged it so that it could be pulled open and up manually.'

Behind the dust-covered, moth-eaten velvet curtains Jas indicated a thick rope on a pulley that attached to the lighting rig above the stage.

'Let's hope this still works,' Jas said.

She turned a metal handle, and the loose-looking rope began to tighten. There was a creaking and groaning as old wood, probably swollen with the damp, tugged and scraped against the moorings. A wood panel began to slide away, and a hole opened up in the stage floor.

'It's too stiff, I can't move it …' Jas said.

Kale placed his hand on the rope. A burst of energy lit up his fingers, and the rope, pulley and handle began to move easily.

The mechanism underneath the stage gave a loud grunt, then a heavy trunk appeared as it rose on a platform up into the hole.

Jas tied off the rope, holding the platform in place. Then the three of them hurried toward it. There was a padlock holding a thick chain wrapped around the trunk.

'I no longer have the key,' Jas said.

Kale pressed the tip of his staff against the lock. It clicked open, and the chain fell away.

'That was easy,' Jas said. 'You can be very useful sometimes, Kale.'

She lifted the lid of the trunk, and they found the store of food still intact. There was a selection of fish, meat, fruit and vegetables in undisturbed cans.

'If the stuff in here is still good, then we won't starve for the next few weeks at least,' Jas said.

3

'It is very strange indeed,' Arven said. 'How could Garuk simply vanish?'

'I do not know, Emperor, but I fear the discontent of the men may have somehow affected him,' Marlin said.

Arven turned to look at Marlin. His gut told him that something was going on. He had an intense dislike of Marlin; something he hid as well as he could. He didn't trust the man, and he was sure that the strange swirl in his eyes – which was sometimes slightly off, not perfectly smooth and pulsing as most Arrak Nah Tiamen's eyes were – gave some indication of what the man was really feeling.

'What do you mean "affected" him?' Arven asked.

'I don't really like to say … I'm not sure it is something you would wish to hear.'

'Try me,' Arven said.

'Garuk said he felt under tremendous pressure. He wanted to help you, but felt that he wasn't the best mage for the job.'

Arven rubbed his chin as he thought. 'If what you say is true, then I need to get a mage who is suitable,' he said. 'Can you suggest anyone?'

'Why, of course, your highness. I have worked with a very adept Al Kuzemen by the name of Prestin. He currently resides in Shandalin.'

Marlin lowered his gaze as Arven tried to meet his eyes, but not before the Emperor saw the swirling irises pulse and freeze in that peculiar off-kilter fashion. Arven had the strangest feeling about the thoughts behind those eyes. He felt unease again. A sense that the man was lying. But about what, he wasn't sure. Was it even possible for a council member to lie to him? Well, of course anything was possible now that Kale had betrayed him and Garuk had vanished, seemingly without a trace.

'Thank you, Marlin. That will be all.'

'Should I send someone to bring Prestin?' Marlin said.

'Not for now,' Arven said. 'I have hope that we may find Garuk and bring him home.'

Marlin bowed and left. Arven watched him walk away, stiff-backed, as though the councillor was making every step as formal as he possibly could. It was unnatural, but nothing unusual among the councillors, and Arven couldn't use the man's oddness as a sign of betrayal. But it made him uncomfortable all the same.

He rose from his chair and walked to the divining pool in the corner of his tent. A tremendous wrench pulled at his heart as he searched for Jas again. Time was moving on. He knew from Garuk that Earth was in a bad state. Now he would have to wait until a new Al Kuzemen could come to him, and he had no clue who to send for. But he suspected that he couldn't trust any recommendation that would come his way. For this reason, he immediately rejected Prestin without further consideration.

At that moment he had an epiphany. The divining pool, given to him by Kale, had never let him down. It was designed to show him images of his first wife and child, and had since been used to allow him to see his new love, Jas. Latterly it had been enhanced by Garuk and used to show him potential outcomes of his actions. But he knew that it could tell him anything if the correct question was asked.

'Find me an Al Kuzemen that I can trust,' he murmured to the pool.

The clear water clouded over. The liquid swirled around like a miniature whirlpool, and Arven stared into its depths until the water cleared.

Kale's face stared back at him. Then a few more faces crowded into view. Arven knew all of the Al Kuzemen whose visages filled the pool one after another. Prestin was conspicuous by his absence, and so was Garuk. *If I cannot trust Garuk, then everything he has told me has been a lie.* All the advice given had been designed for some ulterior motive. But what was that motive, and how could any other Al Kuzemen have betrayed him? Kale's perfidy was enough to have sent the others into a flurry of activity, and he had received many renewed oaths. The Al Kuzemen sect had always sworn fealty to the Emperor, even as the most adept among them qualified in their chosen field.

'Find Garuk,' he murmured, anger bubbling into his chest so hard that he felt he would burst. Had Garuk betrayed him, as Kale had? No, not Kale; he knew that without really considering it. Kale had stayed by Jas. It could even have been a confusion of loyalty. But it had not been, and never would be, the same as any other form of betrayal.

The pool clouded, then cleared. An image of the desert appeared before him. It showed the spot where Jas had disappeared. Then it flipped to the oasis where travellers often stopped to water their horses and el mien mecks. For a moment Arven considered that his wish to see Jas had overpowered his urge to find Garuk, but the more he stared at the oasis, the more he became certain that Garuk was there somewhere. Possibly hiding out. This man was clearly a traitor, and he would find him and force the truth from his lips.

He walked to the entrance of his tent. As usual, a guard stood by the tent flaps waiting for his orders.

'Get my el lien meck and ten reliable warriors,' Arven said.

The soldier blinked, as though surprised by the request. When he failed to react quickly enough, Arven became irritated with him.

'Do it now!' Arven said.

'Yes, Emperor.' The guard bowed and hurried away.

The oasis was deserted. A few dried-looking plants grew from the pale, dehydrated greenery that surrounded the watering hole. The tether pole was made of smooth wood, turned grey with the constant blasting of the day's heat and the sandstorms that picked up on occasion. One such sandstorm had covered all sign of tracks from any recent activity.

Arven pulled his mount to the nearest pole and slipped from the saddle with agility. He flopped the reins over the animal's head and wrapped them in a lose loop over the pole. Behind him the soldiers followed suit, each finding a place to tether their mounts. Once dismounted, they waited for further instruction.

'Emperor?' asked the warrior who had been on guard by his tent. 'What do you require?'

'Search this area. I want you to find any sign of Al Kuzemen Garuk's presence.'

The warrior walked away, and Arven was drawn to the well. He gazed down, noting the clear, clean water below. He knew that Al Kuzemen magic had been placed on the spot, allowing the water to remain uncontaminated.

A short distance from the well stood a tent. It had been erected when Arven had followed Jas and Kale into the desert, when they had run from Sharik. Their vigil had meant an overnight stay, and Arven had been too distracted to order the removal of the structure after Jas had disappeared back to Earth. Later he and Garuk had discussed the idea of following Jas. The tent had remained as a symbol to that idea; he had thought that one day he would need it there again. Now he walked inside, noting the sparse furniture. It contained a bed, a few chairs, a table and some provisions. Nothing more. It was also as undisturbed now as it had been the last time he had been there.

He let the curtain flap fall back down over the entrance as he walked back outside toward the well. He had hoped that Garuk might be hiding inside, but knew the Al Kuzemen would never take it upon himself to enter an imperial tent uninvited. And neither would anyone else.

Even so, he had doubts about his subjects. Loyalty was something he had always been sure of in the past. Things had changed, though, and the insertion of the human women had been the start of it, but not the sole cause.

He could see that now. The Arrak Nah Tiamen race was evolving. It happened sometimes in the course of their history. And those changes weren't always for the good. Arven wondered what his race was heading for. A loss of devoted allegiance might be only the start of something that would change his people beyond recognition.

Evolution was something he couldn't help, though. Or could he? With the right Al Kuzemen, perhaps he could delay or change the course of this strange anomaly. If not, it could, after all, be the thing that destroyed them all once and for all. Like the disease that inexplicably killed their womenfolk had almost done. They were on borrowed time. And, like the dinosaurs of Earth, maybe their extinction would be unavoidable.

'Perhaps it's our time ...' Arven murmured.

He shook his head, forcing back the maudlin thought of their possible annihilation, but the idea wouldn't leave him. He couldn't help but wonder if their merging with humanity had only delayed the inevitable. After all, Earth was on a collision course with finality, wasn't it? And there was nothing they could do to help or change the planet's destiny. He had always known that, and it was one of the reasons he had used to justify their attack. They were, in their own way, saving, not destroying, the human race, as much as they were trying to save their own.

'We cannot always thwart destiny,' Kale had once told him. 'But we can sometimes change its course.'

'Emperor?' said a warrior, now standing a few feet from him.

Arven turned and looked at the man. He was tall, like they all were, with long silver hair and green-flecked eyes that swirled constantly. Arven sensed intense loyalty in the man. He also sensed fear.

'What is it?' Arven asked, his attention fully engaged.

'I've found something,' the warrior said.

Arven followed him away from the well and back toward the first set of tethering poles. The warrior pointed at a small blue stain. Arven marvelled that he hadn't seen it as he had tied his horse at this very spot.

'Blood ...'

'Yes,' said the warrior, though his confirmation was not needed.

Arven studied the spot further. He pushed and prodded the sand at his feet, but there was nothing there to reveal what had happened. The sandstorm had blown away any evidence.

'Search within a two mile radius,' Arven said.

'Yes, Emperor,' the warrior said. Then, bowing, he turned to his al lien meck, untied and mounted the animal.

Arven watched as the warrior instructed half of the men to follow him. The rest remained at the oasis to guard their Emperor.

Arven watched them ride out in different directions, and then he returned to the tent, taking refuge from the heat that had begun to rise in the desert.

Once alone with his thoughts again, he felt anxiety twist his gut. The more time passed between him seeing Jas and knowing she was well, the worse his fear became. He was not thinking just of her now. The child she carried inside her was the symbol that the extinction of his race could be delayed, perhaps indefinitely, if the Arrak Nah Tiamen and human females continued to breed as well as they were. All other births, and there had been many, paled into insignificance when compared with the life of his own child.

An overwhelming urge to go to her again consumed him. Stronger because of the close proximity of the place from which she had escaped him. It was harder for him to not feel that tug and pull when the exit she had taken was so nearby.

He could not help but wonder why Garuk had been out here; and he did not doubt that the man had indeed been here. The pool never lied.

Once again Arven wondered why the scenarios it had shown him had been so diverse and frighteningly negative. If was almost as though something, or someone, had been deliberately interfering with the magic in the pool.

He returned to the tent and lay down on the bed to rest. He was tired, and physical weakness haunted him. But he knew this was a side effect of the absence of his *chio mien*[2]. Hadn't he suffered similarly when his first queen had died?

He closed his eyes. Heart, mind and soul called out to Jas across the galaxies. As he drifted into a fitful sleep, he was convinced that she could hear him.

'Come back …' he murmured.

---

[2] Soul-mate.

4

It was a challenge to sleep in the dirty and decaying theatre. After Kale pulled down the thick stage curtains, bunching them up into dusty makeshift beds, Jas lay down and tried to rest. The theatre smelt of rot and rat faeces. She feared for the health of Julia, barely recovered from her traumatic flight from MD59. On top of that, Jas herself was weaker than she had been for a long time. The awful sickness had returned, but she tried her best to hide it from Kale and Julia, because she didn't want to worry either of them. The lie of it made it easier to believe herself that she was coping. She wasn't though. Pain, both physical and mental, followed her every waking moment. Only when she slept did she get some minor respite.

It was pitch black in the theatre. The curtains they lay on smelt of mould, and Jas could hear the scratching of rats in the corner.

'Why are they even here?' Julia murmured. 'They are usually only attracted to places with food. But other than your stash ...'

'I don't know,' Jas said. 'It is peculiar.'

A low whistling sound made both Julia and Jas stop speaking. Jas could feel Kale tense up in the dark.

'What was ...?' Julia whispered.

Loud laughter echoed through the auditorium. Jas froze in her place. Fear pumped blood rapidly through her heart. She turned her head slowly to look around the theatre, but it was a void, and it was hard to pinpoint from where the laughter came.

'Dogs ...' Jas said, using her old nickname for vicious human scavengers. She sat up and reached for both Julia's and Kale's hands.

They were in the middle of the stage, and despite being completely in the dark, Jas was aware of how exposed they were.

The three of them moved together, shuffling on their bottoms until their backs were against the backdrop curtain. Another bout of laughter from several sources made them freeze where they were.

'Looks like we have a new source of food, boys ...' said a voice.

Jas peered into the dark, as though believing that the more she looked the more she would see. But it was impossible: she could see nothing. It was clear that someone could see them, however, and their stash of food cans. Maybe they had some kind of night-vision eyewear? That would make sense.

She was distracted from her thoughts when a shift in the air told her that someone had just run across the stage. Their movement was swift and silent. It was completely unnerving.

With Julia and Kale on either side of her, Jas strained her eyes to see into the blackness and she began to pick out a shape.

There was a flash of something, like cat's eyes caught in headlights, or the glow of a wolf's gaze in a snow-covered forest. Jas pushed herself backwards as far as she could go. A swirl of air buffeted her face, and she felt the brush of fabric against her cheek.

'Kale …' she whispered. 'Do something …'

Kale stirred. It was as though he had been paralysed with fear and confusion.

Two pin-prinks of red floated before Jas's face. It took a moment for her to realise that they were eyes. A face was before her, level with her own, and she could just make out the shape now. She hit out, and her hand connected with something soft and wet, like the nose of a dog. The thing before her yelped. Laughter answered its cry.

There was no point in trying to pretend they weren't there. These people, or things, could see them. It was obvious.

'Who the hell are you?' Jas said.

A tribalistic whooping picked up as a rush of bodies zigzagged across the stage, taunting them. This went on for some time as the whooping picked up, mingled with laughter. Grubby fingers ran over them as though they were pets that needed to be petted.

Then the moving stopped and silence fell, but several pairs of eyes could now be seen glowing in the dark with a peculiar red light. Jas had never seen anything like it before, certainly not in human eyes, and by the sounds the group were making, she believed they were human. It had to be eyewear. There was no other explanation for it.

Julia's hand tightened in hers. 'What are they?'

'I don't know …' Jas said.

She was surprised by Kale's continued silence, and squeezed his hand.

'Get us out of here …' she whispered.

'I …' was all Kale said.

'What's *wrong* with you?'

Kale didn't answer. She reached out with her aura, something she hadn't done to him since she had persuaded him to help her escape Jinx Town. Although that was merely weeks ago, it now seemed like an age. Her aura soothed the magician. She could feel his terror receding. But why was he so afraid? He was a Jinx and a mage. Surely they could handle this group with his magic and her strength? But then, Jas realised, her energy levels weren't as elevated as they had been. Her concentration slipped as an icy hand touched her face.

Raucous laughter took up as she jumped in surprise. Then she forced her mind back on the task.

'Let there be light,' she said.

Kale's staff tapped on the floor as the mage used it to help him stand to his full height. Then the top illuminated. Light burst into the space, blinding them all with its suddenness. The laughter turned to yelps and screams as their tormenters fell back into the shadows and away from the stage. She saw smoke coming off some of them, as though the intensity of the light burnt their skin.

Jas's eyes adjusted. She looked out into the auditorium, then back toward the wings. They were there, lurking. She knew that if Kale's light failed they would be on them like savage dogs. But what were they?

Julia had released her hand in order to cover her eyes. Now she looked around in the same fashion as Jas.

'Oh my god,' Julia murmured.

'What?' asked Jas.

'I didn't believe it possible. They did it,' Julia continued.

'Explain …' Jas said.

'Drones. They are all drones. But what kind, I don't know.'

'Kale, get us out of here,' Jas said.

'Where?' Kale asked, even as he gripped her hand. Jas took Julia's hand again.

'Take us to Taylor and his men. Their camp by the base … Julia, can you visualise the place?'

Julia nodded.

'Good. When we get there, you're going to tell me what you know about these things. Right?'

Julia nodded again, as though she could not find the words to answer. Jas drew on all of her strength and resources, channelling her mind so that she could read Julia's image of the site and translate it to Kale.

Kale raised his staff. A small vortex began to spin around them. They heard a collective cry from the drones. Jas saw the black corners shift as the three of them entered the void, but knew that the things couldn't touch them now that the vortex was raised. Even so, one of them tried. It braved the storm, running from the shelter of the wings toward the spinning void, and hurled itself forward. Jas saw its face clearly for the first time. Serrated teeth filled its leering mouth, and it had skin the colour of rotting garden waste. Its mouth opened and the stench of decay wafted into the air around them. The eyes were horrible. Bloodshot, luminous red: the pupils were the wrong shape. They were like the eyes of a rabid sheep: the kind of eyes you would associate with the devil. Jas took an involuntary step back as the creature's head penetrated the eddy. And then Kale closed the gap. The head, caught in the loop, spun and twisted, until it severed. Blood and bone splashed up the vortex walls and were sucked away into the ether, even as the head dropped and rolled, coming to rest by Jas's feet.

'Keep focus!' she yelled as she felt Julia slipping.

As the vortex reopened, they stepped out to find themselves on a hillside. Loose shale and rock disturbed by their arrival skittered down around them. The head of the drone was compelled outwards, skittering away from them until it rolled to the edge of the hill. Kale closed the void, and a final flurry of air was enough to send the monstrous head tumbling over the edge and down.

'We're at Llanberis,' Jas said, looking around. 'But we're still a fair way from the base, and the site where Taylor said they would camp.'

The image Julia had sent had been corrupted. Not surprising really, under the stress of their flight. Jas estimated that they were off course by about five miles. But Julia was too tired to attempt a closer leap. Instead they opted to set up camp.

Now they were away from the theatre, Kale was behaving normally again. He bustled with energy and magic. He lit a campfire and created hammocks that floated in the air for them to sit and sleep on, taking them away from the muddy ground.

As they sat around the fire, Jas noted that Julia's hands were shaking. She knew it hadn't been the vortex that had frightened the woman, nor the close proximity of the base. It had been the things she had called 'drones'; and indeed it had been an incredibly unnerving sight when that one had hurled itself into their void. For a moment even Jas had felt that the thing would reach them and those terrible teeth would rip and shred their flesh.

'What were they?' she asked.

Julia shuddered. 'Drones. Definitely.'

'But what does that mean?' asked Jas.

'Before I went to the base, I was privy to lots of confidential paperwork. I used to just type it up without reading mostly; which is harder than you might imagine. It was sensitive material; best not to remember it. But it was hard not to. Over the weeks, I pieced it all together. About the experiments.'

'Experiments? What kind?'

'The worst kind. The kind that can give you nightmares if you know about them. On people. Experiments that changed people beyond recognition.'

Julia paused. The fire crackled, and the sound was oddly comforting, despite the impact of Julia's words.

'They used young men mostly. Teens, once homeless, taken off the streets. Then there were the specific foundations: social security homes, filled with young people that had been taken from their parents for whatever reason. They were homes that were supposed to protect them. But the horrible thing was, they were run by the military. Those kids were there just to be used for some sinister purpose.

'Do you remember, Jas, before this all happened, how obsessed society was with the idea of there being a zombie apocalypse?'

'Yes. There was a new film, new book published, almost every month,' Jas said.

'We didn't believe it would happen, though,' Julia continued. 'We thought it was all just social commentary. A reaction to the military world we were beginning to live in. I recall seeing newspaper reports of "real-life" zombies, where some person would go crazy and start eating another's face. Mostly I dismissed it as the attacker being just insane, or on drugs or something.'

'Me too,' Jas said.

'Then there was that spate of terrible government. Just before it all happened. There was the election, and we feared that a right wing party, who were gaining votes, would actually gain power.'

'Yes. We all feared that. As though they were the new Nazi party; only this time it was the British who were letting them in,' Jas said.

'When the Jinx attacked, I was relieved,' Julia said.

Both Jas and Kale looked at her sharply.

'I hoped it would bring the country together. Make us forget all of this awful nonsense. If we hated the Jinx, then we would stop hating each other. I didn't know then, just didn't realise, that the enemy was already in. The worst kind of misogynists and bigots were our own military. They were the ones planning the coup. All of the political unrest was deliberately orchestrated by them. They controlled the news, they controlled our televisions, they controlled us. And we didn't know it.'

Jas nodded. 'I agree with everything you say. Things just weren't right. Even at the school I worked in, the emphasis was twisted the wrong way. I thought it was me, that I just didn't fit in.'

'You were the normal one,' Julia said. 'That's why you felt odd.'

'But what about these drones?' asked Kale. 'They … frightened me. Something so alien …'

'Interesting that you say that,' Julia said. 'Maybe the technology they use on them is alien. It certainly didn't look human.'

'What technology?' Jas asked. Kale shuddered beside her, and she knew it was the thought of any kind of technology that he saw as evil.

'Brainwashing firstly. With the help of drugs. The documents I saw were about them making super-soldiers. But I saw other things that made me believe that this wasn't the only kind of experimentation they were doing.'

'Those … things today were feral,' Jas said. 'They were also, I suspect, cannibal. I encountered two men like it when I first found the Trafford Centre.'

'Yes. All proper emotion was gone. They were monsters,' Julia said. 'And I thought I'd seen all the monsters I was going to see in the base.'

'Sleep,' said Kale. 'You both need rest. Tomorrow we must find Captain Arch.'

'I don't think I can sleep,' Julia said.

Kale stroked a finger over her forehead. Julia sank back into her hammock, slipping into a deep and restful slumber.

'You can be pretty useful when you want to be,' Jas said.

'Would you like me to help you sleep also?'

'No. We need to talk. What was wrong with you in there?'

'That place …'

Jas thought for a moment. Her last refuge had almost killed them, and something in it had almost paralysed Kale with fear.

'Those … drones. Horrible. And I thought we were the monsters.'

'The Jinx *are* monsters, Kale. There's no getting away from that. What your people did to mine is unforgivable. But we're all in this together now, because there's something far worse than even you guys out here.'

'We needed to survive …' Kale said.

It was an age-old argument to Jas now, and it almost fell on deaf ears, except that she knew Arven and his people *had* been desperate. So desperate that they hadn't cared they were committing genocide of another race.

'I'd like to think that your people can learn a lesson from all of this,' Jas said. 'But I'm not sure they can. Or what we can do to put this right.'

'Earth is dying,' Kale said. 'This planet cannot be put right.'

'I know.' Jas turned away from him.

Anger, hatred and fear rose up inside her again. These emotions were what had brought her here. Any normal woman wanting to survive would have accepted Emin and her new life. After all, heroes and heroines fought for justice in fiction, not in real life. Not really: not when an easier option was left open to them. *I'm no heroine. I'm just a fool*, she thought. Jas knew she wasn't 'normal', not in any sense of the word. Any ordinary person could be forgiven for capitulating in the throes of what, ultimately, wasn't such a bad lot.

This far from Arven and Emin, Jas started to recognise why the other women had behaved as they had. She had criticised them for their acceptance, seeing them as brainwashed sheep. But the truth was, normal people gave in. Normal people did anything they could to survive without fighting. Life wasn't fiction, after all. And hadn't they all been just following the crowd, conforming, on Earth, anyway, before the Jinx had arrived to turn reality upside down?

She had to stop judging others for giving in. Fighting was hard. She had done it for so long and she was tired of it. Weary to the very marrow of her bones. But what choice did she have when life kept throwing in one more obstacle after another?

She lay back on the hammock, tired, but afraid to sleep. She knew the drones would follow her into her dreams. How horrible that such a nightmare had been brought into the real world.

5

'Can you do it?' Taylor asked Archie.

At the site, two soldiers, Carey and Duane, had dug a shallow trench that gave a vantage point overlooking the hatch. The place was just as Julia had described. The hatch had been strategically hidden under a fake grass verge. With the land left unkempt around it, the real foliage had grown up to blend in. Taylor and his men had spotted it immediately, though, because Julia's exit had disturbed the area – although it would not have been obvious to anyone not specifically looking. Taylor and Archie were now getting to work on opening the hatch.

'I think so. It's pretty basic, and I don't think they expected anyone to try to get in through here.'

'Well, the Jinx wouldn't touch it, for certain, based on what we know of their avoidance of technology,' Taylor said. 'And they probably thought we'd never find it.'

'Yeah.'

Archie went quiet as he concentrated on the keypad. He had cracked easier and harder panels than this one, though he was a little out of practice. He took the front of the keypad off and looked at the pressure pads.

'We could try the code that Julia used,' Taylor suggested.

'Yes, we could, but it's likely that they've changed it. This model has an alarm trigger that goes off if the wrong code is entered more than twice,' Archie explained.

'So, what's the plan?'

'I'm going to bypass the code entry, make it believe it has been given the right code, but first I have to disable this wire,' Archie said, pointing to a pale cream wire that looked unobtrusive. 'If this baby is activated, then the base goes into lockdown.'

'So, not that basic after all?' Taylor said.

'Insidious, but not challenging. I can handle it …' said Archie.

Taylor moved away from the hatch, leaving Archie alone to work. He passed through the waiting soldiers and went on to the trench where Carey and Duane were now setting up their weapons. They had an Uzi submachine gun each and plenty of bullet cartridges.

'Maintain radio silence,' Taylor warned. 'If the hatch goes into lockdown, get out of here. I don't want anyone to take any unnecessary risks. We need all the men we can to get back and protect the City.'

'You think they would attack Trafford?' Duane said.

'I don't know what they would do if they knew we'd breached their base. But I have a feeling we've been on borrowed time for a while. They already know we are there – why they haven't contacted us is anyone's guess,' Taylor said.

'Boss?' called Archie.

Taylor turned to see that the hatch was slowly opening on creaky hydraulics. He hurried back, gun at the ready.

Taylor and his men peered down into a black hole. The ladders led a long way down. As Julia had said, she and the other women must have been climbing for a long time before she reached the hatch and opened it.

'Okay,' Taylor said. 'Let's get on this.'

He nodded to Duane and Carey. Then he began to climb down the steps.

Taylor had gone only a few rungs down when the tremor started up.

'What the fuck ...?' said Donovan, who was just about to begin his descent down into the ground.

Donovan jumped onto the grass verge. Taylor pulled himself up through the hatch, to see a vortex opening before them.

It was different from previous Jinx entrances – smaller, and the ground was less disturbed. Taylor moved away and took cover.

'Hold your fire,' he called as his men readied their guns.

The portal opened and Jas, Julia and Kale emerged.

'What the hell are you doing here?' asked Donovan.

'We came because ...' Kale began.

Julia placed a hand on his arm, and the mage fell silent. 'There was an attempted Jinx attack at Trafford City. Everyone is okay, but some of the soldiers became suspicious of Jas and Kale. They forced them to leave.'

'What?' Taylor said. 'Have they taken leave of their senses?'

'A little,' Julia said. 'But the thing is, without Kale, they might not have thwarted the attack. He forced the portal closed. He stopped the Jinx.'

'I can't deal with this now. We're just about to investigate down below,' Taylor said.

Julia looked at the hatch nervously.

'I hope your arrival hasn't alerted the base to our presence,' Donovan said.

'Perhaps you should leave this now, come back to Trafford?' Jas said.

'No. I'm going down there. I need to see this shit with my own eyes,' Taylor said.

Jas placed her hand on his arm, 'Be careful! I have a bad feeling about this.'

Taylor frowned. Her touch confused him, as always. Even as the thought of Dawn and Lucy reminded him he was a husband and father now, and Jas also belonged to another.

Jas dropped her hand away as she met Taylor's gaze. He could see she was unnerved, but didn't know why.

'We need to tell you something else,' Jas said.

'It will have to wait,' said Donovan.

'Davies, take them back to the camp,' Taylor ordered. 'You know what to do if you don't hear from us in the next three hours.'

Davies nodded.

Taylor, Donavan, Archie and three other men began to climb down the steps, disappearing rapidly into the darkness below.

'What did he say you had to do?' asked Jas as she, Julia and Kale followed Davies away from the hatch and back toward their camp.

'Get back to Trafford,' Davies said.

'Oh,' Jas said.

She didn't like the thought of returning without Taylor. She knew Dawn was gunning for her, and that the doctor, Gerald, was threatened by her presence more now than he had ever been. She took Julia's and Kale's hands as they walked back to camp, taking and giving comfort to her two closest friends. They were, apart from Taylor, the only people she trusted on Earth. These days, she wasn't even sure about Andrew. It occurred to her then that Andrew was not with the group, yet she knew he had left with Taylor and many other men who were also not there.

'Where's …?' she began as they reached the small camp.

'Coffee?' Davies asked, cutting her off as he reached for the still warm pot beside the campfire.

'Not for me,' Jas said.

'You should eat,' Kale said. 'It will make you feel better.'

'We can't return to Trafford without Taylor,' she said.

Julia shrugged. 'It will all work out. I think Captain Arch will be fine. Though I must admit I don't see the point of this expedition.'

'Recce,' Davies said. 'Ultimately they want to help the women down there, but they have to discover how to do that first.'

'They can't help them,' Julia said. 'There are too many soldiers, too many drones …'

'You should at least drink something,' Kale said to Jas. He was studying her face closely, observing how sick she appeared to be.

'Water would be good,' she said.

She took a stained mug from Davies's hands and began to sip the tepid liquid. Her stomach groaned, her insides rolled. Then she stood up and ran away from the campfire. At the edge of the camp, she began to heave the liquid back up until her stomach hurt and she had nothing left inside her.

Julia made a move to go to her aid, but Kale stopped her. He walked slowly over to Jas and held out his hand to help her stand.

'I must be coming down with something,' she said, wiping her mouth. Then she took his hand. She felt weak. Fragile. So unlike her normally strong self. She was trembling, and her face was so white the skin was almost translucent.

They were out of earshot of both Julia and Davies, but Kale glanced around to make sure he wasn't overheard.

'Empress … you're with child. I thought you would have realised this by now,' Kale said.

'No. I can't be. I …'

'Come and sit down. You're shaking,' said Kale.

Jas sank down beside the fire. She stared into the flames, newly stoked by Davies, her heart racing.

It was true. She knew it was. Those last few times when she and Arven had made love it had been *different*. No less good, but very different. She had thought that it meant her body was getting used to receiving the pods, but now she knew that in fact it meant Arven's sperm was no longer issuing them. She was already pregnant. His body knew that. He knew that, and he hadn't told her!

Fear, anxiety and a wave of peculiar happiness pushed around inside her. A baby. She was having *his* child. Why hadn't he said, even when she came back to him, drawn across the galaxies on some bizarre, embryonic cord that linked her to him? Maybe it was the child that had caused those blips? In her mind she poured all sorts of blame his way, but she knew deep down there had never been any opportunity to talk.

Ridiculous.

She buried her head in her hands. Then laughed out loud – ignoring the looks that Davies and Julia gave her – as she considered how stupid this whole thing was. She was here on Earth when the man she loved was on another planet. Yes. My god, there it was. She *did* love him. And she hated it. Hated that she could have feelings for someone who had done what he had. Detested her wayward emotions, her weakness, her *pathetic* female nature that could possibly fall for 'the bad guy'. She laughed again. It was all so ridiculous, hilarious really, when you thought about it, that someone like her, someone who had also killed to survive, would even dare to criticise others for that same, very human, instinct.

But then, Jas would not, she believed, have ever become a killer herself if it had not been for the Jinx arrival on Earth.

'I'm so goddamn stubborn,' she murmured, realising that even now she was trying to lay blame anywhere but on herself.

'Are you okay?' Julia asked.

Jas looked up and found Davies, Julia and Kale looking at her intently.

'Just dandy,' Jas said. *Oh my god! I'm knocked up!*

The reality hit her again in a cold wave of anxiety. This was *terrible*, wasn't it? A complete disaster. As if things weren't bad enough.

Fear again. This time not for herself. She placed her hands over her stomach. *Life.* Even when, around her, the world was dying. There was still new life being created, and now she was part of that.

Jas stood and walked away from the fire. The sick feeling had receded and, now that she understood what was wrong, she knew she would deal with it better in future, when she could learn to accept what was happening to her body as well as her heart and mind. Being a mother was not something she had ever seriously considered, or even wanted, if the truth be known. How could anyone want to bring a child into this awful world?

She looked around her, using the landscape as a way to level herself. They were somewhere in Llanberis. She could see the shale peaks of the curving valley. Once she had driven through here; a weekend away with her boyfriend at the time. What was his name? She couldn't remember. Nor could she recall his face. What did it matter anyway? All of that was so long ago.

I've aged a whole lifetime since then, she thought. *Now. That's all that matters. There is no point in looking back with regret.*

She looked up at the peculiar reddish sky and thought about the future. The idea was as obscure as any thoughts of the past were. If not more so. The mystery of what was happening to the Earth was still unsolved. Jas glanced back at the campfire. Julia and Kale were watching her, while beyond them Davies was packing up the camp in preparation for leaving.

Her heart hurt. She was afraid for her child. It was a peculiar feeling, and one that she was so unused to that it was almost surreal.

Why don't I just tell Kale to take us back to Emin? she thought. The idea thrilled and terrified her. Returning with her tail between her legs, having failed to achieve anything by her desertion. And what would Arven do, anyway? How would it look for him if he meekly took his wayward wife back in?

I can't believe that I'm thinking like this. Me. The strong, independent woman. Worried about appearances. What I thought earlier, though, was true. I'm no heroine. I'm just a woman and I'm scared. And now – there's more than me to consider.

But Arven's position on Emin was a valid concern. Before she left, there had already been signs of treachery among his men. Something that had taken him away from her, and given her the opportunity to work on Kale in the first place. The lovesick mage had taken her at her word until the deed was done. Then he had realised how foolish he had been, and so had Jas. It was all a matter of chemistry now. Hers was tuned to Arven. She would never be able to be with another man. The thought of it disgusted her, and it wasn't a view that a 21st Century girl enjoyed taking.

Jas felt vulnerable. Alone. But she knew she couldn't let it show to anyone. Not to Kale, Taylor or Julia. She had to remain, a least on appearance, strong.

'Are you all right?' Julia called.

'Yes,' Jas said, turning back to look at the view. 'I think I'll try some more water now.'

6

Following Julia's directions, the small band of soldiers moved through the boiler room, past steaming pipes and noisy machinery that sounded none too healthy. Silently they stepped through the narrow spaces until they reached the generator room. This was a huge area, larger than they had expected, but as Julia had said, manned by only one single mechanic at any one time.

Taylor moved out of hiding and into the room with practiced silent stealth. The mechanic turned, some instinct telling him that he was no longer alone. The man yelled, ran for the door to raise the alarm, but Taylor was faster than him. Before the mechanic reached the alarm, Taylor swung, levelling the butt of his gun to hit the man on the side of the head. The mechanic crumpled. Donovan quickly secured the now unconscious man, gagging and tying him up as the others in the group streamed into the room.

'What's the plan?' Private Arlington asked.

Donovan and Taylor exchanged glances.

'I think if we can do some permanent damage, force them all back up topside, then that's what we should do,' Taylor said, finally revealing his real motivation.

'Thought so,' said Arlington. 'Knew you wouldn't be able to leave it at a look-see.'

Taylor smirked. 'Archie, you know what to do?'

'Yes, boss. I'm to set charges on the generators. Rig them so that we have time to get out of here.'

'What about the women?' Arlington asked. 'Shouldn't we try to rescue them.'

'No. We can't. Not without compromising our only chance to stick it to Handley,' Donovan said.

'Our chance will come when they start to move them out,' Taylor said. 'Andrew, Harvey and the other team are waiting and ready.'

Arlington sighed. 'And you were going to tell the rest of us when?'

'Need to know … And now you know,' Donovan said.

'Okay. But I'm not comfortable with this. Just so you know. I thought we were here to scout, and possibly help those poor women. This new plan seems a little rash,' Arlington said.

Taylor paused to look closely at the soldier. Arlington was in his early thirties. He had thinning blond hair and pale grey eyes. A former priest, he had been found in the ruins of his own chapel, two years ago. They had made a soldier of him, but the man always kept his conscience: a quality that Taylor wanted in any member of his team. Even so, Arlington never discussed faith. And when religion had been talked about at one of the council meetings, Arlington had been the first to reject the idea of having Sunday school, or sermons of any kind. He had said that people needed to have their own beliefs; and Taylor had supposed it was because the priest had totally lost his faith. Now he was their voice of reason.

'I understand your concerns. Looking at the big picture,' Taylor said, 'an emergency evacuation will wrong-foot them. They won't be expecting this to be our doing. Nor will they be prepared for a surreptitious assault on their medical vehicles topside. This is the only chance we may have of really rescuing those women. We have to be prepared for casualties. We won't be able to help them all. Just remember that.'

'So we aren't going to even try to map the base. To look around?' asked one of the other soldiers.

'No,' said Donovan. 'We never were. Too risky. Now let's set the charges and take this guy up top with us. I don't plan to kill an innocent today.'

'We don't know he's innocent,' Arlington said. 'He could be one the men that has enjoyed inflicting abuse on those poor unfortunates down here.'

'Yes. He probably is,' Taylor said. 'Which is why we will interrogate him when we get clear.'

While the discussion continued, Archie and Donovan began to set the charges. Taylor remained by the generator room door, watching the corridor. Arlington and one of the other soldiers dragged the dazed mechanic back through the boiler room toward the emergency shaft. They then untied the man's legs, but keeping him gagged, hands bound at the front, they made their way back up the ladder while Taylor and the others finished the work below.

As the men gathered at the bottom of the shaft, Donovan said, 'You sure about this?'

Taylor nodded. 'I've barricaded the door. They won't be able to get in here until it's too late. Let's go.'

At the top of the shaft, Duane and Carter helped pull the mechanic out. Then the man was dragged unceremoniously down to the campsite.

'The boss says pack up,' Arlington said. 'We have to be clear by the time the others get back.'

'What's happening down there?' asked Duane.

Arlington shook his head. 'Piece of madness, if you ask me, but who questions the boss?'

Duane and Carter exchanged a look. Then suddenly the mechanic pitched sideways, pulling himself free from their hands. He ran away from the shaft and campsite, with the two soldiers in hot pursuit.

Arlington stared after them, then he glanced back at the hatch. A few seconds later, the soldiers returned with a now unconscious mechanic. The man's face was busted up, too.

'Got a little rough there, didn't you?' Arlington said.

'He fought, we stopped him,' said Duane.

Arlington frowned. It wasn't like those two to get carried away, but then, it was important that this man didn't escape.

'Just don't rough him up any more, okay. Tie him up securely,' Arlington said.

Then he heard movement as the other men began to climb back up from below.

7

Jas was sitting by a campfire. She wasn't wearing the clothing Arven was used to seeing her in, but looked, with the exception of her longer hair, much as she had done when his men had first captured her. Although that had been less than a year ago, Arven felt that time had passed by too quickly. Now, as he scrutinised her, he noted that she was pale, afraid, as though some revelation, newly made, had brought home the gravity of her situation. Arven was certain that he knew what that news was, as she slowly wrapped her arms around her stomach.

He was in some obscure bubble that had opened up in time, and now he also saw the other people with her. His former mage, Kale, another man – human and a soldier – and a woman with a pretty, soft face. The woman fascinated him, because she sat so close to Kale. Arven was aware of a thread between them that was growing into a bond. Curious. He had never seen his mage show any interest in bonding – that was, until he had met Jas and his morals and loyalty had become confused.

Arven turned his eyes back to his wife. There was no point willing her back. She would return when the time was right. She knew now that she was carrying his child, and that would mean the struggle within herself would end sooner rather than later. He hoped.

The sound of galloping el lien mecks pulled Arven from his fitful sleep. For a short time he was disorientated, not recognising the tent he was in, until he recalled lying down on the bed while waiting for his men to search the oasis. He didn't want to wake, or rather to leave the dream of Jas that was still lingering behind his eyes.

There was a whinny as one of the animals came to a stop outside the tent, and Arven could hold on no longer. Pushing his dream – vision – aside, he pulled himself up from the bed and hurried toward the entrance, just as he heard his warrior call him.

'Emperor?'

Arven opened the flap and stepped out of the tent. He blinked. The afternoon had fallen into evening. He had slept the day away so easily that it concerned him.

The warrior was covered in sand from his long ride. His long dark hair was damp with sweat, and he was flustered and red in the face.

'We found the mage,' the warrior said. He dropped to his knees as though he expected some brutal punishment. 'I'm sorry, Emperor.'

'Where is he? Bring him to me!' Arven said.

The warrior nodded, then gestured for two other warriors, who had been waiting behind him, to step forward. Arven saw then that they were carrying something wrapped in a cloak. He knew it was a body.

They placed the corpse down carefully before the tent, then the first warrior unwrapped the robe.

Garuk's emaciated face stared up at Arven. His skin was burnt after long exposure to the desert suns, and his dead eyes were wide and glassy, as though his final moment had come as a great surprise. Something had been eating his face. Al Liens, most likely: sand beetles that were the piranhas of the desert, scavengers that ate anything unlucky enough to die here. Sharik, and the oasis camp, were protected from the things by the magic of the Al Kuzemen, but they were the natural cleaners of the desert.

'How did he die?' asked Arven.

The warrior paused, as though afraid to speak. 'We found a wound, in his back,' he said finally.

'Who would have done this?' Arven said.

All three warriors bowed their heads, as they had no answer for their leader.

'Bring the body back to Sharik. We must give him a funeral worthy of his office.

'Yes, Emperor,' said the warrior.

Garuk's body was wrapped up, and the two warriors removed him respectfully.

Inside the tent once more, Arven picked up the cloak that he had discarded earlier. His thoughts stumbled over each other at the thought that this callous murder had taken place on Emin. Not the first in recent months, true. But why Garuk? It seemed so pointless. What possible enemy could an Al Kuzemen have?

'Why?' he said aloud.

It just didn't make sense. And it was worse than the murder of an ordinary person. This man had been sacred to them. He glanced around the tent. Clean, even though it had been unused for sometime: it had been endowed with magic to keep out desert wildlife and sand, and no dust had settled on any of the surfaces because of this. The Arrak Nah Tiamen relied so much on their magic, and their mages. This was why the obvious murder of one of them was so serious. The Emperor couldn't order the death of an Al Kuzemen – so even Kale, his once most trusted mage, had had no real reason to flee Emin. And had no reason to fear returning. Or did he?

Perhaps Kale knew something that the Emperor himself did not.

The Arrak Nah Tiamen had always kept their emotions in check. It was why they were such good warriors, temperate husbands, patient fathers. Now they were all full of strange feelings. Life had become too complex since the women of Earth had become part of it. Passions were running higher, his men acted out of character. Jealousy of those who had bonded with one of the women had led to arguments and murder. All of which Arven had tried to address. But never in the whole of his leadership had life been so difficult, his job so lonely. His men so distant. The strange thing was, all who had been fortunate enough to bond with an Earth woman would undoubtedly say that their life was now richer. Arven had felt blessed himself. And it wasn't just because of the sex, a wonderful and thrilling revelation in itself; it was because the women were so unique, so intriguing and so unfathomable. So different from their own race, and yet so similar in other ways.

Who among them would really want to change this new order? It could only be those who were not experiencing this new passion first-hand.

He ran through the council members, wondering which of them still supported his reign. It wasn't something they could take from him, of course; it was his birthright and calling, and none could change that; not even he himself, should he wish to walk away from it all. And there had been times when that idea had appealed to him; never more so than now. But he was sure that most of the council members were loyal, even though they had all, at one time or another, disagreed with him. Gallin and Abeken, for instance, had their differences with him, and of late he had begun to feel uncomfortable with Marlin. He didn't fully understand this feeling. The man's eyes were peculiar, but he couldn't really accuse him of treachery: he had done nothing to deserve that. If anything, Marlin was one of the most conscientious councillors. Even so, Arven disliked him. He just couldn't help it. It wasn't Marlin though – or any of the other council members. He was certain of that. They would always have Emin's best interests at heart; because, like the Al Kuzemen, and any other member of their society, their jobs were a calling, a vocation. Something that they did not choose to do, but rather chose them. That was how things worked in their society, and no-one ever went against it.

He pushed thoughts of the council, and possible treachery among them, completely aside, and reflected instead on Jasmine and his unborn child. They were so far from him that they were beyond any real help that he could give. If he did have a traitor among his people, then maybe Jas was safer where she was. For now, at least.

Besides, she was strong. He knew that she could handle anything that happened. She had some destiny to fulfil before she could return – he could see that now – but the separation was made no made easier by this revelation.

Arven's hand fell on the dagger he always kept strapped to his waist. It was not something he was likely to use under normal circumstances, but rather a part of his formal day wear. Now he began to wonder who he could trust, and if his weaponry would at some point have to be used against one of his own people.

'Emperor?' said a voice from beyond the tent.

Arven raised the flap to see the first warrior waiting for him. 'Yes?'

'I wanted to tell you, without other ears around ...'

'Come inside ...'

The warrior stepped in.

'What is your name?' Arven asked him.

'Prins,' the warrior said.

'What did you want to tell me?'

Prins looked around. Arven saw genuine fear behind the man's swirling pupils. 'It is the mage ... I didn't like to say, but he was killed by a *warrior's* sword.'

Arven was silent. He stared off into space, while Prins shuddered as though waiting for some reprimand for his accusation. Then Arven placed his hand on the man's shoulder. The warrior sank to him knees. His terror was real.

'You did right to tell me this,' Arven said. 'Prins, from now on, I will have only you as my personal guard. And one other that you can trust. Stand.'

Prins climbed back to his feet. 'It would be my honour, Emperor.'

It was full night by the time the band of warriors and Emperor Arven rode back into Sharik.

'Take Al Kuzemen Garuk's body to the burial tent to be prepared. Only those who need to, may know of his death,' Arven said to two of the men. They hurried to obey. 'You two men ... ride to Plendura and bring me back their Al Kuzemen, Malachi.' The two warriors bowed, turned and remounted their el lien mecks. Arven watched them ride away, knowing they were already exhausted but would never disobey an order that the Emperor gave. They were, he hoped, two more men he could call upon in the future. 'Prins, come with me.'

Arven returned to his tent, taking Prins and one other warrior, called Elee, inside with him. A few moments later, his manservant arrived with food. A plate of el lien meck cheese, meat, fruit and a jug of wine, which he placed on the table. Arven ignored it, but offered refreshment to Prins and Elee. The two warriors exchanged glances, unsure whether or not to accept the offer. Then Prins took the initiative and poured some of the wine into goblets. He held one out to Arven, who took it, then another to Elee.

Arven drank deeply from the goblet. 'I need men I can trust. Once, I would have said that that applied to all of my warriors.'

'Emperor, my life is yours,' Prins said, and he fell to one knee before Arven. Elee followed suit.

'I would throw myself on my sword if you willed it,' Elee said.

'I need no such proof, no such waste of life,' Arven said. 'Stand. Both of you. You shall be my companions. And I will trust you to recruit key members of my private guard. There is a traitor among us. I need to find out who that is.'

8

They were all safely in the truck when the first explosions echoed around the mountains of Llanberis. The truck was weaving through the valley. Taylor, Donovan, Arlington and the other soldiers were crammed in the back with Jas, Kale and Julia, while Archie drove up front. One other soldier rode shotgun; he was a man Jas didn't recognise. The base mechanic, now unconscious, was stowed on the floor at the very back of the truck.

'What have you done?' asked Jas.

'Put a spanner in the works,' Donovan said.

'We hope that this means MD59 won't be able to operate,' Taylor elaborated. 'They will have to come topside. They will be forced to survive up here like the rest of us.'

Julia said nothing, but Jas could feel her emotions emanating in the atmosphere around her. She was afraid, and the move was foolhardy: an open act of war, and the odds were stacked against the occupants of Trafford City, no matter how brave Taylor's men were. Jas couldn't understand why Taylor would take such a risk. It was obvious to her that the soldiers below would retaliate, or worse still, descend on Trafford City as the only place of reasonable shelter in the area. Then where would the townsfolk be?

Jas took Julia's hand. At the same time, Kale wrapped his large fingers around her other hand.

'Are you all right?' Taylor said. 'Davies told me you were sick.'

'It was nothing,' Jas replied. 'I'm fine.' *Only pregnancy,* she thought.

Julia gasped. Jas squeezed her hand to silence her. She could feel Julia's shock at the revelation that had accidentally leaked from her own mind. Julia was already adept in telepathy on many levels. Jas was only now becoming aware of how much. She clamped her mind shut for a moment, afraid to let the girl see anything more inside her.

I'm sorry, Julia thought. *I didn't mean to intrude. It just happens.*

Relaxing once more, Jas closed her eyes. She focused her mind to have a private conversation with both Kale and Julia. The thought of returning to

Trafford City filled all three of them with a dark depression. Their expulsion had not been good, and now they would be returning to face the jeering crowd that had quite literally tried to kill them.

It was only a few of them, Kale reminded them. *Not everyone is against us.*

True, thought Jas. Indeed it had been only a few. But those few were key, and had influence on the others. What poison had they been spreading since their eviction?

Let's not worry about it too much. Captain Arch will sort things out, Julia thought.

Taylor is not in his right mind either, Jas pointed out. *I mean, what the hell was he thinking, going into the base like that? We stand no chance against that kind of military power. And I'm sure that Trafford City has now been compromised.*

Agreed, thought Julia and Kale in unison.

I wonder how many others here will notice that this was an extreme course of action? Kale wondered. *Or if they, too, have been altered in some way?*

What do you think is happening to them?, asked Julia.

Neither Kale nor Jas answered for a moment, and then Kale showed the two women something that, until then, only he had been aware of.

Images flashed in their minds. The reddened, peculiar sky. The drones in the theatre, with their red eyes, sharp teeth, feral as rabid wolves. The chimneys at a power planet pouring out some particular pollution – a purplish-black smog that bore no resemblance to the ordinary waste one would expect. It was obvious to Kale, and now to the two women, that the planet, and its people, were being poisoned. By the time Kale's montage finished, both women realised that there was significant danger in just breathing the air around them.

Why haven't we been affected yet? Julia asked. Jas could hear the pain and fear she was feeling more intensely, because of the privacy of their telepathic exchange.

It takes time. It is an insidious poison that changes those around them. Empress, I must urge you, we cannot stay on this planet. For the sake of your child ... Kale thought.

How long? Jas asked. *Surely this has taken years to affect them?*

Perhaps. But maybe it is a new thing that has been delivered into the air recently. Maybe it is something that those in the bases are using to control those outside. And if that is so, then all of us are in danger.

'Shouldn't take us too long to get back to Trafford City,' said Arlington.

I have to warn Taylor, Jas thought.

How? Julia thought. *How can we explain that things aren't right here?*

I have an idea, Jas answered.

'You need to know something,' Jas said out loud, turning to Taylor. 'And the only way I can truly explain is to show you what happened before we were forced to leave Trafford City.'

'It was clearly a misunderstanding. I'll sort it out when we get back,' Taylor said.

'Emotions are running high,' Jas replied. 'Sometimes in those circumstances, people aren't in their right mind. But it's more than that. Give me your hand.'

Taylor almost refused. It was a peculiar request, and he still felt uncomfortable about touching Jas in any way. But Jas reached out and took his hand before he could resist.

A vision floated behind his eyes. He saw his wife Dawn in a way he had never seen her before. More soldier, less wife and mother. Her eyes were crazed. A flash of memory overshadowed the vision of her for a moment. It was an image of two men wearing red jackets: men that Taylor knew had been insane, cannibalistic. Those men were long since dead: killed the day that he and his men had found the Trafford Centre and first met Jas. The image flashed between that and a still pause of Dawn and Gerald, as though making a comparison, then the scene continued to unfold.

He saw Dawn and Gerald through Jas's eyes. Felt the fear and terror she had experienced at that moment, and understood something evident in the scene that shouldn't have been there. Gerald and Dawn were somehow connected. It wasn't clear how.

When Jas released his hand, Taylor was trembling. Partly it was because of the mixture of emotions he had experienced from the scene through Jas, but also it was because he was afraid. Afraid of what he had seen. Jas hoped that he recognised this same irrational behaviour in himself, but she had deliberately not touched on that with the images she had sent him. She had also not shown him all that Kale had shared with her and Julia. She wasn't sure why, but the time wasn't right to tell him about the drones in the Lowry, nor about the pollution in the air.

Taylor shook himself. 'Please don't do that again ...'

'I'm sorry,' Jas said. 'But you needed to know.'

'What did she do?' asked Donovan.

'Replayed a scene, in my head. It was ...'

'Captain?' Archie called from the front. 'We've got trouble ...'

Taylor jumped to his feet and looked over Archie's shoulder, out through the windscreen.

About half a mile ahead of them, a group of people were gathering.

'Pull over,' Taylor said.

As Archie brought the truck to a halt, Taylor climbed over the unconscious mechanic and opened the back door.

'Get your weapons and follow me,' he said to his men.

'What is it?' asked Jas.

'I think it might be more of those things, like the red coats.'

'Drones?' said Julia. 'Oh my god.'

'It can't be …' Jas said. 'It's daylight still. They didn't like light, remember?'

'Whatever they are, I don't care for the look of them,' Taylor said.

Taylor climbed out of the back, his men followed, and they gathered around the front of the truck.

Jas went to follow, but Kale put a restraining hand on her arm. 'Stay here,' he said. 'They don't need you, and you must be kept safe.'

'I have to see this for myself,' Jas said, but she listened to Kale and turned instead to look out through the windscreen. 'My god. There are hundreds of them!'

The drones were pouring down the shale rockface on both sides of the Llanberis Pass. They gathered in a shambled group on the road ahead of the truck. In rags, they looked like the abandoned homeless of their old society. And yes, Jas supposed, that was what they were. But weren't they all abandoned now? These, though, were different. They were feral, dangerous creatures, with an agenda that none of the survivors comprehended.

'Fire a warning shot,' Taylor called.

Donovan raised his rifle and fired at the feet of the front row of the drones. They didn't jump back, cry out or react to the warning in any way that a human might. Instead they began to shuffle forward, a collective.

'What do they want?' Archie asked. He was still behind the wheel of the truck, keeping its engine running, ready to move if they had to.

'They look hungry,' said Jas. 'Just like the red coats.'

'Yes,' said Archie. 'Those bastards.'

Julia stood up and looked over Jas's shoulder. 'Definitely drones. Half altered, I'd say. But you don't know what Handley's scientists have been doing. There's no-one to stop them from doing anything unethical now …'

'Fire at will!' said Taylor.

Jas's attention went back to the mob. They were coming faster now, in waves, and there was only one thing they would do when they reached the truck.

Jas turned and scrambled out of the truck. She ran around to the front, catching hold of Taylor's arm.

'Get your men back inside. Drive through them!' she said. 'There's too many, and no way to win this.'

The men began to fire, and the first group of drones fell, only to be trampled by the next in line. As Taylor's men fired again, and the second wave fell, the first staggered back to their feet and, although wounded, continued to march toward them, amidst the third wave. The second group dragged themselves up, now a bloodied mess, and they too resumed their advance. Jas found herself, and the soldiers in front of her, backing up to the truck automatically as the creatures continued their remorseless approach.

Taylor's men went on firing, but to no avail.

'It's not stopping them!' Jas said again.

'I know,' said Taylor. 'But we have to try!'

'We should charge them; bash their bloody brains out if they won't stop,' Donovan said.

'Are you insane?' Jas said. 'You can't win. There are *too many of them!*'

Her words began to sink in. It concerned Jas even more that Taylor and his men were not reacting rationally. She noticed that Donovan's eyes were slightly bloodshot, and he was champing at the bit to dive into a physical fight.

'Get in the truck!' she yelled. 'Before it's too late!'

'She's right,' said Taylor, coming to his senses. 'Get back in the truck!'

He turned, with Jas at his heels, and the men all poured back inside. Before the doors were even locked and secured, Archie pulled away, foot down as hard as possible on the pedal. Fortunately they were going downhill, and this helped them to gather momentum.

As the horde ran up to meet them, Archie drove the truck right through the centre, knocking some of them back like skittles in a bowling alley.

One of the drones caught hold of the side of the truck, jumping up onto the step at the driver's door. Archie yelled as the creature yanked the door open, but the sudden swing of the door outwards caused the creature to lose its hold, and it toppled down into a ditch at the side of the road. Archie pulled the door shut, locking it this time, while driving straight at another oncoming group of drones that were gathering further down.

This time the drones waited for them, expecting to be hit by the truck, but making no effort either to dive on it or to move out of its way.

Inside, Julia buried her head in Kale's arm. The woman was terrified. Taylor climbed into the front with Archie. Then Donovan passed him a rifle. This was all done without exchanging a word; it was obvious that Taylor now intended to ride shotgun.

Over Taylor's and Archie's heads, Arlington and Donovan pointed their rifles toward the front doors on either side of the vehicle. However, as the truck ploughed through the next group of drones, crushing some of them under its wheels, they found that the road ahead was clear.

Duane was monitoring the back window.

'Are they following?' Taylor called.

'No,' said Duane. 'They are just sort of standing there, watching us go.'

Jas stood up and looked back to see the horde receding into the distance. They were away, but it had been a close call. 'They are like zombies,' she said.

'I suspect that was the basis for the experimentation,' Julia said, looking up from Kale's arm at last. 'Colonel James has made his ultimate weapon.'

A couple of hours later, the truck pulled up in front of the Trafford Centre, to the sound of cheers from a group of residents gathered outside to greet their return. The soldiers in the back began to relax and smile, relieved to be home.

Jas closed her eyes, steadying her emotions and fears as she prepared to come face to face once more with what she knew, deep down, were her mortal enemies. When she opened her eyes again, she found Arlington was watching her. His expression was guarded, but clearly too curious. For the first time, Jas began to feel suspicious and uncomfortable around the former priest. Who was he, anyway? How did they know that he, or anyone else, could be trusted?

'I can't believe you brought them back here,' Dawn said. 'After what they did.'

'What *they* did?' said Taylor. 'From what I … saw … was told, Kale stopped a Jinx attack. Who knows what would have happened if he hadn't been here.'

'They – *she* – led the Jinx here. They are dangerous.'

Some of the council members had gathered in Taylor's shop for their first ever private meeting. Taylor, Sylvia and the others had considered it vital that what they discussed should remain confidential - for the time being, at least. With Dawn and Gerald now set against Jas and Kale, it seemed unlikely to Taylor that the Trafford City occupants would once again find common ground without at least imposing some rules on the pair. At his insistence, though, Gerald had not been invited to the private meeting. No-one questioned this; they knew Taylor had history with the doctor and had never fully trusted him.

'I don't understand why you are so negative about Jas, Dawn: she's one of us,' Sylvia said. 'Yes, Kale is a Jinx, but he is the insider that we need to protect ourselves from future attacks. After what Captain Arch has told us about his attack on MD59, we need all the help we can get. Kale was making real progress with some of us. His magic, though something we all considered to be impossible, does in fact have a science of its own. He can wield it, and so it seems can Jas; and now they are generously imparting that skill.'

'I must say,' Arlington said, 'that I did feel the attack on MD59 was ill-advised.'

A roar of discussion erupted in the room. There were mixed feelings about Taylor's decision to interfere with the base, when the original plan had been to observe only.

'Order!' shouted Donovan. When the group fell quiet, he continued, 'So far we have not heard from our rescue party. We don't know if the chaos we caused was enough to force the base occupants up to the surface.'

'But why did you do it?' Sylvia asked. 'It was such a risk. You could bring that whole base down on our heads, and I don't see what has been gained by it.'

Taylor was quiet. He too had been considering the motivation that had caused him to act so rashly. His logical mind could barely understand it either, but some deep urge to destroy Handley and his cohorts had driven him, for a brief and disturbing time, completely out of his mind. Now he could see the implications of his actions all too clearly. And Arlington was right: it hadn't been a good move. Even so, he felt the need to try to justify it.

'I thought that this might be our only chance of ever striking them,' he said slowly. 'It seemed the right thing to do.'

'To me too,' said Donovan, but he frowned, and Taylor wondered if his right-hand man was also having his own doubts.

'I've sent a team out to scout for Harvey, Andrew and the rescue party,' Taylor said. 'We had prearranged a rendezvous point if they got split up. The party will be back soon, and I'm sure we'll have a better perspective on what damage we did.'

'I've also talked to the engineer that was in the generator room,' Donovan said. 'He's not giving much away at the moment, and I'm loathe to resort to unpleasant means of extracting information from him. We'll see if a few days without food and water will mellow him.'

'War is never pleasant,' Sylvia said. 'We aren't savages.'

'Correct,' said Arlington. 'Keep him locked up and watched, by all means, but we can't starve him. That's not us.'

The council members took a vote, and it was decided that, for now, they would treat their prisoner civilly, to make a point that they were different from those he was working for.

'And what if the base decides to attack?' Dawn asked.

'We have men posted to give us early warning,' Taylor said.

'That doesn't answer the question. How can we defend ourselves against them?'

'With magic,' said Caroline.

Donovan turned to look at his wife. So far she had remained quiet throughout the meeting.

'Kale knows how to stop their weapons from working,' Caroline continued. 'That's what the Jinx did to stop us when we were many nations with large armies. We didn't stand a chance, and neither will they. Plus, some of us are developing our own skills. Mine is the ability to move objects with my mind.'

More discussion erupted.

'Then what you're saying is, that we should trust this Jinx to keep helping us?' Dawn said. Her voice was dripping with scorn. 'Because I will never trust him. Or *her*.'

'Enough!' Taylor's anger was evident, and the room plummeted into silence.

'We all have misgivings,' Sylvia said, trying to dissipate the tension. 'But so far Kale and Jas have done nothing but help us. And we all understand your fear, Dawn, and why you and the others acted as you did before. But Jas is not our enemy. We need to be savvy. She could, in fact, be a very important asset in this fight.'

'What do you mean?' asked Arlington.

'She's the Jinx Emperor's wife …'

'So?' said Dawn.

'One day, he is going to want her back …'

The implication of her words hung in the air.

9

Handley was lying in bed, thinking about booking another visit to his favourite P-class female, when the first explosions rocked the base and blew out the electricity supply. His room plummeted into darkness. The air began to tarnish. Within a few moments the emergency generators kicked in and air began to flow rapidly through the air conditioning vents once more. By then, Handley was out of bed and hurrying to his internal com port.

'What the fuck was that?' he demanded when the duty sergeant answered.

'A fire team is over by the sector five generator room drowning the fire,' the Sergeant informed him. 'That's all I know for now. But I'm heading down there to find out more.'

'Forget it. I'm on my way to see what's happening first-hand. Stay by the phone.'

Handley pulled on his uniform and left his quarters. He climbed into the electric-powered buggy that was parked outside of his rooms, and he drove to sector five, which was approximately two miles from the area of the base where his quarters were.

He parked the vehicle near the breeders' building and walked the rest of the way.

One of the fire team was running toward him as he rounded the corner heading toward the officer's mess.

'How bad is it?' he asked

The whole of the corridor, leading from the mess to the engine room, stank of smoke. A thick fog hung in the air. It bit into Handley's lungs with the stench of chemicals as well as burnt metal.

'This whole area is fucked,' said Captain Macken. 'We don't know for sure, but it looks like the engineer went rogue and set charges all around the place.'

'Where is he now?'

'No sign of him. Which does suggest he is either dead under the rubble or he somehow managed to get out through the emergency hatch before he blew the charges.'

'That goddamn hatch again? What the fuck is going on around here?' Handley said.

'Fortunately the explosion cut off the exit point. No-one is coming in or going out through there again. We can't even get through the debris, because the area is compromised. One shift and the roof may tumble in on our heads,' Macken said.

'Has it affected the rest of the base structure?'

'Luckily, no. The designers had the foresight to consider this possibility. The area was self-contained, as are all the generator rooms. The problem is, we now have one less, and the base is being run on the rest. It will be too much of a stretch, long-term, and will mean that we have to rely on power from the remaining plants above ground. Someone will have to go topside to monitor. Repair. All the things we didn't want to be involved in until it was time to resurface.'

'Send a team – and make sure they wear masks above ground,' Handley said.

'Why?' asked Macken.

'The air isn't good up there now. Some form of pollution.'

'Oh,' said Macken. His eyes narrowed, but he knew better than to question Handley further.

'Make sure the other hatches remain on lockdown. Get them rigged to notify security of any interference,' Handley continued. 'And why the fuck wasn't this one on lockdown after last time?'

'I'll look into it,' Macken said. 'It should have been, but then the engineer probably did an override. He was our best guy.'

'And now he's gone …'

Handley left the area. His clothing reeked of smoke and the cloud of fog seemed to follow him. He had a nagging suspicion that there was more to this than just the engineer going rogue. It was too planned, too organised, and yet stupidly futile. Anyone who lived freely on the base would know that this wouldn't put them out of action. Though it would inconvenience them significantly.

Back in his room, he sent an e-mail out to his secretary, giving him instructions for a memo about the power plant expedition. He was worried. He didn't need his men becoming compromised up top. What he had revealed to Macken was only half the truth.

He picked up his phone and called the direct line for Corporal Caine. That was, after all, his only way of contacting General James. James needed to know about this, and Handley needed to make certain his men would be safe if they went topside.

There *was* pollution above ground, but it was being caused intentionally by Handley's science team. A deliberate and subtle poison was being leaked out into the atmosphere. They had been sending out a slow dose for some time, but when the Trafford Centre surveillance was discovered by its occupants, Handley, on James's instruction, had ordered an increase in production. The area that was formerly Manchester was now being drenched in the toxin. It would be making changes to the behaviour of the occupants and any remaining survivors. They would become paranoid, confused, make bad judgement calls. All of which would weaken any resistance when Handley's troops decided to move in.

'Caine?'

'Major?'

Handley filled him in on the incident.

'Strange. Daniel Corben was vetted. He was a staunch advocate of the new order,' Caine said.

'Is there any way that he could have changed his views?' Handley asked.

'Not likely. It seems we've had outside interference.'

'I'm sending some men up to reactivate one of the plants. I'm concerned about the Tradora virus,' Handley said.

'We'll send a supply of vaccine. But you need to contact your man in Trafford. He may have news if Arch and his cohorts were involved in this little inconvenience.'

'You think that's likely?' Handley asked.

'Who else could it have been?'

They talked a few moments longer, exploring the possibilities of any betrayal from within their own ranks. Handley thought it wasn't that unlikely that Corben had betrayed them. After Tremaine's behaviour, he didn't trust anyone. Especially if they weren't being controlled by chemicals in some way.

Handley hung up the phone.

It had been agreed: the move against Arch would be soon, but first they required intelligence on how the occupants of Trafford City were coping. They knew there was a fresh supply of women and children that would be useful to the base, and to Handley's ultimate cause. So far they had left the Centre alone. It had been useful to let Taylor feed and nurture the occupants until such time as they needed them. Now that time was rapidly approaching, and Handley was looking forward to the conflict.

Dr Gerald Avery was listening to classical music in his private rooms, a former shop in the Trafford Centre. He sat with his eyes closed. He heard the door open but didn't look up. He knew who had come to see him. He had been expecting her.

'Have you heard anything?' Dawn said.

Gerald opened his eyes and stared at her. He had, of course, always known who she was. His orders since she had arrived at Trafford City had been to supply her with medication. Gerald had suspected what this was, and had been proved right. It was some form of mind control drug, to cause her to forget, and thus to make her full integration into the community far easier than if she had remembered she was a soldier, under instruction from Major Handley.

'Did anyone see you come here?' Gerald asked.

'I know how to be covert. It's what I did … do,' Dawn said, but he could see she was still uncertain.

'When did you stop taking the meds?'

'A week ago. It's all still a little fragmented, but I remembered today that you are the base liaison. That you have been my supplier …'

Gerald stood up, went to a bureau at the side of the room. On the top there was a decanter of whisky. He poured some into two tumblers and held one out to Dawn.

'Have this. You'll need it.'

Dawn took the drink. Then she sank down into the sofa opposite the chair that Gerald had vacated. She waited until Gerald sat down again. Then she sipped the drink. It tasted peculiar. Strong whisky, but with something else.

'Antidote,' Gerald said simply. 'They are sending some shit into the air around us. It will befuddle these fools, and then we'll be able to swoop in and take things over here.'

'What do you mean, befuddle?'

Gerald shrugged. He didn't elaborate, because he wasn't too sure of the effects of the toxin himself. Just that he had been told to make sure he and Dawn took the cure.

He sat back in his chair. The remedy tasted bitter, but was tolerable in the drink. He sipped it again.

'What about my daughter?' Dawn said. 'Will this stuff in the air *hurt* her?'

'Don't worry about it,' Gerald said, using one of the hypnosis triggers he had been given to control her. '*All will be well.*'

Dawn took another swig of the drink, her body relaxed, and Gerald knew the trigger was still working on her. Despite the drugs being shaken from her system, she was still his to control.

'What do you remember?' he asked.

'Past stuff. How I came to be here,' Dawn told him.

'Good. Then you know your mission?'

'Yes. I was to find other women. Lead them to Taylor … Infiltrate and become a part of this society.'

'And you did that very well, too,' Gerald smiled.

'I've been having headaches,' Dawn said.

'That is understandable. A merge of present and past memories was bound to bring about some form of physical reaction. How bad are the headaches?'

'Migraine at first, but less as the days go by,' Dawn said.

'Then you are adapting. Excellent.'

Gerald's mind slipped back to the first time he had met Dawn: in the base at MD59.

Since the final occupants of his former home town, Stow-On-the-Wold, had been taken by the Jinx, Gerald had been travelling.

It was a long time ago now, and he tried not to think about what he had done, nor the rebellion that his wife, Mallory, had started once she had realised that he had been drugging her and sexually abusing the other women under his protection. He felt no real guilt, but regretted that he hadn't been more careful. He was irritated by his own stupidity. He hadn't wanted Mal to give herself up to the Jinx. Surely at that time she would have thought that suicide? Although Jas was the living proof that it wasn't, Mallory hadn't known that.

When the Jinx had come that final time, Gerald had hung back inside their former home, his dispensing medical practice, with a vault in the basement where he had stored his medicine. They had used the vault to hide in on the rare times when the Jinx had come back, combing the area for any remaining female survivors. Gerald had enjoyed the role of saviour, for a time, until he had realised that he had power over the women. They had been so afraid, they would have done anything he wanted. Better the devil you know than murdering aliens … But then it had all changed.

He tried to push the thought of it all away. But one memory lingered. Mallory and the other women willingly walking into the vortex that had arrived as they fled from him. It was as though the Jinx had been their liberators, not their captors.

Gerald had watched them from the upstairs bedroom window, shaking in anger and frustration. All of them gone in one go. No-one left to control. After that he had filled the car with all remaining fuel and provisions, and had driven for as long as he could, scavenging supplies on the way: there had been no point at all in remaining.

The military had picked him up a few weeks later. He had travelled north, finding himself in the solitude of the Welsh hills, never expecting that a team of men were regularly patrolling the perimeter of an underground base.

They had taken him back to the base.

'I'm a doctor,' Gerald had told them.

He had been made welcome on the basis of his obvious abilities.

He had felt a tremendous relief at the time. No longer alone; a situation that he had begun to believe would drive him insane. And so he had looked with wonder around the base, as he was escorted around like an important person. And he *was* important. He was a doctor, and the Major, Handley, knew that he would be useful.

They let him use the P-class females, wined and dined him. Gerald was given his own room, and it was luxury compared with the long days and nights outside alone. He was safe for the first time in months. And he could indulge his fetishes with the women without judgement. Here were men that understood him, and had the same feelings and emotions about the position that women should now occupy in their lives. Gerald had never thought of himself as a misogynist. But when the levels had changed on the worldwide playing field, he had believed himself to be of the stronger sex, and had reverted to an age-old instinct. A sense of perverse entitlement came into play that he accepted as nature's way of showing the world that it had been wrong for a long time. He had always thought political correctness had gone mad, but in the old days no man had dared stand up to it for fear of being ostracised. Now he didn't have to. It was the way things should be. A utopia of the male kind.

Therefore, Handley and his men indoctrinated a willing disciple. Gerald took to their philosophies as though he had always known and believed in them: in many ways he had, he had merely hidden it. Handley was a god among men to him. A man who had realised early on that this was the way forward.

'The Jinx are strong,' Gerald said during one discussion. 'They seem to be able to smell the women out.'

That was when Handley told him his plan.

'I want you to infiltrate a group of maverick soldiers. They were once under my command. Good soldiers, with a smart leader. If anyone can find a way to tackle the Jinx, Captain Arch can.'

'Why not just bring them into the fold?' Gerald said.

'Arch has … morals that may not fit in with our ideals,' Handley explained. 'But he has his uses. If anyone finds any women out there and protects them, it will be Arch.'

Gerald listened to Handley's proposal. They knew where Taylor and his men were, and he would 'accidentally' find them and offer his medical services. Something everyone needed. The rest would be on a rolling basis. Gerald would also have his own radio with which to contact the base. An old-fashioned Citizens Band radio system that Taylor and his men would not be monitoring, because they all used advanced military equipment. It was the perfect cover.

Handley made many promises. Gerald would one day be able to return to the base on the A-class status he was currently enjoying. He would have access to all the females he wanted. The Major painted a perfect utopian future and sweetened it with a promise of supplies and drugs.

After that Gerald was introduced to Dawn. She was already working covertly in the field, though at the time he didn't know exactly where and how.

Dawn was, Gerald noticed, completely subverted into this strange but wonderful culture. She responded to orders like a robot. She appeared to have no emotions other than a strong desire to serve.

On instruction, she knelt between Handley's legs and gave him a blow job. Gerald was aroused. Not by the sight of the obese Major being serviced, but by the power Handley had over the female soldier. When Handley invited him to participate in the sex, Gerald was so excited that he barely had time to remove his trousers and enter Dawn from behind before he came. It was this power that was Gerald's real fetish. And he had no remorse about using it, and no morals about the women being treated in this fashion. He was the man. He was the hunter-gatherer who would provide for the women. He was God in their eyes. Or so Handley told him he would be, on his return.

Gerald had gone out willingly after that and had remained in covert contact with the base ever since.

Now, Dawn was in his quarters. Her brief had clearly been to go after Taylor, and Gerald had been sure to remain distant from any complication with the Captain. He could have made her satisfy him, but logic had won out and convinced him that was not a good idea. After the disaster that had nearly ended his position with the Trafford City occupants, and Jas's capture by the Jinx, Gerald had virtually gone to ground. With only occasional contact with the base, he knew they too were biding their time. And, with the exception of medical contact, he deliberately avoided the women at Trafford, knowing that one day he would be able to take his pick of them.

'There was an explosion at the base,' Gerald said. 'Do you know anything about that?'

Dawn was quiet for a moment. Gerald frowned. He knew that some of the council had met in Dawn's and Taylor's place. He began to think that the hypnosis had gone too deep and her brain wasn't processing quickly.

'Come back,' he said, releasing some of his hold on her. 'Talk.'

'How would I know anything about it? You are the contact. What did they say caused it?' she asked timidly.

'Engineer gone rogue. How did the mission go? Taylor and his men went to the base, didn't they, to see if they could get inside?'

Dawn blinked, 'Yes. They did. They came back with someone. Possibly your engineer. He's in the weapons room. Locked up in one of the cages. I think they found him wandering outside …'

'Has he told them anything?'

'Not yet,' Dawn said.

'But you don't know if Taylor got inside the base?' Gerald asked again.

'They brought that Jinx and Jas back again with them,' Dawn said.

'Really?' Gerald sat forward in his chair. 'That isn't good. They were making progress with the women, weren't they? On the magic instruction.'

Dawn nodded.

'I'll contact the base for further instructions. But … can you get to the prisoner?'

'Yes. Why?'

Gerald stood and returned to his bureau, opened the bottom drawer and pulled out a small bottle.

'Arsenic. Put it in his food. I doubt that our friends will want the man to tell these people anything useful.'

Dawn stared at the bottle for a moment, then she took it from Gerald's hands, stowed it in her pocket, and listened carefully as he gave her the usage instructions.

When he had finished speaking, Gerald looked at Dawn standing there. He just couldn't resist. He quickly checked outside his rooms. There was no-one there. They were alone.

'Dawn,' he said. 'Program 23. Service me.'

Dawn blinked and looked a little confused as the programming kicked in. Then her face cleared, and she smiled and moved toward Gerald, her hands unbuttoning his shirt as she kissed his sweaty neck.

10

After cleansing himself in the pool, Arven rose from the water. The tent top was open above his head, and he gazed up into the starless sky. It was a warm evening, and his firm naked body shone in the glow of the two moons. It was a peculiar feeling, not one he had experienced before, but the moons had an effect on him. Despite the increasing tension on Emin, and especially in the capital, Sharik, he experienced an overwhelming sense of hope.

In the other room, he heard Prins talking, offering a glass of refreshment, and he knew then that Malachi had arrived and waited for him.

Without hurrying, he rubbed his body dry, then pulled on a robe of blue silk. It would be a crucial meeting, one that could give him the answer he needed to find the traitor that had killed Garuk; but he had to consider first how to broach the subject with Malachi. It would be difficult to explain the death of Garuk. Much must be done to honour the deceased mage, and Malachi would be responsible for using the correct protocol. He would, Arven also hoped, advise him on how they would make the Al Kuzemen's death known to his subjects: so far, Arven had managed to keep it secret from all but his most trusted servants. There had been too many deaths of late. Arven wasn't sure how his people would take this one, as it was a violation of their sacred code. Whoever was responsible had committed treason: the only crime truly punishable by death within their society.

Arven pushed aside the curtain that separated the pool room from the rest of the tent, but he paused to look back at the pool. His mind flashed back to moments of sexual excitement and tenderness with Jasmine. She knew how to make him want her, more than anyone could ever have done, and her uninhibited attitude to sex had made her even more desirable. It was difficult not to recall how she had enjoyed playing with him in the pool as part of their foreplay.

Turning his mind back to the moment, he stepped into the tent. Malachi stood and bowed to him, as did Prins and Elee.

'Please sit,' Arven said, and Malachi did, while Prins and Elee took up position by the tent's main entrance. With a nod from Arven, Elee went outside to stand guard there.

'Before we begin,' Arven said, 'I need you to cast a spell around us. One that will ensure our complete and total privacy.'

'Lord?' Malachi was clearly confused. 'Privacy from whom? We are all your humble servants.'

'From any other Al Kuzemen, especially,' Arven said, sitting down opposite Malachi and looking at him with an intensity that made the mage shuffle slightly in his seat. He didn't know why he felt this was so important, except that an Al Kuzemen would be the only person capable of eavesdropping on their conversation from a distance.

'I … don't understand,' Malachi said. 'All Al Kuzemen are *dedicated* to you …'

'Do as I ask.'

Without further question, Malachi raised his staff, tapping it lightly on the ground three times. A light erupted from the bright red gem that adorned the top, and a large reddish bubble grew. The light-ball stretched and widened until it consumed them and filled the entire tent with a reddish glow.

Arven's ears popped as the pressure around him changed.

'It is done, Emperor,' Malachi said. 'No-one outside of this place, be they seer, mage or mere warrior, will be able to hear what you tell me. And I swear on my life that I will never reveal what you say to another soul, unless you should wish me too.'

Arven nodded. He felt cocooned and safe, and he trusted Malachi: Kale's image pool had shown that he was dependable.

'Garuk is dead,' Arven began. 'He was murdered by one of my warriors, though I have yet to discover who, or why.'

Malachi's skin paled. 'A terrible sacrilege! But how? I felt nothing. And none of the other mages have expressed a concern.'

'He didn't connect with anyone?' Arven said.

'No. This is terrible. The pain of his last moments should have been eased by another Al Kuzemen. It is our way.'

'Perhaps he did fuse memory with someone,' Arven said. 'Someone he trusted.'

Malachi said nothing, but the implications of Arven's words were not lost on him. It meant that there were some mages that could not be relied on. Arven could see that the thought horrified Malachi as much as it did himself.

'But … all Al Kuzemen can be trusted, Emperor,' Malachi still insisted, as though by denying the possibility he could change the reality. 'It is our sacred calling. We cannot be false …'

'And yet Kale helped the Empress escape back to Earth,' Arven pointed out.

'An exception. But …' Malachi stumbled over his words.

He had no real explanation for Kale's defection, or for the murder of one of his colleagues, and Arven could see that the situation horrified Malachi as much as it did himself.

'Our faith, our life has changed. With the addition of the human females. With the … crimes committed against humanity,' Malachi said.

'Crimes?' It was Arven's turn to pale now. His own internal thoughts, his own guilt and torment, were being voiced by the mage. 'Before this, our wars were fought only against those who deserved it,' he admitted. 'What you're saying is that we were wrong. We shouldn't have put our own needs before those of another race.'

Malachi shook his head. 'I was among those who voted for the move. And we sent out many prayers, many requests for guidance before we did. Nothing negative came back from the universe. But it does now seem as though we are being punished. Perhaps it is my vocation that makes me naturally superstitious, but it feels to me as though the divine entity disapproves of our choices.'

'Or maybe not our choices, but mine, in not tempering my men to behave less … violently,' Arven said. 'I know that many innocents died, and it was not necessary. If I had been there, at the raids, maybe …'

'You mustn't blame yourself. Poor decisions are always made on the battlefield. But we knew it would go this way. There was no other road our invasion could travel.'

Arven grew thoughtful. 'And now we must bear the consequences of those actions. We will be punished, maybe die out anyway. Perhaps it was the universe's wish that the Arrak Nah Tiamen would become extinct?'

'No,' said Malachi. 'If that were so, then our efforts to find a suitable race would have failed. We were given a chance, but I think these trials are a test of sorts. One that we must endure with all the stamina that our race has. Otherwise we may not be worthy of survival.'

'So what now?' asked Arven. 'What must I do?'

'I will handle the proclamation of Garuk's death,' Malachi said. 'You must put your enemies on alert by declaring your devotion to finding the Al Kuzemen's murderer. They will be too afraid to make other moves against you when the kingdom rallies to support your cause. Ultimately these men are cowards. They move silently like thieves in the night, but will not openly declare their disloyalty.'

Arven felt the surge of hope again. Malachi was right. His people would be outraged by the murder, and all of the disgruntled thoughts and jealousy among them would be focused onto finding the mage's killer, not on their dissatisfaction about the lack of females, or the defection of the Empress.

'With regards to the Empress,' Malachi said. 'She is with child, is she not?'

'Yes …' gasped Arven. Malachi's powers were stronger than he had suspected.

'I have been watching her, and I know the circumstances under which she fled. Wrongly accused, she believed she had no other choice. But her machinations will end when the time is right, and I see her returning to you – the details of which are still so much fog to me, however.'

'Thank you!' Arven said. 'Your words calm my *chio*[3] somewhat. And your thoughts on our situation give me hope for the future of our race.'

'Even so, I believe we are experiencing a form of *diamah*[4] for our crimes against humanity. But I believe we will put things right. Something tells me the Empress with be a part of that.'

'How?'

'That path has yet to become clear to me,' Malachi said. 'I will meditate on it and try to establish a clearer picture. If your highness with excuse me?'

'Of course. The Al Kuzemen tent awaits you. Rest now, friend. I will have need of your counsel more …'

'All will be well,' Malachi said.

Malachi bowed and left. A while later, the ward he had placed on the tent slowly dissipated. Arven had considered asking the mage, who he now knew was also a powerful seer, to leave the protective aura up. However, it would only have given his enemies cause to try harder to invade his thoughts. While they believed him ignorant of their treachery, he would be monitored less.

He retired for the night, pondering Malachi's last words that 'all would be well': they added to the feeling of hope that he was determined to hold on to.

---

[3] Soul.
[4] Karma.

11

Mallory sat alone in the marriage tent. Her offer to put herself forward for bonding was bound to be rejected by Arven. The Emperor still needed her to be the matriarch of the Earth women and the foundation that cemented their continuing settlement into Arrak Nah Tiamen society. Her own happiness, it seemed, was not important to Arven or anyone else. Besides, she was not as young, or as vital, as the other women had been, even though she was still within breeding age.

Since she had arrived in Sharik, Mallory had done all that she could to make her presence important. Until now, she had actively avoided the marriage ceremony, though she had proactively encouraged the other women to integrate and become part of the Jinx society. After her marriage to Gerald Avery, a lifetime ago now, she had despised men. She had thought of them only as savages, sexual predators; and the Arrak Nah Tiamen were no different. Even so, for survival, she had capitulated in her own way. Then, slowly, she had become obsessed with Arven – to her, he was the one man worthy of her time and respect. As their friendship had grown, she had believed he would one day take her for his own wife; until Jasmine Regis had arrived. Now she knew that this would never happen. Arven loved Jas, and the bonding between them, which she had previously believed was just Jinx magic, she now knew went beyond everything she had deemed possible.

Jas was Arven's *chio mien*[5], and it had taken a journey across time and space to bring them together.

Even though she had no control, and the whole idea was ridiculous, Mallory couldn't help but feel hurt. She wanted love for herself. Real love. Not what her husband, Gerald, had offered. Particularly when she had discovered the inner perversity that he had hidden so well for all of their years of marriage.

She stood up, determined to lay her cards on the table with Arven. She

---

[5] Soul mate.

knew she would be unable to breed, as Gerald had told her long ago that she was infertile, but she would insist on being given the opportunity to find her own *chio mien*. It was the right of every person to find a partner, and her days of fighting it were now at an end. She didn't know what Arven's current state of mind was, but Mallory was hurting, and she felt that he must be too.

A thought crossed her mind. Insane, wild and impossible. Why shouldn't they *comfort* each other? What harm would it do? She would go to him, explain how she felt. There would be no commitment on either side. After all, Arven was a man, just like any other. How could he refuse an offer that gave him no guilt, no redress, but offered so much enjoyment and respite nonetheless?

Mallory looked around the tent once more. Maybe today would be the last day she would spend here for a while. She saw herself sleeping in Arven's tent, in the Emperor's bed. How could he possibly refuse?

'The two tribes …' Arven murmured as he stared down at the map of the galaxy containing Earth.

The universe was infinite, and yet they had been drawn back to the planet of their origination.

'Your supposition is true,' said Malachi. 'The Arrak Nah Tiamen came from Earth. We left, evolved. They changed also, but their faith was turned from the stars to false religions and then to the worst faith of all – science.'

'We are the same. It is why we are compatible.'

'Yes,' said Malachi. 'And why our attack was something of a sacrilege. It went against all of the ancient promises made between the tribes. We broke the treaty.'

Arven ran his hand through his long dark hair. It was wild, unkempt. An outward sign of his inner turmoil and lack of real rest. That day, they had laid Al Kuzemen Garuk to rest, and the secret of his death had been revealed. Malachi had done well to soothe the frazzled nerves of the men and to turn their attention from their obsession with loneliness to the hunt for the killer of the mage. Now they were considering the future, by, Malachi said, examining the past.

'Long ago, we left Earth,' the mage continued. 'A planet that was still in its infancy. Unspoiled, but loved by both peoples. But the Arrak Nah Tiamen have always struggled to settle. Earthlings have a name for our type: *nomads*. We wanted to conquer the universe, and our mages knew how we could travel from one world to the next. With seers, like myself, who could detect the places that could sustain life. Over the years, the truth was lost. We forgot our origins, even though the ancient scrolls existed to remind us. Some of those were later transcribed into books, much as the one you hold,

Emperor. But the books were seen as myth, as fairytale. Only, the words of truth, passed down mouth to mouth through the generations, warned of the truth.'

'We didn't listen,' Arven said. He remembered such stories. One that his mother had told; one that his first wife, Celin, now deceased had shared with his daughter. Celin had known the story because mothers often passed it on to their children. But had his departed wife also understood that it was no myth?

The Arrak Nah Tiamen females, long ago lost, had taken with them a part of their heritage that the men of his race barely recalled. They had been the storytellers and the keepers of history. How had the men forgotten it all so easily?

'We have committed genocide of the second tribe,' Arven said.

Malachi did not reply, but Arven knew for certain it was true. They had committed the worst sin possible, and now they were paying the price. It was no wonder that their own world was in turmoil, that *homilia* – murder – previously a behaviour of the past, was now becoming part of their present society. The jealous squabbles amongst the married and unmarried had at least ceased since the news of Garuk's death had reached the ears of his subjects. But Arven knew that this was a tentative truce. At any moment, jealousy could rear its head once more and bring about more deaths and suffering.

It seemed unfair. Hadn't they suffered enough with the loss of their wives and daughters in the first place?

There would be no reprieve, of course, until they found more women to correct the imbalance. But Earth had few more to offer. Those that had been missed on their raids were surely now dying from the poisonous air. And Emin, a planet twice the size of Earth, had a population to match. They were never going to have a balance in their own world, not for many generations, if nature chose to even the odds.

'The scrolls tell of the first leap through time,' Malachi said. 'That it was both successful and unsuccessful.'

'How could it both succeed and fail?' asked Arven.

Malachi unrolled the scroll and glanced down at the ancient, faded text. 'There is a warning,' he said.

Arven waited for the mage to elaborate, but the Al Kuzemen became lost in thought for a while, and the Emperor did not wish to break his meditation. Finally Malachi came back into the real world and turned his head to look at the Emperor.

'The scroll foretells of a time of doubt. A time when our Emperor will be tested. There is a recommendation: that the Emperor should return to a place that the Arrak Nah Tiamen have not visited since their first leap through time and space.'

'The Eleventh Moon?' Arven said.

Malachi nodded.

'I thought it was nothing more than a legend.'

'Legends are always born from truth,' Malachi explained. 'There are coordinates too.'

Arven looked at the scroll over the mage's shoulder. He saw the directions on the scroll as clearly as Malachi did, yet he knew that this should not be possible. Only Al Kuzemen could *see* the planets: only they could open a vortex and traverse the tunnels of time to reach any destination.

'You think we should travel there? There would be something to learn?'

'The scroll says so. And never has there been a time when our Emperor has been more obviously tested,' Malachi said.

'If we are to go to this place … the Eleventh Moon … then when would you suggest?' Arven asked.

'Soon, highness,' Malachi said. 'But first I must find another mage who can help to focus our journey.'

Arven nodded. 'Begin your search. You must be certain that whoever you pick can be trusted.'

'Emperor,' Malachi said, 'I will need to create a potion that will help me *see* into the souls of the other Al Kuzemen: something to test them without their knowledge. It may take me some time.'

'And when you have found a suitable mage?'

'We will travel to the Eleventh Moon and find the message that has been left for you.'

'You really believe there will be one?'

'Yes,' said Malachi.

'Leave me now,' said Arven. 'I have much to consider. We have bridges to rebuild that have been broken, and I do not, as yet, know how I will go about making those repairs.'

Malachi noted that Arven's metaphor was a very human expression; one he had most likely learned from his Earthling wife, Jasmine. It was an apt description, nonetheless, and it summed up the position perfectly.

A great crime had been committed in their foolish, headlong rush to save themselves. And the punishment was being meted out on them all, even when they were unaware of it. Even so, Malachi had faith that there would be something that could be done to remove this obvious curse. That something was clearly hidden in their past. A past that they must explore in order to regain and repair their present and future.

Malachi left the tent and walked past Prins, back to the tent next door: the official Al Kuzemen dwelling. He thought through all of the spells he knew, but failed to bring to mind any that could blind his colleagues to an attempt to probe their minds for signs of betrayal. He considered that it might, indeed, take quite some time to come up with an effective solution. He only hoped time was on their side.

'I wish to see the Emperor,' Mallory told Prins outside Arven's tent.

The tent flap opened and Mallory was granted admission, as her rank and status as royal translator had always allowed.

Inside she found Arven seated at his table. He was looking closely at the maps that Mallory knew had been used to navigate the galaxies and help his people locate Earth in the first place.

'Emperor … I have come …' she began.

Arven looked up, acknowledging her presence.

'… to … talk to you of the future.'

'I see …' Arven said.

Mallory noticed his gaunt cheeks and wondered how many nights he had stayed up, suffering over the loss of Jas. Would her petition fall on deaf ears? Or would he, now stranded and alone, actually understand her own desperation? Her heart went out to him, and it drowned her doubts about her own foolishness.

She moved further into the room. Her heart was pounding in her chest. What was the worst thing that could happen? He could turn her away, and she would have to live with that, wouldn't she? But in her heart she was certain that he wouldn't – otherwise the risk she was taking now wouldn't have seemed worth it.

'I have been loyal to you. I have helped you, and the women of Earth, to make this mingling of our races work.'

Arven said nothing as she stepped forward again. His pupils mesmerised her with their hypnotic twisting and turning. She was sure they pulsed with passion: a desire for comfort if not for her.

'I know you're suffering. I understand your pain, because I feel the same. I have needs too. I am a woman, after all.'

'What is it that you want?' Arven asked, and Mallory realised that she would have to be more direct.

'Love,' she said. 'Passion.'

Arven frowned.

Mallory was only inches away, and she moved around the desk, hips swaying seductively in her long cream dress. She placed her hand on his arm.

'I know you feel as though you must bear everything alone. But sometimes you *need* a friend. I can be that friend.'

Arven let her embrace him. Comfort, yes … he did need love. Mallory had known, and now she could give him that reassurance. And if Jas never returned, maybe they could console each other forever?

She looked down into his face. He was bemused by her touch, and so failed to react.

She leaned down slightly, lips searching for his.

'I love you,' she said, 'and I wish to soothe you in your need. I ask nothing more than that you accept all I give you.'

Her lips touched his then, and Arven felt an electric current leap into his mouth: it was a burst of lust from her to him.

He jumped up from his chair and stepped back from her. 'No ...'

'Arven ... Let me love you ...'

'*No ...*'

'You reject me? Even now, when you know she will *never* return ...'

Mallory stretched out her hand to stroke his handsome face. She saw his hurt, felt the terrible ripple of pain that tore his soul in two. She could ease that pain: *if only he would let her.*

'Jasmine *will* return. She carries my child,' Arven said.

Mallory pulled back her hand as though burnt. An agonising pain burst into her chest. The biggest rejection of all, that condemned her hope, burning it to ashes that could never rise, phoenix-like, again.

'No!'

'Councillor Abeken was right ... You Earth creatures are different from us. But after all you've seen, can you still not understand how bonding is *forever*?'

Arven saw the pain in Mallory's face and softened his voice. 'I cannot take the comfort you offer, even if I wanted to. I am as much Jasmine's as she is mine,' he said. 'I am grateful for all that you have done for us. Your talents have helped my people, and your friendship has meant much to me. But friendship is all I can give you in return.'

His voice was kind. Mallory, despite her pain, was not blind to the effort he was making to smooth the embarrassment of the situation for both of them. But it made no difference.

'If bonding is so special, then let me go. Let me be put up for auction. Surely I deserve this feeling, this *love*, as much as any other?'

Arven said nothing, and Mallory turned away, eyes blinded by tears as she pushed through the tent flap and hurried away.

She ran for some time, never realising that she was re-treading a path once taken by Jas when she had first arrived in Sharik and railed against her possession by Arven. Now Mallory, who yearned for his love and respect with every fibre of her being, rushed through the tented streets and found herself beside the pens of the el lien mecks. Her eyes stung with tears. Her vision was blurred.

The camel-like creatures grazed the sand at their feet. For the first time in the years since she had arrived in Jinx Town, Mallory looked at the creatures with horror and disdain. They were like and yet so different from Earth camels. The animals were passive by nature, but their razor teeth could sever a limb if they ever had a mind to become feral.

Mallory breathed in gulps of air until she was dizzy. Rejected and hurt, she felt foolish. Why on Earth must she suffer so much? What was wrong with her? She had known his answer before he gave it, yet still she had pushed the point forward. Still she had hoped that she had some magic that made her more desirable than Jas.

'How could I even consider that he would want me? *Me*?'

Even her own husband hadn't really loved her: Gerald was a testament to how despicable a man could be. But Mallory hadn't seen it. Now, as she looked back, she remembered all of those passive-aggressive comments: 'You aren't going out like *that*, are you?' or 'Are you really sure you want to eat that?'

Looking back, Mallory realised that she had been more a prisoner with Gerald than she had ever been with the Jinx. He had controlled her every move. Whether she worked or didn't work; how she spent her free time; what she wore. Even when she slept. She hadn't seen it at the time, though once she had caught a friend rolling her eyes at some comment of his, that she realised now had been an instruction as to how she should behave. She had thought her friend was wrong. She had even severed ties with the woman afterwards. That was another thing that Gerald had commented on too: her friends were never good enough. Once he had even claimed that one of them had come on to him. When she had confronted the woman in question, and been told that actually Gerald had made a pass at her, it had never occurred to her that Gerald had been lying. There had seemed no reason for it, and so she had taken his side in the matter. Why tell her at all if he had been the perpetrator, after all? Now she could see the truth of the situation: Gerald was an abuser. He always had been, and he had often manipulated her into doing exactly what he wanted.

Mallory walked past the animal pens, turning left and heading toward the river that ran alongside. She paused by the bank, looking down into the moving water.

Am I so repellent? she wondered. Glancing down at herself, Mallory gasped. Her skin looked youthful, her body was slender. Her hair, once a dirty blonde, looked bright and shiny, with reddish tinges. She had never looked better in all of her years on Earth. The cleanliness of the air on Sharik had an effect on all of the women. Even the plainest of them had changed. All looked attractive, at least; and those who had married now had devoted husbands. How could this system be so wrong? Why had she thought she had the power to make any change to it? Surely bonding was *real* love?

But of course it went against everything that the Earth women believed in. They still rebelled, in their own way. Mallory knew of all of those tiny rebellions, and now, instead of discouraging them as she had always done, she was tempted to start her own insurgence. How easy it would be to spread discontent instead. But no, as much as she wanted to, out of spite, or hurt, or just plain frustration, she couldn't. Ultimately the women of Earth were happier on Sharik, even though they had no technology, nor the comforts they once enjoyed. Life was simpler. Somehow that was a very good thing.

Fury engulfed her again. She had never thrown herself at a man before: it was upsetting to be rejected. An insult. A slight that was so hard to bear that she wanted to throw herself into the river.

'*Ill elmah reah?*' a voice said behind her.

Mallory turned. She found herself face to face with a warrior she didn't recognise.

'No, I'm not okay,' she said rudely. Her cheeks were tear-stained.

The warrior stared at her blankly. Although she knew his language, she had briefly forgotten that he didn't know hers and had answered him in English.

'*Aluk im,*' she said, which meant *I'm fine.* She wiped her hand over her face, pushing the water from her cheeks.

The warrior smiled at her. Then held out his hand.

'You shouldn't be out alone at this time. The Emperor has told us to be mindful of all women,' the warrior said.

'Chivalry isn't dead yet, then.' Mallory found herself smiling back at him. Like all Jinx men, he had a rugged handsomeness that was both intimidating and interesting. His eyes pulsed with that fascinating rhythm that all the Arrak Nah Tiamen had, only his seemed warmer somehow. There was less distance, and she could sense his innate curiosity as he looked at her.

'What's your name?' Mallory asked.

'Prins …'

12

Dawn sat at the table, drawing on an Etch A Sketch with Lucy. Twisting the dials, she slowly created a picture of a figure carrying a rifle. It was a soldier.

'Is that *you*, Mummy?' Lucy asked.

Dawn stared down at the figure.

'Not all soldiers should follow orders,' said Lucy.

Dawn glanced at Lucy. Her two-and-a-half-year-old daughter's words seemed wise beyond her years; or perhaps they was just childish babble based on things the little girl had heard.

Dawn imagined the soldiers from MD59 coming into their city, taking their children. Categorising the girls. Where would Lucy end up? Would she be one of the lucky few that found a husband among the soldiers, who would grant her a tenuous A-class rating? Or would she become a breeder, a pleasure drone, a servant doing the most menial jobs? Of course, none of this would be decided until she was of childbearing age, maybe 13, 14 years from now. But it was unlikely that Dawn would even see her daughter during that time, as she knew that all children were removed and placed into a care system that from an early age would indoctrinate them on the lowliness of their status. They would never remember any other life.

Things may change down there by then. Women's rights may return once the survival of the race is no longer an issue, she thought.

But no. Dawn knew that would never happen: it was a pipe dream. Handley and James had their little world all tied up. It was never going to change. Never going to be like it had been. Maybe one day, maybe in a few centuries, when they could return to the Earth's surface, find their own places to live as they chose, women would regain their rights, with the help of a few sympathetic bleeding hearts among the men. But not in her lifetime, nor Lucy's.

Even so, Dawn had already started her own mutiny. Lying to Gerald about Taylor's men and their attack on the base had been the start of it. As far as anyone in Trafford City was concerned, they men had carried out reconnaissance and nothing more. Dawn would never be the one to betray

Taylor, because if the other survivors knew the truth, the place would fall into panic. Maybe a few people would leave for fear of retaliation from the base. Dawn considered that possibility now. She could leave with Lucy. But then, where would she go? Nowhere was safe. Especially now she knew of the toxin.

She sighed. There was no need for immediate panic, was there? Handley didn't know the truth if Gerald didn't, and therefore, she hoped, no immediate threat to their lives would arise.

'You must be ready,' Gerald had said. 'At any time you may be called home.'

Home. MD59 was *not* home. It had never been that. It was, as she recalled, torture. Imprisonment. Abuse. Yes, all of the memories were returning – as she had told Gerald – with the drugs now gone from her system. Gerald must not know what was happening until she had decided what to do.

Of course she could tell Taylor the truth about her mission, her brainwashing. All of which might still endanger them, even though she now believed she could fight the awful conditioning that they had subjected her to. But what would he think of her if she did tell him the truth? Would he ever believe or trust her again?

She stroked Lucy's hair.

'Why are you crying, Mummy?' Lucy asked. 'Have I been bad?'

'No. No baby. You're a good girl. The very best girl.'

She held out her arms, and Lucy allowed herself to be picked up, held, hugged, kissed.

'I love you,' Dawn said.

'Love you, Mummy,' Lucy said, and then the little girl wriggled until Dawn placed her back down.

Lucy picked up the Etch A Sketch and shook it. The picture of the soldier disappeared, and the little girl placed her finger on her lips.

'Shh …' she said. 'No-one saw …'

Dawn shook her head: she was sure that fear and sadness were making her hallucinate. Perhaps it was even some form of withdrawal she was suffering from the drugs? Her daughter couldn't really understand what was happening, could she?'

'When the soldiers come,' Lucy said, 'hold my hand, Mummy. I'll look after you …'

Dawn dashed away the tears from her eyes, but more came. Her chest heaved. She left the table, went into the small washroom at the back of the former shop, and rinsed her face, patting it dry. When she returned to the room, she felt stronger.

'No soldiers are coming, darling. Everything will be fine.'

'Yes they are,' Lucy said. 'Mummy, let's draw a bus. I like buses … Do you like buses?'

Confused, Dawn went along with Lucy's babbling. The random change of subject made her realise that it was just baby speak after all. Lucy must have picked up on a conversation at the nursery. She couldn't possibly know or understand that they were under threat. Dawn resolved to speak with Clara about it. The carers needed to be careful what they said around the children. It would be no good for them to pick up on adult fears and concerns.

'Yes, I like buses,' Dawn said. She sat down, and they continued to draw. Lucy twisted the dials, and a shape emerged.

A knock on the door broke into the lovely silence that had fallen between mother and daughter. Lucy had been concentrating so hard she had stopped talking, and Dawn's panic had receded.

Dawn left the table once more. 'Wait there, darling.'

She opened the door to find Gerald standing there.

'Is it done?' he asked.

Dawn's hand went to the poison still in her pocket.

'It will be …' she said. 'The rota was changed and I didn't take the food this morning.'

Dawn glanced back at Lucy, noting that the little girl was still working on her sketch and hadn't looked up to see who was at the door.

'Lucy is growing up fast,' Gerald said. He looked benignly over her shoulder at the little girl.

Dawn frowned. 'Yes. She is.'

'She'll be a welcome addition when we are safely *home*,' he said.

Dawn's frown deepened. Gerald didn't notice; he was watching the child in a way that made Dawn feel uncomfortable.

'You shouldn't be seen here,' she said.

Gerald looked around. 'You're right. If anyone asks, I was making a house call for Lucy. You thought she was sick.'

Dawn nodded. She closed the door, but found she was trembling.

Men like Gerald would decide the fate of Lucy: she couldn't bear the thought. And the memories of how truly awful MD59 was came tumbling into her conscious mind. Panic rose once more in her chest, tears burned behind her eyes and she remembered …

'There's no use in having females in the army,' Colonel James had said. 'Women aren't as strong, fast or deadly as men. You have to prove your stamina or you become integrated into the system.'

Colonel James had wanted her to know the gravity of her situation. She and a few other female soldiers had been taken to the P-class area and shown how the women were treated there. After Dawn witnessed one poor girl dealing with her eighth customer of that day, she felt sick to her stomach.

'We do have rules, of course. No anal sex. We don't want the girls to be damaged, and it is known to cause problems in later life with incontinence,' James said, as though he really cared what happened to the girls, who were clearly little more than unwilling prostitutes being drugged into submission.

After that, James arranged a tour of the breeders' unit. Some of the women there were on a second or third pregnancy in just two years. They looked ruined already, worn down. Like cows in a cattle shed, they were milked of every bit of goodness they had. Around the base, she saw the lot of the other women. A-class status was awarded only to those of particular merit – like the scientist that helped devise the mind-control drugs. Dawn couldn't remember her name, but she saw her as a traitor to her kind. Or certain wives whose husbands were high-ranking – but Dawn knew their position was safe only for as long as those husbands remained satisfied with them. Anyone who was stupid enough to disagree with anything they were told to do would find themselves reassigned. She'd seen it happen: a wife one day could become a breeder, or a whore, the next.

'So now you know how it is,' James said.

Although he never voiced it, there was an underlying threat that they could become any of these things if they did not do as expected. Of course, James hadn't really needed to say it, or to show them the base's reality. The hypnosis and the drugs were already controlling Dawn and the other female soldiers. They made her obey, even when her mind screamed and railed against it. It was as though her real self was shrunk, shrivelled and trapped in a cage of insanity inside her own mind, while this other thing took over.

'It is about alter-ego,' James had once explained. 'We pull the strength in you forward. Make you a better soldier. But we reduce that part of you that would consider too deeply the consequences of your actions.'

Dawn knew that this wasn't strictly true, though. She told herself that real strength lay in the ability not to object. It wasn't the drugs that made her behave the way they wanted, so much as that part of her that wanted to stay alive. The drugs gave her a way to excuse her own fears and cowardice. And while they made her whore for them sometimes, kill for them others, that survival instinct gave her the endurance to suffer the pain of it all. Or so she told herself.

'You know your mission,' Handley had said when she was first assigned her current task. 'Colonel James spoke highly of you. He says you'll get the job done, and I believe you will.'

'Yes, Major,' Dawn had answered. 'Find other women, lead them to Captain Arch.'

Handley had nodded. 'You're to keep taking your medication.'

'Yes, Major.'

'When you find Arch, you make him trust you. Any way you can.'

Dawn had been a good soldier. The meds had controlled the little voice in her head that remembered MD59. They had controlled her. Yet still she had functioned on a normal level: loved Taylor and Lucy as any wife and mother would.

Now that her inner voice was free, and she remembered everything, she wondered to what extent her feelings for Taylor were genuine and to what extent a result of her conditioning. Though her love for Lucy was beyond question.

The issue of her feelings for Taylor was harder to ponder, for some reason. She had been happy before the memories returned. She would never have even questioned the love and loyalty she felt for him, or for Trafford City. Now she no longer trusted herself. What if Gerald had some trigger word that could make her turn on Taylor? Or Lucy? The thought horrified her. Fear of herself surfaced. How could she be trusted around her own child, after everything they had made her do?

I haven't done anything wrong, she thought. *Not really. I only tried to survive. Surely he could forgive me for that?*

'Mummy, why does the doctor have red on his hands?'

'*What?*' Dawn pulled her mind back to the moment. She found herself gazing at Lucy with confusion. 'What did you say?'

'I want to wash my hands …'

'Oh … yes, darling. You should. Let's both wash our hands.'

'It's okay, Mummy. You have clean hands now,' said Lucy.

Dawn looked down at her fingers as cold water ran over them from the tap in the small sink in the back room. She didn't recall going in there, and Lucy was looking at her with a small frown on her tiny brow.

She reached for the towel, rubbed her fingers dry until they hurt. Something was lurking still hidden in her memories. Something she needed to recall. And while her mind probed, and her head ached from the effort, she hoped that whatever it was she had done would not come back to bite her.

13

'I need to talk to you,' Taylor said. 'About what you showed me.'

Jas was sitting by a small water fountain, long since dried up, in the centre of Trafford City. The area was quiet, because most of the occupants were out in the farming fields, or tending cattle, or caring for their families. Living their lives, attending to their duties, as best as they could. It was not lost on Jas that they were almost waiting for the end while pretending to work against it.

'I'm all ears,' she said.

He paused, as though struggling to voice his fears and suspicions.

'Has Andrew returned?' Jas asked.

'Yes.'

'And the women on the base? Were they able to rescue them?'

'No. Handley never came topside. It seems that our attempts barely inconvenienced them.'

'Oh, no. That's awful,' Jas frowned.

Ever since she had met Julia and learnt about MD59, she had wanted to do something to help. But she didn't know what she could do. And now that she knew she was pregnant, she had begun to distance herself from the people at Trafford City. Knowing that sometime soon she would need to make a decision that would change everything. She had to protect herself and her child. She could no longer be responsible for anyone else.

'What will you do?' she asked.

'I don't know,' Taylor said. 'Jas, I'm afraid. For the first time, since all of this started, I really feel we have no future here. And I'm scared for Dawn and Lucy more than for myself.'

Jas met his eyes. She could barely believe that she was hearing him admit to weakness, but she understood completely his need to protect his wife and child.

'I understand,' Jas said. 'More than you know …'

'What you showed me; about Dawn's behaviour … it was enhanced by your own fear at the time, wasn't it? I mean, you didn't really see her as bad as …?'

'Drones,' Jas said. 'They are called drones. Julia told us something about them. It's a form of chemically-enhanced hypnosis in some cases. Complete insanity in others.'

She relayed the information she had learned about MD59's science projects.

'Before we came to you in Llanberis, we stopped at the Lowry Theatre …'

'Your old haunt,' Taylor smiled. 'You always felt safe there.'

'Yes. But not now. The place is inhabited by vermin,' she said. 'There were drones living inside, and they were terrifying. Worse than the two red coats I found here. They weren't even interested in the stash of food I'd left there. They wanted *us*, Taylor. *We* were going to be their next meal.'

'Oh god …' he said. 'What's happening out there?'

'The thing is, you should know … Kale says there's poison in the air that made them that way. That poison is going to reach Trafford City eventually. Perhaps it already has. And then people are going to start changing.'

Taylor grew thoughtful. In his mind's eyes he again saw Dawn and Gerald turning on Jas, Kale and Julia. He also considered again his own lack of judgement in attacking MD59. For the first time, he faced the fury inside him. Anger that had surfaced recently to remind him of his own hatred toward Handley: his resentment at having been abandoned when the Jinx decimated the planet. Underneath it all, he questioned why he and his men had been good enough to die in battle, but not good enough to be included in Handley's plans.

He shook the thoughts away. Of course he knew the answer: he would never have agreed to their treatment of the women. Aside from the fact that it wasn't ethical, it was beyond his comprehension that the Major would want to regress their society so far.

'Show me the drones?' he asked, holding out his hand.

Jas took his hand and sent him the images of what she had seen at the Lowry. She tempered the emotion this time and didn't drown him with her fear as she had previously. Instead she showed him details as she recalled them. The red-rimmed, animalistic eyes of the creatures. The sharp, serrated teeth. The smell of them, like grave-rotted flesh.

'Awful,' he said when she released his hand. 'They are monstrous. Dawn isn't, can't be, like that …'

'No, she isn't like them. But there was something. Ever since I arrived here I've been experiencing all sorts of changes myself. I have more magic than I did. And one thing is for certain: every day I find I have more control over it. I can see things … colours around people. There's something wrong with Dawn … and Gerald, though I don't know what it can –'

Taylor's radio crackled, and a burst of sound broke over Jas's words.

'Captain?' a voice said.

Taylor unclipped his radio and placed it to his mouth. 'Yes, Donovan?' he said.

'Security has spotted military trucks heading our way.'

'How many are there?' Taylor asked.

He was at the perimeter of the Trafford Centre car-park. It was a border control area that the men had established. Andrew and Kline had taken up position with two machine guns and a rocket launcher.

'Enough to wipe us out,' Kline said. 'But the trucks have stopped some way back. They don't seem to be moving in.'

'They are waiting for an order to attack,' Taylor said.

'Should we evacuate the women and children?' asked Kline.

'And take them where?' said Andrew. 'There is nowhere to go.'

An hour later, the lights went off in Trafford City.

14

Kale tapped his staff on the ground, and light burst from the top until the bookshop was filled with a warm yellow glow. Jas and Kale had been waiting for Taylor to return. They both knew that the Trafford Centre had been running on borrowed time for the past three years. Heating, lighting and running water, all being readily available, was something the occupants had come to expect. Now, they had been plunged into near darkness without warning. The only illumination within the building now came from the weak sunlight filtering in through the glass domes above the main walkway. The temperature in the building started to fall soon afterwards, as the heating had also stopped working.

Yells of confusion and fear echoed through the structure, and Jas could see a group of people staggering from their makeshift homes. They were calling to each other, and some had battery-operated torches, others candles.

Jas and Kale looked out from the shop. Though it wasn't nightfall, the domes above their heads were slowly darkening, and a black miasma was forming around the glass.

At that moment, Caroline came hurrying toward Kale's light. She was holding the hands of her two small children. The little girl and little boy both appeared to be calm, despite the confusion.

'Caroline! Where are Taylor and Andrew?' Jas asked.

'I don't know,' Caroline said. 'We were all rounded up from our workplaces and sent inside. Donovan told me to get the children from the day-care centre and stay at home. What's happening?'

'We may be under attack,' Jas said.

'My god! *Jinx?*'

'No …' Jas shook her head. 'They'd be a lot less scary right now …'

'Shit! The military?' What should I do?' Caroline asked. She appeared helpless, afraid.

As if feeling her fear, the two children gathered around her legs, clinging to her thighs as they looked up at Kale and Jas with round, fearful eyes. They were unnaturally quiet. Jas experienced a maternal trepidation at the thought of anything happening to them or the other children of Trafford City. They had all fought so hard, striving for the past few years, after the hell of the end of the world. And now the final hours might suddenly be upon them.

'Gather everyone you can find into the mess area. Let's keep together until we hear what's happening from Taylor,' Jas said. 'Oh, and make sure you find Julia, too. She went over there to volunteer to help serve lunch, and we haven't seen her since.'

'Will do,' Caroline said.

As Caroline left, Jas turned to Kale. 'You can help them, can't you?'

'I can try …'

'Let's round everyone up.'

They walked in the opposite direction to Caroline. The building was slowly getting darker, and so Kale carried his staff as a light ahead of them. Jas glanced up at the glass dome near the former Selfridges store: it was now pitch black outside.

'What is that stuff?' she said.

'Poison,' Kale whispered, though he didn't look up. 'Whatever we do, we mustn't go outside and breathe that in.'

'What about Taylor and the others? They must be still out there!'

Kale said nothing.

They reached another, now empty food shop, and Jas peered into the darkness. She saw someone streak across the room. Then a dull whistling sound came from the far corner of the shop. Jas remembered that there was a storage room and delivery bay over there.

'Hey! Whoever's in there, we are gathering at the …'

Red eyes glowed in the dark. One pair, then two, then several.

'My god,' she stepped back. '*Drones.*'

As they watched, two misshapen figures shambled out of the darkness, their eyes glowing red in the light from Kale's staff.

Semi-clad in rags, hair wild, they were ape-like in the way they loped across the empty interior of the shop. Kale held up his light to ward off the creatures. As he moved it closer to them, they yelped and jumped back into the gloom. Jas pulled the shop door closed.

'Seal it!' she said.

Kale raised his hand and concentrated, his lips moving in silent incantation. There was a hiss, and a stream of smoke emerged from the lock between the doors. Jas gave them an experimental push and they were fixed solid. On the other side, the drones moved closer.

'The doors are glass. It won't hold them for long,' Jas said.

She took hold of Kale's arm and they backed away. Inside the shop there was more movement, and then, suddenly, a large table was thrown against the window. The glass fractured but held. Jas and Kale turned and ran as fast as they could back toward the mess.

Behind them, there was the loud sound of smashing glass as the table was thrown a second time, crashing through the window and into the walkway.

A pack of drones emerged through the broken window. They paused, glancing around the new space, sniffing the air like rabid dogs. As Jas and Kale reached Selfridges, an explosion of glass showered down on them from above. Jas looked upwards just in time to see a group of soldiers, wearing masks and dressed in black clothing, positioned above the dome. They dropped ropes down into the building and rapidly began to descend. The black smog followed soon afterwards.

The drones began to whoop and whistle behind them: hyenas on a hunt. And it occurred to Jas that she was constantly thinking of them in terms of animals, because of their behaviour. Anything other than thinking of them as still human.

'Run!' she screamed, even though both of them were already doing so.

They ran full pelt into the mess area.

'Cover your faces!' Kale called to the startled group of citizens now occupying the area. 'Don't breathe in the poison.'

Above them, the black air curled in, hanging above them as though waiting for the right moment to attack.

The area erupted in chaos as people ran for the main door. Jas and Kale halted by the archway, close to the toilets and an abandoned ice-cream trolley that had been left in place as some sort of tribute to the old life. Kale extinguished the light pouring from his staff and pulled Jas into the food hall.

'Don't go outside!' Jas yelled, but her voice was lost in the cries of panic.

An old woman barged past her, knocking her into Kale. There was a general stampede toward the main entrance.

'Do something!' Jas yelled to Kale. 'If they go outside, they will be right in the middle of the smog.'

Kale tapped his staff. Five balls of light issued from the top jewel. They spun for a second around his head, then Kale sent them spiralling toward the archway, where both drones and soldiers appeared.

'Keep calm,' bellowed Kale. His voice amplified throughout the mess. The room seemed to shudder with the resonance, his words echoing around the room before dying suddenly as the whole space filled with light. The wailing and cries of fear suddenly subsided, and a profound silence fell over the room.

Jas could now see that the soldiers were wearing night goggles as well as some form of gas mask. One ripped off his mask and eyewear in agitation as the burst of light burnt his eyes before he had chance to change the settings on his goggles. He gasped in the air. Then fell to the ground, his body twitching and spasming as the toxin burnt through his lungs. The black mass moved through the soldiers, but having seen its effect on their fallen comrade, the others kept their glasses and masks in place.

A ripple of noise erupted once more from the terrified citizens who gathered behind Jas and Kale to see the soldiers and drones.

Intimidated by the light, the drones fell back as Kale's orbs moved in the air toward them. Light burned above their heads and fell onto the exposed skin of one of the creatures. He screamed and yelled, beating at his own flesh as it erupted. Like an extreme form of bubonic plaque, boils swelled up on his skin. The affliction ran over him until the boils exploded, sending out hot blood and pus. His clothing caught fire as the toxic substance ignited under the glare of the light; his filth-caked hair lit up next. The drone fell, rolling and screaming in agony, while his comrades, abruptly afraid, shrank back into the shadows, their eyes glowing dull red.

'Light …' Jas said. 'They don't like it, so let's have more …'

Kale tapped his staff again. Another burst of light and more glowing orbs rolled out toward the drones and soldiers.

A moment later, a burst of gunfire hit one of the light balls. It crackled and fizzed, then snuffed out like a candle blown in the wind. Seconds later, more gunfire from the invading soldiers took down the other lights.

The mess, with no natural source of daylight, became pitch black once more. The darkness generated more fear among the citizens, who had mostly fallen silent to watch the proceedings, but now began to panic once more.

In the dark, Jas could make out the drones. Eyes glowing, they moved closer. She had no doubt at all that they could see all of the people in the mess: she felt their unearthly, hungry eyes on her as she and Kale backed away.

A peaty odour wafted from the smog, which was now rolling lower above them. Jas could feel the damp, cold fog as it drifted closer. Terrified, she caught hold of Kale's hand.

'Do something …' she said again.

'Empress …' Kale said.

His staff tapped down again. A pale blue glow came from the jewel this time. It surrounded Kale and lapped over Jas, stretching out behind them as it engulfed the occupants of Trafford City. Silence fell as the fear-driven screaming abruptly ceased. The occupants froze in place. A sense of calm returned to the room, and even Jas felt its influence as her heart stopped its fearful pounding. Her mind, no longer panicked, could once again focus on the creatures.

'What are you doing?' asked Jas.

'A protection spell. It will keep that poison away from us for now. It has a calming side-effect.'

'What about the soldiers? And drones?'

In answer to her question, a shot sounded and a bullet whistled through the air toward Kale. It hit the barrier of blue light and sank into it as though it were a warm knife slipping into butter. As it moved, it slowed, and Jas realised she could actually see the bullet.

Kale raised his hand, palm out. The bullet slowed and dropped to the floor before it could hit him.

There was the clatter of gunfire, and bullets rained in their direction. Kale's protection thwarted almost all of them, but one brushed slowly past Jas's head, leaving a bright red burn on the tip of her ear.

'Ouch!'

Kale became furious. His anger rang in the air. The blue barrier shuddered, and all remaining bullets in flight tumbled to the floor. Then Kale pushed his hand forward. The blue glow exploded in front of them, blowing back soldiers and drones. Through the dim light generated by the barrier, Jas could see the front row of soldiers aiming and firing, but to no avail. Their guns had locked. The soldiers looked at their weapons in puzzlement. One of them backfired, throwing the soldier to the ground, his face a mass of blood. Kale had worked his particular magic. The enemy's weaponry was jinxed.

15

'It is time, Emperor,' Prins said.

Arven pushed aside the maps. His search had been, as always, ineffective. Days had passed since the ceremony for Garuk, and he and Malachi were now devoted to discovering other worlds on which they might find women to continue to repopulate their race. However, there seemed to be no other planets with humanoid life. Hadn't they already exhausted every avenue in the past, when Kale had been his loyal mage?

His heart hurt, and he felt the crimes of his race pulling on his soul. A deep, dark pain burned in his chest. They were on the brink of crisis once more, and the council had called an emergency meeting.

Arven left his tent with Prins and Elee by his side and made his way to the council tent.

Inside, Councillor Marlin was seated next to Councillor Abeken. They were in deep conversation as Arven entered. The Emperor saw that all of the councillors were in attendance. All fifty members were crammed around the huge table. Only one seat remained: a large, stout throne that only the Emperor had the right to use.

'Your highness,' Abeken said. 'Thank you for joining us. We were just about to discuss the current crisis.'

Arven took a seat on the throne and nodded to Abeken. 'Please continue.'

Prins and Elee took up point either side of Arven's chair. With folded arms, the two warriors were formidable, but none of the councillors noticed them.

'I will come straight to the point,' said Marlin. 'As you know, even with the addition of the Earth females, we are unable to provide every man with a wife. A problem that is still causing difficulty in many of the towns.'

'Even before our women died, we could not guarantee that all men and women would find soul mates,' Abeken said. He frowned at Marlin. 'Surely the Al Kuzemen in the towns would counsel and advise on this as they have always done?'

'The fault lies with the Emperor,' Marlin said.

Some of the other council members gasped at Marlin's direct accusation.

'What do you mean?' asked Arven. 'I have done everything I can to solve the problem.'

Marlin bowed. 'Of course, your highness, I meant no disrespect. Sadly, though, you did promise a wife for every Arrak Nah Tiamen. The men have taken that quite literally. Even though we know that the bonding process doesn't work that way among us.'

'Earth women have brought along their own complications, as I've pointed out previously,' Abeken said. 'We could not foresee how *they* would affect *us*.'

'Yes. Some Arrak Nah Tiamen have changed. Not all can be relied upon as we would wish,' Marlin commented. He stared directly at Arven as he spoke, but as the Emperor met his gaze, the councillor looked quickly away.

Arven again noted the lack of movement in Marlin's eyes in that split second. He wondered if the other council members felt as uncomfortable with this strange defect as he did.

'Councillor Marlin,' Abeken said. 'You are the person who pushed for this meeting about the future, and yet you seem to have another agenda. Would you care to share this with us, or can the council move on with the pressing matter we came here to discuss?'

Marlin held up his hands: Arven thought it a very human gesture, and had noted when dealing with Jas and other Earth women that it was one used to placate, or indeed back down from an uncomfortable position.

'I have no other subject I wish to discuss,' Marlin said. 'I sought merely to clarify the position as it stands.'

'Good,' said Abeken. 'Then we must move on. Let us hear from Al Kuzemen Malachi.'

Malachi nodded. He was seated at the right hand side of Arven, and he chose now to stand.

'We are addressing first the continued issue of the lack of females. The Emperor and I are spending many hours searching the galaxy maps for signs of potential. So far, nowhere but Earth is suitable. But you know this already. Al Kuzemen Kale's search pointed always to Earth.'

'Yes,' said Marlin. 'And since Kale's defection with the Empress, our journeys to the planet have ceased.'

Malachi ignored the deliberately inflammatory comment about Jas and Kale. The council had agreed to postpone any judgement on the Empress until she could be returned safely to Emin: but he knew that this did not stop Marlin from spreading as much discontent as possible in the meantime.

'We have decimated the population of the planet with our, might I say, your highness, highly aggressive attacks,' Malachi continued. 'Any survivors left are insufficient to make much difference to our population crisis. The Arrak Nah Tiamen males already numbered double the entire population of the Earth. There would, sadly, never have been enough women to satisfy all.'

'What would you have done differently?' asked Abeken, picking up on the comment about aggression rather than the ones about population. It was an argument that had been long discussed and that many disagreed on. 'We had no alternative but to ...'

'Councillors, please,' Gallin interjected. 'There is no need to go over this now. The crisis, though somewhat abated, is still of grave concern. We cannot change what we did, but can only move forward and make new decisions.'

Arven leaned forward in his seat. 'Agreed. But we may have to face our crimes before we can move on.'

'What crimes?' Marlin said. 'We did what had to be done.'

'We saved ourselves at the expense of another race,' Arven said. 'It is something we should never merely dismiss.'

The council erupted into discussion.

'Councillors!' Gallin called again. 'We must keep order! Each man will have a turn to speak, should he wish to. Please continue, Al Kuzemen Malachi.'

Malachi began to walk around the table, and each councillor turned their chair to look at him as he passed by. He met their eyes, and his own pupils spun and warped with his inner excitement and frustration so that each one of them understood exactly how he was feeling. The only councillor who did not meet his gaze was Marlin. Malachi made no obvious recognition of it, but he glanced toward Arven as he passed by Marlin's chair.

'The current reality is that we cannot continue our search until we find an alternative to Earth. Hence why no further raids have been sanctioned. The Emperor and I will, of course, continue our meetings and try to consider all alternatives.

'Now to the other business. The death of Garuk has been a severe blow. We have still to find the perpetrator. On close inspection of the body, I ascertained that it was indeed a warrior's sword that struck the fatal blow. It is hard to believe that one of our own could have done this ... but it was. Finding the culprit is so far proving to be difficult.'

'One of our *own* warriors?' gasped Councillor Teac. He was one of the oldest among the councillors, and his once jet black long hair was threaded with white strands, as was his long moustache.

'Yes,' Arven said. 'The body was left out in the desert for the sand beetles to feed on.'

Cries of 'Sacrilege!' echoed through the council tent.

'Indeed,' said Malachi.

'Which is why Al Kuzemen Malachi is being kept under close guard for his protection,' Arven continued.

All eyes turned to look at the two bodyguards who had been standing by Malachi's chair. It was as though the council had been unaware of their presence until Arven had mentioned it; and indeed they had, for Malachi had weaved an invisibility spell around them, as well as around Prins and Elee, who now appeared before the council at Arven's side.

'So,' Marlin said. 'You believe yourself to be under threat too.'

'I believe that someone among us has a hidden agenda,' Arven explained. 'And until such time as we discover what it is, there will be only a few trusted warriors in my and Malachi's presence. Any others will be thoroughly vetted by a means newly devised by Malachi.'

'What means?' asked Abeken.

'For now, we will not explain. But let us say that we have our suspicions about who is involved. When it is proven, punishment will be swiftly dealt.'

15

The blue shield was holding, but the drones were edging forward toward Kale and Jas, growing ever bolder when they found that the blue light did not corrupt their vile skin. Behind them the soldiers hung back. They looked as though they were guarding a border, but their weapons were now empty threats.

'The drones aren't attacking the soldiers,' Jas noted.

Julia appeared at her side. 'Conditioning. They are trained to obey Handley's men but attack anyone else.'

'We have what we used to call a Mexican standoff,' said Jas. 'We can't go outside, and they can't attack as long as Kale's barrier holds.'

'Precisely, Empress,' said Kale. 'I can send more light to push these creatures back, but it may mean a brief weakening of the barrier.'

'What are the risks?' Jas asked.

'Contamination by the poison ...'

'Then no. We can't risk it. Keep the shield up. I'm going to see how everyone behind us is faring,' Jas said.

'She is a true Empress,' Kale said as Julia joined him. 'Already taking care of everyone but herself.'

'I know,' said Julia.

Jas walked through the gathering of terrified people. Children clung to parents, and parents held them tightly with an equal need for comfort. She stopped by a table where an old woman sat with her hands wrapped around a glass of water. She appeared to be in shock; her face was blanched and her fingers shook. Jas took off the coat she was wearing and wrapped it around the woman's shoulders. She turned to look around at the startled but silent faces of other people. They were all facing the archway, watching the soldiers and drones, but had been calmed by Kale's ward enough to remain patiently with their families.

'Can someone come here? Sit with her? Make sure she's okay? I'm going to check on everyone else.'

'I will,' said a girl that Jas recognised. It was Natasha Healy: the girl who had escaped from the care home. The one that Jas now knew was part Jinx herself. Natasha had been one of the strongest pupils in the magic classes.

'Thank you. I know she will be all right with you here,' Jas said.

'I won't fail you, Empress,' Natasha said.

Jas blinked. None of the residents of Trafford City had ever referred to her by Kale's form of address before.

'I'm not …'

Natasha's eyes met Jas's over the woman's head. 'Her name is Margery. She objected at the first magic session. Do you remember?'

Jas looked at Margery again. She hadn't appeared to be so old the last time she had seen her. Now, shock and fear had turned a middle-aged woman into an old one.

'She'll recover,' Jas said. 'She just needs to feel safe again. We all do.'

Natasha nodded.

Jas left them and found Caroline, who was crouching behind a small table with her two little children. Caroline was nursing her wrist.

'Are you okay?' Jas asked.

'As okay as I can be. I fell when the crowd panicked, landed wrong. It's just a sprain, but I pulled this table down to stop us from being crushed. Everyone seems calm now though.'

'Kale has administered us all with something to help.'

'A drug?'

Jas shook her head. 'Magic. But it helps to dispel panic. This way we can all use our heads and are not driven by fear. Have you seen Taylor or Andrew?'

'No, they must still be outside,' Caroline said.

'I hope not. That stuff in the air …' Jas let the thought drop between them.

'Donovan's out there too …' Caroline said. She frowned, clearly understanding the implication, but the blue ward was working to help her control that dread that even now threatened to overwhelm her.

'If I know Taylor, he will have found shelter,' Jas said. 'I'm sure Donovan will be with him.'

Caroline nodded.

'I'll be back. I just need to check on the exits,' Jas said. She weaved through the crowd of people, who sat or stood calmly, almost sedated, as she passed through them toward the main entrance.

As she reached the old escalator, which was not working since the electricity had failed, Jas came face to face with Dawn.

Dawn was standing by the door, holding Lucy on her hip with one hand and a pistol in the other.

She was looking out at the black miasma, a deep frown on her forehead.

'You could have run outside,' Jas said. 'But you didn't. That was wise.'

Dawn looked over her shoulder, then back at the door. 'There's worse than that black muck waiting for us out there.'

Jas came to her side. 'No sign of our men?'

'No.'

'You haven't had radio contact?'

'No.'

'How did you know to come to the mess?'

'Lucy told me,' Dawn said.

'Lucy?'

'There's bad men in the town …' Lucy said.

Jas looked carefully at the small child for the first time. Though she had seen her a few times in passing since her arrival at Trafford City, the child had been of little interest to her, other than the casual observation that she looked like Taylor. Now, though, as Jas met the girl's pale blue eyes, which looked dark in the gloom, she detected a tiny swirl within the pupils.

The child smiled at her. 'I'm looking after mummy,' she said.

Dawn made no answer, but she accepted the small kiss that the child placed on her cheek.

A small spark jumped like an electric shock from the child to the mother. Dawn didn't react, but Lucy continued to meet Jas's eyes.

'She's been sick,' said Lucy. 'Bad people hurt her.'

Dawn shifted her stance, moving the little girl into a more comfortable position on her hip. As she turned, Jas saw a small mark on her shoulder. It looked like a tattoo, but seemed to have been defaced.

'Shhh …' said Lucy.

'I don't understand,' Jas said.

'They put something in there. I burned it out,' said Lucy.

Despite the blue ward, Jas began to feel a level of confusion and discomfort at the child's words. She was clearly exceptional, and magic was growing inside her at an alarming rate. Jas could feel it in the air. Like a zing of electricity, a feeling that lightning was about to strike. But why? And how did she come to have the swirling pupils of an Arrak Nah Tiamen, unless somewhere in Taylor's or Dawn's lineage there was some Jinx blood?

Something rattled against the door outside, breaking the contact that Jas had with the child.

Following the recent damage to the front door, the panel had been repaired with a sheet of metal. It was difficult to see anything outside through this screen. Then, two figures emerged from the black smog as the front door opened. There was a burst of gunfire. The two men threw themselves inward, slamming the metal-covered door shut behind them. Then they stumbled to their feet, staggering blindly toward the inner door.

Dawn brought her gun upwards.

'Wait!' Jas said. 'It looks like our men.'

'It's daddy,' said Lucy.

The two men were covered in several layers of outer clothing that masked even their faces. There was no way that the little girl could have seen who they were. Even so, Dawn lowered her gun and stepped back from the door as though every word the child said was unquestionably true. Jas noted that Dawn appeared even more subdued than the rest of the people in the mess. She suspected that Lucy was doing something to her mother, but didn't know why or how it was possible.

Some instinct made her believe the child, though, and she too stepped back from the door.

The first man through was quickly subsumed into the blue ward. The second one secured the door behind him, and only then did the blue light lap over him.

The first pushed back his hood, and Jas came face to face with Andrew for the first time in days. She threw her arms around him, and he responded to her hug awkwardly as he always did. The second man unwrapped fabric from around his mouth and nose, and quickly revealed that Lucy had been right. It was indeed Taylor.

'Daddy!' cried Lucy, and the little girl held out her arms to him.

He threw aside his heavy coat first, pushing it into the corner near the door as though he feared it was contaminated. Then he took Lucy in his arms.

The minute the child left her hold, Dawn became less sedentary.

'What the fuck is going on?' she said. It was as though she had just woken from a deep sleep and had found herself sleepwalking.

'MD59 soldiers are all around the perimeter,' Taylor said. 'What happened to the lights in here?'

'Everything went dark about an hour ago,' said Jas. 'They've entered the building through the domes. Kale has been holding them, and the smog, off. There's a ward around us all.'

'The structure is undermined. My god, that stuff is poison out there. We've seen several men taken down just by breathing it in,' said Andrew.

'I know. One of Handley's men died horribly that way too,' Jas said.

As Jas spoke, a nervous prickle worked its way up the back of her neck. She turned to find Dawn holding the gun up once more. This time it was pointed in her direction.

'What the fuck are you doing?' Taylor said. 'We've got enough trouble right now going on outside.'

'Have. To. Deal … with the alien …' Dawn said.

'What are you talking about?' Andrew said.

'Jinx … She's Jinx …'

'Put me down, Daddy,' Lucy said.

But Taylor wasn't paying attention. Instead he turned his body aside so that Lucy was blocked from Dawn.

'Dawn, put the gun down. Jas is not our enemy,' Taylor said.

'Ruined everything …' Dawn said. 'All going well …'

'Mummy …' said Lucy.

Andrew and Taylor exchanged glances, and Andrew began to shift forward, placing his own body between Jas and Dawn.

'You think I won't kill you too?' Dawn said.

'What's gotten into you?' asked Taylor.

Dawn didn't look in his direction. 'A good soldier follows orders.'

'Dawn …' Taylor said.

Dawn wasn't listening. Instead, she was moving back toward the door, her hand outstretched behind her.

'Have to return for instruction …' she said.

'For goodness sake don't go out there!' Jas called.

'I'll kill you. Just for the fun of it. You're tainted. You stink of them,' Dawn said, looking at her over Andrew's shoulder; and Jas knew that her threat wasn't empty, which was the only reason she remained behind Andrew. She hoped that Dawn's previous loyalty to the occupants of Trafford City would still be there in whatever subconscious was left – keeping Andrew safe from attack unless he did something stupid.

'Something's controlling her,' Lucy said. 'It's not Mummy's fault …'

Taylor glanced down at his daughter with the first realisation that the child knew something that he did not.

'Put me down, Daddy,' said Lucy, and she placed a kiss on his cheek. A spark of energy left her and entered him. Taylor's eyes glazed over and he placed the little girl down on her feet before him.

'Mummy …' Lucy said, slowly walking toward Dawn.

'Don't come near me …' Dawn said. She turned the gun to point at the small child. 'Don't *touch* me …'

'Mummy … You have to remember …'

'Stay away …' Dawn's gun hand trembled. Her left hand came forward, and now she gripped the weapon with the stance of a soldier, two-handed, with one hand balancing the weapon in order to offset recoil.

Lucy was almost at her side again, one small hand outstretched to reach her mother.

'No …' Dawn said. A frown warped her brow, colour rose in her cheeks. She appeared to be having some sort of inner struggle with herself.

Lucy stopped short. She made no attempt to touch her mother.

'Remember, Mummy … *I believe in you.*'

Dawn pulled back the safety on the gun and her finger twitched on the trigger.

16

The trembling took up again as Dawn fought with herself; every part of her body was rebelling against something in her mind that was forcing her to behave out of character. Her knees, arms, hands and torso shook with the effort she was making to overcome her conditioning. Pain burst behind her eyes as a migraine threatened to overwhelm her.

The gun lowered, her thumb reluctantly knocked the safety back in place. Then the weapon dropped from her fingers onto the ground.

Andrew hurried to pick it up.

Lucy finally touched Dawn, clutching her around the knees, even as the strength left her mother's limbs and she slumped. Taylor caught her before she fell, and Lucy clutched her mother's hand, squeezing it tightly as she pressed some of her energy into her.

'I knew you could do it, Mummy,' Lucy said. 'You've fought the bad man. All on your own.'

'I don't understand,' Taylor said.

Dawn hugged him but didn't answer.

'She will tell you soon, Daddy,' Lucy said.

'I've been in a deep, dark hole …' Dawn said.

Shouts from the front drew Jas's and Andrew's attention away from the moment.

'Andrew, come with me. Kale may need a soldier to keep back the drones,' Jas said.

'What about the Captain?'

'I think he needs to stay with his wife and daughter …'

Jas turned away from the still hugging family and hurried through the crowd, who were now nervously moving and talking again. She was closely followed by Andrew, clutching his semi-automatic Uzi.

They reached Kale and Julia just in time to see a drone sinking through the blue ward skin. Andrew raised the Uzi and fired a burst of bullets directly into the creature's face. Vile, brackish blood burst from its head as teeth and gore speared out. Kale and Julia jumped back, narrowly avoiding being splashed. The blue ward juddered after the intrusion. Jas looked up and saw to her horror that more of the drones were descending on it.

'Why isn't it repelling them?' she said.

'They are still part-human,' Kale explained. 'The ward is designed to protect from the smog and gunfire, but they can pass through it – as could the soldiers, if they wanted to.'

Andrew aimed again, this time at the line of the blue ward, as two drones began to push through. But they had intelligence, despite their animalistic behaviour, and they were far enough apart that only one of them was actually hit by the first rain of bullets. The second and then a third followed rapidly on the first one's heels, dived at the blue ward and fell through it as the body of the first crashed onto the floor before Kale.

The Al Kuzemen turned his staff upside down and, pointing it directly at the creature as it stumbled to its feet, sent out a light ball that exploded into the drone's face. The creature fell back, out through the ward, in a rupture of light, illuminating the whole area behind him. Further drones, who had been heading toward the ward, halted, shrinking back into the shadows. Light appeared to be the only thing they were truly afraid of.

The soldiers began to move forward now. Their weapons couldn't work, but they had their hands, and Jas saw one of them pulling a hunting knife from a sheath at his belt. The others soon followed suit. Andrew was ready though, and he fired a torrent of bullets through the ward, pushing them backwards.

The soldiers retreated, but to Jas's horror, she could see more now joining them, having newly climbed down into the structure. There were also more drones. More than she could have imagined existed. Looking out, with only a bare minimum of light behind them, Jas could see that the soldiers and drones were now rows deep.

'Where have they all come from?' Andrew said.

'Outside,' Julia replied. 'These were people living outside of our borders. They've all been slowly poisoned, then manipulated by Handley, no doubt, as the fog took hold of their senses and changed them from people to … monsters.'

'We're never getting out of here!' a voice erupted from behind them. It was Margery; already unstable, the woman had been tipped over the edge by what had happened in last few moments. Noise from the other occupants of the ward began to escalate once more.

'I'm losing my control on them,' Kale said. 'There are too many.'

'What about Donovan? Where's Donovan?' cried Caroline behind them.

Jas turned and she saw that panic had brought all the people crushing closer to the border of the ward.

'Stay back! Please keep calm!' she called. 'If you panic, all is lost. Those creatures will get in here, and that smog will kill us all.'

A surge of screaming echoed through the crowd as various people awakened: the ward was no longer dampening their fear.

'Oh my god,' Jas said. 'I don't know what to do. If they lose it, we're all dead.'

'Keep calm, Empress,' Kale said, and his words made her recognise her own rising anxiety.

She took a deep breath, steadying her heart as she glanced back at the mage. Beyond him was a sight that brought further panic bubbling into her chest: the soldiers were advancing again.

'Kale!' she yelled.

The Al Kuzemen turned back to look at the advancing enemy. He raised his staff, tapped down on the floor three times and then, stepping back, grabbed Jas's hand. He placed her palm around the staff and the jewel at its head began to glow white and luminous with their combined power.

'You know what to do. Keep focused …' Kale said.

'What?'

'We have nowhere else to go!' Kale said.

'No, not there. We can't go back.'

'Do you think that anything on Emin can be worse than this?'

Jas gasped. She looked over her shoulder at the people behind her, then back at the marching enemy. The sheer volume of numbers meant that they had no choice. They could never win. There really was only one way out.

She gripped Kale's hand, focusing her memory on the oasis on Emin. A clear picture rose in her mind. Kale nodded, the focus was good.

'Julia,' he said. 'Get everyone ready to cross through the vortex.'

'What the hell's going on?' asked Andrew. 'We can take these guys.'

'No, Andrew. *Look*. We *can't*,' Julia said. 'Help me round everyone up. This is our only chance.'

Andrew looked through the ward, his frown deepened, and then the choice was taken from him. The ground began to shake, and overhead the large fake sky of the Trafford Centre Orient cracked. A lump of plaster tumbled down, was caught briefly by the ward, then slipped inside, crashing to the ground as three people dived aside, narrowly avoiding being crushed.

Kale was shaking with the effort of holding the shield in place, while calling the vortex at the same time. Jas used all of her skills of concentration to help steady him and maintain her own focus, even as the air before them opened up.

The swirling vortex appeared and the smell of sand filled the atmosphere, along with a rush of noise that sounded like the torrent of a waterfall as you stand in a cave behind it.

'Get inside!' Jas called.

Kale sent a final surge of calming magic into the atmosphere, and the people of Trafford City began to walk, docile, into the raging eddy. Julia stood at the open mouth of the vortex, guiding them in, as Andrew worked from the back ,pushing them forward.

'What are you doing?' cried Taylor, appearing by Jas's side.

He was holding Lucy in his arms, and Dawn clung to his arm as though she believed that if she let go she would plummet back into the dark realms that Handley's scientists had consigned her to.

'You have to trust us. Get inside. We are taking you somewhere safe,' Jas said.

'Where?'

Jas glanced at Dawn and Lucy. 'Somewhere that I feel you will be welcomed. Somewhere that I'm now starting to see as home. This planet is fucked. You know that, right?'

'The Jinx planet? *Are you out of your fucking mind?*' Taylor yelled. 'Get those people out of that thing. Right now!'

'If you get them out, then they are dead!' Julia said. 'For god sake, let's get out of here and discuss it later. We can always come back, you know.'

'Where's Donovan?' Caroline said. She was about to cross the border with her two children.

Taylor looked at the children's cherubic faces. They gazed up at him as though he could save them, and he knew then that he couldn't.

'Caroline, take the children and get in that thing. Donovan was okay the last time I saw him. Dawn, take Lucy. Go in. I'm going outside again to try to find any of our remaining soldiers.'

'Don't leave us!' Dawn said. Sobs wracked her chest as she stared at the vortex before her.

'Get inside. We can't hold the drones and soldiers back for much longer,' Kale said.

'Jas ...' Taylor said. 'You do know you are probably condemning any men and male children among these survivors, don't you?'

Jas looked at him sharply. 'No. I won't let that happen. I'm taking us to an oasis, away from Sharik. With Kale's help, I can keep us all hidden.'

'I hope you know what you're doing ...' Taylor said.

Jas didn't answer for a moment, then she said, 'Take your family inside. We can come back to look for the others when we are better placed.'

Bullets suddenly whistled past their heads from behind them, toward the vortex. The bullets ricocheted off the growing shield around the vortex and fell into the line of the blue ward. As the ward worked only one way, the bullets tore out into the drones and soldiers on the other side, pushing them back from the edge. By default, it gave the Trafford City survivors a few more minutes' breathing space.

Cries from behind Jas, Kale and Taylor, as well as the gunfire from that direction, made them all turn to see a group of men running through the centre toward them.

'They've broken in through the back now that it is defenceless,' Andrew yelled.

'No,' said Taylor. 'Hold your fire! It's our men!'

'Everyone, this is the last chance. We need to get inside the vortex. Kale and I are losing it,' Jas said.

The vortex shuddered, and the blue ward blinked like a light in a power surge.

As the group of Trafford City soldiers reached them, Taylor pushed Dawn and Lucy toward the vortex.

'Captain?' said Harvey, pushing aside the fabric that was covering his face. 'The enemy is surrounding us. And now the Jinx ...?'

'Get everyone inside. We have to get out of here,' Taylor said. 'I'll explain later.'

The final few people entered the vortex, Kale and Jas going last. The front spun quickly around them, then began to close.

The blue ward fell, and Handley's soldiers and drones pushed forward. There were battle cries of the most haunting kind. The face of a drone pushed up against the shrinking vortex and was ripped apart by the power as it closed.

Jas looked back and smelt one final whiff of decay before the wormhole closed and all that could be sensed was warm air and the scent of sand.

17

It was morning. Arven and Malachi stood in a clearing near the oasis. Behind them the tent rippled in the gentle breeze that flowed over the sand. There was a small band of warriors around them, and via a telepathic connection, Malachi was linked to Taeran, another of the Al Kuzemen mages that he had deemed trustworthy. Malachi had been working his way through his assessment of the other mages, and now had cleared all but four of them of suspicion. The remaining four had for some reason refused to connect with him: though there was little point in their refusal, as ultimately they would be forced to prove their loyalty to the Emperor.

'We are ready, highness,' Malachi said.

'You are certain this is what we need to do?' Arven asked. Even though he did not doubt Malachi, he wondered at the necessity of this trip when so many more pressing matters needed his attention.

'In our life journey it is rare that we reach a point of prophecy,' Malachi explained. 'The signs have been there. We did not read them.'

A few days earlier they had discovered the scroll. Now Malachi held it in his hands and unrolled it as Arven waited.

'Emperor, if I may ...?'

Arven nodded.

'The scroll is in the old language. It tells of a planet with "two moons, two suns; a world of peace and perfection". Obviously Sharik, where our race finally settled. "No longer warriors and travellers, the settlers face their greatest challenge. As the two moons rise in the final year of the Goddess Almia, a pestilence will descend. Lives will be lost. The peoples of the first tribe will return to the stars."' Malachi paused.

'The first tribe. That's us?' asked Prins.

'Yes. "Through time and space the search will begin, and so too will the curse of the two tribes."' Malachi said.

'We are cursed,' Arven explained. 'First by the death of our women, doomed to extinction; and then, because we dared to fight for our existence, we are cursed for our attack on the second tribe.'

'But why?' Elee said. 'Why does this all have to be a curse? And if it is one, then how can we free ourselves from it?'

'All questions we have been asking ourselves,' Arven said.

'By reading the scrolls, we have learnt that the curse originated on the Eleventh Moon,' Malachi said.

'The Eleventh Moon is a story told to frighten children,' Prins said.

'No. It is real. It existed. And the curse was written down into the scrolls and carried through our lifetimes, passed by word of mouth from mother to child as a story to remind us to beware,' Malachi explained. 'But we still forgot the true meaning of it all. Lost in our lives as we were. And later, buried in the tragedy of the death of our women and children, we ignored the signs.'

'This is Al Kuzemen Kale's fault, then?' asked Prins.

'Not really,' Malachi said, defensive of all of his order – and Kale was still one of theirs, even though he was absent and his behaviour had been questionable. 'He cannot be blamed for not discovering the scroll. It was buried among others in his tent, true. But his objective was to look for signs of life in the other galaxies, not for any portent of disaster. He, like all of us, was under pressure to save our race. He would not have given a scroll of this nature much credence, even if he had read it. The Al Kuzemen order have never been carriers of history. We focus on magic; our teachings are about this only. And, like you all, we believed these stories were things of myth, not magic, not reality. Though we are exploring now how that perception was wrong.'

'The scroll goes on to tell us that we would err in our attempts,' Arven explained. 'By decimating Earth, we would commit a great crime against the second tribe. We have broken a treaty, and that has in effect caused the second curse. And that curse was set in motion when Jasmine was granted the power of persuasion.'

'The Empress has magic?' asked Prins.

'Yes,' said Malachi. 'All the Earth women here do. We had thought it an anomaly, but now realise that it a result of their contact with us. You see, when the two tribes parted, one relied on magic, the other on science. We took all magic from Earth with us, because we were the only people who had knowledge of it. Those who remained on Earth turned away from our ways and travelled the path of their science. A science that we know is destructive, dangerous and is now bringing about the final phase of the obliteration of Earth's resources.'

'We came from Earth? That dying, poisonous planet?' Elee said. 'I could smell death as we arrived there that first day. Even before we began …'

Malachi nodded. 'And therein lies our possible salvation …'

'I don't understand,' another warrior said from the back. 'How? If we have committed some terrible breach … then how can we make amends?'

Malachi's pupils swirled with a fire that reflected the suns above their heads. 'I have an idea, but cannot be sure. I think the answer lies on the Eleventh Moon. Now we begin.'

Malachi turned to face the desert once more and walked forward, farther from the camp and out toward the spot where Kale and Jas – and, unknown to the Emperor's loyal followers, Marlin and Garuk – had previously opened a vortex. It was far enough away from the oasis not to disrupt the magic protecting the area, and yet near enough to be only a short walk back to relative shelter, and to their mounts, on their return.

Arven, Prins, Elee and the other warriors followed the mage at a reverent distance, pausing just behind him as he stopped and stared out at the expansive landscape. Malachi raised his staff, then brought it down into the soft sand. Almost immediately the wind picked up and the sand began to swirl around their feet.

'The connection with Taeran is strong,' Malachi said. 'We are calling on our ancient lineage, an inherited memory, to show us the map.'

A dark spot appeared in the air before them, then expanded. Arven stepped closer to look at the growing blackness. He recognised the solar system surrounding Sharik, then watched as the map changed and a pathway through the stars opened up. It was a brilliant wormhole that led into another galaxy. This galaxy was so far from their home that the distance was unfathomable. It didn't matter though, as the vortex would take them there in just a few physical steps, leaping through time and space effortlessly.

With a tap of his staff, Malachi began to raise the vortex, and the sand swirled around them, churning the ground up in huge waves that indicated more to the warriors the implication of distance. This place they were going was beyond Earth, maybe twice as far again, and none of them knew what they would find there.

The vortex opened, a howling maw, and the Emperor followed Malachi inside, accompanied by his nervous warriors. All of the men had removed their swords from their ornate scabbards. They now stood in readiness for whatever horror they might find. Just as the vortex began to close, another swirl of wind picked up outside.

'What was that?' Arven said, stepping forward to look out, but the breach closed too quickly, and Malachi was now in a deep trance, brought on by the depth of concentration needed to sustain the distance to the Eleventh Moon.

A few long moments later, the atmosphere in the vortex changed. Arven shuddered as a cold chill permeated the spinning walls. The vortex rocked slightly. The warriors and Emperor staggered on the walkway, though Malachi remained steady. Unusually the eddy noise began to echo inside. As the gateway opened once more, a howling wind screamed inside, with air so thin that the warriors felt their breath being sucked from their lungs.

Malachi stepped forward as the void opened, and then halted. Arven stepped out beside him, and the two Arrak Nah Tiamen looked out on an unfamiliar, terrifying landscape.

18

It was a bright day, and the occupants of Trafford City had barely seen sunshine for years. But this was a different sun. In fact, two of them. Despite the brightness, they didn't burn. The suns gave off a perfect heat that warmed the skin.

Jas stepped out of the vortex with Kale, and they moved aside as the people followed them onto the sands of Emin. There were several hundred of them, men, women and children. And they blinked and looked up at the sky, knowing instinctively that this was a foreign world.

Jas felt the rays of the Emin suns, and the pull of the two red moons, which currently were not visible in the bright blue sky. The air was fresh. She breathed it in, clearing her lungs in one breath of the weeks of pollution that she had ingested on Earth. When the heavy feeling left her, it was then that she realised how anxious she had been since leaving Sharik.

Jas looked around at the people of Earth as Kale closed the vortex. The soldiers who had joined them at the eleventh hour were all divesting themselves of the protective layers of clothing they had been wearing. Jas saw Caroline walking with her children among the soldiers, looking for Donovan. But he wasn't there. She felt her heart go out to the woman. It probably meant that he was dead, or at the very least had been overwhelmed and captured by the soldiers. Better than the alternative of the drones.

The survivors gathered in the sand around the well, and noting the large tent, one or two wandered inside to investigate.

'There are animals here. Tied up!' one of the men called. 'They look like camels.'

'Where are we?' asked Harvey.

'Somewhere in the middle of an Arabian desert is my guess,' said Kline.

Jas took a breath, but Taylor spoke before she had time to explain.

'We're on the Jinx planet,' he said. 'Look above you. Two suns. Not Earth. Definitely not Earth.'

Some of the people nearby heard Taylor's words, and there were some sharp intakes of breath and urgent muttering.

'This was a trap,' Mack Bennett, Sylvia's husband, said. He walked forward, holding his wife's arm. Sylvia's white hair seemed to glow in the bright light from above. 'You came back to Earth just to capture us for the Jinx.'

'Mack, darling, of course they didn't,' Sylvia assured him. 'Don't you see, they just saved all of our lives?'

'But for what?' sobbed Margery. 'We'll be fed to the Jinx.'

'The Jinx aren't cannibals,' said Jas. 'And right now we are safer here than back on Earth. The planet is doomed, and we need to try to find a way to live with ...'

'Are you insane?' asked Dawn. 'I mean, *really*?'

'If you'll let me finish ...'

'You were about to say, you'd like to find a way for us to live with the Jinx. Right?'

'Well, yes ...' Jas stuttered. 'But it's not going to be so simple. We need to keep you safe. Hide you all until ...'

'Until what? Until your boyfriend finds us and kills all our men?' Dawn sneered.

'I won't let that happen,' Jas said. 'I give you my word.'

'She's the Empress,' Natasha said.

Lucy slipped her small fingers into Dawn's hand and squeezed.

'We're safe from the bad men now, Mummy.'

'Okay,' Jas said. 'We're here, and I'm sure there's not one of us who'd prefer to be back on Earth right now. Would you rather be here ...' she gestured around her, emphasising the quiet, the cool breeze, the sunlight and the fresh air. '... or back at the Centre?' She paused for a moment and saw the slow realisation cross the others' faces that this was indeed a much safer place to be.

'So let's be practical,' said Julia. 'I see there's a well here. Kale, where can we find food?'

Kale smiled. He could feel his Al Kuzemen power returning. It was as though a tap had been switched on, and he truly realised how much the distance and pollution on Earth had impeded him. He tapped his staff in the sand three times, and the oasis was transformed. Dark green grass sprouted from the ground beneath their feet. Trees and plants began to grow around them, some bearing unusual-looking fruit.

'We shall not starve,' said Kale. 'But I think it is safe to remain here only for a short time. Someone else was here a while ago and may return. I will prepare a camp further into the desert for us to hide. It will just take longer than this to do.'

'How does he do that?' asked Sylvia.

'Jinx magic,' Julia said. 'Can't you *feel* it?'

Sylvia shuddered as though a chill wind had whisked around her. Jas met her eyes, and knew that the council member understood perfectly well what Julia meant.

Jas walked away from the group. The air around them swirled with unseen energy, and she had never been more aware of Jinx magic than now, after escaping the oppressive atmosphere of Earth. It was clean and wonderful, and above all enchanting.

She gazed off in the direction that she knew led to Sharik. Arven's presence should have pulled at her. She was prepared to resist it, because the time was not yet right to go to him – though soon she would need his help. Still, she sensed him strongly around the oasis, yet …

'What is it?' Julia asked.

Jas glanced at the woman, who even without touching her appeared to have some empathy and connection with her emotions.

I can't sense Arven … She sent the thought as an experiment, but Julia caught it and nodded.

Kale came to her side. He glanced around, back to where their own vortex, now closed, had opened. Jas could feel a wave of energy coming from the mage as he sent out his own search.

'This is not good,' he said quietly. 'The Emperor is not on the planet.'

'But where …?' Jas asked.

'He may have gone to Earth to find you,' Kale said.

'My god. He'll come face to face with those …'

Kale nodded, but they left the sentence unfinished between them.

'The Emperor will have his warriors, though. We are stronger, faster than any Earth men,' Kale said.

'Even those … *things*?' asked Julia.

The three of them fell silent.

'I think it best that we move out into the desert as soon as possible,' Kale said. 'Other Al Kuzemen may sense my presence: if Arven is not here, then I am unsure what kind of greeting either of us might receive.'

'Yes. And we need to keep these people safe. I made them a promise,' Jas said.

Jas turned back to the survivors. By some instinct they remained mostly huddled together.

'Listen everyone!' Jas said.

There was little chatter, but those talking together stopped and turned at the command in her voice.

'We need to move away from this site. It is used regularly by the Jinx, and the time has not yet come to reveal our presence here.'

The people listened to her proposal, and soon they were moving out and away from the point of their arrival, further into the desert, following Kale and Jas into an unknown future.

19

Arven stepped out of the vortex into the rushing wind, followed by Malachi, Prins, Elee and the other trusted warriors. Then the eddy of the vortex faltered.

'This land is too unstable, highness,' said Malachi. 'We must either return home or close the vortex now.'

'What would happen if it remained open?' Arven asked.

'I fear that there would be repercussions on Emin,' Malachi explained. 'The vortex works two ways. I would not like to risk any effect on our own world.'

'Then close it,' Arven said. 'We can raise another when we have finished our investigation.'

'Very well. lord,' Malachi said.

Malachi melded his mind with Taeran, explaining the position.

'He will be waiting for me to reconnect when we are done,' explained Malachi, and then at a tap of his staff the vortex closed, shrinking slowly until it was nothing more than a dot of light. The dot blinked and disappeared.

The party turned to begin their search of the Eleventh Moon. They did not know precisely what they were looking for, but Malachi was certain that the answers they sought were somewhere on this long forgotten planet.

'They've gone to the Eleventh Moon,' Al Kuzemen Prestin explained as he and Marlin looked over the scroll that Malachi and Arven had left spread out on the table.

'What do they hope to find?' Marlin asked.

'It is a wild el lien meck chase,' Prestin said. 'They can learn nothing by researching into a child's fairytale.'

'Are you so sure?'

Prestin studied the scroll carefully before responding. 'It seems they are looking at the curse of the two tribes,' he said. 'And now I see why this foolhardy trip is taking place. Here … there is talk of curses.'

As Prestin read on, he began to understand the implication of the curse, just as Malachi had.

'This is not good,' the mage said. 'They believe that we have sinned against the humans. If they come back with some form of proof, then our world will be in turmoil.'

'What kind of turmoil?' Marlin said.

'They may insist on giving the human women free will. A choice to remain with their new husbands or not.'

'But of course they will remain. They have bonded,' Marlin said.

'So had the Empress with the Emperor. But it did not stop her from choosing to leave him,' Prestin said. 'An anomaly that none of us can understand under the circumstances. But these creatures are strong-willed, independent. It may be the opportunity that they require to give them the courage to refuse their new lives. And should they do that, then our race, and theirs, will die.'

'Then we must make sure that whatever the Emperor learns does not come back to Sharik,' Marlin said.

He glanced around the Al Kuzemen tent; signs of Malachi's occupation were evident in the rows of potions and portents on shelves by the tent entrance.

'This is a fine mage's abode,' Marlin said. 'You'd fit in well here.'

'What are you saying?' Prestin said. 'I couldn't take over here unless …'

'Unless Malachi didn't return?' Marlin asked, leaving the question hanging in the air.

'If Malachi didn't return … then neither would …' Prestin said.

'The Emperor …' Marlin finished.

'I couldn't!' said Prestin, shocked and afraid.

'Dear friend, you need do nothing, except perhaps put some kind of force to block anyone from entering or leaving the Eleventh Moon.'

'But that would mean …'

'We don't need to voice this,' Marlin said. 'You can block the raising of a vortex, can't you?'

'Yes …'

'Then do it,' Marlin said.

'Where do we start?' Prins asked.

'The source of knowledge is close by. The co-ordinates were specific,' Malachi said. He removed a necklace from around his neck. It was an amber stone, held on a long leather thong. He held the jewel up in the air.

'What is that?' asked Elee, his eyes full of wonder as the gem began to glow.

'This is the jewel of Almia. It will lead us to the knowledge and wisdom we seek.'

'I thought the jewel was a legend?' Prins said.

'So did I,' said Arven. 'Where did you find it?'

'I have always held it,' Malachi said. 'Each Al Kuzemen is given an ancient gift on the day of his induction. This treasure was mine.'

Arven and the others knew little of the Al Kuzemen induction ritual, as these ceremonies were attended only by the mages.

'I didn't know,' he said now.

The light cast an impossible beam forward.

'This way,' said Malachi.

The Al Kuzemen led the small group into the howling wind. Arven held back a moment, wrapping a scarf around his head to protect his nose and mouth from the swirling dust. The storm, if indeed that was what it was, gave him a sense of foreboding. He glanced back at the point where their vortex had been. The ground around the spot was churned up, the surface destroyed. He knew that their travel harmed the destination on their arrival, but it was a price he was willing to pay in order to find answers.

They were cursed; he had to find out how to resolve that, if his people were to survive.

'Emperor?' called Malachi.

Arven looked forward to see that the group waited for him. He stepped deeper into the world of the Eleventh Moon, not knowing that this abandoned planet had just become their personal prison.

THE STORY CONTINUES IN *JINX BOUND*

About the Author

Award winning author Sam Stone began her professional writing career in 2007 when her first novel won the Silver Award for Best Novel with *ForeWord Magazine* Book of the Year Awards. Since then she has gone on to write several novels, three novellas and many short stories. She was the first woman in 31 years to win the British Fantasy Society Award for Best Novel. She also won the award for Best Short Fiction in the same year (2011).

Stone loves all genus fiction and enjoys mixing horror (her first passion) with a variety of different genres including science fiction, fantasy and steampunk.

Stone lives in Lincolnshire with her husband David and her two cats Freya and Shadow.

Her works can be found in paperback, audio and e-book.

Praise for Sam Stone

'A deceptively readable date with darkness – watch your step! This book is lit for the much more discerning chick (and cock) who likes to walk in the shadows. Relax with it, but be prepared for sudden jewels and little masterpieces and the rug to be pulled from under your feet.' Tanith Lee on *Killing Kiss*

'Stone has such fun reinventing the material and running it through a horror-come-steampunk grinder that it works and marvellously well … The obvious progenitor in this field is *Pride and Prejudice and Zombies* but Stone's work is far more engaging and less forced than that one-joke outing.' Peter Tennant on *Zombies at Tiffany's*

'Sam Stone without doubt is a mistress of the grisly and the glutinous. I believe that we can look forward to seeing Sam Stone develop into a major influence in the realm of blood and shadows and things that wake you up, wide-eyed, in the middle of the night.' Graham Masterton

'*Zombies at Tiffany's* reminds me a lot of Alan Moore's *League of Extraordinary Gentlemen* or the work of H G Wells … this is a brilliantly authored piece of steampunk literature, and then some.' Jim Reader, *Exquisite Terror*

More Titles by Sam Stone

<u>THE VAMPIRE GENE SERIES</u>
Horror, thriller, time-travel series.
1: KILLING KISS
2: FUTILE FLAME
3: DEMON DANCE
4: HATEFUL HEART
5: SILENT SAND
6: JADED JEWEL

<u>KAT LIGHTFOOT MYSTERIES</u>
Steampunk, horror, adventure series
1: ZOMBIES AT TIFFANY'S
2: KAT ON A HOT TIN AIRSHIP
3: WHAT'S DEAD PUSSYKAT
4: KAT OF GREEN TENTACLES

<u>JINX CHRONICLES</u>
Hi–tech science fiction fantasy series
1: JINX TOWN
2: JINX MAGIC
3: JINX BOUND (2017 TBA)

POSING FOR PICASSO (2017 TBA)
Supernatural Thriller

THE DARKNESS WITHIN
Science Fiction Horror Short Novel

ZOMBIES IN NEW YORK AND OTHER BLOODY JOTTINGS
Thirteen stories of horror and passion, and six mythological and erotic
poems from the pen of the new Queen of Vampire fiction.